A Cold Red Sunrise

A Cold Red Sunrise

An Inspector Porfiry Rostnikov Mystery

Stuart M. Kaminsky

OVERLOOK DUCKWORTH
New York • London

This edition published in the United States and the United Kingdom in 2013 by
Overlook Duckworth, Peter Mayer Publishers Inc.

NEW YORK:
141 Wooster Street
New York, NY 10012
www.overlookpress.com
For bulk and special sales, please contact sales@overlookny.com

LONDON:
30 Calvin Street
London E1 6NW
www.ducknet.co.uk
info@duckworth-publishers.co.uk

Cataloging-in-Publication Data is avaliable from the Library of Congress

Printed in the United States of America

ISBN: 978-1-4683-0681-1 US
ISBN: 978-0-7156-4633-5 UK
2   4   6   8   10   9   7   5   3   1

This book is dedicated to Shirley, Belle and Al in St. Louis, which is, I am told, rather a long distance from Siberia.

I stood there and I thought: what a full, intelligent and brave life will some day illuminate these shores.

ANTON CHEKHOV,
1890, in his travel notes,
on seeing the Yensei River in Siberia

ONE

Commissar Illya Rutkin tucked his briefcase under his arm, adjusted his goatskin gloves, pulled down his fur hat to cover his ears and tightened the scarf over his mouth before opening the door of the wooden house and stepping out into the Siberian morning.

He had been reluctant to get out of bed, reluctant to dress, reluctant to light the small stove, heat his day-old tea, eat the smoked herring left for him in the cupboard. He was a Commissar. The old woman should have prepared his breakfast, given him some attention, but he had been warned

Tumsk was not only Siberia but a small weather outpost near the Yensei River between Igarka and Agapitovo well within the arctic circle. Tumsk had barely been touched by the move to modernization which had, since the days of Stalin, been part of the propaganda of a harsh but promising new land beyond the Urals. Siberian towns sprang up to mine copper, diamonds, gold, to develop power from wild rivers, to revive the fur trade with the Evenk natives who have paid little attention to six hundred years of history.

Tumsk had not resisted change. Tumsk had not even been threatened by it. No one had cared. A few dozen people lived in the town just beyond the banks of the river, worked in the weather station, lived out their days as political exiles, made plans or hid. Tumsk was not a town in which to invest one's reputation and future.

Rutkin put out his right foot and tested the snow. It was brittle on top and took his weight reasonably well. In a few minutes or so the plow from the naval weather station on the slope would come to begin its rounds creating temporary paths, but Illya Rutkin did not have time to wait. He took another step out into the frigid, dark morning clutching his briefcase tightly and stood panting. What was the temperature? Sixty below? Ridiculous. Probably more like forty below. He stood with his arms out at his sides like an overbundled child in his fur coat under which he wore another coat and thick underwear.

The Commissar waddled rather than walked toward the People's Hall of Justice across the town square, glanced at the statue of Ermak Timofeyevich who had, with a band of cossacks, conquered most of Siberia in the name of the Czar early in the sixteenth century. Ermak, in full armor, a cap of snow on his head, was pointing east, contemplating the Siberia which he had taken. Ermak was badly in need of repair.

Rutkin took a few more steps, stopped and looked west, toward the Ural mountains more than a thousand miles away that stood like a great wall stretching from the Caspian Sea to the Arctic Ocean and separating Russia from the vastness of Siberia.

There was no one on the square. Something sounded to his left and Rutkin turned awkwardly to look toward the river, but the river was hidden by a low ridge covered, as was the world, with snow. He looked toward the taiga, the massive forest that came within a hundred yards of the town on three sides. Nothing. No one.

The Commissar sighed and started again toward the low stone building where he was to conclude his investigation into the death of the child. Normally, a Commissar would not have been dispatched from Moscow to Siberia for such an investigation, but there were two factors which made it a reasonable action. First, the child was the daughter of Lev Samsonov, a well-known dissident physician and scientist who had been sent by a court tribunal to Tumsk a year earlier. The hope had been that the world would forget Samsonov while he was in exile, but, apparently, the world had not forgotten him. Somehow word of his thoughts, life, efforts to return to Leningrad got to the outside world, even as far as the United States. The decision had been made only a month ago to allow Samsonov, his wife and daughter to leave the country. Arrangements were being made. The date of departure was only days away and so, now, the suspicious death of such a man's child had to be given serious attention, a Commissar at least, and, Rutkin had to admit to himself, he was probably considered one of the least busy of all available Commissars.

Rutkin had been given careful instructions. He had made "mistakes" in the past, he had been told by Party District Leader Vladimir Koveraskin, mistakes relating to certain alleged abuses of power for personal gain. Rutkin knew well what he meant, knew that the assignment to Tumsk was a warning, a taste of the Siberia in which he could easily find himself on a permanent basis. Illya Rutkin, who puffed his way through the snow, was expendable. If he failed to resolve this situation and it led to negative outside publicity, it would be Rutkin who would be blamed, demoted and punished. If he succeeded, he had a chance to survive, keep his title, his influence, his dacha near Yalta. At the age of fifty-four, he did not look forward to starting a new life above the arctic circle. His wife, Sonia, would certainly not join him. She would keep the apartment or, if necessary, go to live with their son and his wife and child in Odessa. Rutkin had no doubt and mixed feelings about the knowledge that Sonia would not be at his side blaming, grinding her teeth in sleep, hating his failure.

Barbaric, he told himself, looking at the ring of concrete buildings alongside almost ancient wooden and brick structures. The buildings around the square and the houses on the slope circled Ermak, who looked ever eastward. These people, he thought. Some of them, the older ones like that fool of a caretaker, still said spasi bog, may God save you, rather than spasibo when they wanted to say thank you. The place, even the wooden church building where no services were held, was part of a useless past that would not simply die. The entire town had no reasonable function for existing other than the weather station. Well, there was another reasonable function: to isolate people like Samsonov. Siberia was dotted with exile towns to receive those who, for various reasons, the State did not want to put into the more formal prisons farther east. One cannot be a martyr if he or she lives to a ripe old age.

But Illya Rutkin did not want to think of such things. He was, in fact, feeling good this morning, hopeful about the future. He knew something, had through careful investigation discovered something startling about the case that would save his career. Well, if he were to be honest, the information had come to him through luck and not investigation, but he had no need to be honest about this and nothing to gain from such honesty. So he trudged on, wanting to be the first person present for the hearing, to give the impression to these exiles, hooligans, ancients that he was constantly alert, that the State was constantly alert.

He would show these people, show Samsonov and the outside world that Commissar Illya Rutkin was not a man to be fooled, trifled with. He would be swift, efficient, and then he would make a show of presenting his information and the documentation on the child's death, closing the hearing and re-packing his briefcase before he departed. He had already made the call to Igarka to pick him up that afternoon, told them that he would have the entire matter settled, but he had refused to tell Famfanoff, the local

MVD officer, what he had discovered. No one was going to take credit for this but Illya Rutkin.

He looked up, took a deep breath and another step toward the People's Hall of Justice. He had no more than thirty yards or so to go but he could not hurry. The icy air would not let him hurry, the snow would not let him hurry, his heavy clothing would not let him hurry and years of neglecting his body would not let him hurry. So, he did not hurry.

Were his hat not so tightly pulled against his ears, Commissar Rutkin might have heard the sound, the slight wooshing sift of snow, but he did not hear and so the sudden apparition was all the more startling.

"Wha . . ." Rutkin cried at the hulking animal-like figure before him. The creature had risen from the snow like an extension of it, a massive snow man.

Illya Rutkin was startled but not frightened. He was a practical man who represented the Soviet Union. He faced the creature and waited for it to move away or speak, but it did neither. It stood facing Rutkin.

"What do you want?" Rutkin said.

The creature said nothing.

"Are you drunk?" Rutkin went on. "I am a Soviet Commissar. I am conducting an important investigation and you, you are in my way."

The creature did move now. It moved toward Illya Rutkin who stepped back, clutching his briefcase protectively to his chest.

"What do you want?" Rutkin shouted. "You want trouble? You want trouble? That can be arranged."

The creature closed in on him.

"Stop," Rutkin shouted, hoping someone in one of the shuttered houses on the square would hear and come to his aid, but no one responded and the statue of Ermak continued to point east.

The creature did not stop and fear came to Commissar Illya Rutkin.

"Stop," Rutkin repeated, seeing something now in the hand of the creature, something that made him want to run, run to the safety of the People's Hall of Justice.

He tried not to think about dying. Not here, he thought, not here. All thought of the hearing, of his future, was gone. Rutkin couldn't take in enough air. There wasn't enough air in the world to satisfy him and so he stumbled, mouth suddenly dry, nostrils acrid. He clutched his briefcase and trudged, stumbled, fell and rose to look back at the creature that was now a few yards from him. Yes, he was much closer to the Hall of Justice, much closer but it was still so far. Rutkin tore off his hat, hurled his briefcase at the creature and tried to force his iron legs to move, to hurry, but they did not move.

Rutkin screamed, now only a few feet from the door. The creature hovered over him and he screamed and from far beyond the village an animal, perhaps a wolf, perhaps the companion of this creature, howled into the dawn.

The door. If he could simply open the door, get inside, close it and throw the latch. Was that too much to ask of his body, his legs, whatever gods might exist and in which he did not believe?

His hand actually touched the wooden panel next to the door but he did not get the opportunity to clasp the handle. He had a moment, however, before he died to regret what he did next. He turned his head to see how far behind the creature was, and the icicle in the creature's hand penetrated through his eye and into his brain.

It should be cold, Rutkin thought. I should be dead. He shivered once and slumped against the stone stoop of the People's Hall of Justice thinking that he would survive this, that he would pretend to be dead and that he would be found and taken by helicopter to a hospital where he would somehow recover. Yes. It did not hurt. He would survive. And with that thought, Illya Rutkin died.

Inside the People's Hall of Justice of the Village of Tumsk, Sergei Mirasnikov looked out of the frosted window and adjusted his rimless glasses. Sergei clutched his broom and watched the creature gather in something brown that looked like a huge book. Sergei's eyes were not good even with the glasses. At the age of eighty-three, he was content that God had allowed him to live this long in relatively good health. One sure way to end that life and show his ingratitude to God would have been to open the door and try to come to the aid of the fool of a Commissar who had strongly hinted that Sergei was too old to continue to hold his job. Had he gone through that door to face the creature with his broom, Sergei was sure that there would now be a dead Commissar and a dead caretaker in the square.

Now there would be another Commissar coming, another investigation. It wouldn't end. Sergei watched the creature amble into the far snow, move toward the taiga, and then disappear into a clump of birch trees.

Sergei put down his broom when the creature was out of sight and looked around to be sure no one was there to see him. It was then that he saw the other figure standing silently near the row of birches at the edge of the forest just beyond the square. He could not make out the face of this other figure, but he knew from the stance, the fur parka, who it was. This other figure had also witnessed the death of the Commissar. Sergei blinked and this figure near the forest disappeared. Perhaps the figure had never been there. Perhaps the memories of age were playing tricks on Sergei. Perhaps the Commissar wasn't dead at all, hadn't been murdered by the creature.

Before he went to the door to check, Sergei Mirasnikov backed away from the window so he couldn't be seen, and crossed himself.

TWO

Porfiry Petrovich Rostnikov pushed away the sleeve of a jacket that brushed against his cheek and shifted his weight on the battered wooden stool to keep his partly lame left leg from growing too stiff. He would probably need to move quickly when the moment came to act.

He was sitting in the closet of an apartment on the third floor of a building on Babuskina Street in Moscow just four blocks from his own apartment on Krasikov Street. In his left hand, Inspector Rostnikov held a small Japanese flashlight whose bulb was threatening to reject the Czech batteries which he had recently put into it. In his right hand, Rostnikov held a paperback copy in English of Ed McBain's The Mugger. He had read the book five years earlier and about four years before that. It was time to reread it and so, while he waited for the three strong-arm robbers to return to the apartment, Rostnikov sat silent, shifted his more than 220-pound bulk, and hoped that the batteries would hold out.

If the flashlight did fail, Rostnikov would put the book away and sit silently waiting, contemplating the dinner of chicken tabaka, chicken with prune sauce and pickled cabbage, that his wife Sarah had promised him for that night if she did not get another one of the headaches she had been plagued by for the past few months.

Rostnikov read: "For as the old maid remarked upon kissing the cow, it's all a matter of taste." He had read the line before but for the first time he thought he understood the joke and he smiled slightly, appreciatively. Americans were most peculiar. Ed McBain was peculiar, including in his police novels pictures of fingerprints, maps, reports, even photographs. Delightful but peculiar.

And then Rostnikov heard the door to the apartment begin to open. He turned off the flashlight and stood quickly and silently in spite of his bulk and muscles tight from years of lifting weights. As the three men entered the apartment talking loudly, Rostnikov placed the flashlight in the left pocket of his jacket and in the right he carefully placed the paperback book. He did not use a bookmark, would never consider turning down a corner of the page to mark his place. He had no trouble remembering his place in the book.

The first man through the door was named Kola, Kola the Truck, a great bear of a man with ears turned in and curled by too many drunken battles. Kola, who would be celebrating his thirty-ninth birthday in two days, shaved his head and wore French T-shirts that showed his muscles. Unfortunately, T-shirts did nothing to hide his huge belly though no one would have the nerve to tell this to Kola, not even Yuri Glemp who was the second man into the apartment. Yuri was even bigger than Kola and ten years younger, probably even stronger, but Yuri was afraid of the older man who didn't seem to mind being hurt, didn't seem to be afraid of anything. Yuri, on the other hand, did not like to be hurt though he thoroughly enjoyed hurting others.

Together, for almost two years, Kola and Yuri had made a more-than-adequate living by robbing people on the streets at night and beating them severely if they did not have much money. They also beat them if they had money, but not with as much zeal. Watches, wallets, belts and even shoes they sold to Volovkatin.

Yuri, who paused in front of the small mirror to admire his neatly combed hair, kept track of the number of people they had robbed and beaten. His count was fifty-one. Kola had no idea and no interest in the number. He didn't even seem to have a great interest in the amount of money they had made. Between robberies Kola tended to be quiet and morose, drinking vodka, looking for arguments and watching television.

Yuri didn't know how to record the last two robberies since they had taken on the "kid," Sasha, the third man to enter the apartment. Yuri didn't like Sasha who had met them in the National Bar on Gorkovo. Sasha, who looked as if he should be in school with his hair falling in his eyes, his teeth white, had bought them vodka and mineral water chasers, started a conversation. Later, when Yuri and Kola had had enough of him, they had left, more than a little drunk, and started toward their apartment. No more than a block from the hotel, Sasha had stepped out of a dark doorway and pointed an old Makarov 9mm pistol at them. He meant to rob them. Kola had smiled and stepped toward the kid. Yuri had touched his partner's arm to stop him. The kid looked like he meant to shoot.

"Just give me your money, your watches," the kid had said, holding the gun steady and looking around to be sure they were not interrupted.

Yuri had cursed and reached for his wallet. Kola had stopped and laughed.

"We're in the same business, boy," Kola said.

"Good," Sasha had answered. "Just give me your money, and do it fast."

"How long have you been at this?" Kola asked. Yuri had already handed over his money and his watch.

"A few months. No more talk. Give me the money."

"I like you," Kola had said. "You've got a stomach for this."

"Shit," Sasha had answered, his hair falling even further over his eyes. "Money."

"You're not afraid of a little blood, are you, boy?" Kola had said.

"You want to find out?" Sasha had hissed.

"Join us," Kola had said.

"Just give him the money," Yuri had whispered.

"Why should I join you?" Sasha had asked.

"You'd be a good front. Yuri and I look like robbers. You look like a kid. No one would be afraid of you. Can it hurt you to talk about it?"

"We can talk," Sasha said. "But I'm doing fine on my own."

They had talked; at least Kola and the kid had talked after the kid returned the money he had taken from Yuri. The kid agreed to join them for a while, to see if he made more money, if they were careful enough for him.

"I like this boy," Kola said to Yuri, putting a huge arm around Sasha's shoulder.

He's turning queer, Yuri had thought, possibly with some jealousy that he did not acknowledge to himself. But Yuri had said nothing. Now, more than a week later as they entered the apartment and Yuri checked his hair, he was sure they had made a mistake. They had committed two robberies and Sasha had not engaged in the beatings that followed, had even claimed to hear someone coming before they could really teach a lesson to the second victim whom they had left about an hour ago with a closed eye and bleeding nose just outside the Dobryninskaya Metro Station.

"Let's split it up," Kola said, closing the apartment door.

Yuri could tell that Kola was not content. He had not finished with the victim, would be looking for a fight, someone to smash, and Yuri was planning to be careful so that it would not be him. Perhaps he could manipulate it so that Kola took out his rage and frustration on Sasha.

"Yes, let's split it," said Yuri, moving to the wooden table in the center of the room. Sasha had sat in one of the three unmatched but reasonably comfortable stuffed chairs near the window.

"Now," Kola said and Sasha got up and joined the other two at the table.

Kola, who held the money from the robbery, pulled it and a watch and ring from his pocket.

"Fifty-four rubles," he said. "Eighteen each. The watch and ring go to Volovkatin."

"Volovkatin?" asked Sasha.

"Volovkatin. He has a jewelry store on Arbat Street, gives cash, hard rubles in hand for things like this," said Kola.

Kola had taken a few drinks before the robbery and he was talking too much. This kid might go back on his own and deal with Volovkatin without them. Kola should have kept Volovkatin to himself. Kola should eat something, but Kola pointed to the closet and Yuri knew that he wanted the vodka from the shelf.

Yuri got up and swaggered toward the closet. If Kola kept drinking like this, Yuri might soon, but not too soon, have enough nerve to challenge him. Yuri Glemp knew he was smarter than Kola but smarter didn't determine who was in charge. Soon, soon, if Kola kept drinking, things would be different.

Behind him Kola whispered something to the kid and laughed. Yuri knew it must be about him, some joke. Yes, he would get Kola, but first he would get Sasha alone and take care of him. He clenched his fist in anticipation and opened the closet door.

Before him stood a man who looked as if he were waiting for a bus. He was a square, squat man in his fifties with a nondescript Moscow face. The eyes of this man seemed to have a light dancing behind them. The man, who wore a brown shirt and a dark jacket, seemed to be quite at home standing in the closet.

In the same split second, Yuri's mind registered the figure before him and decided to do two things at once: close the door and turn for help. Both decisions were poor ones. As he tried to close the door, the bulky figure stepped forward, held the door open with his left hand and struck out at Yuri with his right hand. The blow hit Yuri's midsection, sending him staggering backward into the room.

Rostnikov stepped from the closet as quickly as his leg would allow him. The other two men in the room took in this barrel of a man and Kola rose quickly, pushed past the staggering Yuri and rushed forward with a smile. He roared at Rostnikov knowing that this man, be he police or burglar, was not to be reasoned with and Kola had no wish to engage in reason. He wanted to punish this man who had come from the closet. Kola, his arms out, threw his body into the intruder expecting to send the man staggering back into the closet, but when they met with a loud grunt the man did not stagger back, did not move. Kola was surprised but also delighted. He had expected it to be easy, perhaps unsatisfying. He thought vaguely that if this were indeed a policeman there might be other policemen nearby and if he were to get any satisfaction, have any chance of getting away, he would have to smash this man quickly, but he didn't want it to happen too quickly.

Kola looked into Rostnikov's eyes, saw the dancing light and had an instant of doubt, though he clutched the older man in a bear hug, a hug with which Kola had crushed the chest of at least three victims in the past two years. Kola could hear the man's breath and was surprised that it was not in the least labored. Kola locked his hands and squeezed, imagining Sasha sitting in wonder and admiration. Kola grunted, watching for the fear and pain in the eyes of the man in front of him, but there was no pain, no fear. The man even seemed to smile or almost smile and Kola felt the veins on his bald head swell with strain. Still the man smiled.

Behind him Kola heard Yuri catching his breath, hissing, "Turn him, Kola, so I can shoot."

Kola was enraged. He had lost face. Yuri could see that the bear hug which had never failed him before was not having its effect. And so Kola changed tactics. He let out a savage growl and stepped back with clenched fists to pummel the man in front of him, but he never got the chance to use his hands. Rostnikov reached out swiftly to grab Kola's right wrist with his left hand and his corded neck with his right. Kola tried to step back and free himself from the grip of the smaller man but he couldn't break free. He hit the man's hand with his left fist and tried to ram his head into the placid face before him but Rostnikov yanked at his left wrist, bent over as Kola leaned forward, grabbed his leg and put his head under Kola's arm. Kola found himself over the shoulders of the barrel of a man. He screamed in rage and humiliation but Rostnikov lifted him over his head and Kola found himself falling, flying toward Yuri who stood in front of Sasha. Kola hit the table, crushing it, sending wooden legs crashing, skidding into the air and across the room. Before he passed out, Kola thought he heard someone far away playing a balalaika.

Yuri had danced back as Kola's body shattered the table. He had stood back, gut burning from the punch he had taken, to watch Kola kill the intruder, but it hadn't happened. Kola had been the one beaten. And so Yuri stood now, pistol held firmly, and aimed at the wide body of this man from the closet who stood in front of him. Yuri had no choice and wanted none. He would shoot if the man moved. He would shoot even if the man didn't move. There was nothing to think about. He raised the gun and fired, but something had hit his hand and the bullet, instead of entering the intruder, thudded into the leg of the unconscious Kola who jumped, flopped like a fish with the impact.

Yuri was confused, afraid. What had happened? What would Kola do when he was awake and sober and knew that Yuri had shot him? Yuri raised the gun again, unsure of who he should kill first, Kola or the man from the closet who was limping toward him. He was not given the opportunity to make the decision. Something hit his arm again and the pain made him drop the gun which fell gently into one of the cloth chairs. And then, as the washtub of a man reached for him, Yuri understood and looked at Sasha who tossed his hair back and punched Yuri in the face, breaking the bridge of his nose.

Yuri staggered back in pain, hit the wall and slid down, reaching up to try stop the blood that spurted from his nose.

"Call down to Zelach," Rostnikov said, checking his pocket to be sure his book hadn't been damaged. "He's waiting down in a car."

Sasha Tkach nodded and hurried to the window. An icy blast entered the room as he threw open the window, leaned out, shouted and nodded.

"He's coming," Sasha said closing the window and turning back to Rostnikov. "I noticed him when we came in. I was afraid they would see him too."

"Yes," sighed Rostnikov. "Zelach is a bit conspicuous."

Sasha looked at Kola's leg while Rostnikov lifted Yuri from the floor after pocketing the gun that had landed on the chair. Rostnikov propped Yuri against the wall as Zelach and a uniformed MVD officer burst into the apartment, breaking the lock. Zelach and the young officer both held weapons. Zelach's was a pistol. The young man held an automatic weapon that could have dispatched a regiment with a touch.

Rostnikov sighed and motioned with his hand for the two to put the weapons away.

Zelach, his mouth open as usual, looked around the room as Rostnikov went back to the closet to retrieve his coat and hat.

"Call an ambulance for the one on the floor," Rostnikov said. "Take the other one too. Have someone fix them up and bring the one with the broken nose to my office. Watch them both. Inspector Tkach will fill out the report. And find a jewelry store operator named Volovkatin on Arbat Street. Arrest him for dealing in stolen goods."

Zelach stood, mouth open.

"Do you understand, Zelach? Are you here, Zelach?"

"Yes, Inspector. Volovkatchky on Lenin Prospekt."

"Sasha," Rostnikov said. "Go with him. Get Volovkatin."

"Yes," said Sasha, moving toward the door.

"There's no phone here," said Zelach looking around the room.

"That is correct. There is no phone," Rostnikov confirmed. "Why don't you send Officer—"

"… Karamasov," the young man said.

Rostnikov looked at the brown-uniformed young man with interest but saw nothing to be particularly interested in other than a literary name and shrugged.

"Karamasov can call the ambulance and you can wait here and then accompany these two to the hospital. Sasha, you and Zelach go to Arbat Street. You understand?"

"Perfectly," said Zelach, blinking. "Oh, they called."

"They did. Who are they?" said Rostnikov, buttoning his coat, thinking about dinner, deciding to make another attempt tonight to reach his son Josef by phone.

"Colonel Snitkonoy," said Zelach, trying to remember an approximate message. "You are to report back to him immediately. Someone has died."

"Someone?" asked Rostnikov.

Kola groaned on the floor and reached for his wounded leg. Yuri, his face bloody, looked as if he were going to say something, ask something, but changed his mind and moaned once. Karamasov looked around once more and hurried out of the apartment to make his call.

"Someone," Zelach repeated.

It was late, but there might be time to get to MVD headquarters, meet with Snitkonoy and still get back home at a reasonable hour. It was annoying. He was no more than a five-minute walk from his apartment, but Rostnikov was accustomed to annoyances. He would walk to the Profsojuznaja Metro Station on Krasikov and finish his paperback novel on the train.

"Anything else, Inspector?" Zelach asked.

"Yes, don't break down doors if you don't have to. It is very dramatic but it makes unnecessary work for some carpenter."

"I'll remember, Inspector," Zelach said seriously, moving to stand over Kola who was now definitely waking up.

Rostnikov clapped Tkach on the arm to indicate that he had done a good job. The inspector surveyed the room one last time, returned to the closet, retrieved the small stool and put it back in the corner near the sink where he had found it.

He stepped past the broken table and broken robbers and headed into the hall on his way back for what he feared would be a long lecture from the Gray Wolfhound.

One hour later, Rostnikov was uncomfortably seated at the conference table in the office of Colonel Snitkonoy, the Gray Wolfhound, who headed the MVD Bureau of Special Projects. Rostnikov had drawn a coffee cup in his notebook and was now thoughtfully shading it in to give the impression that some light source was hitting it from the left. He had been drawing variations on this coffee cup for several years and was getting quite competent at it. From time to time, he would look up, nod, grunt and indicate that he was pensively listening to the wisdom being dispensed by Colonel Snitkonoy who paced slowly about the room, hands folded behind his back, brown uniform perfectly pressed, medals glinting and colorful.

The Gray Wolfhound believed that Rostnikov was taking careful notes on his superior's advice and thought. This caused the white-maned MVD officer to speak more slowly, more deliberately, his deep voice suggesting an importance unsupported by the depth of his words.

Rostnikov had recently been transferred "on temporary but open-ended duty" to the MVD, the police, uniformed and nonuniformed, who directed traffic, faced the public, and were the front line of defense against crime and for the maintenance of order. It had been a demotion, the result of Rostnikov's frequent clashes with the Komityet Gospudarstvennoy Besapasnosti, the State Security Agency, the KGB. Before the demotion, Rostnikov had been a senior inspector in the office of the Procurator General in Moscow. The Procurator General, appointed for a seven-year-term, the longest term of any Soviet official, is responsible for sanctioning arrests, supervising investigations, executing sentences, and supervising trials. Too often, Rostnikov's path had crossed into the territory of the KGB which is responsible for all political investigations and security. The KGB, however, could label anything from drunkenness to robbery as political.

Now Rostnikov worked for the Gray Wolfhound whose bureau, everyone but the Wolfhound knew, existed because the Colonel looked like the ideal MVD officer. Colonel Snitkonoy was trotted out for all manner of ceremonial events from greeting and dining with visiting foreigners to presenting medals for heroism to workers at Soviet factories. Colonel Snitkonoy's bureau was also given a limited number of criminal investigations, usually minor crimes or crimes about which no one really cared. Rostnikov and the three other investigators who worked for the Wolfhound would conduct their investigations, and if the doznaniye or inquiry merited it, the case might be turned over to the Procurator's Office for further investigation and possible prosecution.

"Surprise, yes. Oh, yes," said the Wolfhound, pausing at the window of his office and turning suddenly on Rostnikov who sat at the table across the room in the Petrovka headquarters.

Rostnikov was not surprised, but he did look up from his drawing to make contact with Snitkonoy's metallic blue eyes.

"We will surprise them, Porfiry Petrovich," the Wolfhound said. "We will conduct the investigation with dispatch, identify those responsible, file a report of such clarity that it will be a model for others to follow for years."

Rostnikov adopted a knowing smile and nodded wisely in agreement though he had no idea of what this performance was all about. Snitkonoy began to stride toward Rostnikov who turned over the page of his notebook with the unfinished drawing. Snitkonoy approached, polished brown boots clicking against the polished wooden floor. He stood over Rostnikov with a sad, knowing smile.

"I have in this past month you have been with us come to rely upon you, Porfiry Petrovich. You and I have the same attitude, the same outlook on dealing with the criminal mind, coping with those who pose a threat to the ongoing struggle of the Revolution."

Rostnikov's deep brown eyes met the Wolfhound's soberly and he nodded in agreement, though he agreed with almost nothing the handsome military figure in front of him had said. Rostnikov had been with the MVD for more than four months. He was certain that his and the Colonel's views of the criminal mind were not at all similar, partly because Rostnikov did not believe in a criminal mind. There were evil people, true—stupid, selfish, brutish people—even a good number of quite insane people, but few who thought themselves so. Mostly there were people who considered themselves quite decent, quite compassionate, quite reasonable. They got carried away with their emotions, beliefs or assumed needs and broke the law, sometimes quite violently. The only minds that Rostnikov thought might reasonably be identified as criminal belonged to certain kinds of bureaucrats who had the opportunity and desire to engage in ongoing illegal activities.

As for the Revolution, Rostnikov had struggled with a nearly useless left leg for over forty years as a reminder of the Revolution that never ended. When he was fifteen in 1942, Rostnikov had lost most of the use of the leg in defending the Revolution against German invaders. No, the differences between the Wolfhound and the inspector known by his colleagues as the Washtub went beyond the contrast of their appearance, but, in spite of this, Rostnikov had developed a certain affection for the caricature of an officer who paced the room before him. There appeared to be no malice in the colonel and his naïveté was sincere as was his loyalty to those who worked under him whether they deserved it or not. All the colonel expected in return was admiration. So Rostnikov did his best to project admiration while retaining as much dignity as possible.

"So," said Snitkonoy standing to his full six-feet-three, "you understand what must be done."

"No," said Rostnikov amiably.

The colonel shook his head, a patient patronizing smile on his firm lips. He stepped to the polished dark table and leaned forward toward Rostnikov.

"Commissar Illya Rutkin," the Colonel whispered. "Do you know him?"

"The name is somewhat familiar," answered Rostnikov putting down his pad, beginning to sense a potential threat. Rutkin was, he knew, a relatively incompetent assistant to Party District

Leader Vladimir Koveraskin, who was far from incompetent and had the reputation of a man to be avoided. Rutkin was an expendable, one of the dispensable underlings Party members keep around to throw to the KGB or whomever might come nipping for corruption or scapegoats. Koveraskin had something to do with keeping track of dissident movements, or at least he was rumored to have such a function.

"He is dead," the Wolfhound whispered dramatically.

"I am sorry to hear that," said Rostnikov shifting his left leg which threatened, as it always did when he sat too long, to lose consciousness.

"A man destined for greater service for the State," the Wolfhound said softly, sadly.

"Dead," Rostnikov repeated before the eulogy reached proportions worthy of Tolstoy.

"Murdered," said the Wolfhound.

Rostnikov shifted and put his notebook in his pocket alongside the novel he had finished reading on the metro. Rostnikov's thoughts, up to this moment, had been on dinner and on some urgency to get down to his desk for a quick interrogation of the dealer in stolen goods he had sent Tkach to arrest. Rostnikov did not like the sound of the colonel's voice which suggested something of great moment. He did not like where the conversation was going but he could do nothing to stop it.

"And we . . . ?" Rostnikov began.

"Precisely," said Snitkonoy with satisfaction. "We have been given the task of investigating the murder of this important figure. We are responsible for the investigation and the quick resolution. There are ramifications to this case, Porfiry Petrovich."

Yes, Rostnikov thought, I'm sure there are, but I am not sure you know what most of them are. Murders of commissars were not usually turned over to the Wolfhound. Someone was not terribly interested in the outcome of this murder case. Rostnikov might be reacting with too much suspicion, but it was better to be suspicious and survive, as he had managed to do, then to underreact and find that it is too late. There was no help for it. It was coming and he would have to deal with it.

"And I am to conduct the investigation," Rostnikov said. "I'm honored."

"We are all honored," said Snitkonoy. "This important investigation assigned to us indicates the high esteem in which we stand."

Rostnikov nodded and hoped that the case was a nice simple one, robbery or a domestic conflict that simply required a cover-up. Snitkonoy strode to his desk, boots clicking again, and reached for a brown file which he picked up and brought to Rostnikov who didn't want to touch it but did so.

"Bad business," the colonel said. "He was investigating the death of a child, the death of Lev Samsonov's child, a young girl."

Rostnikov did not nod, did not respond. This was getting worse and worse.

"You know who Samsonov is?"

"Yes," sighed Rostnikov. "The dissident."

"The traitor," hissed Snitkonoy magnificently. "He and his wife are scheduled for deportation. It was feared that without the investigation Samsonov demanded, he might go to France or whatever decadent nation would have him and cause embarrassment, imperil Premier Gorbachev's magnificent and courageous attempts to bring world peace. And ... "

"... And in the course of his investigation of the death of Samsonov's child, Commissar Rutkin was murdered," Rostnikov cut in.

The Colonel did not like to be interrupted. He fixed his fourth most penetrating glance at Rostnikov who looked back at him blandly.

"It is all in the report. You are to investigate the murder of Commissar Rutkin. You need not address the death of the child. Another representative of Party District Leader Koveraskin's office will be dispatched later to deal with that. However, it is possible that the two deaths are related."

"There are many violent subversive people in Moscow," said Rostnikov.

"Moscow?" the Wolfhound said, halting in his pacing as someone softly knocked at his door. "Commissar Rutkin was murdered in the town of Tumsk, where you are to go immediately to conduct your investigation and report back within three days."

"Tumsk?"

"Somewhere in Siberia on the Yensei River," the Wolfhound said, ignoring the now insistent knock. "Arrangements have been made for you. Check them with Pankov. Take the report. It is a copy. Guard it carefully. It contains information on Rutkin, Samsonov, the child. You have my support and confidence and three days."

"Thank you, Colonel," Rostnikov said getting up carefully and clutching the file. "Can I have some assistance in this? Perhaps I can settle this with even greater dispatch if I have someone to do the legwork. Someone we can trust."

The colonel had a smile on his face which did not please Porfiry Petrovich. The colonel put his hands behind his back and rocked on his heels.

"I've anticipated your request, Gospodin, Comrade," the Wolfhound said. "Investigator Karpo will be accompanying you."

"As always, Comrade Colonel, you are ahead of me," Rostnikov said.

"Porfiry Petrovich, do not fail me. Do not fail us. Do not fail the Revolution," Snitkonoy said from his position near the window where the setting sun could silhouette his erect form.

"The Revolution can continue in confidence with its fate in my hands," Rostnikov said, hand on the door. It was as close to sarcasm as Rostnikov could risk with the colonel, but the inspector's dignity required the gesture.

"Ah, one more thing," said the colonel before Rostnikov could get the door open. "An investigator from the office of the procurator will be accompanying you. Someone from the Kiev district. The Procurator General himself wants him to observe your methods, learn from your vast experience."

Rostnikov opened the door where the colonel's assistant, Pankov, a near-dwarf of a man, stood ready to knock again. Pankov was not incompetent but that was not why Snitkonoy had chosen him. Rostnikov was sure that Pankov owed his position in life to the striking contrast he made to the Wolfhound. Pankov's clothes were perpetually rumpled, his few strands of hair unwilling to lie in peace against his scalp. When he stood as erect as he was able to stand, Pankov rose no higher than the Wolfhound's chest. Rostnikov had recently decided that Pankov looked like a refugee from the pages of a novel by the Englishman Charles Dickens.

"Is he upset?" Pankov whispered in fear to Rostnikov.

"Not in the least," Rostnikov whispered back.

"Pankov," the Wolfhound bellowed and Pankov almost shook.

"I'll check back with you in half an hour to make arrangements for my mission to Siberia," Rostnikov told the frightened little man who looked at the silhouetted colonel.

"Sometimes," whispered Pankov, "I think I would live longer if I were in Siberia."

"Perhaps," Rostnikov whispered back, "it can be arranged."

"Stop whispering and get in here, Pankov," the Wolfhound shouted. "I haven't all night, my little friend."

Rostnikov stepped out, closed the door, tucked the folder under his arm and slowly headed for his office. He did his best not to think, to concentrate on nothing at all, to select in his mind the novel he would take with him on the trip. Rostnikov had never been to Siberia. He had no curiosity about Siberia. He did not want to go to Siberia. But, and this was much more important, he had no choice in the matter.

THREE

ICE CREAM IS THE SOVIET UNION'S MOST POPULAR DESSERT. It is eaten not only in the summer but in the winter. It is eaten in enormous quantities. In Moscow alone more than 170 tons of ice cream are consumed each day and visitors report that the ice cream in Moscow runs second in taste only to that of Italy and is probably equal to that of France and the United States.

Business, however, was not particularly good that morning at the ice cream stand in the Yamarka, the shopping center behind the Education Pavilion of the USSR Economic Achievements Exhibition, the VDNKh, in North Moscow. Boris Manizer, who had sold ice cream at the stand for four years, knew why. Visitors, who usually stood in line at the stand, would approach with an eager smile, see Boris's new assistant and change their minds.

Boris's new assistant was not just sober. He was positively forbidding. The man was tall, over six feet, lean with dark thinning hair and very pale skin. He looked corpse-like and his dark eyes radiated a frost more cold than the ice cream they sold or, today, failed to sell. The white sales-coat simply added contrast to his new assistant's pale skin. The man did not serve many customers and when he did he moved his left hand a bit awkwardly, as if he had recently been injured. Boris had decided that he did not like his new assistant, but he had no choice. The man had appeared two days earlier, shown his MVD identification and informed Boris that he would be working with him "for a few days." There was no further explanation.

And so, this morning as every morning Boris Manizer took the metro to the VDNKh Station and walked past the massive Space Obelisk pointing into the sky to commemorate the progress of the Soviet people in mastering outer space. Five years ago on a summer day, Boris had heard two educated men in front of the Obelisk saying that religion had been replaced in modern Russia by the Soviet space program. It had struck Boris as a wonderful, secret truth. He began to notice how many space stamps, space ashtrays, space desk ornaments were being sold. Even grocery stores and beauty shops had names like Cosmos and Sputnik. It had, in the last few years, began to change a bit, but it was still evident that the people were waiting for something new to happen in space, something new to celebrate the way he heard the crazy Americans celebrated the anniversaries of rock singers like Elovis Presahley and movie stars like Marilyn Munrue.

The wind had been blowing across the Peace Prospekt this morning and Boris had hurried beyond the Alley of Heroes, with its busts of Yuri Gargarin and the other Soviets who had been in space, and to the main entrance of the Exhibition, the biggest museum in the city including 100,000 exhibits, frequently renewed, in 300 buildings and 80 pavilions with open-air displays when weather permitted. He had tramped left, past the Central Pavilion and the stature of Lenin in front of it, avoided the frozen path lined with winter-white birch trees where skaters would soon flash back and forth laughing, their noses red. He had walked around the Education Pavilion and down the path into the shopping center.

Boris could talk knowingly with his customers about the many exhibits and pavilions though he had actually been in only a few of them. Boris liked to talk, to suggest to his customers that they visit the Circlarama theater, the bumper cars in the fun fair, the Animal Husbandry Pavilion and the Transport Pavilion. Now Boris fleetingly considered talking to the policeman who had given him no name, but one look at the gaunt face changed his mind.

A few weeks earlier business had been booming. People had come, in spite of the cold weather, as they always do to the annual Russian Winter Festival. The exhibits were crowded and people coming in from the troika rides were hungry. Now, standing beside the vampire of a police officer, Boris began to worry about how long the stand would stay in business. Already, he knew, the next nearest ice cream stand, the one managed by Pugachev, had almost doubled its business since the coming of the ghost. And so Boris stood glumly and watched the customers pass him by, glance at the policeman and hurry on to another stand or to one of the shashlyk grills.

"What are you looking for?" Boris finally asked as the day wore on and the pale man stood unblinking. "Since it is destroying my livelihood and starving my wife and children, I would like to know."

The man looked down at Boris. Almost everyone looked down at Boris who stood slightly over five feet tall. Boris wore a clean, white linen cap with a peak to give the illusion of a few added inches to his height, but it simply made him look like a very little man with a peaked cap.

"There is no need for you to have that information," the man said flatly.

"What about my business? No one will buy ice cream from us but blind people. I'm sorry to tell you you are not a welcoming figure. You know that?"

"I can do nothing about that," the man said.

"You could smile," Boris said looking hopeful at a mother and child who were headed for the ice cream stand.

"I cannot," the policeman said. The policeman, whose name was Emil Karpo, had attempted a smile before the mirror in the wash room at Petrovka years earlier. It had looked grotesque, reminded him of the character in a book he had been forced to read as a child, a French book called The Man Who Laughs about a man who has his face twisted into a permanent grin.

"Maybe not, but what about my business?" wailed Boris.

"The business of the State takes precedence over the interests of the individual," the man said, his eyes scanning the crowd.

"True," sighed Boris as the mother and child saw Karpo and veered off toward a nearby restaurant, "but what is the business of the State here? If my wife and three children are to starve for the State, I would like to know why?"

Karpo's eyes fixed on two young men, heavily clothed, moving resolutely, hands in pockets, toward a group of Japanese tourists who were taking pictures of everything but Boris Manizer's ice cream stand.

"Three children is too much," Karpo said, not looking at Boris.

"Right, eezveenee't'e pashah'Ista, please forgive me. I'll kill two of them as soon as I get home. I might as well. I can't feed them any longer," Boris said sarcastically.

"That won't be necessary," Karpo said, his eyes still on the young men. "The State will provide if they will do their share."

Boris had been shifting the ice cream cartons as Karpo spoke. He looked up to be sure that the man was joking but the pale face gave no indication of humor. Before Boris could pursue the issue, a customer appeared, one of the Japanese complete with camera around his neck.

"Yah tooree'st," said the small Japanese man who was bundled in a bulky black coat.

"What a surprise!" Boris said with a smile. "Who would have thought you were a tourist? I would have taken you for a member of the Politboro."

"Mah-ro-zheh-na," the Japanese man said, deliberately looking back at a group of his friends who admired his courage.

"What?" said Boris.

"He thinks he asked for ice cream," Karpo said.

"Da," the man agreed.

Boris got the ice cream and the Japanese man motioned to his friends to join him. A few seconds later the stand was surrounded by Japanese tourists holding out ruble notes. It wouldn't be enough to make it a profitable day, but it wouldn't hurt. He turned to the policeman for help with the crowd, but the man was gone, his white jacket and cap lying on the floor beside the stand.

As he scooped and handed out cones, Boris looked over the heads of his Japanese customers to see the policeman moving swiftly through the crowd toward the two young men he had been watching. The young men, one of whom had removed his hat to reveal long red hair, were talking to the woman and child who had veered away from Boris's stand only minutes before.

"Choco-late," said one Japanese man.

Boris had no idea what he was saying and handed the man a vanilla cone. The man smiled and paid.

Boris tried to concentrate on business but he couldn't help watching the policeman who was only a few feet from the young men who were standing very close to the mother and child, both of whom looked quite frightened.

And then something quite strange happened. Two men in black coats stepped through the crowd and stood in front of the pale policeman who stopped and reached quickly into his pocket.

One of the two men in black coats had something in his hand and the pale policeman removed his hand from his jacket and spoke. The two men in black looked back over their shoulders at the young men and the mother and child and then turned back to the gaunt policeman. The two youths had now taken notice of the gaunt man and the two in black coats. They began to back away from the mother and child.

Boris handed out ice cream after ice cream pulling in coins and paper, handing out change, not quite sure if he was doing it right.

As Boris served his last tourist he watched the red-haired youth and his companion turn and run, coats flapping behind them, in the general direction of the Metallurgy Pavilion. The pale policeman pointed at the fleeing pair but the men in black coats did not turn to look. They remained, hands at their sides, directly in front of him while behind them the mother and child stood trembling, confused. Boris could stand it no longer. He hurried around his stand and moved as quickly as he could through the crowd to the mother and child as he would want someone to do if his Masha and one of his children were standing frightened, alone like that. The boy even looked a bit like his Egon.

"Are you all right?" he asked the woman and child. Though the boy was no more than ten, he was nearly as tall as Boris, taller if Boris took off his peaked hat.

"They threatened us, me, Alex, but . . . " she said looking around for the youths.

Alex's nearly white hair was a mass of unruly curls. His mouth hung open.

"Come. I'll give you both an ice cream and you'll feel better," Boris said, looking around the crowd for any sign of the policeman, but there was none. Boris led the mother and boy toward his stand, praying to the gods that didn't exist that he would never see the pale man again. And the gods that didn't exist granted the wish of Boris Manizer.

The trip to Dzerzhinsky Square in the KGB Volga took less than twenty minutes. Karpo sat silently next to one of the black-coated men while the other drove. They took the center lane, the lane of the privileged, straight down Mira Prospekt, around the square past the statue of Felix Dzerzhinsky, who, under Lenin himself, headed the Cheka, the forerunner of the KGB. The car pulled up smoothly in front of Lubyanka, a massive block-square mustard yellow building. Karpo did not glance at the white-curtained windows of Lubyanka nor at the shiny brass fittings on the door as he walked up the steps flanked by the two KGB men who had left their car at curb.

Lubyanka had begun life as a turn-of-the-century insurance office. It was converted under Lenin to a great prison and interrogation center and now it was the headquarters of the KGB.

An armed guard in uniform inside the door scanned the three men without moving his head. At a desk about twenty paces farther on, behind which stood a duplicate of the armed man at the door, a woman in a dark suit looked up, recognized the KGB men and nodded for them to pass. People, almost all men, passed them carrying folders, papers, notebooks, briefcases. Flanked by the two, Karpo walked quickly down a corridor, past a desk where a dark-suited man sat with yet another young, uniformed soldier behind him carrying a machine pistol at the ready. The trio turned right down another corridor and one of the black-coated men motioned for Karpo to halt at an unmarked door. The second KGB man remained behind Karpo. It was more a question of routine and procedure than any thought or fear that Karpo might run or go mad and violent. It did not matter who Karpo was. There was a way of bringing someone in and that way had to be followed or the consequences could be quite severe.

They entered the small reception area that looked more like a cell. There were wooden benches against the wooden walls. Four photographs of past Party heroes were on the walls, one on each. A photo of Lenin at his desk looking at the camera was slightly larger than the other three photographs.

One of the KGB men nodded at the bench. Karpo sat, back straight, eyes apparently focused on the wall ahead while the shorter KGB man stood near him and the other walked to the inner door and knocked gently.

"Pa-dazh-DEEk-tye, wait," came a deep voice from within and the KGB man stepped back a bit too quickly as if the door upon which he had knocked were electrified.

They waited, one man standing over Karpo, the other pacing the room and occasionally glancing at Karpo or the door. The pacing man's face was square, solid, cold but beyond it Karpo, who never looked directly at him, could see the fringes of anxiety. The man wanted to get rid of his responsibility and be free of this cell of a reception room.

Five minutes, then ten passed with none of the three speaking. And then the inner door opened and a thin, balding bespectacled man of about forty, wearing a brown suit that looked almost like a uniform, stepped out and fixed Karpo with dark blue eyes. Karpo looked up and met his eyes. Karpo's eyes showed nothing.

"Out, both of you, now," the man said.

Karpo's escorts moved to the door. They did their best to give the impression that they were in no hurry to leave, an impression that they failed to deliver.

When the two men were gone, the man motioned to Karpo to follow him. Emil Karpo rose and entered the inner office which continued the monastic motif of the outer office. There was an old, dark wooden desk containing nothing but a telephone, no carpeting on the clean but worn wooden floor and four wooden chairs, one behind the desk, three facing and opposite it. There was one white-curtained window and on the wall across from the desk, a painting of Lenin signing a document. Karpo felt quite comfortable in the room for it was not unlike the one in which he lived.

"Emil Karpo," the man said. "You may sit."

"If you wish," Karpo said watching the other man adjust his glasses and move around to his chair behind the desk. They stood looking at each other, both unblinking.

"I wish," the man said, and Karpo sat in one of the wooden chairs. The man did not sit.

"I am Major Zhenya," the man said.

Karpo nodded.

Zhenya opened the drawer in the desk without looking down and removed a thick file.

"This is your file, Inspector Karpo," he said. "It is a very interesting file. There are things in it which you might find surprising, not surprising in their existence, but surprising because we know them. Would you like some examples?"

"My wishes are clearly of no consequence," Karpo answered, and Zhenya studied him for a sign of sarcasm but he could detect none for the simple reason that there was no sarcasm. Karpo had no use for sarcasm or imagination.

"You are a dedicated investigator," Zhenya said without looking at the report, "a good Party member. Recently, with your acquiescence, you were transferred from the Procurator's Office to the Office of Special Services of Colonel Snitkonoy in the MVD to work under Inspector Porfiry Petrovich Rostnikov who has also recently been transferred, a definite demotion for both of you."

He paused for response and Karpo met his eyes.

"I believed that my association with Inspector Rostnikov who was out of favor would hamper my continued services to the Procurator General," he said. "Therefore, when offered the opportunity to continue to serve under Inspector Rostnikov, even in a reduced capacity, I accepted."

"I see," said Zhenya glancing down at the folder. "Are you a bit curious about why you are here?"

"No," said Karpo.

Major Zhenya removed his glasses, cocked his head and looked at Karpo with disbelief but Karpo's dead eyes met his without flinching.

"Let us then try a few of those surprises," said Zhenya. "Twice a month, on a Wednesday, you have an assignation with a telephone operator and part-time prostitute named Mathilde Verson. Your next such assignation will be this coming week."

"Prostitution has been eliminated from the Soviet Union," said Karpo.

"You deny this assignation?" asked Zhenya.

"I quote official statements of the Office of the Premier," said Karpo. "That I meet this woman is true. That our meeting is intimate is also true. That it represents a weakness I also confirm. I find that I am not completely able to deny my animalism and that I can function, do the work of the State to which I have been assigned, with greater efficiency if I allow myself this indulgence rather than fight against it."

"You recently had an operation on your left arm," Zhenya went on, hiding the fact that he was annoyed by the failure of his first surprise. "An operation performed by a Jewish physician who has been excluded from the Soviet State medical service, a physician who happens to be related to the wife of the same Inspector Rostnikov."

"Such an operation did take place," Karpo agreed. "The arm was injured three times in the performance of my duty, once in pursuit of a thief, the other in an explosion which caused the death of a terrorist in Red Square and the third time on a hotel roof while subduing a sniper."

"I'm well aware of the circumstances," Zhenya said with a small smile to hide his frustration.

"I was hospitalized in a State hospital and informed that I would never be able to use my left arm and hand and that I might have to consider having it removed to prevent possible atrophy and infection," Karpo went on. "The Jewish doctor whom you mention indicated that the arm could not only be saved but could function. With great reluctance because of my faith in the State medical service I allowed the man to operate on my hand and arm and to suggest a regimen of exercise and therapy. It was my belief that the law allowed me this option. I checked legal passages on medical treatment and Article 42 of the Constitution of the Union of Soviet Socialist Republics."

"And," Zhenya said, unable to keep the sarcasm from his voice, "I am sure you could quote those legal passages and the Constitution."

"The Constitution, yes," agreed Karpo giving no indication that he recognized the sarcasm, "but not all the legal passages though I did take notes on them and have them in my room, at home.

"We've checked the room where you live, Emil Karpo," Zhenya said walking around the desk, folding his arms and sitting back against it to look directly down at Karpo. "We've seen your cell, looked at the notebooks on all your cases. You live a rather ascetic life, Investigator Karpo, with, of course, the exception of your animal sojourns with Mathilde Verson."

"I'll accept that as a compliment from a senior officer, Major," Karpo said.

"Are you trying to provoke me, Karpo?" Zhenya said, standing.

"Not at all, Major," Karpo said evenly.

"You have no secrets, Karpo, no secrets from us," he said.

"I have no secrets to keep from you," Karpo responded.

"Then why the thin wire on your door, the feather which falls if someone enters your door?"

"I've made enemies among certain criminals in Moscow," said Karpo. "As you know from looking at my notebooks, I continue to seek criminals on whom the files at Petrovka have been temporarily closed. It is possible that some of them might wish to stop me. I think it best if I know when and if they have discovered my pursuit and might be waiting for me or might have placed an explosive device within my home."

"When you go home you will find your wire and your feather exactly where they were," said Zhenya softly, adjusting his glasses. "If we wish to enter your room, we will do so and you will never know."

"Am I to gather from this, Major, that you wish something from me?" said Karpo.

Major Zhenya did not like this situation. It had not gone as he had planned. Major Zhenya had taken over his office only a few months ago after the death of his superior, Colonel Drozhkin. Major Zhenya wanted to make a quick name for himself. The KGB was at the height of its power. KGB chief Viktor M. Chebrikov had been elevated to full membership and was the first member to announce his support for Mikhail Gorbachev's policy of change. In return, the KGB was being given even more responsibility for surveillance on the performance of economic and agricultural enterprises. New KGB chiefs, younger men, had been appointed in five of the fifteen Republics of the Soviet Union. The situation could change quickly as it had in the past but Major Zhenya wished to take advantage of the moment. He wanted to be Colonel Zhenya and to remain permanently in charge of an important section of internal criminal investigation of which he was now only acting director. There were several bits of unfinished business that he might put in order and thereby impress his superiors. He was attempting to address one of them at the moment.

"This afternoon or this evening you will be informed that you are to accompany Inspector Rostnikov to the town of Tumsk in Siberia. Do you know where Tumsk is?"

"A small town on the Yensei above Igarka," said Karpo. "I believe it was one of the small summer ports established by traders in the fifteenth century."

"You are a remarkable man," said Zhenya.

"Siberia is the source of great power and potential," Karpo said.

"You've been reading Soviet Life, Inspector," Zhenya said.

"When I can," agreed Karpo.

"Commissar Rutkin—and I'm sure you know his entire life story and that of his ancestors—was murdered in Tumsk under somewhat unusual circumstances. He was in Tumsk to conduct an inquiry into the death of a child, the daughter of Lev Samsonov, the dissident who is scheduled to be deported to the West in a short time. Inspector Rostnikov, you and an observer from the Procurator's Office in Kiev will depart by plane as soon as possible to conduct an investigation."

"I will do my best to assist Inspector Rostnikov," said Karpo, "and I will consider it an honor to serve the State in an investigation of this importance."

Zhenya shifted impatiently and leaned forward, his hands palms down on the desk.

"You will take careful notes on the investigation, notes on Inspector Rostnikov's handling of the entire situation. You will take these notes confidentially, in detail, including every violation, every infraction of the law and acceptable inquiry. You will call this office the moment you return from Tumsk and you will report to me directly with your notes. You understand what I am telling you?"

"Your words are clear, Major," said Karpo.

"Do you have some sense of the reason?"

"You have cause to believe that Inspector Rostnikov may operate in violation of the law," he said.

"He has given some cause for concern and we wish simply to check," said Zhenya backing away, arms still folded. "You are a loyal Soviet citizen. I expect you to carry out this assignment without question."

Karpo was quite aware that no questions he might have would be answered and so he nodded. Loyalty also extended to Rostnikov who, Karpo knew, was a bit too independent and had come into conflict with the KGB on at least one occasion. It would do no harm to keep notes and file a report. Zhenya was quite correct and within his jurisdiction in asking for such a report and Emil Karpo had every intention of carrying out the assignment.

"Good," said Zhenya unfolding his arms and going around the desk. "You may leave. I'll expect your report within an hour of your return to Moscow."

Karpo rose slowly as Major Zhenya reached for Karpo's folder, put it in front of him and opened it, his eyes examining the words before him or pretending to for Karpo's benefit.

Less than half an hour later Emil Karpo sat in his small room, efficient handbag packed with two changes of clothing and two notebooks. He paused, checking to see if he had forgotten anything, and as he checked he found that he was troubled by his meeting with Major Zhenya. Emil Karpo would have preferred to think that the KGB was efficient, unfailing, but experience had demonstrated that this was not always so. Zhenya's ambition had been quite evident. Ambition was personal, destructive. It hampered efficiency. It was Major Zhenya's ambition that had prevented Karpo from catching the two youths who had been preying on visitors to the Exhibit of Economic Achievements. Had they given him but one minute more he would have had the redhead and the other one. Efficiency would have dictated that they allow him to do so. Nothing would have been lost, since they had waited for Major Zhenya even after arriving at Lubyanka. And now the duo might harm, possibly kill a Soviet citizen. It disturbed Karpo, who had changed into his black wool sweater and black pants, that the KGB should be so inefficient.

It also disturbed Karpo to find that while the wire and the feather on his door were, indeed, back approximately where they had been, possibly even close enough to have fooled him, the KGB men who had come through his door had failed to find the single thread of his own hair which he had stretched across the lower hinge. Karpo had no doubt that someone had entered his room.

It was at that point that a sense of loyalty to the State and concern for Porfiry Petrovich Rostnikov entered into an unconscious battle deep within and unknown to Emil Karpo, who did not believe that an unconscious existed.

FOUR

ROSTNIKOV FINISHED HIS BENCH PRESSES, FIFTEEN WITH TWO hundred American pounds, and with a soft grunt let the weight back onto the two padded chairs just above his head. He sat up on the flat plastic coffee table with the steel legs that he used for his lifting and began to breathe deeply as he watched Sarah set the table.

There were many things Porfiry Petrovich Rostnikov would have liked. He would have liked a real weight-lifting bench like the Americans made. He would have liked a small room where he could go to lift his weights instead of a corner of his living-dining room. He would have liked more room to store his weights instead of having to place them neatly inside the cabinet in the corner where the good dishes would be kept if he and Sarah had good dishes. He would have liked their son Josef back safely in Moscow or, at least, not in Afghanistan where he was now. And he would have liked to avoid telling Sarah about the trip to Siberia he would be taking the next morning.

He had come through the door that evening prepared with a vague excuse for being late and with an offering in his hand to make up for his tardiness. He had clutched a bag of garden vegetables—a squash, two onions, something that might be a cucumber. A nervous man with exceptionally bad teeth had set up one of those quick-moving folding stands outside the metro station to sell some of the vegetables. Rostnikov had the good fortune to be there when the man was setting up and was standing in the line that formed even before anyone knew what the man was selling. By the time Rostnikov had filled the little sack he kept in his coat pocket, the man was almost sold out, though the line still contained about twenty-five people.

Sarah had been late. Her latest job was in a small bookshop on Kacholav Street where, she said, she felt far more comfortable than she had working at the Melodiya Record Shop or for her cousin who sold pots and pans. Rostnikov did and did not believe her. In any case, the bookshop had been opened late to accommodate a special customer of high rank who wanted to pick up an American book.

Sarah had explained all this after she entered the apartment wearily and greeted Rostnikov who, at the moment, had been doing one-handed seventy-pound curls while seated on the edge of the bench.

Rostnikov had grunted as she took off her coat and he sensed her moving across the room toward him. She touched his head from behind with cool fingers and then moved toward the small kitchen into his line of vision. For an instant Rostnikov lost count of his repetitions. Sarah looked unusually tired and he sensed that something weighed upon her. Sarah was forty-six, solidly built, with a remarkably unlined face considering the life she had led. She wore round glasses. When she was listening carefully to what someone said, she would tilt her head down and look over the glasses. Her dark hair with highlights of red was naturally curly and she kept it cut short partly, he knew, because Rostnikov had frequently admired her neck.

She smiled back at him when she discovered the vegetables on the small table near the equally small refrigerator and then set to work on heating his chicken tabaka, which she had prepared and cooked the night before.

"Are you having more headaches?" Rostnikov said panting from the workout, wiping his face with the moist corner of his gray sweat shirt.

Sarah didn't answer at first. She only shrugged, and then she muttered, "It comes. It goes. Nichevo. It's nothing."

At that point, she smiled, looking at him over her glasses. In one hand she held a knife. In the other, the possible cucumber he had purchased. He thought she looked quite beautiful.

"You should talk to your cousin Alex, the doctor," Rostnikov said, getting up slowly to keep his left leg from complaining.

"I'll call him tomorrow. You want to wash up? The chicken will be ready soon."

He grunted and went through their small bedroom to the bathroom smelling both his own sweat and the aroma of chicken. The tiny bathroom was Rostnikov's triumph. He had learned to repair the frequently broken toilet himself knowing that the building superintendent, whose job it was, would never get it done. He had learned to fix the almost-as-frequently functionless shower. He had begun his amateur exploits as a plumber out of a determination to triumph over adversity, but he had discovered that he enjoyed reading about conduits and pipes and plunge valves, that he enjoyed identifying the problem, locating its origin and repairing it. A few of the neighbors had even learned to come to him, though it was quite illegal to bypass the People's plumber for the district and everyone knew that you could almost never get one of the assigned repairmen to the building and if you did you would have to pay a bribe of at least five rubles to get any decent work done, even though the repairs were supposed to be free. The neighbors figured that since Rostnikov was a policeman the normal rules of the Socialist Republic did not necessarily apply.

They had encountered the system often enough to know that this was generally true. And the nice thing about Rostnikov was that he did not expect a bribe. He even seemed to enjoy himself when fixing a toilet or a sink.

Sarah had suggested to him that plumbing repair was just another form of detection with different tools.

"Yes," he had agreed, "but toilets are much simpler. They may complain and talk back but they don't make you weep. And when you find out what is wrong, you fix it. It is simple lonely detection."

She had understood. Sarah usually understood, Rostnikov thought as the cool water beat against his hairy chest. And he usually understood her. For months they had not spoken about leaving the country. He had tried, had even engaged in an attempt to blackmail the KGB, but he had failed and endangered both them and their son Josef. And so they had stopped speaking of leaving and Sarah had remained just as supporting and loving but her smile was not as ready, her step not as hopeful. And the headaches had come.

If Sarah were not Jewish, perhaps, she would not have thought, dreamed of leaving. It would not have entered her mind, but she was Jewish and their son Josef was, on his records, listed as being half Jewish and Rostnikov was identified as having a Jewish wife, all of which gave rise to the idea of leaving. Officially, the Soviet Union, whose Constitution, in Article 34, declares that all "Citizens of the USSR are equal before the law without distinction of origin, social or property status, race or religion," draws a distinction between Russians and Jews or Russians and other ethnic minorities. This distinction is made quite evident on the passports of Soviet citizens, and Jews are sometimes sneeringly called pyaty punkty, fifth pointers, because it is on the fifth line of the Soviet passport that nationality is indicated and the line on which a Jew is identified as being different from the rest of his countrymen.

Rostnikov turned slowly to let the water hit his lower back and then his leg. It would have felt better to have the water beat down, massage, but there was seldom enough water pressure for this to happen. Sometimes in the shower Rostnikov made a sound like singing or humming to tunes or near-tunes that ran through his head, but he did not feel like singing this night.

When he turned off the shower and stepped into the bedroom to dry himself, Rostnikov considered once again how best to tell Sarah about Siberia. It struck him, as it often did, that getting through life was a minefield and one did it successfully by constant worry or by developing a sense and sensitivity.

"Ready?" Sarah said calling to him.

"Coming," he replied with a sigh as he finished putting on his pants and tucked in his white pullover shirt.

Sarah was seated. The pot was steaming in the center of the table as it rested on a block of wood. The salad stood next to his plate and there were glasses of red wine. He tasted his and smiled.

"Saperavi," she said sipping from her own glass.

Like most Russian wines, Saperavi came from Georgia.

"You said you liked it," Sarah said, taking the lid off the pot and pointing to it, indicating that Rostnikov should eat.

"I like it very much, but it costs . . . " he began as he reached forward to serve himself.

"A celebration," Sarah interrupted.

"What are we celebrating?"

Sarah shrugged and looked at her plate.

"I don't know. Your favorite dish. Your favorite wine."

"You know the story about my cousin Leonora," he said after tasting the chicken and telling her it was delicious. "For some reason she thought I loved cold mashed potatoes. I don't know where she got the idea but she served me a plate of them one day when I came to visit her—I couldn't have been more than twelve years old. It was before the war—and I didn't have the heart to tell her that she was confusing me with someone else or something else I may have said. I seldom visited my cousin Leonora after that."

"When are you going?" Sarah asked softly, delicately removing a small bone from her mouth.

Rostnikov wanted to rise, hug her to him. Perhaps later.

"Tomorrow morning, early. A car will come for me."

"How long will you be gone?" she asked not looking at him.

"Not long, I hope," he said looking at her. "How did you know?"

"I don't know," she said with a sigh. "Perhaps it's because you acted this way two years ago when you were sent to Tbilisi on the black market business. You brought home a chicken instead of vegetables. And you told the same story about the mashed potatoes. Where are you going?"

"Siberia," he said and she looked up, fear in her wide brown eyes magnified by the glasses.

"No," he laughed. "It's work. A murder. I can't say more."

"Why you? Are there no inspectors in all of Siberia?" she said, continuing to play with her food and not eat it.

"Who knows?" Rostnikov shrugged. He picked up a piece of the cucumber thing in his fingers and took a cautious nibble. It wasn't bad.

"Who, indeed," Sarah said. "I'll pack with you. You always forget simple things like your toothbrush."

They said no more during dinner and finished the entire bottle of wine. After dinner they both cleared the dishes and when Sarah had finished washing them, he motioned for her to join him on the battered sofa in the living room. She dried her hands and came to him.

"Do you want to read, talk, watch television?" she asked. "Channel 2 has a hockey game on, I think."

There was a tightness above her eyes that troubled him. Rostnikov touched her forehead and she closed the eyes.

"I'd like to go to bed," he said. "And then we'll see."

She looked at him over her glasses and shook her head.

"You want to . . . ?"

"Yes," he said. "And you?"

She smiled at him and the pain in her face faded a bit as she touched his rough cheek with her hand. It might be many days before he saw her again.

Rostnikov was ready, his Yugoslavian-made, blue-cloth zippered case at the door, when the knock came at precisely 7 a.m. the next morning. Sarah had already left for work and Rostnikov had been sitting at the window watching people on Krasikov Street shuffling to work or school or in search of a bargain.

"A moment," Rostnikov said when the knock came. He rose, moved as quickly as his leg would allow him and opened the door where a serious-looking woman in a gray uniform faced him. She was pink-faced, about thirty and rather pretty if a bit plump.

"Inspector Rostnikov," she said seeing his blue bag and stepping in to pick it up. "I am your driver."

"I was hoping you were not a particularly bold suitcase snatcher," he said as she stood up.

"I assure you I am your driver. I should have showed you my identification," she said, starting to put down the bag.

"That will not be necessary," Rostnikov said reaching for his coat on a nearby chair.

She nodded, waited for him to put on his hat, coat and scarf and led the way out into the hall pausing for Rostnikov to close his door. She began by moving quickly and realized that the

Inspector was limping a dozen steps behind. She stopped and waited for him.

"I'm sorry," she said. "Comrade Sokolov is waiting in the car and we have only an hour to get to Sheremetyevo Airport."

"I too am sorry that Comrade Sokolov is waiting in the car," Rostnikov said, catching up to her, "but I believe they might hold the airplane till we arrive."

"No," the woman said, flushing healthily. "I didn't mean I was sorry that Comrade Sokolov was in the car. I just . . . "

"I understand," said Rostnikov. "I was attempting to be amusing."

"I see," she said, relieved. He said nothing more till they got out on the street and into the waiting black Chaika. The woman opened the back door and Rostnikov stepped in to join a round-faced man with a thick black mustache which matched his coat and fur hat. In the front next to the driver who had placed Rostnikov's bag in the trunk and hurried back to her seat was Emil Karpo, also black-clad but hat-less. Karpo did not look back as the car pulled away from the curb.

"I am Sokolov," the pudgy mustached man said, showing a large white-toothed grin.

Rostnikov nodded, noting that both the teeth and grin were false.

"I am in from Kiev," he explained as they turned toward Gorky Street. "I'm an inspector with the Procurator's Office. The Procurator's Office thought I might learn something of procedure from you. I've been with the All-Union Central Council of Trade Unions as an investigator for almost a dozen years and I've just moved into criminal investigation. I hope you don't mind. While I'm pleased to be joining you, I assure you it was in no way my idea."

"I do not mind, Comrade," Rostnikov said looking out the window as Gorky Street became Leningrad Highway. Tall apartment houses flashed past as the woman sped down the center lane of the 328-foot-wide highway.

Sokolov continued to talk and Rostnikov responded with a nod.

"I've heard much about you," Sokolov said with a smile. "You are much admired, Comrade."

"I have done my best to serve the State with the abilities I have been fortunate enough to possess," Rostnikov said as they passed Dynamo Stadium and Rostnikov had a memory flash of Josef years ago at his side at a Moscow Dynamos' soccer game. Josef was ten or twelve, his straight brown hair combed back, his eyes riveted on the field.

"You have children, Comrade?" Rostnikov said.

"Children?" Sokolov said. "Yes."

"You have photographs of them?"

"Of course," said Sokolov reaching into his inner jacket pocket to remove his wallet. "My daughter, Svetlana, is fifteen. My son, Ivan, is fourteen. See."

Rostnikov took the wallet, looked at the picture of two smiling blond children.

"They were younger when the picture was taken," Sokolov said taking the wallet back, glancing at the photograph with a smile and returning it to his pocket. "I mean they were younger than they are now."

"They are handsome children," Rostnikov said.

"Thank you, Comrade," Sokolov said softly. "I've heard that it is very cold along the Yensei this time of year. I've brought extra layers."

"A good idea," Rostnikov said.

The Petrovsky Palace shot past them on the right. The Palace now housed the Soviet Air Force College of Engineering. It was built some time in the eighteenth century and, Rostnikov knew,

Napoleon had stayed there for a few days after he was forced to abandon the burning of the Kremlin. Twenty minutes further, Rostnikov caught a glimpse of an izby, a traditional log cabin. It was one of the last of the structures which used to spot the countryside.

Sokolov went on talking. Rostnikov nodded.

In less than an hour, Rostnikov saw the twin glass buildings of the Hotel Aeroflot and the Ministry of Civil Aviation. Behind them he could see the Moscow Air Terminal. The woman driver, either out of zealousness to complete her mission or a desire to discharge her passengers, accelerated as they passed the giant sculpture in the shape of an anti-tank barrier. Rostnikov remembered when real anti-tank barriers circled the city and he knew that this sculpture stood at the exact spot where Hitler's armies were stopped in 1941.

The driver pulled around the main terminal building and entered a side gate after showing identification to the armed soldiers on duty. She drove directly onto the field, skirting the main runways, clearly knowing where she was going. Sokolov stopped talking as the woman headed toward a distant plane which, as they approached it, Rostnikov identified as a YAK-40.

The car came to a stop directly alongside the plane and the driver leaped out, closed her door and hurried to the trunk of the car. Karpo, Rostnikov and Sokolov got out of the car, closed their doors, and took their luggage from the woman who did not insist on carrying any of it.

Sokolov lumbered ahead and Karpo slowed down to join Rostnikov as the car behind them pulled away.

"KGB?" Karpo asked, looking at Sokolov who was mounting the aluminum steps to the plane.

"I don't think so," said Rostnikov. "I believe he is from the Procurator's Office, but I doubt if he is making the trip to learn from us. It is more likely that he is along to report on how we conduct the investigation."

Karpo looked away and nothing more was said till they were seated and in the air. The crew had been expecting them and had held the plane. There were other passengers but they paid no attention, or appeared to pay no attention as these important latecomers were ushered to seats in the middle of the plane.

Rostnikov had taken the aisle seat and Sokolov had taken the window seat next to him. Karpo sat across the aisle next to a white-haired man who kept his nose in a technical book and did his best for the entire flight to avoid looking at the ghostly figure next to him.

Porfiry Petrovich Rostnikov hated airplanes, especially jet planes. There was no dealing with such an airplane, no sense of control. It either stayed up or it went down. You couldn't land a dying one and the passengers couldn't grab parachutes and leap to safety. He didn't like the way the engines made strange sounds. He didn't like the lightness in his stomach.

Sokolov babbled for the next hours, through a sandwich dinner and later sucking on a piece of hard candy that had been passed out by a crew member. When, after stops in Kirov and Berezovo, they arrived in Igarka in near darkness, Rostnikov's leg refused to respond to threats, pleas and will power. He had to wait while the other passengers deplaned before he finally coaxed his leg into movement.

"War wound?" Sokolov said sympathetically.

As you probably well know if you've done your work, Rostnikov thought.

"War wound," he acknowledged.

Though he was well bundled, the cold hit Rostnikov as he made his way down the metal stairway that swayed in the wind. Sokolov was holding his suitcase against his chest and Karpo was standing before them in the snow, holding his travel bag at his side, showing no effect of the cold.

"Cold," said Sokolov as they looked across the small field at the houses with about three feet of snow on their roofs. The airport building was a wooden structure in front of which sat several small airplanes mounted on skis.

"The air here is good," said Karpo. "It is easy to breathe. The frost is intense, but it is much easier to bear than in Russia."

"Easier to bear?" Sokolov said as a man in a flowing coat moved forward to meet them and they moved toward the airport building. "You find Siberia easier to bear than Russia?"

"I was quoting Lenin," Karpo said as they walked. "In a letter to his mother. He was on his way to three years of exile in Novosibirsk as a political agitator."

"Of course," said Sokolov as the man from the terminal came face-to-face with them and guided them to one of the small planes with skis. They scrambled into the plane, nodded at the pilot and took off following the Yensei River north into darkness toward Tumsk.

At the moment Inspector Porfiry Petrovich Rostnikov was landing just beyond the town of Tumsk in Siberia, Sasha Tkach sat at his desk in Petrovka writing a report and trying not to look up at Zelach who sat across from him in pursuit of thought, an almost hopeless venture.

"We can wait at his house, at the shop," Zelach said.

"You can," Tkach said still looking down at the report.

"Yes," said Zelach, "at the shop and the house."

Zelach looked at Tkach who brushed back his hair and suddenly met Zelach's eyes. It was not Sasha Tkach who had lost the buyer of stolen goods. He had indicated to Zelach how they should go about the arrest and it had almost come to pass. They had entered the shop on Gorkovo after looking in the window at a particular piece of jewelry which interested neither of them. Carefully, without letting his eyes appear to wander, Tkach had searched without success for their man. Finally, they found a salesperson, identified themselves as policemen and asked for Volovkatin. The saleswoman had said that Volovkatin was at a nearby stoloviye, luncheonette, and had given a description from which they might be able to identify him.

They had moved swiftly to the stoloviye, stepped in and looked around. In the back of the crowded shop, not far from the cafeteria line, Tkach spotted a man who fit the description of Volovkatin. He was about thirty-five, average height, with his dark hair brushed straight back. He was smoking a cigarette in a holder and nodding sagely. Working their way through the crowd would be a bit difficult and Tkach could see a rear door a few feet from their man who was talking animatedly to two women who sat with him as he ate from what looked like a bowl of cabbage soup.

Zelach spotted the man too and said, "There he is."

"Quiet," Tkach said. "Get in line. Get something to eat. Look around for a table."

Zelach moved to the counter, ordered a meat-filled kotleta and a side order of potatoes with a glass of kvass. Tkach, moving behind him and keeping his eyes on Volovkatin, ordered nothing, but when the waitress behind the counter reached over for payment Zelach had already begun to move away with his hands filled with food. Tkach paid the two rubles and turned to find Zelach and Volovkatin staring at each other.

There were three tables with several standing people between the two policemen and the suspect. Zelach looked over at Tkach and Volovkatin followed the look while one of the women with him said something to which he nodded his head.

No doubt now. The man knew he was spotted, that two men, probably policemen, were moving toward him.

"Now," Tkach said to Zelach.

"My food," Zelach whined.

Tkach tried to push past a fat man who stood between him and Zelach and as he did so Volovkatin stood, dropped his cigarette holder and took a quick step toward the rear door.

"Where are you going?" Tkach heard one of the women ask Volovkatin.

He didn't answer and Zelach, who was closer to him than Tkach, looked around for an open table on which to place his food.

"Get him," called Tkach past the fat man.

Zelach looked back at Sasha, looked down at his food and shrugged.

"Drop it," Tkach shouted. "Get him."

Volovkatin had his hand on the door and was starting to open it when Zelach, who could not handle two ideas at the same time, finally dropped his plate and glass in the middle of the nearest table. The kvass spilled on a matronly woman who got up screaming. Tkach managed to get past the fat man but Zelach was still closer to the suspect who was now going through the rear door. Zelach made a lunge past the table at the closing door but he was too late. Zelach turned the handle on the closed door as Tkach leaped over a fallen chair and joined him.

"Locked," Zelach sighed.

They had worked their way back out of the store with Zelach pausing to retrieve his kotleta from in front of the matronly woman who cursed him and demanded money to clean her dress. He shoved the meat pie into his mouth and followed Tkach toward the street where, after fifteen minutes of searching the area, they failed to find Volovkatin.

"Two rubles," Tkach said as he looked across his desk.

Zelach looked at him blankly. Two rubles was far too modest a bribe for keeping quiet about the disaster Zelach had caused.

"For the food," Tkach explained, seeing Zelach's confusion.

Zelach understood and reached into his pocket with enthusiasm to find the money which he quickly turned over to Tkach.

"What are you writing?" Zelach asked. "What are you going to say?"

"I'm going to lie," whispered Tkach. "I'm writing lies because both of us will look like fools if I write the truth."

"Good," said Zelach blowing a puff of air in relief as a pair of detectives moved around the desk talking about someone named Linski.

And so Sasha Tkach finished the report, read it, realizing full well that it was unconvincing. He considered their next step. He would probably do what Zelach had suggested, but he doubted that they would catch Volovkatin who probably had false identity papers and was on his way to the Ukraine. Most likely, if he were a reasonably clever and careful criminal, "Volovkatin" was probably not his real name and he was on his way somewhere with his own quite legal identification papers. The report Tkach has just written would surely go to the KGB and there would surely be hell to pay for letting an economic criminal get away.

Tkach signed the report and handed it to Zelach to sign. Zelach read it.

"Looks good," Zelach said with a grateful smile.

"It's terrible," said Tkach.

As he took the signed report back, a clerk came down the aisle between the desks and paused at Tkach's desk to drop off a file and a note. He recognized the neat handwritten notes as soon as he opened the file.

The note said that Tkach was to replace Inspector Karpo in the investigation of the young men who were intimidating visitors to the USSR Economic Achievements Exhibition. Not only was he to investigate but he was to go undercover that afternoon and evening as an ice cream salesman, which meant that his daughter Pulcharia would be asleep when he got home and his wife Maya would be up to remind him that he had been promised a regular day schedule when the strong-arm case ended.

"Good news?" asked Zelach.

"Wonderful," Tkach sighed sourly.

"I'm glad," said Zelach. "You want to get something to eat?"

FIVE

THE NAME SIBERIA MEANS "SLEEPING LAND" AND FOR MORE than a thousand years while the rest of Europe and Asia were developing a history most of Siberia slept. Beneath the sleeping giant whose five million square miles could swallow all of the countries of Western Europe and could hold almost two countries the size of the United States lay vast riches including coal, oil, iron, gold, silver and diamonds. On the sleeping giant's back grew millions of square miles of timber in the sprawling taiga, the forests which even today serve as massive havens for wolves, tigers and bears who have never experienced civilization and know nothing of its existence. Other animals, fox, mink, sable, roamed and multiplied and still roam wild.

The first known Siberians lived 40,000 years ago. For more than 32,000 years the descendants of these first aboriginal tribes spread throughout Siberia, cultivated cattle, used tools made of bronze and copper, began settlements; then, about 1,000 B.C., Mongol tribes began to move upward from China bringing iron tools, introducing agriculture and war. From the northwest the Huns began to move downward through Siberia pushing both the Mongol tribes and the aborigines into less hospitable parts of the sleeping giant.

The Huns gradually lost control and abandoned their Siberian settlements or mixed with the Mongols and aborigines. By the thirteenth century, Siberia was a storybook land of small multiracial tribes, states and small kingdoms scratching to stay alive on the back of the slowly waking sleeping giant.

And then Ghengis Khan rode into the vastness with an alliance of Mongols and Tartars who, even after Khan's death, dominated not only most of Asia including parts of China and India, but all of Siberia, all of Russia and much of Western Europe beyond Hungary right up to the gates of Vienna. But Khan's empire was too vast and eventually broke into powerful khanates, the largest of which, the Golden Horde of the Tartars, controlled both upper Russia and all of Siberia.

The Mongol/Tartar occupation united Russians for the first time. They had a common enemy, and the Russian princes who existed as Tartar puppet rulers put aside their major differences and united with Moscow as their focus. In 1380 a force of Russians marching under the banner of the principality of Moscow defeated the Tartars in the battle of Kulikovo. Russians throughout the divided land began to declare loyalty to Moscow. In 1430 the united Russians pushed the Tartars back behind the Volga. And then, in the middle of the sixteenth century, Czar Ivan IV, Ivan the Terrible, finally drove the last of the Tartars beyond the Ural mountains and into Siberia.

The Siberian Tartar Khan, Ediger, fearing a Russian invasion of his land, petitioned Ivan to make Siberia a Russian province and commit the Czar to support Ediger against his tribal enemies. In return, Ediger promised to deliver one sable skin for each of his male subjects. The Czar agreed.

In spite of the agreement, Ediger was soon overthrown by a rival, Kuchum, who hated the Russians, denied the agreement, murdered the Russian ambassador to Siberia, refused to pay taxes and moved his capital further east, away from Russia, to Kashlyk near present-day Tobolsk.

The Czar, fearing that he could not win a major war in Siberia against Kuchum, enlisted the aid of the enormously wealthy Strogonov family, a powerful, independent merchant clan whose territory covered much of the land on the broad western slopes of the Ural mountains. The Strogonovs were summoned to Moscow and given by the Czar Ivan a deed to most of Siberia. All they had to do was take it from the Tartars and hold it.

The Strogonovs found a mysterious cossack, Ermak Timofeyevich, to head the expedition against Kuchum. Ermak took seven years to raise and train an army of 540 men, mostly fellow cossacks and mercenaries. The Strogonovs ordered an additional 300 of their own men to join them and, outnumbered by more than sixty to one, Ermak and his well-armed band crossed the Urals and attacked.

The Tartar hordes who had only a few flint rifles and fought mostly with bows and arrows were driven back. In less than a year Ermak was on the Tura River sailing toward Kashlyk. In a final major battle, Kuchum's army attacked and was defeated. Kuchum and his allies fled deep into the wilderness.

Ermak occupied Kashlyk and proceeded to clear large areas of Siberia forcing the local tribes to declare loyalty to the Czar. Ivan the Terrible declared Ermak "the Conqueror of Siberia" and sent regular Russian army troops to join him and secure the territory for the Strogonovs.

A year later, in 1854, a vengeful Kuchum ambushed Ermak who, weighed down by his heavy armor, drowned in the battle. Ivan sent further troops who routed the last of the Tartar resistance.

With the death of Ermak and the end of Tartar resistance, the vastness of Siberia opened to adventurers and Russian mercenaries who rushed in, conquering villages, towns and tribes, laying claim to territories in the name of the Czar.

The tide was halted to the south with resistance by the Chinese who fought against Russian expansion into their country. Peace was achieved and the southern Siberian border established. To the east the Russians continued to expand their territory. Under a merchant, Gregori Shelekhov, Russia developed a plan to include much of North America, the Hawaiian islands and the entire Pacific coast of America all the way to Spanish California. By 1812 Shelekhov and his partner Baranov had almost achieved their goal.

On March 30, 1867, the Czar, fearing that he could not control the vast eastern lands, decided to pull back, and sold the American territory and Alaska to the United States for $7,200,000 in gold. The Czar had even been willing to throw in a good part of Siberia for the gold but the Americans showed no interest.

And so Siberia, fed over the years by forced immigrations of peasants, criminals and political dissidents, survived as part of the Russian state in spite of rebellions, successful attacks by the Japanese in 1918, and occupation by the White Russian army under Admiral Kolchak following the Revolution. It wasn't till 1923 that Siberia was finally unified under the Soviet government.

The first person Porfiry Petrovich Rostnikov met in Tumsk after the small plane landed was Miro Famfanoff, the local MVD officer, who informed his visitors proudly that the temperature was -34 degrees centigrade and that Ermak himself, whose statue stood before them in the town square, was reported to have spent three days in the town in the summer of 1582.

Rostnikov had nodded, pulled his wool cap more tightly over his ears and tightened around his neck the red scarf Sarah had made for him two years ago. Sokolov touched his mustache which had already stiffened in the frost and Karpo looked at Famfanoff, a heavily bundled-up overweight man in his forties with a face turned red probably not as much by the frigid air as by vodka.

"You should wear a hat," Famfanoff suggested to Karpo nervously.

Karpo nodded and looked around the town square where Famfanoff had led them. The statue of Ermak in armor, right hand raised, pointing into the wilderness, stood in the center of the square. Around him were houses, about a dozen of them, most of them made of wood, spread out in no particular order. The town consisted of a concrete structure with a metal tower on a slope to the right, which Rostnikov assumed was the weather station; a collapsing wooden church, obviously not in use, with part of the cross on its spire missing and its windows glassless and yawning; a wide log building with a broad cedar door; and another concrete building to the left which they were about to pass. Set back on the slope not far from the weather station stood three more wooden houses about thirty yards apart.

"This way. This way," Famfanoff said, pointing to the right at a two-story wood building. He trudged through the snow and urged them to follow him. They formed a line behind the man, Karpo first, followed by Sokolov and Rostnikov in the rear.

Rostnikov glanced to his left at the lopsided concrete building over whose door was a faded wooden plank with "The People's Hall of Justice and Solidarity" painted in red letters. A curtain parted slightly in the window of the Hall and Rostnikov saw the frightened face of an old man.

"I don't live here in the village," Famfanoff said when they were inside the two-story wooden building. "Our office is Agapitovo. I'm responsible for periodic visits and responses to calls from the south. Kusnetsov is responsible for the north. I don't live here."

"But other people do," said Rostnikov. "And after we eat I would like to know about them."

"I am at your service," said Famfanoff.

Famfanoff escorted the visitors into the wooden building and up to the second floor where there were three small bedrooms each furnished with a military cot. Rostnikov asked for the smallest because it faced the square. No one objected. Rostnikov's room contained a wooden chair and a small white metal cabinet with drawers that was meant to serve as a dresser. Sokolov and Karpo had similar furnishings. The bathroom in the hall was the only other room on the floor.

The house, Famfanoff explained as he stood in the doorway while Rostnikov took off his coat and unpacked his bag, was built by government fur traders in the last century but the last Mongols had long since moved beyond the massive forest, the taiga, which almost reached the town. When the traders left, the Navy moved the first weather station into the house and only recently, about five years ago, the new concrete weather station had been completed. Since then, the building they were in had been maintained by Mirasnikov, the janitor at the People's Hall of Justice and Solidarity which served as a town hall, recreation center, meeting ground and office space for Tumsk.

Rostnikov nodded as Famfanoff, his coat open to reveal a less-than-clean MVD uniform underneath, reached into his pocket for a foul-smelling papirosy, a tube cigarette which he lit without pausing in his banter.

"The weather station was built under the direction of the Permafrost Research Center in Igarka," he said. "It's on steel beams hammered deeply into the ground. The permafrost softens every summer to about six feet down. The stilts have to go down twenty, thirty feet maybe. Before they came up with the idea of beams all the buildings had to be wood or they would sink into the ground in the summer. Even those would start to sag after four or five years. The wooden houses of Tumsk have all been reinforced with steel beams. You may have noticed that the People's Hall sags. It was shored up by some steel beams about a dozen years ago but, if you ask me, it was too late. It should probably come down or be abandoned like the old church. One of these summers both of them will collapse. No doubt of it. It should come down, but no one seems interested enough in it to make a decision. I tell you, Inspector, Tumsk is a dying town, a dying town."

Rostnikov walked to the window and looked out at the white square, the buildings with smoke coming from their chimneys and the white expanse behind the village leading to the forest. Then he looked at Ermak's statue which, now that he looked at it carefully, seemed to tilt slightly to the right.

"The statue, is that mounted on a steel beam?"

"I think so," said Famfanoff with a shrug.

In the window of the People's Hall of Justice and Solidarity, the old man looked out and up at Rostnikov from the parted curtains. Their eyes met and the old man stepped back letting the curtains fall back across the window. Rostnikov moved the single chair near the window and sat looking out.

"You want my theory?" Famfanoff asked as Rostnikov turned back into the room which was rapidly filling with the smoke and smell of the policeman's ropey cigarette.

"Da, kane-shna, of course," said Rostnikov as he moved the chair closer to the window.

"A bear," said Famfanoff pointing at Rostnikov with his cigarette. "Commissar Rutkin was killed by a bear."

"Are there many bears around here?" asked Rostnikov.

"Not many, but some," said Famfanoff confidentially and quietly, probably, Rostnikov thought, to keep the bears from hearing. "And tigers. There are still tigers. And wolves, of course wolves, a great many of them. I, well, not I exactly, but Kustnetsov had to kill a tiger just three years ago. Of course that was four hundred kilometers north of here but it was a tiger and I've seen bears many times, believe me."

"I believe you," said Rostnikov. "I will consider your bear theory. Is someone getting us something to eat?"

"To eat? Yes, of course. Mirasnikov's wife. She's the wife of the janitor in the People's Hall of Justice," said Famfanoff. "She'll keep the house warm. Plenty of firewood."

"You have files on everyone in town, everyone who lives in town?" Rostnikov asked, looking up at the policeman who appeared to be waiting for an invitation to sit, though there was nowhere to do so but the cot and the single chair on which Rostnikov sat. Rostnikov didn't want to prolong the visit.

"Yes, of course, Comrade," Famfanoff said. "I'll get them for you. You want them all? Even the sailors in the weather station?"

"All," he said. "How many are there?"

"Let me see. Fourteen, fifteen, if you don't count the few Evenks who wander through and you don't count me, and you shouldn't count me. I don't live here. That doesn't mean I'm not a real siberyaki, a devoted Siberian who takes pride in the rigors of the land of my fathers." Famfanoff straightened his tunic, looked down the small corridor and then moved toward Rostnikov and spoke softly. "However, as a matter of fact, Commissar Rutkin before his untimely death indicated that he would recommend a transfer for me someplace a bit larger, possibly Irkutsk where my loyalty, my knowledge of Siberia could be put to better use. I have a wife, a child and perhaps . . . "

"After the investigation is complete, assuming your cooperation is thorough and efficient, I will make the recommendation," Rostnikov agreed.

Famfanoff beamed and clutched the cigarette in his teeth in a grin.

Rostnikov doubted that the dead commissar would have made such a promise to the slovenly and probably less-than-competent policeman. Famfanoff was probably where he belonged. For once the system had not failed. In a larger MVD unit he would probably have trouble surviving. Rostnikov had not lied. He wanted and needed the man's loyalty and cooperation. He would write the letter of recommendation, certain that it would have no effect because he lacked the power Famfanoff believed him to possess.

"Two more things, Sergeant," Rostnikov said.

"Anything, Comrade Inspector," Famfanoff said, removing the cigarette from his mouth and standing straight in something that resembled attention.

"First, I'd like you to draw me a simple map indicating who lives in each of the houses in Tumsk. Bring it back to me later. Second, I want to know if there is any weight-lifting equipment in town?"

"Weight lifting?" asked Famfanoff, puzzled.

"Yes."

"I will see if the sailors have any. I don't think they do. Ah, Dimitri Galich has something like that. I'll inquire and I'll have the map for you within the hour."

"Good. Now I would like to rest. Get the files. Find out about the weight-lifting equipment and call us when the food is ready. Now please close the door on your way out so I can get some rest."

Famfanoff considered saluting, started to raise his right hand, saw that Rostnikov wasn't looking at him and decided to leave. In the corridor he passed the closed door of the one who looked like a vampire and the open door of the other one, the one called Sokolov with the soft smile, the mustache and hard eyes. Sokolov wasn't in his room. The bathroom door was closed.

Famfanoff walked slowly, hopefully down the narrow wooden stairway, determined to please Inspector Rostnikov whom he could not figure out. The man was shaped like a crate and had a face so common that one might easily forget it after being introduced if it weren't for the sad brown eyes and the mouth that looked as if it were just about to smile. Inspector Rostnikov looked like a man who knew a tragic yet comic secret about you.

Buttoning his coat and pulling his hat down over his ears, the policeman made an agenda. First, to remind the Mirasnikov woman to get the visitors' food ready. Second, to pull together the copies of all the files on residents of Tumsk. This was easy since he had already done the job for Commissar Rutkin and had the files locked in the cabinet at the People's Hall of Justice. He would let Rostnikov think he had pulled them together quickly. The third task, the weight equipment, was relatively easy but puzzling. Did Rostnikov have some wild theory that Commissar Rutkin had been killed with a weight-lifting bar? Or did he think the killer was so powerful that he had to be someone who used such equipment? Famfanoff had glanced at the medical examiner's report that had come in from Noril'sk where they had taken the body. Nothing seemed to support any interest in weight equipment.

Famfanoff went out into the cold, deciding to get a drink from his own room in the house of Dimitri Galich where he stayed when he came to Tumsk. He could, at the same time if Galich were home, ask about the weights. He crossed the square hoping that Rostnikov was not insane or stupid. Famfanoff did not care if Commissar Rutkin's killer was found. He thought his bear theory perfectly acceptable and possibly even correct. He did care that Rostnikov not look bad. The inspector's promised letter might be his ticket out of the frozen exile. Yes, things were looking better and he definitely needed a drink to celebrate.

"Ah," said Sokolov after smoothing out his mustache and reaching for a piece of coarse black bread, "sometimes it is good to get away from the watchful eyes of Moscow and Kiev, isn't it?"

They ate at a wooden army mess table with no cloth. There were four chairs, wood and so old that Rostnikov imagined himself collapsing to the floor.

"It is good to experience the magnificent diversity of the Soviet Socialist Republics," replied Rostnikov without pausing in his consumption of shchi, a thin cabbage soup containing a hint of potato.

"And," added Sokolov, "it is good to get back to our history, the simple food of our peasant past." He pointed at the food on the table: bread; soup; a bowl of kasha; and golubtsy, cabbage rolls, two for each of them, probably stuffed with potatoes; a bottle of amber vodka and a bottle of spring water.

"Shchi da kasha, Pischcha nasha: cabbage soup and gruel are our food," said Rostnikov repeating the old Russian saying.

Karpo, Rostnikov noticed, drank his soup slowly, ate one piece of bread even more slowly and drank only one glass of mineral water while Rostnikov and Sokolov consumed everything on the table including the two golubtsy which would have been Karpo's, but which he declined when Sokolov gestured to one of them with his fork when he had consumed his own share. Rostnikov had taken the other one.

"We will grow healthy on such fare if we stay here long enough," said Sokolov sitting back to drink his vodka.

"No balance," said Karpo still at his bread. "The myth of health of the peasant was fostered by the landowners, the church and the aristocracy to ease their own consciences."

"Lenin," said Sokolov toasting Karpo.

"Engels," said Rostnikov.

"Politics," sighed Sokolov.

"Economics," said Karpo.

"The same thing," Sokolov came back pouring himself another vodka.

"We agree," said Karpo.

And with that the old woman who had served the meal came in from the kitchen behind Karpo. She looked at the table, saw that there was nothing left to consume, and began to clean up. Rostnikov guessed the woman's age at eighty, perhaps more. She was small, thin, bent and wearing a heavy black dress. Her sparse gray hair was pinned to the top of her head and her wrinkled face held no expression, but her eyes were a deep blue.

"So, Comrade," Sokolov said with a smile, protecting his glass and the vodka bottle from the old woman. "How are you going to proceed?"

"Spasee'bo," said Rostnikov to the old woman who nodded and then, to Sokolov, "I will begin in the morning after I've read the files Sergeant Famfanoff has brought me. Inspector Karpo will conduct some of the interviews. I will conduct others."

"And how long will this take?" asked Sokolov.

Rostnikov shrugged and refused the offer of a drink. He watched the old woman move slowly in her work and was sure she was listening.

"You are the wife of the janitor?" Rostnikov asked her as she made a second trip to the table to continue cleaning.

"Yes," she said without pausing.

"I will want to see him," he said.

The woman bit her lower lip, nodded and left the room.

"Is it cold in here?" Sokolov asked. "I'm cold."

No one answered.

They were all wearing sweaters. Rostnikov's was a solid brown with a gray line, knitted by Sarah. Sokolov's was a colorful creation with two reindeer facing each other on a field of white. Karpo's was plain, black and loose.

"Well," Sokolov said when the old woman had finished clearing the table and the last of the vodka was gone, "tomorrow we begin."

"Tomorrow," agreed Rostnikov shifting his aching leg.

And then silence. The silence lasted several minutes before Sokolov reminded Rostnikov to wake him in the morning and excused himself. Rostnikov and Karpo waited till they heard Sokolov walking about in his room above them.

"He did not ask to see the files," Karpo observed.

"I'm sure he has his own copies, had them before we left Moscow," said Rostnikov.

"Yes, but he should have asked to see them," said Karpo. "That was a mistake."

Rostnikov shrugged. There were many possible reasons for Sokolov's failure to ask about the files. Perhaps he wanted to appear slightly naïve. Perhaps he wanted to test Rostnikov, put a doubt in his mind about his observer. Perhaps he wanted to disassociate himself from the public investigation.

"We will not be able to avoid dealing with the death of the child," Karpo went on.

"Ah, there's the rub," said Rostnikov.

"The rub?"

"It's Shakespeare," explained Rostnikov. "We have been ordered to leave the investigation of the child's death to a Commissar who is supposedly coming after us. Yet Rutkin, whose death we are investigating, was himself investigating the Samsonov girl's death. It is not unlikely that the two are related."

"It is very likely," agreed Karpo, his eyes fixed on Rostnikov's face.

"Your arm seems to be fine," said Rostnikov.

"It is almost normal," said Karpo.

"You have something you wish to say, Emil?" Rostnikov said slowly, rising with one hand on the back of the chair and the other on the table.

"Nothing, Comrade Inspector," said Karpo.

"Then tomorrow you begin with the sailors at the weather station," said Rostnikov. "Do'briy v'e'cher, good night."

"Good night," said Karpo.

When Inspector Rostnikov had made his way slowly up the stairs, Emil Karpo turned off the light, went to his room and spent the next two hours reading the files Porfiry Petrovich had given him. There was no doubt that this investigation was a test for Rostnikov. While he was searching for a killer, Sokolov would be searching for a mistake and Karpo would be expected to confirm any error the Procurator General's man observed.

It would be a dangerous few days for Rostnikov.

In the back of the People's Hall of Justice and Solidarity was a room which had been designed as the chamber of the regional Party member who would serve as presiding judge for all disputes and legal injustices in the region. However, a decision had been made before the building was even completed in 1936 that all disputes and legal injustices in and around Tumsk and six other towns north of Igarka would be heard in Agapitovo.

And so, because no one seemed to care, Sergei Mirasnikov, the thirty-two-year-old town janitor, had moved with his wife into the chamber, where they had continued to live for the next fifty-one years.

Nominally, the officer in charge of the weather station was the ranking official in Tumsk, but in fact few of the many officers who had been through Tumsk on three-year tours of duty cared much about the running of the town and no one had ever questioned Marasnikov's right to the chamber or inquired about the work he did.

The large room had a bed in one corner and odd pieces of unmatched furniture abandoned by various naval officers and others who had been exiled to Tumsk that sat around the room in no particular arrangement.

Sergei was sitting at the table which they had obtained from an engineer named Bright in 1944. Bright had suddenly left the town accompanied by some men in uniform. Sergei had waited a respectful two years before confiscating Bright's furniture.

At the table Sergei slowly ate the two cabbage rolls his wife had withheld from the table of the visitors.

"What did they say?" he asked her.

"I'm nearly deaf," she answered, sitting across from him and drinking her soup like tea from a dark mug.

"Did they say anything about me?" he asked.

"No, not when I was in the room. Why would they say anything about you?"

Her hollow cheeks sucked in and out as she drank. She saw no need to tell him that the heavy one had said he would be talking to Mirasnikov. If she told him, they would have a miserable night in which he would wail and complain about the burden of his life.

"The one who looks like a tree stump," he said. "He was looking at me."

"Don't look back," she said.

"That's your advice? Don't look back? He's going to come and ask me questions. I know it. He can drag me by the neck, take all this from us, throw us into the forest if he doesn't like my answers," he whimpered.

"Then don't answer when he asks," Liana said.

"Don't answer, she says," he mocked with a bitter laugh.

"Then answer," she came back.

"Answer, she says," he mocked again.

The old woman looked up at her husband. She could think of no other course of action than to answer or not answer.

"Then what will you do?" she asked.

"Nothing," he said. "He doesn't know that I know anything. How can he know? I'll do nothing. I'll play the fool. I'll lie."

"Sounds like a good plan to me," she said finishing her soup by tilting back the cup. A small trickle of soup went down her chin. Sergei watched it blankly and repeated, "Nothing."

Those eyes could not force the secret out of him. He pressed his lips together and felt them rubbing against the few odd teeth which remained in his mouth. He would simply avoid the eyes of the man who was built like a tree stump.

As the soup trickled down the chin of Liana Mirasnikov, the person responsible for the death of Commissar Illya Rutkin sat in a dark room looking out the window toward the center of Tumsk with a pair of binoculars. The night was cold but clear with the moon above almost full. A wind, not the worst of the past few weeks, sent the snow swirling about the town and between the houses.

In the house where the three investigators were staying, a single second-floor light remained on. In the window of that second-floor room, the heavy-set inspector sat looking out. Unlike the killer, the inspector did not seem to care if he were seen. It would be simple enough for him to turn out the light and watch in the safety of darkness as the killer was doing. Perhaps he actually wanted to be seen.

The killer watched as the inspector scanned the square and looked toward the darkened houses. At one point, the inspector's eyes fixed on the room in which the killer sat, but the killer was safely back, invisible in darkness. Nonetheless, the killer's breath held for just an instant as killer's and policeman's eyes seemed to meet. And then the policeman broke the contact and returned his gaze to the square.

What was he looking at? What could he see? There was nothing there. No one. No one would be out tonight. There was nowhere to go and the temperature had dropped to almost 45 below zero. And yet the policeman looked. He seemed to be looking at the window of the People's Hall of Justice and Solidarity, but that window was dark and there was nothing in there to see but old Mirasnikov and his wife. But a second look convinced the killer that Rostnikov was, indeed, watching the window.

What could he know after only a few hours in Tumsk? The killer watched the policeman for almost two hours and was about to give up for the night when the inspector rose slowly, moved out of sight and then, about twenty seconds later, the lights went out.

The killer put aside the binoculars and went to bed. Tomorrow promised to be a most challenging day.

"It's not my business. I know it's not my business, but wouldn't it have made more sense if you sold flowers or worked in one of the restaurants?"

The question came to Sasha Tkach from the small man named Boris at the moment Porfiry Petrovich Rostnikov had first sat down at the window of his second-floor bedroom in Tumsk.

It was a reasonable question. Karpo had been undercover at the same ice cream stand. It was at least possible that the young men who were mugging people around the Yamarka area would stay away from the place where they had almost been caught. It was also possible that they had seen Karpo at the ice cream stand and would, even if they were stupid enough to return, check anyone new at the stand. It made no sense, but one could not always expect sense from the Procurator's Office or the MVD, at least no sense that could be explained to an investigator who would simply be given orders.

The little man in white kept talking but seemed to be reasonably happy.

"But I must admit that you look more like an ice cream salesman than the other one," Boris said looking up to examine Tkach between customers. "The other one looked like an embalmer. You want an ice cream?"

"No," said Tkach adjusting his white cap and scanning the crowd.

He had called home to tell Maya that he would be late but she had been out. Instead he had reached his mother, Lydia, who lived with them. Lydia had a hearing problem and a listening problem.

"Mama," he had said. "I must work late tonight."

"No," said Lydia.

"Yes, mama," he said.

"Tell them no," she insisted.

"I cannot tell them no, mama," he said with a sigh. "I can only tell them yes."

"Your father would have told them no," she insisted loudly enough so that he was sure Zelach, who was sitting across from him, would have heard if he were not preoccupied with preparing a report.

Tkach remembered his dead father well enough to know that he would rather have cut out his tongue than disagree with a superior who issued him an order. His father had never even had the nerve to disagree with his own wife.

"I'm not my father," Tkach said.

"Now you talk back," Lydia shouted.

"I'm not talking back," Tkach said looking over at Zelach who still appeared to hear nothing. "I've got to work. Tell Maya I'll be home late."

"You're not going to tell them no?"

"I am not."

"You are a stubborn child," Lydia shouted.

"I have not been a child for some time, mama."

"Be sure to eat something," she said. "And don't stop at a movie before you come home the way you always do."

Once, when he was fourteen, Sasha had stopped at a movie before he returned home from school. That one incident had, over the years, turned into "the way you always do."

He had hung up depressed and the depression did not leave him as he made his way to the shopping center, found the indoor ice cream stand and informed the little man that he would be working with him.

"You have children?" Boris asked after they had served a pair of families.

"A little girl," said Sasha watching the crowd, hoping for a stroke of luck.

"Little girls are better," said Boris.

Tkach waited for the reasoning or emotion behind this observation but Boris appeared to have none.

"Your wife ever see the exhibition?" Boris said, hands on his hips.

"Once, before we were married."

"Why not have them come tomorrow? We'll give them a free ice cream," said Boris.

Tkach liked the idea and smiled at Boris.

"I've decided in the last hour you're good for business," said Boris. "The women like you. You are coming back? Not the other one."

"He's in Siberia," said Tkach, looking past a pair of giggling girls who were looking at him and walking toward the ice cream stand.

"Just for failing to catch those kids?" asked Boris incredulously.

"An investigation," Tkach corrected as the two girls ignored Boris and ordered ice creams from Sasha.

Boris was pleased. He hoped the muggers stayed away and this policeman remained working with him for weeks. He imagined expanding, hiring relatives, getting a bigger cart, becoming a capitalist. Stranger things had happened, happened to his own brother-in-law Oskar, and Oskar, that big, lumbering oaf, deserved beets growing out of his ears, not financial success. Boris began to dream of a dacha in the country, a week in Yalta. The week had started badly but it could well turn out to be quite profitable.

SIX

THERE WAS NO DAWN IN TUMSK, NOT IN THE WINTER. THE SKY went from black to dark gray and the moon faded a bit. Rostnikov had managed to wake up a little after six. It was not difficult. He seldom slept through any night. He would normally awaken three, four or five times each night to a stiffening of his leg and rolled over to check the time by switching on the lamp near his and Sarah's bed. She never awakened to the light. He would then go back to sleep.

And so, in spite of the morning darkness, Rostnikov had awakened just before six, had checked his watch and decided to get up and read the reports. He used the white pad he had brought with him to make a list.

Assuming no one had come in from the outside, an assumption for which he had no evidence, he had a limited list of suspects. He would assign the least likely to Karpo and take the troublesome and the possible himself.

He had already decided how to handle Sokolov. He had considered simply ordering him to accompany Karpo and tell him the truth, that he did not conduct initial investigation interviews well with someone observing. It tended to interfere with making personal contact with the person being interviewed. He would also keep notes and turn them over to Sokolov for discussion. Sokolov might not like it but he would have difficulty overcoming the order without exposing himself. For the present he would simply leave early and claim that he had been unable to wake him.

Rostnikov dressed, wrote a note for Sokolov and left his room, closing his door quietly. On the wooden table at the foot of the stairs he found a warm kettle of tea and a plate with three smoked fish. He sat down with a grunt, poured himself tea and reached for a fish. Behind him he sensed rather than heard movement.

"Good morning, Emil," he said softly without turning around.

"Good morning, Inspector," replied Karpo.

"Fish?"

"I've eaten," said Karpo, moving around the table to face Rostnikov who carefully peeled his fish and tasted it.

"Good," said Rostnikov.

Karpo placed a small pile of handwritten notes in front of Rostnikov who glanced down at them and continued eating and drinking.

"I interviewed the sailors on the night shift at the weather station," Karpo said. "Those are my notes."

Rostnikov removed a small bone from his mouth and looked at Karpo who seemed, as he had last night, to be struggling with something.

"What are your thoughts, feeling about the sailors?"

"The interview material is all . . . " Karpo began.

"Intuition," Rostnikov said, turning the fish over, savoring its smell and touch.

Karpo sat silently for about thirty seconds while Rostnikov ate, and finally said, "I think they are innocent of any participation in or knowledge of the murder of Commissar Rutkin. "And I believe that when I question the day shift, I will likely conclude the same about them. The weather station is well equipped, autonomous, and the sailors do not interact socially with the residents of Tumsk. When they are given two days off, they go to Igarka."

"And so, following your questioning of the day sailors, we can tentatively eliminate half the residents of Tumsk from our suspect list," said Rostnikov.

"Perhaps we can give them somewhat lower priority," suggested Karpo.

"Let us do so," said Rostnikov.

"And Comrade Sokolov?"

"He was snoring this morning as I passed his door. I knocked lightly but failed to rouse him and so I've written this note."

Rostnikov rubbed the tips of his fingers together and removed the note from his pocket placing it against the kettle. Sokolov's name was printed clearly on the folded sheet.

"I believe," Karpo said slowly, "we should proceed with caution."

"Always a good idea," agreed Rostnikov, putting aside the neat bones of the fish. "Now, you can talk to your sailors and I will have morning tea with the residents of Tumsk. Wait. Add the janitor at the People's Hall to your list, Mirasnikov."

"Yes, Inspector," said Karpo.

A few minutes later, after checking the location of the various houses on a crude map Famfanoff had made for him, Rostnikov bundled up from head to foot, wrapped the scarf Sarah had made for him around his neck and stepped into the town square of Tumsk. The cold greeted him with a slap and a frigid hug as he moved to his right. There had been no additional snow during the night but the wind had filled in the footprints.

He trudged past the pointing statue, glanced at the window of the People's Hall of Justice and Solidarity and moved slowly in the morning darkness. A mechanical rattle and then a motor catching broke the silence and Rostnikov paused, looking at the weather station on the slope across the square. A yellow vehicle with a snow plow mounted low in front rolled slowly, noisily around the building and began to move toward Rostnikov.

Behind the wheel a young sailor in his dark uniform and tight-fitting hat nodded at the policeman and began to clear the main section of Tumsk. A few lights went on in the houses on the hillside toward which Rostnikov was headed. The morning naval plow was probably the alarm clock of the village. Rostnikov tried to remember what time Rutkin was supposed to have died and he made a mental note—it was too cold to take his hands out of his pockets and write—to check it.

With the rattling of the plow behind him, Rostnikov made his way up the gentle slope to the first house beyond the weather station. A light was on inside. He knocked on the heavy wooden door and a voice called almost immediately, "One moment."

And then the door opened and Rostnikov found himself facing a burly man with a head of long, curly white hair and a smile of remarkably even white teeth that did not look false. The man wore a short fur jacket, thick pants and fur mukluks that came up just below his knees.

"Inspector Rostnikov?" the man asked stepping back to let him in.

"Dimitri Galich?" Rostnikov counter-questioned as he stepped into the house.

"Let me take your coat, get you a cup of tea," Galich said, helping Rostnikov remove his coat.

Outside, the plow roared in the twi-morning as Rostnikov looked around the room. The walls were dark wood. Colorful rugs hung on the walls and the combination living-dining-work room was furnished in solid, dark wooden furniture. Wooden cabinets lined the walls except for one floor-to-ceiling bookcase.

A broad worktable covered with odd-looking pieces of metal and glass stood at the rear of the room near a floor-to-ceiling window beyond which stood two similar houses; beyond stood the forest.

"I'll get the tea," Galich said putting Rostnikov's jacket, hat, scarf and gloves on a nearby heavy chair. "Look around if you like."

Galich disappeared to the right behind a stairway and Rostnikov wandered toward the worktable. As he approached he could see that the various items upon it included a ceramic pot filled with unfamiliar coins, a rusted and very ancient rifle, several cracked pots and something that looked like a door hinge. He was reaching for the door hinge when he heard the deep voice of Galich behind him.

"That was on two pieces of wood I found less than a week ago near the river," he said handing Rostnikov a steaming mug.

"What is it?"

"I don't know," said Galich picking it up with his free hand, turning it over. "But I'll figure it out. The books," he said nodding at the nearby shelf, "will help me. Usually I spend the winter working on the pieces I find in the summer. It is rare that I'll actually pick up an artifact in the winter but the new hydroelectric plant north on the Yensei has shifted the river bed slightly. All up and down the river for over a thousand miles hydroelectric plants are going up. There are over twenty-five of them now. Here, look at this piece."

Galich took a quick sip of hot liquid and reached for the rusted rifle. He picked it up in one large hand and handed it to Rostnikov. It was surprisingly heavy.

"Probably sixteenth century, maybe a bit earlier," said Galich taking the rifle back. "Could have belonged to one of Ermak's cossack's, maybe Ermak himself. It could be. This area is a treasure of history. I've found pieces that date back to Khan.

But most of what I find date back to the late 1500s. There was an ostrog, a cossack fort, not more than four hundred feet from here, overlooking the river."

"Fascinating," said Rostnikov.

"The cabinets are filled with pieces," Galich said with pride. "I'm cataloging, organizing. In three, possibly four years I'll have a major museum exhibit ready with a series of monographs covering the history of the upper Yensei."

"The tea is very good," said Rostnikov moving to one of the straight-backed chairs.

"Indian, imported. My one vice," said Galich amiably, sitting opposite Rostnikov on an almost identical chair. "To what do I owe the honor of being first on your list this morning?"

"How did you know you were first?"

Galich laughed and shook his head.

"Visitors are major events in Tumsk," he explained. "I'm sure that everyone in the village was up early looking out the window, waiting for you or the one who doesn't blink."

"I started with you because Famfanoff said he was staying here," Rostnikov said. "Is he up? I need some information from him."

"He sleeps deeply," said Galich looking up toward the ceiling. "We can rouse him later. Perhaps I could help you."

"I also started with you because I am looking for weight-lifting equipment I can use, a few weights will be fine."

"No difficulty," said Galich beaming. "I have a small but adequate supply of weights left by a naval officer a few years ago. I can show them to you later."

"I would be very grateful," said Rostnikov, finishing his tea.

"More tea?" asked Galich, jumping up to reach for the policeman's empty cup.

"No, thank you. Questions."

Galich nodded.

"You are a priest?"

"I was a priest, Russian Orthodox Church," said Galich. "Surely your records contain this information."

"I like to listen," said Rostnikov, sitting back and folding his hands in his lap. "Why did you leave the church?"

Galich shrugged. "Crisis of faith. No, actually there was no crisis of faith. It was a question of too much passion. I simply accepted one morning when I was about to go to the church that I had never had any real faith, that I had endured the church because my family had always been leaders in the church back in Suzdal. The oddity is that had it not been for the Revolution, the Party, I would have left the church as a young man. I said things, did things even then that did not fit the image of the contemplative priest. I persisted, entered the priesthood because I didn't want to be considered a coward. Ironic, isn't it? I convinced myself that I believed but I knew that I could not reject the church because my family, the congregants, would think I was afraid of the Party."

"But you did quit," Rostnikov said.

"I did."

"Why?"

"I became sixty years old and stopped worrying about what others thought. Sometimes I think I waited too long. I have much work to do here and probably not enough time to get it done. But I'm babbling. I think you'll find many of us in Tumsk will babble. We are not accustomed to outsiders and we sometimes grow tired of each other's company. You want to talk about the Samsonov child?"

"About Commissar Rutkin," corrected Rostnikov. "He spoke to you."

"Several times. Would you like some pickled vegetables while we talk?"

"No, thank you. What did he ask you?"

"Commissar Rutkin? He asked where I was the day the Samsonov child died. What I did. What I saw. What I thought."

"And you told him . . . ?"

"I told him," said Galich, "that I spent most of the day at the river. I have a very passable twelfth-century Mongol cup I found that day. It's in the cabinet behind you. I saw no one from town. And what did I think? I thought the child's death was an accident. I cannot imagine anyone would harm her. Why would they?"

"Because of her father, perhaps," said Rostnikov.

"Inspector, what monster would kill a child to punish the father?" Galich shook his head. "And for what? This is a town of exiles. A dissident is nothing new here. I am a voluntary exile. So is General Krasnikov. Most of us here, except for the sailors, are out of favor with the Party."

"Yet the child is dead and monsters do exist," said Rostnikov.

"Of a sort," agreed Galich with a sad shrug. "I am well aware of our history. Perhaps that is why I am trying to retrieve some of the more distant and possibly more colorful parts worth remembering. Am I talking treason?"

"Reason," said Rostnikov. "And the day Commissar Rutkin died? You were?"

"Famfanoff said it was early that morning. I was in here, certainly not up yet. It must have happened before the sailors plowed the square or else everyone would have seen the body. I don't even know who discovered Commissar Rutkin's corpse."

"It was Samsonov," said Rostnikov. "There was to be a hearing at the People's Hall of Justice and Solidarity on the child's death. Samsonov wanted to get there early."

"I think, if you want my opinion," said Galich, "Samsonov is making all this fuss not only out of grief but of guilt. He was forced to bring his wife and child here because of his politics. And this is not a place for a child. The girl was here for a year with no other children. She didn't even go to the school in Agapitovo. She spent a lot of time here with me and my collection," he said looking around the room. "I knew about the hearing, of course, but I . . . what can one say? I can't say I liked your Commissar Rutkin, but I didn't dislike him, either. Rutkin was . . . self-interested. The child's death did not seem to touch him."

"And no one came into conflict with him, argued with him," Rostnikov tried.

Galich hesitated, rose and opened his broad hands palm up as if he were about to deliver a sermon.

"Samsonov," Galich said. "I'm sure you know that. He was outspoken and quite bitter. He quite openly declared that the government had purposely sent an incompetent to conduct the investigation so the truth would never be known."

"There is something in the reports to that effect. And you, Comrade Galich. Did you agree with him?"

"I'm a historian and amateur archeologist," replied Galich. "Until further information is available, I choose not to form an opinion."

"Wise," said Rostnikov, standing. "Perhaps we can talk again."

"I gather you do not believe, as does Sergeant Famfanoff, that Commissar Rutkin was killed by a bear from the taiga."

"Considering the nature of the wounds, it is highly unlikely," said Rostnikov, moving slowly toward the chair on which his coat rested. "Is there anything else you could tell me that might be of some assistance?"

"No, nothing I can think of at the moment," said Galich, rubbing the back of his head. "But you might hear some nonsense from the janitor Mirasnikov and his wife. Shamanism is still practiced among the few Evenk natives remaining in the area and superstition is remarkably powerful. The word 'shaman' itself is a creation of the Evenks, the native Siberians who live in the forests. The atheist rationality of the Revolution has failed to conquer much of Siberia beyond the limits of the larger towns and cities. There was even talk that Commissar Rutkin was killed by a snow monster called up by an Evenk shaman to destroy the godless intruder."

"Interesting," said Rostnikov getting into his coat. The noise of the plow outside suddenly stopped.

"You're mocking," said Galich.

"Not at all. I find it very interesting. Please have Famfanoff find me when he finally awakens but please do not wake him. From here I'll be going to the Samsonovs' and then to General Krasnikov's."

"You have much to do," said Galich. "Let me show you my modest collection of weights."

Rostnikov followed the big man to a door off the wooden stairway to the right. Galich opened the door and stood back to let Rostnikov in. The small room with a tiny frosted window contained a sizable collection of weights piled neatly on the floor. Bars were neatly hung on racks and four barbells were lined up evenly against the windowed wall.

"If this meets your needs, please feel free to come back at any time and use them," said Galich.

"It more than meets my needs," said Rostnikov.

"I find the weights very satisfying, very therapeutic and reassuring," said Galich stepping back to close the door.

Before he put on his gloves, Rostnikov shook Galich's hand.

"Then you'll return?" said the former priest. "Perhaps before you finish your work in Tumsk you'll even join me for dinner. I've visited Moscow many times and I'd like to hear about how it is now, if you wouldn't mind."

"I would not mind," said Rostnikov.

The square was plowed as were paths along the hills. Rostnikov slogged into the nearest furrow and made his way higher up the slope to a nearby house almost identical to that of the former priest.

Like the other houses the front faced down the hill toward the town square. Rostnikov moved off the plowed path and through the snow to the door. Before he could knock the door opened.

"Doctor Samsonov?" Rostnikov asked.

The man before him was lean, tall and somewhere in his forties. His hair was dark and thin and his face placid. Beneath the placidness Rostnikov sensed a seething anger. The man wore a black turtleneck sweater. He pulled up the sleeves slightly as he examined the policeman at his door.

"You find it necessary to interrogate me in my home," Samsonov said, not backing away from the open door to let Rostnikov in.

"If you prefer, we can go to the People's Hall or to the house in which I am staying," said Rostnikov.

"Let him in," came a woman's voice from within the house.

Samsonov shuddered, played with his sleeves again, ignoring the cold that must be cutting through his body, and then stepped back to let Rostnikov in.

When the door was closed behind him the chill of the outside lingered.

"You may keep your coat on," said Samsonov. "I would like this visit to be as brief as possible."

"As you wish," said Rostnikov. "Though I would prefer to sit. I have a leg which gives me some trouble from time to time."

The house was identical in structure to Galich's but the atmosphere was a world away. The wooden floor was covered by two rugs, one very large and oriental. The furnishings were upholstered and modern, the kind Rostnikov had seen in the

Moscow apartments of Party officials and successful criminals. On the walls were paintings, very modern paintings with no subject and no object.

"You are surprised?" Samsonov said leaning back against the wall and folding his arms.

"At your inhospitality or the furnishings?" Rostnikov asked.

"I owe you no hospitality," Samsonov said. "You have exiled me, taken me and my family away from my practice, my research, driven me out of my country. If you had not driven me to this corner of hell, my daughter would be alive. My daughter is dead and you people have done nothing. What hospitality do I owe you?"

"I did not exile you. I did not drive you out. I am not responsible for what happened to your daughter," said Rostnikov softly. "I am not the government. I am an inspector looking for the killer of a deputy Commissar and I am a man who has a son and feels deeply for a man who has lost his daughter. Do you have a picture of your little girl?"

"What has that to do with your investigation?" asked a woman who emerged from the darkness beyond the stairs.

Rostnikov turned to her. She was dark, slender, quite beautiful. Ludmilla Samsonov wore a red and black close-fitting knit dress that would have been stylish even on Kalinin Prospekt.

"It has nothing to do with the investigation," replied Rostnikov unable to take his eyes from the lovely pale woman. "My son is grown. He's a soldier stationed in Afghanistan. Each day my wife and I hold our breath in fear."

"You have a picture of your son?" Ludmilla Samsonov asked, stepping even closer.

Rostnikov had expected the illusion of beauty to drop away in the light, but the woman looked even better as she drew closer. He wondered what she would look like smiling and knew that he would never know. He reached under his coat, removed his battered wallet and took out a photograph of Josef and Sarah. The photo was three years old but Josef had not changed much. Sarah, however, looked quite different.

Ludmilla Samsonov reached out to take the picture and her cool fingers touched Rostnikov's.

She examined the photograph and held it out to her husband who turned away, gave Rostnikov a cold stare and then looked down at the picture. His face betrayed nothing. The woman handed back the photograph which Rostnikov put away carefully.

Samsonov shared a look with his wife and pointed to a desk by the front window. Rostnikov walked to the desk and picked up the framed picture which rested on it. The girl in the picture was smiling at him.

"Beautiful," said Rostnikov.

A single sob escaped the woman behind him and he put down the photograph and turned back slowly to give her time to recover. She was standing closer to her husband now but they were not touching. Rostnikov sensed a terrible tension between the two.

"You perform perfectly, Inspector . . . " Samsonov began.

"Rostnikov. May I sit?"

"Sit," said Samsonov tersely.

Rostnikov moved to the nearest straight-backed chair and sat with relief.

"An old injury?" Samsonov said referring to Rostnikov's leg.

"A very old injury," agreed Porfiry Petrovich.

"And it still causes you pain?" asked Samsonov, his tone changing to one of professional curiosity.

"From time to time, mostly discomfort."

Ludmilla Samsonov turned and left the room as quietly as she had entered it.

"Leg dysfunctions used to be my speciality before I began my research," said Samsonov not moving from the wall. "Especially war wounds. I treated quite a few soldiers who had been in Afghanistan."

"This is a war wound," said Rostnikov.

"May I look?" asked Samsonov.

"If you wish," said Rostnikov sitting back.

Samsonov moved from the wall with confidence and knelt on one knee before the policeman.

"I have had very little opportunity to practice here," said Samsonov, his fingers running the length of Rostnikov's left leg. "And no opportunity for research. Remarkable muscle tone. You must be a very determined man. In most people this leg would have atrophied."

"We endure," Rostnikov said as Samsonov stood.

"Whether we like it or not," agreed Samsonov. "Do you take any medication?"

"No," said Rostnikov.

"I can give you the name of an American muscle relaxant which should help you if you can get it. You take one a day for the rest of your life. I assume that since you are a policeman you have connections for such things."

"Perhaps," said Rostnikov.

"I may have a bottle of the medicine among my things. I'll see if I can find it. I can also give you a set of exercises that should ease the pain and make walking easier," said Samsonov moving to a chair. "Are you interested?"

"Very much."

"I'll ask Ludmilla to type them up and get them to you before you leave."

"And now?" asked Rostnikov.

"And now," said Samsonov, as his wife came back into the room carrying a tray with three matching cups and a plate of small pastries.

"I'd like you to tell me about your contacts with Commissar Rutkin," said Rostnikov, accepting a steaming cup of tea offered by Ludmilla Samsonov. She placed the tray on an inlaid table to Rostnikov's left.

"He was a fool," Samsonov said, the anger returning to his voice. "They sent a fool. It took the death of a fool for them to send you to find out what happened to our Karla."

"I'm going to tell you something," said Rostnikov, putting down the tea and leaning forward. "I want you to hear me out, not interrupt me till I am finished."

"Say it," Samsonov said impatiently.

"I have told you that I have not been sent here to investigate your daughter's death."

Samsonov clenched his fists and closed his eyes. He looked for an instant as if he were going to cry out. His wife touched his shoulder and Samsonov laughed.

"You're only here to look for the one who killed that fool," he said. "God."

"I asked you to hear me out without interruption," said Rostnikov.

"And I never agreed," said Samsonov.

"Let him finish," said the woman.

"Why bother?" asked Samsonov.

"Let him finish," she repeated quietly looking at Rostnikov.

"I think it possible, probably even likely, that the two deaths are related," he said carefully. "I have been told that someone else will be sent to investigate your daughter's death, but I do not see how I can conduct the investigation of Commissar Rutkin's murder without knowing something about what happened to your daughter. Do you understand?"

Samsonov cocked his head to one side and examined Rostnikov.

"You have been ordered away from Karla's death but you intend to pursue it anyway," Samsonov said.

In answer, Rostnikov reached for one of the pastries which he plunked into his mouth.

"Very good," he said.

"I made them myself," said the woman. "I do a great deal of baking since . . . I do a great deal of baking. How can we help you?"

"A few questions. A few answers," Rostnikov said resisting the urge to reach for more pastries. He looked at Samsonov. "You are the only doctor for several hundred miles. I assume you examined Commissar Rutkin's body."

Samsonov bit his lower lip, took a deep breath and clasped his hands in his lap.

"I would think you had the pathologist's report," Samsonov said. His wife reached over to touch him again.

"Yes, of course," said Rostnikov, "but you were first, possibly you saw, noted something that they might later miss and, as you know, each pathologist is different, searches in his or her own way. You understand."

"Yes," said Samsonov with a pained grin. "You don't trust them. Good. Neither do I. My daughter died of trauma. Rutkin made it clear that he thought she fell from the rock near the river. Her bones, her body . . . She was hurled from the rock. She was murdered and I told him as I tell you, if the murderer is not identified I shall carry the story with me into the West. It is too late to stop us from leaving. The world already knows I am leaving."

Rostnikov took a small sip of the tea, a very small one. Soon he would need a washroom, but he did not want to stop. He would have to be more careful, more precise with his questions. He had not wanted the man to conjecture about the death of his daughter. His questions had clearly been about the dead Commissar.

"I understand you discovered the body of Commissar Rutkin," he said.

Samsonov looked at his wife and nodded his head to confirm the policeman's understanding.

"Tell me about it," Rostnikov said.

"Tell you about it," Samsonov said, shaking his head and touching his hair as if he suddenly felt unkempt. "I got up early, before the plow. I wanted to be there when Rutkin arrived to conduct his hearing, present his findings. I wanted him to face me. I knew that he planned to find that Karla had died of an accidental fall. I did not intend to let him get by with that."

"So," Rostnikov prompted to get the man back to the subject, "you got up early."

"Early, yes. I was out by six, possibly a bit earlier. I didn't see the body till I was almost at the door to the People's Hall."

"So you heard nothing? Saw nothing?" asked Rostnikov.

"No shouts. No screams. No whimpers. No regrets," said Samsonov looking up at Rostnikov.

"How long had he been dead when you found him? Could you tell?"

"Minutes. The temperature was 40 below and the blood had not yet frozen," said Samsonov. "Cause of death appeared to be a puncture wound through his left eye and into his brain and a second about two centimeters across just above the shoulder blade, barely into the neck. It appeared to be deep and, judging from the hemorrhaging into the eyes and mouth, I think it penetrated the carotid artery and cut through the esophagus. I am not a pathologist. I did not get an opportunity to examine the body very closely, but this all seemed obvious."

"So the killer knew what he was doing, how to kill?" asked Rostnikov. "I mean in your opinion."

"Who knows?" sighed Samsonov reaching for a cup of tea, picking it up, changing his mind and putting it back down again. "It could have been luck. I've seen accidental trauma, a fall, a car crash that caused incisions that looked as if they had been done by a skilled surgeon."

"Do you think someone caught him unaware?"

"Impossible," said Samsonov. "He was in the square, the open square. The snow hadn't been plowed. Get out there some morning. You can hear the slightest change in the wind. He was running away from whoever got him. You could see the footprints in the snow. I told that fool Famfanoff. I tell you."

"So, if Commissar Rutkin saw someone coming at him with a weapon, he had time to call for help."

"Probably," Samsonov agreed.

"But no one heard him call," said Rostnikov. "The report says . . ."

"The square itself is a small, silent canyon, but if the wind is blowing toward the river, you would have to be right in the square to hear someone yell," said Samsonov. "What's the difference? I knocked at the door of the People's Hall and Mirasnikov helped me bring the body inside before it froze."

"How long did it take for him to answer your knock?"

"I don't know. Not long. Almost immediately."

"Was he dressed?"

"Dressed? Yes," said Samsonov with irritation. "He was dressed, but . . ."

"If Commissar Rutkin shouted in the square, would someone inside the People's Hall hear it?" Rostnikov continued.

"Probably. Who knows? If you mean Mirasnikov, he is an old man. So is his wife. I don't know what they can hear and can't hear."

Rostnikov said, "I see," and with an effort he tried to disguise, stood up. He was still wearing his coat and felt perspiration under his arms. He was reluctant to pass too close to Ludmilla Samsonov as he moved toward the door.

"That is all?" asked Samsonov.

"For now," said Rostnikov.

"But what about Karla? You have my warning," said Samsonov.

"A foot at a time," said Rostnikov, buttoning his coat. "A foot at a time and patience. Someone once said that you can get to town faster after a storm by walking around the fallen trees and rocks than by following a straight path and climbing over them."

"Someone once said . . . ?" Ludmilla said, reaching out to take Rostnikov's hand.

"I think it was Gogol," Rostnikov admitted.

"Do your best, Inspector," she said.

Rostnikov could smell her cleanliness and his own sweat.

"You will hear from me," he said, including Samsonov in his parting comment, but Samsonov was still sitting, his hands clasped, his face turned away.

"I will remind him about the medicine and the exercises for your leg," she said quietly as she opened the door.

"Spasee'bo," said Rostnikov.

Rostnikov resisted the impulse to turn back and look at Ludmilla Samsonov as he went down the wooden steps and onto the plowed path.

Questions, questions. Porfiry Petrovich needed some space and time for thinking but he decided to make one more visit before going back to his room.

SEVEN

SASHA TKACH WOKE UP SUDDENLY WITH THE EMPTY FEELING that he was late for work. He looked around the living room at the baby's crib, at his sleeping wife, at the dull winter sunlight coming through the window and for an instant he could not remember if he was an ice cream vendor or a policeman. He had to reach over and touch Maya to restore reality.

She stirred and rolled toward him, her dark, straight hair in disarray over her closed eyes, and laid her right arm over his bare stomach. Sasha wanted to pull her to him but he didn't want to waken her. He lay back looking at the ceiling, listening to the sound of his mother's snoring in the bedroom, even though the door to the bedroom was closed.

Lydia had been given the bedroom because a better sense of partial privacy was possible with the assumption that at night the living room/dining room/kitchen was the territory of Sasha, Maya, and the baby while the bedroom belonged to Lydia. Neutral time was spent in Sasha and Maya's space but Lydia knew that she was to retreat to the bedroom about an hour after dinner which, in any case, was close to her bedtime. None of this had ever been openly discussed. It had been arrived at through trial and error, argument and near argument, compromise and conflict. It had been arrived at in the Tkach household as in hundreds of thousands of households in cities throughout the Soviet Union in much the same way.

"I don't sleep for hours after I go to my room," Lydia had once confided to her son as if it were a secret to be kept from his wife. In fact, Sasha and Maya could tell from Lydia's snoring that she was in bed and asleep almost every night within half an hour of going to her room.

Sasha turned his head toward the window and considered getting up.

"You are awake," Maya whispered in his ear.

"Yes," he answered. "I have to get to work in a little while. I'm selling ice cream today."

"I love ice cream," she said in her Ukrainian accent which always sent a thrill through him.

"Bring the baby today to the Yamarka at the Economic Exhibition. You can see the bears in the zoo having fun and me dressed like a fool and I can watch the two of you eat."

She smiled. Her teeth were white. She pulled him down and kissed him. Her tongue played with his lower lip.

"My mother will be getting up in a few minutes," he whispered. "And the baby . . . "

"I don't care," said Maya touching his stomach and reaching down into his pajama bottoms.

Sasha wanted to tell her that they should wait till that night, that he was in a hurry, but his body responded and he felt that he owed her the demonstration of love which he felt. He hoped they could stay under the blanket in case Lydia burst into the room. He hoped they could make love quietly. He hoped, but he didn't expect it. He reached for his wife's hands and moved them to where they felt best.

After they had made love with no interruption except a movement by Pulcharia in the crib, Sasha kissed Maya who clung to him not wanting to let him go.

"I hear her," he whispered looking up at the bedroom door.

"When we get the new apartment in North Zmailova," she said, "we get the bedroom with the baby and Lydia gets the small room off the living room."

"I remember," he said, disengaging her arms and kissing her on her warm, exposed shoulder.

"And remember you said you would call the housing registry to see why they haven't called us," Maya said as he stood up and reached for his underwear.

"I'll call today," he promised. "Are you going to come with the baby?"

"Yes," she said. "It sounds like fun."

This time he was sure he heard Lydia moving behind the bedroom door. Sasha finished pulling on his underwear and was yanking on his pants when his mother came through the door and said, "Why did you move the towels?"

Lydia thought she was whispering but, being more than a bit hard of hearing, the whisper was a hoarse shout that immediately awakened the baby. Pulcharia began to cry in fear and Maya reached for her worn robe.

"The towels," Lydia repeated.

"In the lower drawer," Maya said, throwing her hair back and wrapping the robe around her as she moved for the baby.

"In the lower drawer?" Lydia asked. "It's harder to reach the lower drawer. What sense does it make to put towels in lower drawers?"

Sasha buttoned his shirt and moved to the closet for his blue tie.

"Something has to go in a lower drawer," Maya said picking up and rocking the baby.

Lydia made a tsk-tsk sound that made it clear she found the answer insufficient. She returned to the bedroom leaving the door open behind her.

Sasha moved over to smile at his daughter. She saw his face and returned the smile.

"Don't put the tie on," Maya said. "You need a shave."

"I shaved last night," Sasha complained.

"Virility is making your hair grow faster," she said with a smile, brushing the hair from her face.

"I'll shave," he said, pausing to kiss his daughter before moving to the sink in the kitchen corner. "An ice cream vendor should be immaculate."

"A husband should be immaculate," Maya said, picking up and cuddling the baby. "Sasha, we must get that apartment. We must."

"Yes," he agreed, reaching for his razor on the shelf above the sink.

In the small bathroom off the bedroom, Lydia hummed a completely unrecognizable song. Pulcharia looked as if she might cry again but Maya offered her a nipple which the baby took with glee.

In less than half an hour Sasha would be on his way to the Exhibition to sell ice cream and Lydia would be on her way to the Ministry of Information where she worked filing papers. Maya would be alone with the baby, her thoughts and the shopping before she could take the metro to the Economic Exhibition. It wouldn't be a bad day.

"... and I've been vorking like uh dug," Lydia sang-shouted the Beatle song in terrible English. Sasha and Maya looked at each other and laughed. The baby paused in her sucking, startled, and then continued drinking.

It wouldn't be a bad day, Sasha thought. Not a bad day at all.

He turned out to be quite wrong.

"He's coming. He's coming," Liana Mirasnikov shouted from the window of the People's Hall.

"Coming here. The square one?" wailed Sergei wide-eyed from across the hall.

"No, the other one, the ghost," she said without turning.

"Oh no. Worse and worse," the old man groaned. "Is he wearing a hat?"

The old woman squinted through the curtains.

"No hat," she announced. "He is mad."

"We are undone," he moaned.

He had prepared for this moment. He had gone through everything that they had accumulated over the years and decided whether they had a right to each piece. If they did not, he moved the piece—an old pair of candlesticks, a chair with a worn velvet covering, a movie projector that he had never tried to use—to the loft which could not be reached without a ladder. The loft already contained a collection of articles which Mirasnikov had kept just in case. These articles included paintings of Stalin and Khrushchev and even a small painting of someone Liana thought was Beria and Sergei was sure was Trotsky. The large painting of Lenin with the flag remained in place in the main hall as it had for almost fifty years. Lenin was always a good, conservative art investment.

Sergei took a last, quick look around the hall as the door opened and the pale man stepped in.

"Mirasnikov," the man said in a deep voice. It was, the old man thought, like the voice of the devil calling for him, telling him it was his time and he should know it.

"I am Mirasnikov," the old man admitted.

The ghostly man stepped forward and looked around. The big hall was clean and relatively empty except for the old oak table with three chairs behind it, the painting of Lenin, and a broom leaning against the wall. The folding chairs which had been pulled out for the rare meeting were usually stacked inside the large closet.

"I am Deputy Inspector Karpo," the man's voice echoed through the empty room. "I have a few questions to ask you concerning the death of Commissar Rutkin."

"A good man," said Mirasnikov quickly.

"I am not concerned with his virtues," said Karpo. "Only with his actions and your knowledge of them."

This man, who looked rather like a Tartar, had stopped in the middle of the hall and looked at Mirasnikov. And this man named Karpo did not blink, which caused Mirasnikov to blink uncontrollably for both of them.

"Of course," said Mirasnikov. "Would you like to sit? Would you like some tea or maybe we even have coffee. Liana, do we have coffee for the inspector, anything for the inspector?"

"I don't . . . " the old woman near the window stammered in confusion.

"I want no tea or coffee," said Karpo. "Come."

Mirasnikov followed the man to the table where Karpo moved around to sit in the chair in which, in the old days, the visiting procurator would sit. Mirasnikov took a chair as far from the man as he could get and Liana was forced to take the remaining chair nearest the inspector. She had seen him the night before when she served and cleaned up the dinner for the three visitors. She had avoided his eyes the night before but now she could not.

Had someone told Karpo he was frightening the couple, he would have been surprised and curious. He had no intention of frightening them. On the contrary, he wanted to put them at their ease, to get his answers as quickly and efficiently as possible and then to get back to his room to prepare his report for Rostnikov.

"Who murdered Commissar Rutkin?" Karpo asked when the old couple was seated.

It was the very question which Mirasnikov had most feared and for an instant he sat, mouth open and silent.

Karpo looked at the old man. It was a standard question. One to which he had expected no answer beyond conjecture which might feed into other conjecture. But the old man had reacted and Karpo considered a new line of questioning.

"You saw the murder of Commissar Rutkin," Karpo said. It was not a question but a statement.

"Nyet. No," said Mirasnikov shaking his head vehemently. "I saw nothing."

"I do not believe you, Comrade," Karpo said.

"He saw nothing," the old woman chirped.

"You were with him on the morning of the murder?" asked Karpo, looking at the old woman next to him. She shrank back against the chair.

"No. I was still asleep," she said.

"So you were not together," said Karpo turning his eyes on the old man. "You were up early. You were in here preparing the hall for the hearing."

"I . . . maybe," Mirasnikov said with a shrug. "I was moving chairs, making noise. Then Doctor Samsonov knocked and I went to help him. The Commissar was dead. I had made tea for everyone. I can show you the tea pot."

"What did you see?" asked Karpo.

The old man looked at his frightened wife before he answered.

"Nothing. Nothing."

Karpo sat silently, white hands on the table. He was dressed, as always, entirely in black, which contrasted with his white face. Something creaked in a corner.

"What did you think of Commissar Rutkin?" Karpo asked breaking the silence.

"He was a Commissar," Sergei answered, unaccustomed to anyone, even his wife, asking his opinion. Mirasnikov was unaware that he had any real opinions—was, in fact, convinced that opinions were very dangerous things to have.

"That is not an opinion," said Karpo.

"It's not?" Mirasnikov said looking at his wife for help, but she looked forward resolutely as if she were being pestered by a stranger she wished to ignore.

"Was he admired, respected?" asked Karpo. "Did people like or dislike him? Did they cooperate with Commissar Rutkin? Did you?"

"Cooperated," Mirasnikov said eagerly. "Everyone cooperated."

"But what did you, others, think of him?"

The old man was backed into a corner with no way out.

"I don't know," he said.

And then Karpo began his questioning in earnest.

Sokolov was slogging up the plowed path behind Rostnikov who realized that he could not avoid the man and so turned to wait for him. Sokolov was bundled in fur with only his eyes, nose and a bit of his mustache showing.

"You didn't wake me," he said through the scarf which muffled his voice.

"You didn't answer my knock," Rostnikov said with a shrug, which was true though Rostnikov was certain that his knock had not been loud enough to awaken a frightened bird. "I left a note."

"I found it. Please knock harder next time," Sokolov said through his scarf. "I don't wish to miss anything."

"I'll bear that in mind," Rostnikov said, turning to walk further up the slope toward the next house. "Won't you join me?"

Sokolov grunted and moved to Rostnikov's side.

"Who have you spoken to? What have you done?" Sokolov said trying to hide his irritation. The problem was obvious.

Sokolov had already failed to stay with the man he was assigned to watch. Sokolov could be in trouble.

"I've talked to a few people," said Rostnikov moving toward the next wooden house up the slope. "The Samsonovs, Galich, the former priest."

"What?" Sokolov asked, stopping.

Rostnikov stopped him. Sokolov's talking was soaking his scarf.

"The Samsonovs, Galich," Rostnikov repeated.

Sokolov's eyes scanned Rostnikov's face but whatever he was seeking wasn't there.

"Your reports. I'd like to read your reports on these interviews," Sokolov said, trying to hide his nervousness.

"No report," said Rostnikov. "Just informal conversation at this point."

"But you must write up each interview," said Sokolov. "It's procedure."

"Interview, yes. Conversation, no," said Rostnikov. "I will be happy to tell you what passed between us, Comrade. Believe me, you missed nothing which would inform you about investigative procedure. I'm about to talk to General Krasnikov. Would you like to join me?"

"Yes, yes," said Sokolov whose nose was quite red. "Let's get out of this cold."

Rostnikov nodded and stepped into the snow to knock at the door of the house they had moved to. It was a triplet of the previous two houses but, like those houses, it had a bit of its own personality, a personality Rostnikov guessed belonged not to the present inhabitant but to some past transient. Krasnikov's house had narrow painted blue trim above the door and along the front of the house. No one answered the knock. The windows were shuttered and no light shone out.

Rostnikov removed the glove on his right hand and knocked again.

"Perhaps he's still sleeping," said Sokolov.

"Perhaps," said Rostnikov, knocking louder.

"Perhaps he is out," Sokolov tried.

"No," said Rostnikov. "No footprints in the snow. Look."

"The back door," said Sokolov irritably. "He could have gone out the back."

"He is inside," Rostnikov said, knocking again.

This time something stirred inside the house.

Rostnikov put the glove back on his frigid hand.

The sun had by now whispered to the sub-arctic sky giving the gray darkness a glow, a gentle glow. Rostnikov remembered the ghost of a winter morning when he was a child. He couldn't quite place himself in that memory but it was strong and had something to do with an aunt who lived near Porfiry Petrovich and his parents in Moscow. It was a bittersweet memory of childhood he would have liked to grasp but the door opened and he lost it.

"What is it?" said the man who opened the door, looking at the two men on the step below him.

He was tall, erect and younger looking than Rostnikov had expected. His face was surprisingly unlined and youthful though his straight white hair betrayed him. Krasnikov was, Rostnikov knew, fifty-three years old, nearly his own age. The man wore a faded flannel shirt and jeans that looked American. The former general stood straight, head up, hands at his sides, ignoring the blast of frigid air that slapped his bare cheeks.

"I'm Inspector Rostnikov. This is Inspector Sokolov. I am investigating the death of Commissar Rutkin."

"I'm not feeling well today," Krasnikov said, looking like a healthy Olympic wrestler.

"We won't be long," Rostnikov said soberly stepping up on the wooden stoop.

Krasnikov who stood about four inches taller than Rostnikov blocked the entrance.

"I'd appreciate it if you would let us in," Rostnikov said softly. "It is cold and it is important that we get on with our investigation. Others have cooperated fully."

Krasnikov smiled but there was no amusement in the smile. He stood looking at the policeman, almost toe to toe continuing to block the way.

"I would appreciate your cooperation," Rostnikov whispered so that Sokolov could not hear. "Sokolov is monitoring my investigation and it will look bad for me if you don't cooperate."

Krasnikov's mirthless smile turned to a real one as Sokolov moved forward to try to hear.

"I'm a soldier," Krasnikov whispered. "I know how to read a man's eyes. You aren't afraid of being monitored by this one."

Rostnikov shrugged.

"Concerned," he said.

"And if I refuse to let you in? I suppose you'd try to force your way," said the General.

"I would do my best," Rostnikov said softly.

"And I have a feeling it might be enough," said Krasnikov. "I also know how to read a man's body."

"I think it best if you let us in," said Sokolov menacingly.

Krasnikov glanced at Rostnikov to show his disdain for the threat and backed away to let the men in. Rostnikov waited for Sokolov to pass him with a satisfied look in his eyes. Rostnikov followed behind him and Krasnikov closed the door behind them.

It was probably no more than 40 degrees above zero in the room but it felt hot to Porfiry Petrovich, who found himself not in a large room as in the two similar houses but a much smaller room, roughly but comfortably furnished with unupholstered wooden furniture. A desk stood in front of the window and, Rostnikov could see, from the chair behind it Krasnikov could looked down at the town square. On the wall across the room a bear's head was mounted. The bear's mouth was open in an angry snarl showing sharp yellow-white teeth.

Rostnikov looked at the bear's head and back at Krasnikov.

"You like Stalin?" Krasnikov nodding at the bear head. "I killed him last year. An old Evenk mounted the head in exchange for the meat and the hide."

"You shot him?" Rostnikov asked opening his coat.

"No," said Krasnikov his eyes widening. "I strangled him with my bare hands."

"Impressive," said Sokolov.

"Ridiculous," answered Krasnikov. "Of course I shot the bastard. I was out for a hike. If I hadn't had my rifle with me, he would have torn me to pieces. I filled him so full of holes I didn't think there was enough left of the hide to make it worth having, but the Evenks can work miracles. They can't fight but they can hunt. Sit, but don't expect tea or little cakes."

"Thank you," said Rostnikov moving to a nearby chair. "I've had enough tea today."

Sokolov, who had removed his coat, sat in an almost identical chair to the one Rostnikov had chosen. He inched the chair a little closer to Rostnikov who looked back over his shoulder out the window.

"Very nice view," he said.

"There is no other view," said Krasnikov moving to the only remaining chair, which was large enough for two people but which he managed to fill by putting one booted leg up on it. "In the back you can see trees. Out that way," he said, pointing to a small window in the wooden wall, "you see the Samsonov house and snow. The other way, more trees and snow."

"And so," said Rostnikov, "you sit at the desk and watch."

"I sit at the desk and work," Krasnikov said with irritation. "I'm not a petty sneak or a gossip. You want a sneak, talk to the old man. You want gossip, see the priest."

"Mirasnikov, the janitor?" asked Rostnikov. "He is a sneak?"

"Of course," sighed Krasnikov.

"And, may I ask, what work do you do at the desk?" asked Rostnikov.

Krasnikov shrugged.

"Military articles," he said. "Alternatives to great battles in Russian history, particularly the war against the Nazis. Strategy is, or was, my specialty."

"I would very much like to see some of your writing if I may," said Rostnikov.

"Perhaps you may," said Krasnikov. "Now, if you have questions, ask them. I have work to do. A routine becomes very satisfying when one is deprived of an outlet for one's skills, especially if one is accustomed to a disciplined military career."

"We will do our best to vacate ourselves from your routine at the earliest possible moment, Comrade," Sokolov said grimly.

"General," Krasnikov said. "I have not been stripped of my title or dignity, only of my responsibility."

"I stand corrected," said Sokolov. "General."

"Commissar Rutkin interviewed you on three occasions," said Rostnikov.

"Two, three, four. I don't remember," said Kraskinov rubbing his hands together. The hands, Rostnikov could see, were rough, calloused.

"And what did you talk about?" Rostnikov asked.

"If you've read his reports, then you know," said Krasnikov.

Since Rutkin's reports had apparently been scattered to the winds when he died and were now buried in snow or lost in the woods or river, the opportunity to examine them had not been afforded to Rostnikov or anyone else. However, Rostnikov did not plan to share this information with the general.

"There is a story," said Rostnikov, "that Field Marshal Mikhail Kutuzov before the Battle of 1812 called in his artillery officer and asked for a report on positions of Napoleon's army. The officer made his report and was ready to leave when Kutuzov asked him once more to give his report on French positions. The officer, in some confusion, gave his report again and turned to leave. Once more Kutuzov asked for the report. Once more the officer reported and this time, before he turned, he asked the Field Marshal why he had wanted the same report three times. Kutuzov replied that in the third telling the officer, in an attempt to vary his presentation, had added information which he had not given before, information which he had not thought important. Kutuzov told the officer that the added information about movement on the left flank in the cavalry cover would significantly alter his plans for counterattack."

"I've never heard that story," said Krasnikov.

"Maybe it isn't true," said Rostnikov.

"Maybe you made it up," said the general.

"Perhaps if I repeat it you will find some detail that will confirm your suspicion," said Rostnikov.

"Very clever, Inspector," Krasnikov said with a smile. "But remember the real Kutuzov was responsible for abandoning Moscow."

"... and thereby saving the Russian army," added Rostnikov.

"You know military history," said Krasnikov.

"I know Tolstoy," responded Rostnikov.

Sokolov sighed deeply, clearly impatient.

"I think I like you, Inspector," said Krasnikov, putting both booted feet on the hard wood floor with a clap. "Or, at least, I may have some respect for you, which is even more important."

"What did you tell Commissar Rutkin?" Sokolov said.

Krasnikov fixed Sokolov with what was probably his most withering military look, then he turned to Rostnikov, whose eyes and hands went up to indicate that he knew the question at that juncture of the conversation had been out of order but, perhaps, it might not be a bad idea for the general to answer it. At least that was what Krasnikov got from the look.

"Commissar Rutkin questioned me about the death of the Samsonov child," said Krasnikov, a touch of emotion suddenly coming into his voice. "He seemed to think that the child had been murdered."

"And?" Rostnikov prompted when the general stopped.

"The child fell from the rock by the river," he said. "She should not have been playing at the rock. She simply fell. Her father could not accept this fact, could not accept the responsibility and so he began to scream murder and Rutkin came running up here to hold his hand and humor him. Everyone is so concerned about the feelings of a dissident. Everyone is so afraid that he will take his accusations to the West."

"And," Sokolov interrupted, much to Rostnikov's annoyance which he did his best not to show, "you are confident that the child did not meet with foul play?"

"Foul play?" said Krasnikov, not trying to hide his annoyance. "Why would anyone want to kill the child? She was a quiet, gentle little thing. She couldn't even go out most days because of the cold and wind. She had no one to play with, no other children."

"And so you spent time with her?" Rostnikov asked, opening his coat a bit more.

"A bit," he admitted. "She was a smart child. Mostly she spent time with the priest Galich."

"And you got along well with her parents?" Rostnikov continued.

"He's a fool," Krasnikov said, striding across the room past Sokolov to his desk where he picked up an iron paperweight.

"And the mother, Ludmilla?"

Krasnikov looked down at Rostnikov who had turned awkwardly in his chair to face the general.

"She is no fool," Krasnikov said, shifting the paperweight from one hand to the other.

"She is quite beautiful too," Rostnikov observed.

Sokolov shifted in his chair and cleared his throat to indicate his irritation with these diversions from the issue.

"I've seen more beautiful women. I've not always been here," Krasnikov said, looking around the room and then over his shoulder out the window. "I've seen the women of Rome, Budapest, even Paris."

"Do you have some idea of why anyone might want to kill Commissar Rutkin?" asked Rostnikov.

"To rid the world of one more fool?" Krasnikov answered with his own question.

"Comrade General," Sokolov said with intensity. "This is a serious investigation of the death of a high-ranking Party member."

"High-ranking?" countered Krasnikov with yet another question.

"A Party member," Sokolov amended. "Do you have anything to tell us about his murder?"

Krasnikov smiled and, ignoring Sokolov, threw the piece of iron in his hand to Rostnikov who caught it and felt its cool power.

"Meteorite," the general said. "Dimitri Galich finds them all over the area. You might ask him for one as a souvenir."

Rostnikov rose and threw the piece of iron back to the general who caught it without removing his eyes from Rostnikov's face.

"We will talk again," said Rostnikov, buttoning his coat and heading toward the door. Behind him he could hear Sokolov getting up quickly.

"I have a few more questions, Comrade Inspector," Sokolov said.

"By all means," said Rostnikov pausing at the door to look back at the other two men. "I am going to go back to my room and then to Dimitri Galich's again."

"I'll meet you there," said Sokolov.

"He has some weights. I plan to use them. You may join me if you wish."

"All right then. I'll meet you at the house in which we are staying," said Sokolov.

Rostnikov agreed and moved to the door. "Don't forget to ask for a meteorite," said the general.

"I won't," said Rostnikov who opened the door and stepped into the skin-freezing morning.

EIGHT

A DEDUSHKA, A GRANDFATHER WITH A MASSIVE, OLD-FASHIONED white mustache, held his bundled-up grandchild by the hand and ordered an ice cream. Sasha, who was now growing accustomed to using the ice cream scoop, served them while Boris Manizer watched his new assistant critically. The child, no more than two, was wearing a snowsuit that made him or her look like a cosmonaut.

The grandfather paid and held out the ice cream for the child to lick. The child was wrapped too tightly to bend his arms.

"He likes it," said the grandfather revealing an almost toothless mouth.

"Good," said Boris pulling Sasha back behind the stand where two waiting customers, probably foreigners, stepped up to be served.

"Do you see them?" Sasha said looking around the shopping center.

"No," whispered Boris. "I just wanted to remind you to scoop like this. Like this. You leave a little hollow space in the ball. You use a little less ice cream. By the end of the day, you save gallons. You understand?"

"Yes," Sasha whispered back. "You cheat the people."

Boris stepped back and put his right hand to his heart.

"Cheat? Me? The people? Never," he said. "I keep innocent children from eating too much ice cream and getting terrible cramps. Children will do that. I have children. They do that. I'm doing them a service."

"You are a hero of the Revolution," Sasha said.

"Can we get ice cream?" a fat woman demanded. Next to her was an almost identical fat woman. They were either mother and daughter or sisters.

"See," whispered Boris. "You think they need a fat scoop of ice cream? No. They're never going to look like French women but we can help them a little."

"I recant," said Tkach looking down at Boris. "You are a saint, not a hero of the Revolution."

For the next few hours the two men worked in relative silence. Boris said no more about how to scoop. He served and watched the crowd for the possible return of the two criminals, an event that Tkach was certain would not take place.

"An ice cream, please," came the woman's voice above the noise of the afternoon crowd when Tkach was turned away. Before he could respond to Maya's voice, Boris was serving her.

Behind Boris's back, Sasha turned and showed his white uniform to his wife and to Pulcharia who looked blankly at her father from the carrying sling on her mother's back. Maya, wearing her insulated blue coat, smiled, almost laughed at her husband who shrugged as Boris reached down to gather a hollow scoop. Sasha moved forward, put his hand on Boris's shoulder and shook his head 'no' when the little man turned to him.

"I'll take this customer," Sasha said.

Boris considered reminding Tkach who was in charge of this ice cream stand but he stopped himself, remembering that this smiling youth was a policeman. It was difficult to remember that he was a policeman. He looked like . . . like a kid standing there with that smile, serving the pretty dark woman with the baby on her back. The woman smiled at this Sasha almost brazenly. The world, Boris thought, was falling into chaos. Muggers, thieves, young women with babies who throw themselves at young ice cream sellers. No young woman had ever thrown herself at Boris Manizer.

The young woman licked the ice cream and looking back held it over her shoulder for the baby to lick. The child, wearing a wool hat that revealed only its round face, leaned over to put its mouth on the ice cream and then, having tasted it, lean forward to plunge its whole face in the cold, sweet delicacy. The pretty young woman and Sasha shared a laugh. The child looked happy. Boris tried not to but he too smiled.

The woman said something to Sasha. Boris couldn't hear it over the noise of the crowd and the music that was now being piped throughout the pavilion. It sounded like something English or American. Boris didn't like it.

The pretty woman with the baby took another lick of the ice cream, smiled at Tkach and moved into the crowd.

"Very nice," Boris said looking at the woman and child.

"Very nice," Tkach agreed, adjusting his white cap.

A group of customers surged to the stand and began to order at the same time.

"Get in a line," Boris called over the noise and the music.

Tkach continued to watch his wife who looked back at him, waved and reached back to raise Pulcharia's arm in a wave. Tkach raised a hand and Boris, who watched him from the corner of his eye, shook his head but kept working.

When the surge had cleared, Boris, who was lower than almost everyone in the pavilion, looked up to where the woman with the baby might have been. She was there, with her baby, deep in the crowd near a shop where little rockets and space trinkets and toys were sold. She was there, her eyes wide, talking to two young men, one of whom had red hair.

"There," said Boris. "There they are. The two you are looking for."

"Where?" asked Tkach, scanning the crowd.

"There, by the Cosmonaut Shop," cried Boris jumping up and pointing. "With the woman who was just here, the woman with the baby."

Tkach ripped the cap from his head sending his straight hair down over his forehead. He looked suddenly frantic.

"Where? I can't see them."

Boris pointed and, through the crowd, Tkach saw them, saw the two young men, his wife and child cornered between them, pressing her backward toward an alcove, talking to her. Then he lost them in the crowd. Tkach leaped up on the ice cream stand for a better view, and spotted the redhead. Passing visitors paused to look up at the mad young man atop the ice cream stand and the little man in white who was shouting at him to come down.

Tkach caught a glimpse of his wife's frightened face looking in his direction. Tkach leaped down into the crowd as the redhead turned to see what Maya was looking at. Tkach had no way of knowing if the young man had seen him leap. Pushing his way through the crowd, Tkach tore off his white jacket and flung it back in the general direction of the ice cream stand. My fault, he thought, told himself, perhaps even said softly aloud as he pushed his way past people, glared madly at a burly man who grabbed his arm to slow him down, and moved quickly without running toward the Cosmonaut Shop.

Maya and the baby were out of sight now, pushed back into the alcove next to the shop. The dark-haired youth wasn't in sight, must be in the alcove with them. The redhead blocked the alcove entrance with his body and looked back to see if anyone was watching. Tkach slowed down, looked to his right at a woman walking near him, forced himself to smile and nodded.

He wanted to run, to scream, but they might hurt Maya and the baby, might even grab them as hostages. It was maddening. Why had he told her to come there? And how could these two have the nerve to come back?

The redhead backed into the alcove, arms out at his side. Tkach had made his way to the right of the alcove. He now walked along toward it, looking over his shoulder at the shop window. His heart was pounding. He could feel it, take his pulse by it as he forced himself to move slowly, slowly, and then he was alongside the space between the shops, the alcove where the redhead was stepping into the shadows.

Tkach paused, smiled and asked, "The oobo'rnaya, is it in here?" he asked.

"No," said the redhead, who wore a punkish haircut with his head shaved on the sides. He had some kind of accent that made it difficult to understand him. "Get away. We're working here."

Pulcharia was weeping. Sasha could hear her in the darkness, over the noise.

"I'm sorry," Tkach said, forcing his most winning smile, "but I've got to get in here."

Before the redhead could respond. Tkach stepped into the alcove, leaned forward and threw his right hand out sharply, his knuckles connecting with the young man's stomach. The redhead grunted, staggered back in surprise and fell to his knees leaving just enough space for Tkach to get past him. Sasha could see outlines of people further in the darkness and, as he moved past the redhead who called out the name Ben and reached out to stop him, Tkach rammed his left knee between the groping hands and felt it connect with the redhead's face.

The dark-haired youth, whose name was Ben, called back something in a foreign language and Tkach lunged forward. Now he could see Maya and the baby, fear on his wife's face, the dark-haired youth pulling her hair back, forcing her down to the ground. Pulcharia was crying out of control.

The dark-haired youth named Ben turned and saw that it was not his friend coming toward him, but a slender young man. Ben was stocky, physically confident. He showed no fear, only disdain for the smaller, delicate man hurrying toward him. His friend was probably behind this fool, ready to take him. But that did not happen and Ben had to let go of the woman's hair and turn to face the advancing idiot.

Ben could see beyond the advancing man now, could see his red-haired partner on his knees holding his face, could see the people passing by the mouth of the alcove looking in but not pausing, not wanting to get involved, could now see the furious face of the young man coming toward him. It took less than a few seconds and, had he not been holding the pretty woman by the hair with one hand and touching her with the other he would have had his knife out. He was just reaching in his pocket for it, sure he had time to get it out, when the slender man threw himself forward with an anguished scream and fell on Ben who tumbled backward in the narrow space, landed on his back, striking his head on the concrete. He punched at the man's side and ribs, punched hard, punches that should have sent the man tumbling off of him in agony, but the man was possessed, insane. The man ignored the punches, screamed and began to punch at Ben's face.

Ben told him to stop, said that he had enough, said that he gave up, but the man continued to beat him. Ben felt his nose break, heard the young woman behind him shouting for the man to stop.

You tell him, lady, Ben thought. This lunatic is going to kill me. And that was his final thought before he passed out.

Rostnikov was sitting on the chair in his room. He had pulled the chair to the window and was looking out at the square, looking, more specifically, at the window of the People's Hall of Justice and Solidarity.

The day had been busy. He had gone back to Galich's house and had been readily admitted and allowed to lift weights in the small room off to the side. Galich gave Rostnikov permission to alter the weights on the bars and then excused himself and returned to the large room where Rostnikov had talked to him early that morning. Galich had, he said, a small, ancient vase that required his attention.

Rostnikov was impressed and pleased by the weights. He worked for nearly forty minutes, humming occasionally, concentrating on the weights, trying to think of nothing but the resisting iron. There had been one interruption: Famfanoff who, red-faced and obviously having had a drink or two, came puffing into the small room, his uniform coming loose in spite of a clear attempt to pull himself together.

Famfanoff apologized for not being up early, offered his services again, asked for an assignment, a task.

When Rostnikov had completed the curls he was doing, he put the weight down, took a deep breath and gave the policeman an assignment, a confidential assignment which Famfanoff gratefully accepted with the promise that he would tell no one. Hope of a transfer was evident in Famfanoff s open red face. He left looking like a man with a secret.

When Rostnikov had finished his lifting, he dried himself with the towel he had brought and sat waiting to cool down before moving quietly to the main room where, at the rear, Dimitri Galich sat at his large, crowded table.

"Finished?" Galich asked.

"Yes, thank you."

"Come back tomorrow if you like," said Galich looking up at Rostnikov from the unimposing vase in his hands.

"I will. Could I, perhaps, invite you to join me for dinner tonight?" asked Rostnikov.

"You needn't repay me," Galich said.

"I'd feel better," said Rostnikov. "And we can talk about things other than murder. History, perhaps, Moscow or lifting."

"Not much to say about lifting," said Galich, "and much to say about history. I lift, read, walk, talk to convince myself that I am not as obsessed a creature as I know myself to be. I sometimes fear that I'll become one of those madmen who spend all their time examining some small part of the universe and block out all the rest. It turns into a kind of meditation. You know what I mean?"

"Yes," said Rostnikov. "I believe so. Dinner?"

"I would be happy to, but I would prefer your coming here," said Galich. "I'm less than comfortable in social situations since I came here a few years ago. I know you are with two others. I've seen them both and would prefer your company alone. I hope I am not offending you."

"Not at all," said Rostnikov.

"Eight o'clock?"

"Eight o'clock," agreed Rostnikov. "Oh, by the way, General Krasnikov showed me the meteorite you had given him."

Galich put down the vase and folded his hands in front of him.

"The meteorite," he said softly. "Yes. An interesting specimen, but it pre-dates human history. It is human history in which I am interested. If you like, I can give you a similar meteorite. I have plenty. A memento of your visit to our community."

"I would like that," Rostnikov said. "I'll pick it up this evening after dinner."

"I look forward to it," said Galich, hands still folded.

Rostnikov returned to the house on the square, took a cold shower since there was no other kind to take, changed clothes and made himself two sandwiches of hard cheese and coarse black bread he found in the kitchen. When Karpo knocked at the door of his room an hour later and handed Rostnikov his report, the inspector was about to begin his second sandwich. He glanced at the neatly printed, many-paged report and nodded. Then his gaze returned to the window. Rostnikov knew that Karpo had made a copy for his own files, his private files.

"Emil," he said. "I would like you to take the reports on the case that I brought with me from Moscow. Get the local report from Famfanoff. Take them and your report from this morning along with the notes you will find on my bed later when I go out for dinner. See if you can find any discrepancies."

"Discrepancies?"

"Items, pieces of information which do not coincide, perhaps something, something small that is in one report and not in the others," Rostnikov explained.

"Yes, Inspector. You should know," Karpo said as he watched Rostnikov looking out the window, "that someone has entered my room and read my notes. Whoever did it was quite experienced. They were placed back almost but not quite lined up with the pattern on my bed quilt."

"The same is true of my reports, Emil," Rostnikov said, taking a bite of his sandwich. "Someone entered my room and read them."

"Sokolov?" asked Karpo.

"I don't think so," said Rostnikov without looking up. "But it may have been."

Karpo left, closing the door behind him.

About two hours later, Sokolov knocked at the door to the Inspector's room. Rostnikov told him to come in and Sokolov entered finding Rostnikov on his chair by the window looking out.

"May I now read your reports, Comrade Rostnikov?" Sokolov asked coolly.

Rostnikov grunted and pointed at the bed without looking away from the window.

Sokolov picked up the reports and looked at them.

"These reports are by Inspector Karpo," Sokolov said. "What about your reports?"

"Later," Rostnikov said. "I'm busy now."

"Busy?" said Sokolov, deciding that Rostnikov was making his job very easy. His investigation was sloppy, self-indulgent, meandering. He didn't do his paperwork and instead of pulling together information he sat, apparently for hours, looking out the window at nothing. Perhaps Rostnikov was simply going mad. It was possible, but it was more likely that he was simply lazy.

"I took the liberty of interviewing Samsonov, Galich and a few others," Sokolov said. "If you would like to go over notes with me . . ."

"Tomorrow," said Rostnikov softly, not looking back.

"Well, we can discuss the investigation at dinner," Sokolov tried.

"I'm having dinner with Galich," Rostnikov said.

"I see," said Sokolov, holding in his anger. He had done this kind of thing before and knew that if he were patient he would eventually be sitting across the table from this man, driving him into defensive corners, tearing into his actions, his loyalties, his very thoughts. Sokolov thought about this moment, picked up Karpo's report and slowly left the room.

Rostnikov sat for four more hours. He had, with the exception of the time he took to walk around the room to keep his leg from going rigid and the hour he took to read Karpo's reports before

Sokolov came to his room, been at the window for almost six hours. He had been rewarded twice by the sight of the old janitor in the People's Hall, Sergei Mirasnikov, who came to the window and looked directly up at Rostnikov. The sight of the inspector looking down at him had each time sent the old man staggering back into the Hall. When he worked up enough courage to move carefully to the window again and under cover of the curtain to look up, Mirasnikov was struck with terror. The inspector from Moscow was still there, still looking down. He would be there all the time. Mirasnikov shuddered and vowed not to look any more, not to imagine that man staring down at him, waiting, watching.

Sergei Mirasnikov decided that he needed something a bit strong to drink.

When Sasha Tkach returned to Petrovka after accompanying his wife and daughter home, there was a neatly typed message on his desk held down by the small rock he kept there for just such a purpose. The message instructed him to report immediately to the office of the Gray Wolfhound on the seventh floor.

Sasha was in no mood to report. He had barely brought himself under control after his attack on the youthful muggers. He remembered much of what happened rather vaguely.

He remembered Maya and the baby crying and Maya telling him to stop hitting the mugger who jabbered at him in some strange language. He remembered the little ice cream vendor, Boris, behind him telling someone, "That's him. That's him."

He remembered someone in uniform taking the two muggers away while Maya, who should have been comforted, instead comforted Sasha. Someone in uniform drove Sasha and his family to their apartment and somewhere on the way Sasha began to pull himself together. By the time they were at the building, he had regained enough control to reassure himself that his wife and child were, as they appeared to be, unhurt.

"It's all right," Maya comforted him quietly while holding Pulcharia close to her breasts in the rocking car.

The driver kept his eyes fixed straight ahead and had the decency not to look at them in the rearview mirror.

"I thought he, they . . ." Sasha began.

"No," Maya said with a smile. "They just frightened us a bit. I'm fine though I have a small headache. The baby is fine. Look at her. Look at us. I'm more worried about the way you are behaving."

"I, too, am fine," he said, taking his wife's hand.

And so he had left Maya and the baby at the apartment and gone back in the car to Petrovka to prepare his report. The message on his desk might be about a new assignment. He had only recently been transferred from the Procurator's Office to the MVD and wasn't yet familiar with all the procedures. Perhaps his success at catching the muggers had earned him a choice assignment or, at least, a commendation or a letter of approval.

Zelach wasn't at his desk but other investigators and a few uniformed policemen made phone calls, walked past with folders or sat preparing reports.

Sasha adjusted his tie, brushed back his hair, examined his face in the window of the office behind him to be sure he was not bruised, and headed for the stairway.

In the outer office, Pankov, the Wolfhound's assistant, pointed to a chair, barely looking up from something he was writing. Tkach sat. Tkach listened to the sound of voices inside the office. He couldn't make out the words but the deep, confident voice of Colonel Snitkonoy was unmistakable. He seemed to be arguing with someone who spoke very softly. After three or four minutes, the office door opened and Deputy Procurator Khabolov stepped out. A few beads of sweat dampened Khabolov's very high forehead in spite of the coolness of the room and he looked at Tkach with triumph. The look did not surprise Tkach who met Khabolov's eyes and held them till the older man strode away.

Khabolov had reason to dislike Sasha Tkach. Rostnikov and Tkach had caught the Deputy Procurator illegally confiscating black market video tapes and video tape machines for his private property and use. They could have turned him over to the KGB. Khabolov's actions were, if the KGB wished, sufficient to earn a firing squad. Instead, they had made a deal with the Deputy Procurator. Tkach and Karpo were transferred to the MVD under Rostnikov. There was no doubt in Sasha's mind that Khabolov would be very pleased to see the men who knew about his indiscretion moved even further away from his office.

"Investigator Tkach," said Pankov as soon as Khabolov closed the other door behind him. "You may enter."

Tkach adjusted his tie again, nodded to Pankov who still did not look up and went into the Wolfhound's office.

"Close the door," the Wolfhound said. He was standing behind his desk, hands clasped in front of him. He looked as if he were posing for the cover of Soviet Life. The medals on the chest of his brown uniform glistened in the path of light coming in from the west and the setting sun.

Tkach closed the door and stepped forward. The Wolfhound nodded at a large wooden chair with arms, across his massive polished desk. Tkach sat. The Wolfhound made Sasha nervous. Everything the man said and did seemed to take on such importance, as if his every word were being recorded for posterity. The Wolfhound never perspired, never looked as if he even needed to use the toilet or eat food.

"We live in very delicate times," the Wolfhound said, fixing his clear gray eyes on the junior investigator.

Tkach was not sure if he was expected to respond. He elected to nod very, very slightly in agreement. The Wolfhound unclasped his hands and leaned forward over the desk. Another pose.

"We live in a world of diplomacy and compromise," the Wolfhound said. "The Revolution has not fully ended, may not end for years, may not end, Tkach, in our lifetime or even that of our children, but we do not despair. Constant vigilance is essential. Our allies must be clasped to us with strength and support. Enemies must be given constant notice of determination. You understand this?"

"I understand," said Tkach.

"You did a fine job today, a fine job," said the Wolfhound.

"I'll have a full report ready in less than an hour," said Tkach, now sensing that something was wrong, but not sure how wrong. The Wolfhound's words and furrowed brow suggested that nations were at stake.

"Of course," said the Wolfhound. "Your report. What I'm really interested in is your return to the search for the missing dealer in stolen goods. What is his name?"

"Volovkatin," Tkach supplied. "I'll get back to that immediately."

"And concentrate all of your effort on finding this enemy of the State," Snitkonoy said, his voice rumbling with determination.

"I'll devote my full attention to it with time out only to complete the report and attend the Procurator's hearing on the two we apprehended today at the Yamarka shopping center."

The Wolfhound stood up straight and walked to the window. He said nothing for almost a full minute and then turned to Tkach.

"There will be no hearing on the two young men you caught," said the Wolfhound.

"No . . . ?"

"The two young men are sons of high-ranking members of the Cuban Embassy," Snitknonoy explained. "Their parents have been informed and it has been suggested that the two young men be sent back to Cuba."

Tkach gripped the handles of the chair and tried to keep his jaw from tightening. He glared at the Wolfhound who did not meet his eyes.

"They attacked my wife," Tkach said, angry at the small catch he heard in his voice. "My daughter could have been . . ."

"Yes," said the Wolfhound, "But there are greater issues, greater consequences for the State. Individualism in this situation as in most is counterproductive."

"I see," said Tkach as the Colonel turned once again to face him. The Wolfhound had positioned himself with his back to the sun coming through the window. He was an outline, a rearlighted black specter. Five minutes earlier Tkach would have been impressed.

"Sometimes we must take a small step backward in order to take great strides forward in the future," said the Wolfhound, and Tkach felt the urge to shout out, to tell him that he didn't care about the State, the future, Soviet/Cuban relations. He cared about his family.

"There are some good things here," Snitkonoy said, stepping out of the light to reveal his face and a paternal smile. "The Procurator's Office has decided not to investigate certain irregularities in your handling of the situation though the Cuban Embassy has demanded an explanation. The Cubans must also live with diplomacy and reality."

"Irregularities?" asked Tkach, feeling rage but speaking softly.

"There are some reasonable questions," said the Wolfhound. "Why were your wife and daughter at the site of an undercover investigation? Why did you beat the two suspects to the point that they had to be examined by a physician?"

"They were going to rape my wife," Tkach exploded.

"Inspector," the Wolfhound said firmly, resonantly. "You will control yourself. There is no reason to believe they were going to sexually address your wife. They have done nothing of the kind before. And the young Cubans claim that they offered no resistance and you continued to beat them in spite of their cooperation."

That, at least, Tkach thought, is partly correct. He sat silently.

"So," said the Wolfhound, confident that he had the situation under control again. "The Procurator's Office has agreed to forget the irregularities, though a notation will be made in your file. We, in turn, will not file a report."

"So there is no case," said Tkach. "We will act as if nothing happened and hope that the Cubans send those two home."

"I'm sure the Cubans will administer punishment or issue consequences," said the Colonel.

"I'm sure," said Tkach. "Now, if I may be excused I would like to get back to the investigation of the buyer of stolen goods."

"Yes," said Snitknonoy returning to his desk. "We must all get back to work. I have a talk to give at the Likhachov Automobile Works, the Zil truck division. They have exceeded their half-year quotas."

"I'm elated," said Tkach, rising.

"So are we all, Comrade," the Wolfhound said with a touch of warning in his voice. "So are we all. Tread softly and you'll break no eggs. You may leave."

And Tkach left. He closed the office door behind him and without looking at Pankov strode across the outer office and into the hall, being careful not to slam the door behind him.

He stood still in the hall outside the Wolfhound's office for almost half a minute. An older woman he vaguely recognized from the records office strode by him. She wore a dark suit and glasses and looked at him with motherly concern. He would have none of it and made it clear from his look. She walked on.

When Tkach felt that he was capable of moving without striking the nearest window or door with his fists, he headed for the stairway. His first thought as he walked down the stairs was that he needed to talk to Porfiry Petrovich. He would know what to do, how to deal with the Wolfhound, how to find a way to punish the Cubans, but Rostnikov was in Siberia and there was no knowing when he would be back. Sasha would have to deal with this alone and, he was beginning to realize, he would have to deal with it by putting the day behind him and going on with his work.

NINE

"He's not there," Sergei Mirasnikov shouted, removing his glasses. "Thank God. He's not watching me anymore."

Liana Mirasnikov shook her head and went on eating her bread in the next room.

Her husband's voice had echoed across the meeting room of the People's Hall in which she spent little time and through the door to their room where she sat. With each passing year, Liana grew more brittle, more cold, dreading the long winters of ice which came so gray and close together. She had begun to grow angry at the brief summer, talking to it, accusing it of teasing her with its brevity, of telling her that she would experience few more of such interludes before she joined her ancestors.

"Why do you keep going to the window?" she said when he came back into their room and closed the door. "Just stay away from the window."

"I can't," he said, anxiously looking at her. "I know he is there, looking. I don't want to go to the window but I can't help it. He knows I can't help it."

Sergei paced the room and in spite of or because of his fear he seemed younger than he had for years. Worry seemed to agree with him, at least physically.

"Just so the other one doesn't come back, the ghost," she said, popping the last crumb of bread in her mouth and looking around the room and at the frosted window before crossing herself. "It will be hard enough to go over there and serve their meals. I think I'll just put out the food and stay away till they're finished."

"What does he want from me?" Mirasnikov muttered, ignoring her words.

"Possibly the truth," she said.

"Do you know what might happen to us if I told him?"

"I know," she said. "Don't tell him."

Sergei straightened out as best he could and, as firmly as he could, said, "I won't."

And with that he strode back to the door and opened it.

"Where are you going?" Liana called.

"To see if he is back at the window, just to see, to peek. I'll just be a second. Less than a second."

She heard his footsteps stride quickly across the hall, felt the draft from the big room because he had not closed the door behind him, and she started to get up so she would have an early start preparing dinner for the visitors.

"He's still not there," Sergei called.

"Good," she said, moving from her soft chair to the closet where she kept her coat. She had not removed her boots when she came in earlier. They were a bit tight from the snow and it was the devil to get them on and off. She looked forward to coming back and taking them off later.

"Still not there," Sergei said, striding back into the room as she tied her babushka under her chin.

"Good," she repeated.

"But he will be back," he said, adjusting his glasses and looking at the closed door. "He will be back."

Rostnikov had left his post at the window reluctantly, but he had agreed to join Galich for dinner and he was hungry. The two sandwiches had not been enough nor had he expected them to be.

When he opened the door of his house for Rostnikov, the former priest looked even more like a woodsman than he had that morning. He wore the same flannel shirt and jeans but he also wore a fur vest. He had shaved and combed his hair.

"Come in," he said heartily. "I hope you like fish."

Rostnikov closed the door quickly behind himself and said, "I love fish. In fact, as my wife will affirm, I feel a certain affection for almost all foods. She sometimes accuses me of being more interested in quantity than quality."

"And," said Galich, taking his guest's coat, "is she correct?"

"She is correct," said Rostnikov with a sigh, "but my interest in quality should not be entirely discounted."

They ate at Galich's worktable. He had cleared a section at one end and set out a rough tablecloth. On the table was a bottle of vodka, a bowl of boiled potatoes, a roughly shaped loaf of warm, dark bread and four large fish which had been baked whole.

"Caught them in the river this afternoon," Galich said after they had sat down. He let Rostnikov serve himself and the policeman did so generously. "If you're here long enough, I'll take you fishing through the ice. That's about the only fishing we get to do here for months. The Yensei, at this point, is frozen more than two hundred days a year."

"And when it isn't frozen?" asked Rostnikov.

"Ah," said Galich, a piece of boiled potato bulging in his cheek, "when it isn't frozen it roars north to the Arctic Ocean. Rolling waves chase one another forming great whirlpools. It's magnificent, mighty, more than 2,600 miles long. And its banks and depths hold treasures of history in spite of everything that has been swept by its force into the ocean."

Galich paused in his chewing and seemed to be gazing into the depths of the Yensei of his imagination.

"I should like to see that," said Rostnikov.

"Yes," said Galich returning to the present, nodding his curly white-maned head and resuming his chewing. "It must be experienced."

"You love it here," Rostnikov observed reaching for a second fish.

"Yes," agreed Galich. "If I weren't so old, perhaps I would become a taiozhniki, a forest dweller. There are Evenks in the taiga beyond the town who don't encounter civilization for years. No one knows how many of them there are. The government can't find them, keep track of them. The forests have been theirs since God created man. They named the river, Yensei, "big river," a thousand years before we came. You mind if I refer to God?"

"Not at all," said Rostnikov. "Do you mind if I help myself to more vodka?"

"Not at all," said Galich, "but you have really had very little. Are you trying to keep a cool head while you get me to talk, Inspector?"

"Perhaps a little," Rostnikov agreed. "But just a little. It is as difficult to stop being a policeman even for a brief time as it is to stop being a priest."

"Sometimes more difficult than one would like," Galich agreed, downing the last of his glass of vodka and reaching for the bottle.

"There are Evenks nearby?" asked Rostnikov.

"A few, from time to time," said Galich. "Even a shaman, name of Kurmu, though the government thinks there aren't any shamans left. There are plenty of them. Shaman's a Evenk word. It means priest-healer, not witchdoctor. Shamans are both religious figures and healers. In some places shamanism has been wedded with Buddhism, particularly among the Buryats. It's even been merged with Christianity among the Yakuts. In this territory along the river, in the taiga and up to the Arctic Ocean it seems to have kept its base in ancient pantheism."

"Fascinating," said Rostnikov with a smile, holding his hand over the top of his glass as Galich reached over to try to refill it.

"I'm a bit drunk," said the former priest. "It's not often I get a guest who is willing to listen to my ramblings. I had the new captain at the weather station over for dinner once about four months ago. Too young. No imagination. No fire. No interests but permafrost. Who wants to spend a night talking about permafrost?"

"You speak the Evenk language?"

"A little," Galich said with a shrug, pouring himself another glass of vodka. "I have much time to learn, think."

"What do you think of Samsonov?" Rostnikov said picking up a small, elusive piece of fish with his fingers.

"See," laughed Galich, "what did I say? I get drunk and you go to work, but I don't care. Not tonight. Samsonov is a weakling and I'm sure Kurmu is better at curing if it comes to that."

"But he's had the nerve to become a dissident," Rostnikov prodded. "To ask to leave the country."

"I don't know how much of it is his idea," Galich said looking up at Rostnikov.

"You mean his wife wants to leave?" asked Rostnikov.

"You are an observer of men. I am an observer of details," said Galich. "I hear little pieces of information, see small artifacts and I put them together into a story. Then, with each piece of new information I reshape the story hoping that it comes closer to the truth. Is that the way you work?"

"Very much," Rostnikov admitted.

"Yes," said Galich confidentially, reaching over to pat the inspector's arm with his hand, "but the difference is that sometimes you can have your story confirmed. Mine remains forever conjecture. I must be careful not to be too creative or I lose the truth."

"The same is true of my work," said Rostnikov, allowing the former priest to pour him just a bit more vodka. "Ludmilla Samsonov?"

"A lovely woman," said Galich raising his glass in a toast. "A very lovely woman."

"A very lovely woman," Rostnikov agreed raising his glass to meet that of his host.

The glasses pinged together and the men drank.

"Are you getting what you want from me, detective?" asked Galich after he had drunk more vodka.

"Yes," said Rostnikov, "some information, a good meal and good vodka. Let me ask a direct question before we are both too drunk to make sense. What is the General writing?"

Galich grinned and shook his head.

"Magnificent," he said. "You noticed too. It took me a long time to figure it out and then it struck me."

"He's not just writing articles on old military battles," Rostnikov said.

"He is not," agreed Galich. "The desk is facing the window so he can see anyone coming and hide whatever he is working on. The desk would be better where mine is. It would catch more light, but he is afraid of being come upon suddenly. From the front you can see anyone coming and have plenty of time to hide things. And he talks too vaguely about his articles, never shows them. Not that he is uninformed. On the contrary, I'm sure he could write articles, but I think he is working at something, working even harder at it than I do at my work and he seems driven as if he still has battles to win. One would expect a military man in exile to be a bit more depressed now that he is away from

141

that for which he has been trained. No, our little general has a secret."

"You should have been a detective," said Rostnikov toasting his host.

"Perhaps, if the Evenk are correct about reincarnation, it may be so in another life. I'll be a fisher of men," Galich toasted back. "God, I can't get rid of the religion."

"It runs through the blood like vodka," sighed Rostnikov feeling more than a little drunk himself though he had consumed far less than his host.

"It runs warmer than vodka and it won't wash away," Galich said in a voice that may have betrayed some bitterness. "Would you like to see some armor, some mesh armor I've been restoring? Found it near the rock, the great rock where . . . " he paused, remembering.

"Where Karla Samsonov died," Rostnikov finished.

Galich nodded but didn't answer.

"I'd like very much to see the armor," Rostnikov said.

Galich got up slowly, carefully, and walked toward the cabinet against the wall. Outside, through the window, Rostnikov could see the moon over the forest. The tops of the trees were silver white. Rostnikov felt quite content. Ideas were beginning to take shape. A story was starting to tell itself deep inside him.

"Definitely Russian thirteenth century," said Galich, fumbling at the door of the cabinet, but before he could get it open someone knocked at the front door.

"Famfanoff," said the former priest. "Would you let him in?"

Rostnikov agreed and, with a bit of difficulty, got up from the table. He should have moved his leg around a bit more during the long meal, but he had forgotten and now it was complaining.

The knock was repeated twice before Rostnikov made it to the door, threw open the latch and opened it. It was not Famfanoff but Emil Karpo illuminated by the nearly full moon, an erect black-clad figure with a face as white as the snow behind him.

"Come in," Rostnikov said. There was something, an urgency on the face of Karpo that was unfamiliar. Karpo stepped in.

"Ah," called Galich from the cabinet where he now stood holding a mesh net of metal. "Your sober friend. Bring him in for a drink."

"I do not drink, Comrade," Karpo said evenly, not taking his eyes from Rostnikov. "Comrade Inspector, a message has come through at the weather station from Colonel Snitkonoy's office. You are to call your wife."

The glow of the vodka disappeared. He had been encouraging, nursing it, but now it was gone. He had feared this call for months, feared the message that meant his son, Josef, were injured, possibly . . . He had feared this call.

"I must leave," he told Galich who had been listening.

"Of course," the former priest said. "This," he said, holding up the armor, "has waited for more than five hundred years. It can wait a bit longer while you deal with the present and I get some sleep."

Rostnikov thanked his host for dinner, hurriedly put on his coat and followed Karpo into the night.

"I can quit," said Sasha Tkach pacing the space near the window of his apartment. He spoke quietly because, in the darkened area across the room, Pulcharia slept fitfully.

Sasha's mother was out for the evening at his aunt's and uncle's apartment near Proletarian Avenue off of Bolshiye Kamenshchiki Street. Her absence was a blessing.

Maya seemed to have recovered from the afternoon better than her husband. There was a slight bruise on her cheek, but no other injury, and she shared none of her husband's anger when she found that the two young men who had attacked her would get away without further punishment.

"You sent them both to hospital," she had said gently, touching his arm. "And Pulcharia and I are fine."

"It's not enough," he had said.

"What is it you want?" she had asked.

"I don't know. Justice. Punishment."

The conversation had gone on like this after they ate. Maya had spent the afternoon in stores with the baby. She had wanted to return to the normalcy of daily life, to return the baby to the comfort of the usual routine and she wanted to prepare a comforting meal for Sasha who, she was sure, would be upset and need reassuring even more than his wife and child. She had never seen him like that before, never seen him as he had been when he attacked those two at the shopping center of the Economic Exhibition. Sasha, who was always so gentle, had been a raging madman. There had been something exciting about it, but also something very frightening and she was sure that the transformation would leave him shaken. And so, Maya had gone shopping. She selected cheese, butter and sausage. Each was in a different section of the store and each had a separate line for selecting the items and finding the price. Maya bypassed the price line and stood in three more lines, one for each item, to pay. She knew what each item cost. After paying in those three lines and receiving receipts, she moved to three other lines with a less-than-content baby on her back to turn in her receipts and pick up the food. She got into only one argument with someone, a small terrier of a woman with a net bag who tried to get into line ahead of her. It took Maya almost an hour to pick up the dinner.

It had not been a good day but it appeared to be an even worse day for Sasha who was now pacing in front of the window.

"I can sell ice cream," he said. "I'm good at it."

"They wouldn't let you quit," she said, nibbling small crumbs of cheese by picking them up with the tip of her finger and raising them to her lips. Sasha looked over his shoulder and watched her as he paced.

"There are ways," he said. "Others have done it. I just fail to do the job, make mistakes, mostly mistakes in reports. After a while I'd be told to find other work. It's been done. Remember Myagkov? The old man with the funny ears."

"No," she said.

"Well, he was separated from the Procurator's Office two years ago," said Sasha. "They said he had proved to be incompetent. He was so incompetent that he's now running an automobile shop, has his own car and lives in a big apartment near Izmailovo Park."

"What kind of car?" asked Maya.

"A Soviet Fiat-125," he said, "and . . ." He stopped his pacing and looked down at her. "Are you humoring me?"

"I'm trying to," she said smiling up at him, a point of cheese on the tip of her finger near her mouth, "but I'm not doing as well as I would like."

Sasha shook his head.

"I'm not going to quit, am I?"

"No," she said, "but if it helps you to pace and complain, I'm happy to listen."

"Enough complaining," he said smiling for the first time since that morning. He leaned over and kissed her. She tasted like cheese, and Sasha felt excited. "Do you think we have time before Lydia gets home?"

"Why not call your aunt and see if she's still there? It takes her at least an hour to get back."

Tkach moved beyond the baby's crib. He had turned on a small light on the table near the phone and was about to call his aunt when the phone rang. He picked it up after the first ring and looked back at the crib to be sure the baby hadn't awakened.

"Tkach," he said softly.

"It's me, Zelach."

"Yes."

"Volovkatin. I found him."

"Where?"

"He came back to his apartment building, through the back. I was waiting. He's up there now. You want me to go up and get him?"

"No. Go inside. Get somewhere where he can't get past you, where you can watch his door. If he starts to leave before I get there, take him. I'm coming."

He hung up and looked at his wife.

"I'm sorry," he said feeling strangely elated.

Maya moved past the crib to her husband, put her arms around him and kissed him deeply, the way she had seen Catherine Deneuve kiss some thin man in a French movie she and Sasha had seen last year.

"I was very proud of you this afternoon," she whispered. "It made me very excited to see you like that. Is that a little sick, do you think?"

"Maybe a little," he whispered rubbing his nose against hers, "but don't lose the feeling."

Less than two minutes later he was out the door, on the street and running for a taxi parked at the stand on the corner.

The person responsible for the murder of Illya Rutkin stood in the darkened room near the window. Light came from some windows in Tumsk and the moon helped to brighten the square, but no one was about and no one was likely to be about except those who had no choice. The temperature had dropped again. Even with layer-upon-layer of clothes and the best Evenk-made furs, no one could remain outside tonight without pain. The killer watched, waited, going over the encounter with Rostnikov.

Rutkin had been lucky, had stumbled on a truth, but this one, this quiet block of a man seemed to be working it out.

His questions suggested a direction, an understanding, and his suspicion was evident in his watching eyes which belied his stolid, bland peasant face.

There was no point in trying to make his death look like an accident. With two deaths in the small village within a month, it was unlikely that a third death, the death of a man investigating a murder, would be accepted as accidental, regardless of the circumstances. It could be covered up, obscured, but it couldn't be ignored. Perhaps the assumption would be that a madman was at large. It wasn't important. At this point it was simply a matter of slowing things down for five days. In five days or so it would all be over.

The killer poured a drink from the bottle on the table and waited, waited and watched. The secret of success was surprise, patience and anticipation. The killer knew that, had been taught that, had already gone out in the snowy night to take care of the possibility of temporary failure.

And so the waiting continued and was eventually rewarded. Just before midnight a round, bundled figure stepped out of the door of the weather station and limped slowly, even more slowly than he had come up the slope, down toward the square. He was alone.

At his present pace, it would take Rostnikov no more than three or four minutes to get back to the house on the square.

The killer lifted the nearby binoculars and scanned the frost-covered windows of the houses around the small square. No one was visible. It was time for the killer to act.

The rifle was oiled, ready and waiting near the rear door.

Rostnikov had a great deal on his mind. Normally, the cold would have driven him down the slope as quickly as his leg would allow, but he barely noticed the cold. All he could think about was the phone call. He was but dimly aware of where he was and where he was going. It almost cost him his life.

The sailors in the weather station, an efficient, comfortable box of a building with walls painted white, were in gray sweaters and matching sweat pants and they all looked young, even younger than his Josef, even the commanding officer whose face was serious and pink. The large room in which they were congregated held a variety of odd machines with dials, pointers and cylinders. The machines hummed and clicked as Rostnikov looked around for a phone.

"This way, Comrade Inspector," the officer said. He obviously knew something was happening, something that suggested that sympathy was in order for this limping man.

Rostnikov thanked him and followed the officer through an open door to a small office with very bright overhead lights and a small desk that looked as if it were made out of plastic. The decks, walls and even the phone were the same gray as the casual uniforms of the sailors.

"I don't know how to . . ." Rostnikov began.

"Let me," the officer said with a very small, supportive smile. "Let me know the number you want and I'll see if I can get you through. It should be easy. This is a military phone."

Rostnikov gave him the number of his apartment in Moscow and the man made contact with an operator almost immediately.

"Sometimes the lines . . ." the officer began. "Ah, here it is."

He handed the phone to Rostnikov and left the room quickly and quietly, closing the door behind him.

Rostnikov listened to three rings and then the phone was picked up in Moscow.

"Sarah?" he said before she could speak.

"Yes, Porfiry, who else would you expect to be here?" Her voice would have sounded perfectly calm to anyone but him. He detected the strain. "I should have known they would call you. I didn't want them to. It could have waited till you got back."

"Is it Josef?" he asked softly.

"No," she said. "On the contrary. He is fine. At least he was last Thursday. I just got a letter from him."

"Then . . .?"

"It's me," she said softly.

"The headaches," he said.

"They think I might have some kind of growth, a something on the brain," she said.

"They think," he said, sitting on the steel chair behind the desk.

"They know," she said. "They did a machine thing with my head."

"I see," he said.

"It's probably nothing much," Sarah said.

He imagined her sitting on the dark little bench near the phone, her left hand playing with the loose strands of auburn hair at the nape of her neck. She paused and he said nothing.

"Porfiry, are you still there?" she asked.

"Unfortunately, I am still here and not in Moscow," he said, his voice dry, very dry.

"Will it be long? Will you be long?" she asked quite matter-of-factly.

"I'll try to get this finished in a few days. I'm doing some things to move it along. Who did you see? What are they going to do?"

"My cousin Alex sent me to a friend of his, another doctor. She did the test. I'm afraid it will cost, Porfiry Petrovich. She is a private doctor, private clinic just outside of Moscow. She'll try to keep it down, but, I'm sorry."

"We will pay. We have some money," he said. "What are we paying for?"

She laughed, a sad variation on her familiar laugh.

"An operation," she said.

"When?"

"As soon as possible. It can wait three or four days for you to get back. She assures me that I should be fine. It doesn't look as if it is anything to worry about."

"Allow me the indulgence of worry," he said.

"I'll join you."

"I'll try to get Josef back on leave," Porfiry Petrovich said, looking around the room for something to focus on, finding a small bookcase whose technical volumes were neatly lined up. "I might be able to . . ."

"You can't," she said gently. "Don't waste your time trying. I know you'd like to."

"What is the doctor's name? The one who will . . ."

"Operate? Dr. Yegeneva. Olga Yegeneva. Remember when Josef went with that girl named Olga?"

"Yes."

"This one is nothing like her, but she is young, a child almost with big round glasses like mine, clear skin and her hair cut short. I like her."

"Maybe we can make a match," he said with a smile.

"I think she's married," Sarah said. "Who is paying for this call?"

"The navy. Don't worry."

"What is it like there?"

"Cold, dark. Peaceful on the surface. Boiling beneath. How are you feeling?"

"Surprisingly, not bad. I feared the worst for weeks and hearing it was a terrible relief. You understand?"

"Yes," he said. The room seemed a bit blurred.

"I don't know how you feel, Porfiry Petrovich. I'm never sure how you feel and I don't think you know how you feel. The irony is that you seem to understand perfectly how everyone else feels but yourself, but that is a bit deep for a phone conversation in the middle of the night from Siberia. The line is very clear."

"I think they do it by satellite or something," he said.

Silence again, a slight crackling sound on the phone. For an instant he feared that they would be cut off.

"Sarah," he said. "I love you very much."

"I know, Porfiry Petrovich. It would help if you said it a bit more often."

"I'll do that."

"Enough," she said. "Get your work done. Find whoever or whatever they sent you to find and get back. I've dusted your weights. Do they have weights for you there?"

"Yes," he said.

"Good. Stay strong. Goodbye."

"Goodbye," he said and she hung up.

He sat holding the phone for a few seconds and then put it down. Galich's vodka or empathy sent a pain through his head, a cold pain as if he had bitten into an icicle. He shuddered and picked up the phone again.

Trial, error, persistence and the use of the fact that he was a policeman got him Olga Yegeneva on the phone within six minutes.

"Dr. Yegeneva?"

"Yes." She sounded very young.

"This is Inspector Rostnikov. You have seen my wife."

It sounded awkward, formal, wasn't what he wanted to say at all.

"Yes, Inspector," she said, perhaps a bit defensively.

"You are going to operate on her. Is that correct?"

"Yes." She was growing more abrupt. He had reached her at home.

"How serious is the situation?"

"Can you call me back tomorrow, please, at the clinic," she said coolly.

"I am in Tumsk, Siberia. I don't know if or when I can get a phone or a line tomorrow."

"I see. It is serious, but it does not appear to be malignant. However, it is in a position where it is causing pressure and even if it is not malignant the longer we wait the more difficult the surgery."

"Then operate immediately," he said.

"She wants to wait for you."

"I cannot get back for at least two days, possibly three or four."

The doctor paused on the other end just as his wife had a few minutes earlier, and Rostnikov felt that he had to fill the vacuum of time and space but he did not know what to add.

"It can wait a few days, but not many," she said much more gently than she had been speaking.

"I'll get there as soon as I can," he said.

"As soon as you can. And Inspector, I really do not think that the danger is great. I cannot deny that some exists but I have done more than forty similar operations and seen quite similar cases. I believe she will be fine."

"Thank you," he said. "Forgive me for calling you at home."

"Oh, that's all right. I just got home and I was spending a few minutes with my little boy before he went to bed."

"How old is he?"

"Two years," she said.

"A good age," said Rostnikov. "Goodnight, Doctor."

"Goodnight, Inspector."

Rostnikov left the office, thanked the young officer, nodded at a sailor with very short hair and freckles who looked up at him, and went out the door of the weather station and into the night.

The path which the navy plow had made that morning had long been filled by drifting snow. He had to move down the slope slowly, carefully. He was no more than a dozen feet from the door of the house on the square when the first shot was fired. It probably would have torn off the top of his head had he not been stumbling slightly. He had stumbled more than a dozen times coming down the slope. Had he looked up and behind him there was a chance, a slight chance that he would have seen a movement in the shadows near the forest higher up the slope between the wooden houses, but he had no reason to do so.

Even as he rolled to his right and the second shot came tearing up a furrow of snow as if an animal were tunneling madly past his head, Rostnikov was aware of the irony. The leg which he had dragged behind him for more than thirty-five years had finally repaid him by saving his life.

He knew now or sensed where the shots were coming from and before the third bullet was fired he was crouching behind the statue of Ermak. A small chunk of Ermak's hand shattered, sending small shards of stone over Rostnikov's head.

The fourth shot came from further right and Rostnikov looked around knowing that he would have to make a move if someone did not come out to help him quickly. There was no thought of running. Rostnikov could not run.

It was at that point that the door of the People's Hall of Justice and Solidarity banged open and Mirasnikov, the old man Rostnikov had been watching all day, came out, his boots not fully tied, his coat not buttoned, the fur hat on a mad angle atop his head. In his hand he held an old hunting rifle.

"Where?" the old man shouted at Rostnikov.

"Up there," Rostnikov shouted back. "On the slope. By the trees. But don't step out. He'll . . ."

The old man stepped out, looked up toward the slope, put the rifle to his shoulder and fired three times in rapid succession before the rifle on the hill responded.

Mirasnikov tumbled back from the shot that appeared to hit him in the chest.

It had been no more than ten seconds between the time the first shot was fired and Mirasnikov had tumbled back wounded. Other doors were opening now and Rostnikov thought he saw a movement on the slope. The killer was running.

Rostnikov rose and moved as quickly as he could toward the fallen old man. The light from the open door of the People's Hall of Justice made a yellow path on which Mirasnikov lay.

"Where?" Someone behind Rostnikov shouted as the inspector knelt by the fallen man.

"On the slope by the trees," Rostnikov shouted back without looking. He had no hope or expectation that anyone would see the assailant. "How are you, old man?" he asked Mirasnikov gently.

An expanding circle of red lay on the old man's jacket just below his right shoulder.

"Did I get him?" Mirasnikov asked.

"I don't think so, but I think you saved my life."

"If I had my glasses, I would have gotten him."

"I'm sure you would. You can't lie out here. I'll take you inside."

"My glasses. My rifle," Sergei Mirasnikov said.

"Your glasses are on your head and your rifle is safe," said Rostnikov picking up the man easily as Karpo, wearing his coat but still bareheaded, came running to his side.

"Are you all right, Inspector?" he asked.

"I am fine," he said. "Get up to Dr. Samsonov's house. Bring him down here immediately."

"Immediately," Karpo said.

"One more thing, Emil," he said and he whispered his order as Mirasnikov's wife came stumbling out the door of the Hall wailing.

The naval officer and two of his men were working their way down the slope toward them and lights were going on in the houses on the slope.

"Of course, Inspector," Karpo said, and something that only Rostnikov would recognize as a smile touched the corners of Emil Karpo's face before he turned and hurried past the sailors coming toward him.

Rostnikov moved past the wailing woman with a strange feeling of elation. The killer had made a mistake, a terrible mistake in letting Rostnikov know that something had happened to frighten him, to make the killer think that Rostnikov knew something that required his death. He would go carefully over what he knew when he got back to his room. But that was not the only mistake the killer had made.

Given enough mistakes and a bit of luck, Rostnikov could possibly identify the killer quickly enough so that he could be back with Sarah in a few days.

"A bed," Rostnikov said to the wailing woman who followed him as he looked around the hall.

"In there," she said pointing to their room.

"Stop howling, woman," Mirasnikov groaned from Rostnikov's arms.

"Howling," she shouted following them. "Howling, he says. I'm grieving."

"I'm not dead yet," Sergei mumbled, but only Rostnikov heard.

Five minutes later Samsonov, with the help of his wife, was working on the old man. Everyone else had been told to go home and Mirasnikov's wife had been banished to the meeting room.

Rostnikov stood carefully watching Lev and Ludmilla Samsonov while Karpo whispered to him. When Karpo was finished speaking, Rostnikov nodded.

"Our killer is very clever, Emil."

"Yes, Inspector. Very clever. May I ask about your wife?"

"She needs an operation," he said. "If I were a religious man, I would say that with God's help we will be home in a few days."

"But you are not a religious man," said Karpo.

"There is no God, Emil Karpo. You know that."

There were times when Karpo could not tell if Porfiry Petrovich Rostnikov was making a joke. This was certainly one of those times.

"He's still in there," said Zelach as Tkach came panting up the stairs taking them two or three at a time.

It was one of those 1950s concrete block buildings with no personality. This one was on Volgogradskij Prospekt and Volovkatin's apartment was on the fifth floor.

Zelach was standing on the fifth-floor stairway landing behind a thick metal door. The door was propped open just a crack with a piece of jagged wood.

"There," Zelach said pointing through the crack at a door. "You can see it." The lumbering investigator with only minimal ability to think did have a skill, a skill which had resulted in his finding the man who had evaded them the previous day. Zelach was single-minded. If he was told to find Volovkatin, then he would doggedly pursue Volovkatin for years following false leads, even ridiculous leads and vague possibilities if no one gave him a direction in which to go. In this case, he could think of nothing but to go to the apartment and wait in the hope that the dealer in stolen goods would return.

The vague possibility of Volovkatin's return had prompted Zelach, who had been in the man's apartment, to leave everything as it was. He did not want Volovkatin to return to an empty apartment and run away. As Inspector Rostnikov had once said, the rat does not step into a trap without cheese. It was the kind of truism that Rostnikov often fed Zelach like a simple catechism. Rostnikov himself tended to discount such simplicities which, though they were often true, were just as often false. In this case, there was a magnificent supply of cheese.

If Volovkatin had not returned, Zelach would have continued his vigil during his free time till other assignments or a direct order forced him elsewhere. Luck had been with him this time as it had a surprising number of times in the past.

"Good," said Tkach leaning over and clasping his knees to catch his breath. "We'll do this right."

"He's trying to be quiet in there," said Zelach, "but he is not being very successful."

"We are not concerned with his success," said Tkach straightening up, "but with ours. Let's go."

Tkach pushed the door open and stepped into the hall with Zelach right behind. Sasha stood to the right of the door and Zelach to the left. The procedure in this case was clear. They would continue to wait in the hope and expectation that Volovkatin would be leaving. He knew the police were after him and that coming to the apartment created some danger but the cheese had proved too tempting.

If Volovkatin did not leave within an hour, they would have to try the door and even knock. It would end the surprise and Volovkatin might be armed, might do something foolish. There was no other way out of the apartment but, knowing the severity of his crime and the likely punishment, the dealer in stolen goods might do something foolish, might dive through the window or decide to remain in the apartment till they broke down the door, in which case someone other than Volovkatin might be hurt. So the policemen stood against the wall on each side of the door and waited and listened and watched.

Five minutes later an old man staggered drunkenly through the stairway door singing something about rivers. The old man didn't see the two policemen at first. He was a stringy, gray creature with his cap tipped dangerously close to falling on the back of his head. A cigarette burned down close to the old man's lips as he concentrated on searching through his coat and pants pockets as he sang. At the moment he fished his apartment key out of one of his inner pockets, he looked up in triumph and saw the two men leaning against the wall.

The old man swayed, stepped back in fear, his cigarette dropping from his lips.

Tkach put a finger to his own lips with his right hand and pulled out his police identification card with his other hand. The old man gasped and his moist red eyes showed fear.

"I'm just drunk," wailed the old man. "That's still no crime. Is it a crime now?"

Tkach looked at the door, put away his identification card and continued to put his hand to his lips to quiet the old man. Then he stepped forward quickly and clasped his hand over the old man's mouth. He could feel the man's stubble and the sticky moisture of his mouth. Tkach leaned close to the man's ear and whispered, "We are not going to arrest you, little father," he said. "We are waiting for the man in that apartment. I am going to let you go and you will go very quietly to your apartment. You understand?"

The old man nodded, Tkach's hand still clasped on his mouth.

"Good, very good," whispered Tkach. "We appreciate your help."

He removed his hands from the old man's mouth and immediately wiped it on his own jacket.

"You sure . . ." the old man said aloud.

Tkach put his hand back on the man's mouth but the old man was nodding now. He understood and put his own grimy hand to his mouth. In doing so he knocked his already tilted cap onto the floor. He started to lean down for it, but Tkach stopped him, retrieved the cap and placed it firmly on the old man's head. The old man opened his mouth to say something but Tkach shook his head no and the old man smiled in understanding and closed his mouth.

"I don't live here," the old man whispered.

"Then go where you do live," whispered Tkach.

"I don't know how to get there," the old man whispered again.

His breath was green-brown and foul but Tkach stayed with him, wanting to open the door and throw him down the stairs. He looked over at Zelach who shrugged.

"What is your name?"

"Viktor," said the old man, swaying and looking at the key in his hand.

"Viktor," Tkach whispered. "Go down to the bottom of the stairs and wait for us. Wait as long as it takes. When we are finished, we will take you home."

"All the floors look alike," said Viktor trying to focus on the doors down the hall. "I think I live down." He pointed at the floor.

"Then go down to the next floor and see if you live there. If you don't, then go to the floor below that. Work your way down and if you fail to find your apartment we will find you waiting at the bottom and will take home."

"What if I live up?" Viktor said softly in triumph, pointing to the ceiling.

"We will find out later," whispered Tkach, resisting the terrible urge to strangle the old man. Nothing was ever simple.

"I don't think I live in this building at all," Viktor announced, pulling a bent cigarette out of his pocket and putting it into his mouth so he could continue this fascinating conversation at leisure. "I have no match."

Tkach had a flash of inspiration.

"Well," he whispered. "Knock on that door and ask for one. The man in there has matches. Don't let him tell you otherwise. And don't mention us. You understand."

"Am I a fool?" asked Viktor, swaying and pointing at his chest with his key.

"Knock and ask," Tkach said, and the old man staggered to the door and knocked.

"Louder," Tkach whispered looking at Zelach, who grinned showing his quite uneven teeth.

Viktor, bent cigarette dangling from his thin lips, knocked again and called out, "I need a match."

Volovkatin's apartment was silent. Tkach mimed a knock for Viktor who nodded in understanding and knocked five times.

"I need a match, Comrade. I am a drunken old fool in need of a match and I know someone is in there. I was told by . . ." Tkach put up a warning hand and Viktor winked. ". . . a little brhat, a brother."

He knocked again and sang, "I need a maaatch."

Something stirred in the apartment. Zelach and Tkach went flat against the wall and pulled out their pistols. Viktor looked at them with new interest and as the door started to open Tkach motioned for the old man to look at the door and not at them. It was beyond his ability.

The door came open a crack while Viktor stood staring to his right at Zelach's pistol.

Tkach stepped out, kicked at the door, pushed Viktor out of the way and jumped into the apartment his gun leveled and ready but it wasn't necessary. Volovkatin, his hands going up automatically, stepped back looking at Tkach and Zelach.

"Don't shoot me," he said.

Tkach's eyes took in a warehouse of a room, a floor-to-ceiling collection of phonographs, cameras, coats, hats, tape recorders, television sets, even three computers. There was barely enough room amid the mismatched furniture and boxes containing, as Tkach saw, watches, jewelry and wallets, to fit three people in the room.

"We don't intend to shoot you," said Tkach.

"I saw something like this in a magazine or a movie or on the television or something," Viktor said, stepping into the already crowded room and looking around.

"Volovkatin," said Tkach. "You are arrested."

"Arrested," sighed Volovkatin touching his forehead, looking over his glasses in panic. He wore a threadbare suit and tie but the tie was loose and off to one side. He needed a shave. "We can come to an understanding. Look, look around. There's plenty here. You want a television? Take a television. Take a television for each of you, a television and a watch. I've even got Swiss watches, American, French, anything."

"I'll take a watch and a television and that chair," said Viktor trying to step past Zelach on his way to the television.

"Comrade," Zelach said reaching over to grab the old man by the neck. "Go out in the hall."

"He gave me a television," Viktor insisted. "I'm a Soviet citizen, have been since before any of you were born."

"Get him out," Tkach cried and Zelach turned the old man and marched him out the door into the hall.

"There's enough here to make you rich," Volovkatin said to Tkach, looking at the door beyond which they could hear Viktor shouting about his rights. "I'm waiting for a friend with a truck, a truck will be downstairs in a few minutes, maybe even now. I could fill it up, leave things for you, anything. Or we can drop them right at your home, yours and the other policeman's. You never saw me."

"I see you," Tkach said. "I see you very clearly. Zelach," he called, and Zelach came running in. "There's a truck downstairs or will be in a minute or two. Arrest the driver and call for a car to take us all to Petrovka."

Volovkatin gave up and Tkach felt a strange mixture of triumph and failure. This didn't feel as good as he had expected. It didn't quite compensate for what had happened this afternoon, but it would have to do.

Ten minutes later, the two policemen and two suspects were on their way to Petrovka. One minute after they had left, a drunken old man who had regained a bit of his sobriety opened the unlocked door of Volovkatin's apartment, turned on the light, looked around at the treasures before him and began to weep with joy.

"Hardly the most antiseptic conditions possible," Samsonov said stepping back from the bed on which old Mirasnikov lay with his eyes closed. Samsonov had put his instruments and bandages back in the black bag he had been working from. "He will probably live."

Liana Mirasnikov heard, gripped her bulky dress with withered white knuckles and let out a wail of relief or anguish. Sergei Mirasnikov opened one eye and looked at her with distaste.

Samsonov's blue sweater was spotted with blotches of blood. There were also spots of blood on his cheek and hands. Ludmilla Samsonov, whose hair hung down on one side and whose hands and gray dress were flecked with blood, stood next to her husband smiling, and touched his cheek.

"The bullet went through," Samsonov said, taking his wife's hand. "Quite a bit of blood and he may have trouble using his right arm though the muscles are generally intact. For an old man, he is in remarkable condition. A Moscovite his age would be dead."

Rostnikov had trouble keeping his eyes on the doctor rather than the doctor's wife, but he forced himself to do so.

"Thank you, Doctor," Rostnikov said.

"Someone will have to stay with him all night and call me if his breathing changes," Samsonov said looking back at his patient.

"I'll stay," said Ludmilla.

"I think it a better idea that Inspector Karpo and I take turns remaining with Mirasnikov," Rostnikov said confidentially over a sudden renewal of wailing by the old woman. "The person who shot him might want to make another attempt."

"Why would anyone want to kill Mirasnikov?" asked Ludmilla moving close to her husband with a shudder.

"The object of the attack was not Mirasnikov," Rostnikov explained. "I was the one shot at. The old one came out to help me."

"Does that mean you know something about Karla's murder?" Ludmilla Samsonov said hopefully. With the excuse to look at her, Rostnikov turned his head and smiled.

"Probably more about Commissar Rutkin's murder," he said gently. "The problem is that I'm not sure what I know."

"I don't . . ." she began, looking with puzzlement at Rostnikov, Karpo and her husband.

"And what are you going to do, Inspector?" Samsonov demanded rather than asked.

"I have several ideas. For now, and forgive me for moving into your province, I think Mirasnikov should get some rest."

"Yes," agreed Samsonov, "and if you will forgive me for moving into your province, I remind you that my daughter's killer is somewhere in this town in bed sleeping when he should be dead."

"I'll not forget your daughter's death," Rostnikov said, his voice a promise.

"Ah, but I almost forgot," said Samsonov reaching into his black bag. "I found some of those muscle relaxants I mentioned to you for your leg. They are not the American ones but the Hungarian. Almost as good." He handed the bottle to Rostnikov who thanked him and put the bottle into his pocket. The simple mention of his leg awakened a tingling prelude to pain.

Samsonov helped his wife on with her coat and then put on his own. The doctor guided her across the room ignoring the thanks of the old woman. Ludmilla, however, paused to hold the woman by both shoulders and whisper something reassuring to her.

When the Samsonovs had left, Rostnikov beckoned to Karpo while he moved to the bedside of the old man. Liana's wrinkled face, a dry wisp of white hair sticking out wildly from under her babushka, looked up as Rostnikov approached.

"Sergei," Rostnikov said softly, sitting on the bed near the old man. "You're awake. I can see your eyelids fluttering."

"I've been shot," Mirasnikov said. "I deserve rest, a week off."

"You deserve rest and my thanks," agreed Rostnikov. "You saved my life."

Mirasnikov smiled.

"But my friend," Rostnikov said, "you have a secret. I've seen it in your eyes and you've seen in mine that I know about it."

"Nyet," squealed the old woman.

"No, she says," Mirasnikov whispered. "We're beyond no."

"But he'll kill you," she cried.

"What do you think this is, woman?" Sergei Mirasnikov pointed with a finger of his left hand at his shoulder. "I could be dead by morning. I'm weary of being afraid."

"Afraid of what, Sergei?" Rostnikov asked gently. "Did you see who killed Illya Rutkin?"

Mirasnikov nodded in affirmation.

"Who?"

"Kurmu."

"The Evenk shaman?" asked Rostnikov.

The old woman let out a terribly shriek and hurried from the room into the assembly hall.

"You saw him stab Commissar Rutkin?"

"No, he called to the da-van, the great ruler, and a snow demon arose and killed the man from Moscow," Mirasnikov whispered, looking around with wide eyes to be sure that no one else was present.

"You saw this?" Rostnikov repeated.

"I saw this," Mirasnikov confirmed and closed his eyes.

"Sleep," said Rostnikov rising from the bed and moving toward Karpo. The pills Samsonov gave him were jiggling in his pocket.

"You heard?" Rostnikov asked quietly.

"Yes," said Karpo looking at the sleeping man.

"And . . . ?"

"He is delirious," said Karpo.

"Perhaps, but he believed what he said even before he was shot. I've been watching him, as I said. He was frightened. He did have a secret."

"I don't believe in Siberian gods or snow demons, Porfiry Petrovich," Karpo said evenly.

"Nonetheless," said Rostnikov. "I think we have some questions for Kurmu the Shaman. Maybe he will have some ancient medicine for Mirasnikov. He is feverish already."

"Shall I call the doctor back?" Karpo asked.

"No, I'll sit with him. If his temperature goes much higher, I'll have the old woman watch him while I go for Samsonov."

"And what shall I do?" Karpo asked.

"Bring me your report on the comparison of information. I assume you've prepared it."

"I've prepared it," said Karpo.

"Good. Then after you've given me the report, I want you to go to the house of Dimitri Galich. It will be dawn soon. He speaks Evenk and knows the taiga. Tell him I want to speak to Kurmu. Go with him to find the shaman. Accept no answer from Galich but yes and no answer from Kurmu but yes. You understand."

"I understand," Karpo said. "Anything else?"

"Yes, tell the old woman to make tea, a great deal of tea and to bring it to me. And tell her gently, Emil Karpo."

"I will do my best, Comrade Inspector," Karpo said, his unblinking eyes betraying nothing.

"I know you will, Emil. You have my trust."

The sense that Karpo had something more to say struck Rostnikov again and, normally, this would be the time to pursue it, but this was not a normal time, a normal place, a normal situation and Rostnikov wanted, needed to be alone.

TEN

NEITHER KARPO NOR GALICH HAD SPOKEN FOR MORE THAN half an hour.

The burly former priest had answered his door in a dark robe looking bleary-eyed and confused, his white hair sprouting out wildly. He had ushered Karpo in quickly. Karpo had explained that Mirasnikov had been shot and that he had claimed the shaman Kurmu had sent a snow demon to kill Commissar Rutkin.

"And Rostnikov wants to arrest Kurmu for this?" Galich had said with a pained smile.

"Inspector Rostnikov wishes to talk to him," Karpo explained. "Can you find him?"

Galich had run his thick hand through his hair and said, "I can get to a place where Kurmu will know we want to talk to him. If he doesn't want to talk to us, we can forget it."

"Then let us go," said Karpo. "I can get Famfanoff's vehicle."

"No vehicle," said Galich, moving back into the house. "There's no room in the taiga for a vehicle to get through the trees. Wait. I'll be ready in a few minutes."

Then he looked at Karpo.

"And I'll give you something warmer to wear," he said. "We have a half-hour walk both ways. Dressed like that you'll be dead before we get there."

Karpo had not argued and when Galich returned with his arms filled with clothing, sweaters, an ugly wool hat that proved too large for Karpo's head, and a pair of snowshoes, the policeman accepted it all and Galich's directions on how to put them on.

When they were fully dressed, Galich said, "All right. Follow behind me. Keep your face covered. There should be some morning haze to aid the moon in about fifteen minutes. And no talking until we find Kurmu . . . if we find Kurmu. And, one more thing: I speak enough Tunga to get basic ideas across, but if it gets too complicated we may have trouble."

"I will keep the conversation simple," said Karpo. "Let us go."

And they began the walk by moving behind Galich's house, across the open white space of about one hundred yards and into the forest. Karpo followed in the prints of Galich's snowshoes, surprised at the older man's steady stride and his ability to find relatively solid pathways through the snow-covered ground and the trees which seemed to be an endless repetition of cedars, larch, birch, pine and spruce.

Karpo's migraine had begun the moment they left Galich's house. He had expected it because he had smelled flowers, roses, quite clearly even before he left the People's Hall of Justice and Solidarity. The headaches were almost always announced by an aura, a feeling and a smell from his past. When they reached the first line of trees in the forest, the pain had begun on the left side of his head, just above the ear. It remained with him, spread like an old enemy, in some ways a welcome, challenging old enemy.

The cold heightened the pain, almost made him blink at the broad back of Galich in front of him. Pain, he reminded himself, was a test. To withstand pain, distraction, emotion and do one's job was the major satisfaction of life. Emil Karpo, plodding through the snow of a Siberian forest in the moonlight, reminded himself that he was not an individual, didn't want to be. To be effective for the State, he had to see through the demands of his own body, the pleas of others.

Meaning, in his life, was determined by his value to the State. There were criminals. Each crime drained the State, made it vulnerable. The task of Emil Karpo was to identify and locate criminals, take them, with the help of the system, out of society. It was his life, and the pain of a headache was simply a test of his determination. Thoughts, feelings wanted to enter. The vague, amused smile of Mathilde came to him. He concentrated on a shifting shadow in the coat of Dimitri Galich and the smile became the fluttering of fur. The voice of Major Zhenya whispered in the humming wind through the trees, reminding him that he would have to report on Porfiry Petrovich when he got back to Moscow. Emil Karpo let the chill pain of his headache take over and pierce the voice.

They walked. Once some animal rustled to their right. Once a wolf howled so far off that Karpo was not sure he really heard it. The only other sound was the wind, the swishing of their snowshoes and the shift of their bodies moving through the snow. The forest was dark but a faint change had come as they walked, not exactly dawn but a lighter grayness. A bright Moscow dawn would have torn at Emil Karpo's head. He would have accepted it but he knew that bright light would have made it difficult for him to function.

"Here," said Galich through the scarf covering his mouth and face. He stopped and pointed.

It was his first word since they had left his house. Karpo looked at the man who was pointing at a slight ridge that looked no different to Karpo than dozens of others they had passed.

Galich led the way up the slight slope and motioned Karpo to move to his side. Karpo did so and found himself looking down at what appeared to be a road through the woods.

"Stream," explained Galich. "Frozen solid. Luckily for us. If this were summer, we'd never find Kurmu. Much of this is a bog and there are ticks, insects whose bite can kill, wild animals who don't have enough experience to fear men. The winter is safe, except for the cold."

"And now?" Karpo said, the left side of his head throbbing.

"We wait. We sit on these rocks for a minute or two. We drink some of the tea I brought in my canteen. We walk around. He knows we're here, probably knew it when we entered the taiga. If he means to come to us, he'll show up soon."

And so they drank, moved around and spoke very little. Karpo's headache allowed him to ignore, even welcome the cold that clawed at his face. His body was surprisingly warm, even perspiring under the six layers of wool and fur that Galich had dressed him in, but his exposed face tingled electrically. Galich looked at him and gestured for Karpo to cover more of his face with the scarf he had been given. Karpo did so.

He was just getting up from a minute or so of sitting on the rock when Karpo saw the man. He was standing no more than two dozen yards away next to a cedar tree. The man was a motionless, dark, faceless figure in a parka.

"Wait," Galich said as Karpo took a step toward the shaman. "He hasn't made up his mind yet."

"If he tries to run, I will have to stop him," Karpo said, his eyes fixed on the man near the tree. "He's an old man."

Galich laughed.

"He'd be gone before you got five steps. No, we wait."

And so they stood waiting, watching each other for perhaps five minutes. Suddenly the man in the parka waved, turned and was gone. Karpo stepped forward, each step sending a shock of agony through his head, but Galich held out his hand.

"He'll be back. If he weren't coming back he wouldn't have waved. He would have simply disappeared."

When Kurmu returned it was not to the base of the same cedar tree. This time Karpo turned to the frozen stream and saw the shaman standing still on the path of ice and snow looking up at the two Russians. The Evenk carried something slung over his shoulder. Karpo's eyes found those of the shaman and only then did the Evenk move forward and up the slope to the rock where the two men stood.

The shaman's bearded, craggy face turned first to Galich and then to Karpo. His eyes were narrow and dark. While looking directly at Karpo he spoke, his words a soft clattering, words running together.

Galich answered in what sounded to Karpo like a slow imitation of the old man.

"He says," said Galich, "that he has something for your pain."

"How does he know I am in pain?" Karpo asked.

"You really want me to ask him that?"

"No," said Karpo.

The shaman reached into the sack over his shoulder and pulled something out, something that clacked and echoed in the gray forest. He looked at Karpo and then said something else.

"He wants to know," said Galich, "if you would rather keep your pain. I think he said it is yours and he doesn't know why you might want pain but he thinks you might."

"What does he have?" Karpo said, the right side of his head welling in tempoed heat.

The shaman held out his mittened hand to Karpo showing what looked like a necklace of thick stones.

"It's amber beads," said Galich. "He wants you to put it around your neck."

Karpo reached out, accepted the necklace and put it over the oversized hat and around his neck. The shaman nodded.

"Give him my thanks and tell him we would like him to come with us to Tumsk to talk to the inspector. Tell him Mirasnikov has been shot."

"I'm not sure my Tunga is good enough for all that," sighed Galich. "Remember I said you have to keep it simple. I'll do what I can."

But before Galich could speak, the old shaman chattered out what sounded to Karpo like one long word.

Galich answered even more briefly and turned to Karpo with a shake of his head and a smile.

"He said we should get started. He has to be very far from here by tonight. He knows about Mirasnikov."

Karpo looked at the shaman who returned his unsmiling gaze. The eyes of the old man scanned Karpo's face and came back to rest on his eyes.

Kurmu said something else and Galich said, "He says he sees the color of your pain. It's very . . . something. I don't understand. He says the color is surrounding your soul and you should let your soul breathe through."

"He sees the color of my pain?"

"He's a shaman, remember," said Galich.

"And he's a Soviet citizen," Karpo reminded Galich.

"Is he?" Galich said with a deep laugh. "These people have ignored our history. Most of them never knew the Mongols had ever been through here."

The shaman spoke again and Galich answered before turning to Karpo.

"He wants to know if you're a Tartar?"

"No," said Karpo reaching up unconsciously to touch the beads around his neck.

Kurmu spoke again.

"He says, good. Let's go."

Before they were down the small slope and into the forest again, Karpo had the sensation of bright, scorching yellow and knew that his headache was already beginning to fade away.

It was just before dawn when Sasha Tkach entered his apartment. Maya sat at the table near the window breastfeeding Pulcharia who turned her head toward the clack of the door.

"Is Lydia here?"

"No, she had to leave early. What happened?"

Sasha brushed back his hair and touched his face. His hair grew quickly though his beard was light. Nonetheless, he needed a shave.

"What happened?" he repeated her question, moving to the table, kissing his wife on the head and looking down at his daughter who had returned to her feeding.

Sasha opened his jacket and sat in the chair where he could watch his wife and daughter.

"We found the black market. We found Volovkatin," he said. "We found him, brought him in, and the Deputy Procurator on duty sent a team to the apartment. And you know what they found?"

"No," said Maya concerned about the strange smile on her husband's face.

"Nothing. They found nothing," he said. "Everything Zelach and I saw there was gone. Someone had cleaned out every piece of stolen property. There was no evidence."

"But who . . . how?" she said softly, trying not to frighten Pulcharia who sucked away, her eyes partly closed.

"An old drunk," said Sasha. "There was an old drunk there named Viktor when we took Volovkatin. He must have sobered up quickly and gotten help in cleaning out the apartment. Now I've got to go out and find the drunk. It's a cycle. It never ends."

He laughed, shook his head and glanced at the window. In profile, Maya thought her husband looked very strange and very tired.

"So they had to let this Volovkatin go?" she said gently.

"No," laughed Tkach. "Kola the Truck and Yuri Glemp have already signed confessions. Zelach and I will testify to what we saw. The Procurator wants Volovkatin, claims he is a major fartsovschiki, black marketer. No little thing like missing evidence will get in the way of a conviction, particularly a conviction concerning economic crime. The Procurator wants to show the KGB that he is alert, swift. The Wolfhound will probably even get another medal."

"So?" said Maya puzzled.

"So," repeated Sasha. "You get attacked. I catch the hounds who did it and they get spanked and sent home to their parents. I catch a dealer in stolen goods who has probably never physically harmed anyone in his life and he'll go to jail for years, without evidence. If the KGB gets involved he might even be shot."

"How do you know he never physically harmed anyone?" she asked as the baby paused to catch her breath before continuing.

"Actually," he said with a laugh, "I don't know. He's probably murdered hundreds of innocent people. He had a gun when we caught him. I was just trying to set up a contrast so I could feel even more put upon by the system."

Maya laughed and Tkach felt better, much better. He even considered laughing but he couldn't quite bring himself to do it.

Mirasnikov moaned through the night, moaned and ranted, growing feverish, perspiring, going quiet and cool for brief periods and then burning with fever.

After three hours, Rostnikov had the old woman sit with her husband while he dressed, went out and made his way across the square and up the slope. He doubted if the killer would make another attempt on his life. It was possible, but the killer would have to be waiting up all night in the hope that Rostnikov would come out of the People's Hall of Justice and Solidarity. In addition, it was much lighter out now that what passed for day in this part of Siberia was coming. The killer would find it much more difficult to hide.

Rostnikov stopped at Galich's house and knocked at the door. There was no answer. He pounded mightily and the sound of his pounding vibrated through the village. Finally he heard movement inside and Famfanoff in his underwear opened the door.

"Comrade Inspector," he said.

"Get dressed, go down to the People's Hall of Justice and guard Sergei Mirasnikov," said Rostnikov. "I've got to get the doctor."

"What happened?" Famfanoff asked half asleep.

"Mirasnikov was shot last night," Rostnikov said. "You heard nothing?"

"I . . . I was . . ." Famfanoff stammered, resisting the urge to scratch his stomach.

"Get dressed and get down to the People's Hall," Rostnikov said and closed the door.

Famfanoff cursed, turned and moved toward his small bedroom, wondering if he had lost his last chance to escape from the arctic circle. I was drunk, he thought, hurrying to his room to get into his badly wrinkled uniform. His wife had warned him but he hadn't listened. Now it would be different.

"No more drink," he said aloud to himself. "Tonight, right now you begin. No more and that's final."

But even as he spoke, deep within him Famfanoff knew it was a lie.

Ludmilla Samsonov answered the door when Rostnikov knocked. She was dressed in green, her hair pinned up on top of her head.

"Please come in," she said. "We've been unable to get to sleep. Is Mirasnikov worse?"

"I am afraid he may be," Rostnikov confirmed.

"And you?" she said examining his face with her large, moist brown eyes. "You look very tired. Let me get you some coffee. We have real coffee we save for special occasions."

"Thank you," he said, "but I would appreciate your telling your husband that I think he should come down and take a look at the old man."

"I will," she said, starting toward the rear of the small house and then pausing to look back and add, "I heard about your call to Moscow. I hope your wife will be well."

"Thank you," Rostnikov said, sinking back into the same chair he had sat in the last time he had been in the house.

"How long have you been married?" she asked.

"Twenty-nine years," he said. "And you?"

"Lev and I have been married for almost two years," she said.

"Then Karla was not your daughter?" he asked yawning and closing his eyes.

"Inspector," she said with a small smile. "You must have known that."

Rostnikov held up his hands in mock defeat.

"It's difficult to stop being a policeman."

"I loved the child very much," Ludmilla said, her eyes growing more beautifully wet. Rostnikov regretted not having paused to shave before coming up the slope. "She was so . . . I'll get your coffee and my husband."

Rostnikov was dozing, probably even snoring when he felt the presence of someone in the room and came suddenly awake.

Samsonov stood nearby, his coat on, his black bag in his hand. He looked tired. At his side stood his wife holding a cup and saucer. Rostnikov rose with a grunt and stepped forward to accept the cup of steaming coffee.

"I warned you," said Samsonov. "He is an old man, conditions here are not the best even for a simple procedure such as I performed last night. Add to this that I've not worked with shoulder trauma in years."

"No one blames you, doctor," Rostnikov said, sipping the black, hot coffee, feeling both its liquid heat and caffeine surge through him.

"Is that right, Inspector? I am blamed for a great deal but I also hold others responsible for a great deal. What have you discovered?"

"About your daughter's death? Very little. About Commissar Rutkin's death, possibly quite a bit more. Perhaps when we find out about one we will find out about the other."

He gulped down the last of the coffee, returned the cup and saucer to Ludmilla Samsonov and gave her a small smile before turning to her husband.

"Shall we go," he said.

A moment later the doctor and the policeman stepped out the door and looked down the slope. The frantic figure of Famfanoff was rushing toward the People's Hall, his flowing coat only partially buttoned, his hat perched precariously atop his head.

By the time Rostnikov and Samsonov reached the square, the navy vehicle had broken the silence of the morning by cranking to life. In moments, a sailor would drive around the corner of the weather station and start the morning ritual of clearing a path.

Samsonov entered the People's Hall of Justice and Solidarity first. After the doctor entered the building, Rostnikov paused for an instant to look back around the town. In the window of his own room across the square he caught a glimpse of Sokolov who danced back out of sight. Rostnikov turned and entered the People's Hall, closing the door firmly behind him.

Rostnikov followed the doctor across the wooden floor and into the room where Mirasnikov lay on his bed, his wife kneeling next to him. Famfanoff tried to rise to stand at attention.

"All is secure, Comrade," Famfanoff announced.

"I had complete faith in you, Sergeant Famfanoff," said Rostnikov as Samsonov moved to the bed, pulled a chair over, examined Mirasnikov's face, eyes and wound and pulled a stethoscope out of his bag.

Liana Mirasnikov looked at her husband, the doctor and the two policemen for answers but they had none for the moment. She let out a wail of pain and frustration and Rostnikov wondered where the old woman got the energy for all this grief after being up all night. He suppressed a fleeting image of himself at the bedside of his wife Sarah, her head bandaged, a woman doctor with huge glasses hovering over her and clucking sadly, refusing to give Rostnikov attention, an answer.

Rostnikov met the old woman's eyes and motioned with his hands for her to be calm.

It took Samsonov no more than three minutes to complete his examination and change the bandage on the old man's shoulder. Mirasnikov groaned when his body was moved. He opened his eyes, looked around in fear and closed them again.

"Give him one of these now," he told the old woman, handing her a bottle of capsules. "And another every two hours. Wake him if you must but give them to him."

Samsonov got up and moved to the door. Famfanoff still stood at what he took to be attention. Rostnikov motioned for him to be seated and the policeman gratefully moved back to the chair.

In the assembly room with the door closed behind them, Samsonov took off his glasses, put them in a black leather case, placed the case in his pocket and told Rostnikov, "There is nothing to be done for him. The wound is infected. I've cleaned it, given him an antibiotic. I suppose we can call in a helicopter and have him evacuated to the hospital in Igarka but I think he would die from the movement. He is a very old man."

"I understand," said Rostnikov.

"If you have grief in you, Inspector, give some of it to my Karla," he said, weariness dulling the bitter edge he sought.

"I have and I will," Rostnikov said. "I'll not forget your daughter."

Samsonov looked up suddenly, angrily, to search for irony in the policeman's sympathy, but he could see none because there was none to be seen. Samsonov considered thanking the man but he couldn't bring himself to do it, not now, not yet. Words, looks were something but deeds were more important.

"We will see," said Samsonov. "We will see."

He turned from Rostnikov and hurried across the room, opening the door through which the sound of the navy plow came screeching. When he closed the door, the sound did not disappear but it was muffled, a little further away.

There was one more person to see before he could rest, Rostnikov thought. One more person. It was not quite together yet. He had a picture but he did not trust that picture. It needed some changes. It needed, among other things, the shaman for whom he had sent Karpo. It would be best if he could get some rest first, but there was no time. Sarah was alone in Moscow.

He buttoned his coat and went out to find General Vassily Krasnikov.

The killer returned to the window and looked out at the square, at the ever-pointing Ermak. Things had not gone well.

The policeman was not dead and seemed to be even more eager to pursue his investigation as if he had some deadline, near as the next full turn of the clock.

Perhaps, thought the killer, the attempt to shoot Rostnikov had been a bit rash. Perhaps the man knew nothing. It would be best if he were gone but now was the time for retrenching, pulling in, putting on the mask. Just a few more days and it wouldn't matter what the detective found or thought he found.

The killer looked out of the window and sipped from a glass of wine, a morning glass of French table wine, a small one which always seemed to help clear the mind.

And then something interesting happened. Rostnikov came out of the People's Hall and looked up the slope. The killer did not move away from the window, did not want to risk being seen moving away from the policeman's eyes. Better to simply stand there, look down. Rostnikov turned his head and began to move around the square and onto the just-cleared path. But before he could get ten yards, the door to the old building across the square opened and the other one, the one with the mustache, Sokolov, came running out to head off Rostnikov.

He blocked the other man's way and spoke quickly, apparently with anger and much movement of his hands and arms; the killer could hear the voices but none of the words. Rostnikov looked up the slope wearily and then answered Sokolov with apparent calm and no histrionics.

Whatever he said infuriated Sokolov even more. He pointed a finger at the inspector who moved past him and he kept shouting as Rostnikov followed the plowed path upward past the weather station. Rostnikov did not turn back, did not acknowledge the shouting man in the square standing next to the ruins of the old church. Sokolov shouted once more and then gave up and stalked back into the house slamming the door.

Rostnikov was out of sight for the moment beyond the bend, blocked by the concrete weather station. The killer stepped back from the window, put down the empty wine glass and waited in the expectation that Rostnikov would in a few moments be knocking at the door.

ELEVEN

"YOU LOOK WEARY, INSPECTOR," GENERAL KRASNIKOV SAID AS he ushered Rostnikov into the house.

Rostnikov grunted, unbuttoned the top of his coat, tucked his hat into his pocket, glanced at the furious stuffed head of the bear and moved to the firm wooden chair he had sat in before.

Krasnikov was dressed in a quasi-military suit of boots, gray neatly pressed pants, white shirt and tie and gray jacket. Rostnikov looked up at the General who wandered to his desk by the window, looked out and then turned back to look at his visitor.

"Your Comrade Procurator is not pleased with you," he said nodding toward the window. "I happened to be looking out the window a few minutes ago."

Rostnikov said nothing. He nodded and rubbed his nose.

"I can't say I liked the manner of the man when you two were here yesterday," Krasnikov went on, standing, hands clasped behind him, legs spread slightly. The pose reminded Rostnikov of the Gray Wolfhound, which reminded him of Moscow, which in turn reminded him of Sarah.

"He wanted to come with me to talk to you," Rostnikov said. "And?"

"I didn't want him to come," Rostnikov went on, opening his eyes but still rubbing the bridge of his nose. "I wanted to speak to you alone."

"Good," said Krasnikov firmly. "I do not like the man. He confuses duty with power."

"A common military mistake?" Rostnikov asked, looking away from the General to a vague spot on the dark wood wall.

"Yes."

Outside the navy plow groaned into the gray morning. The two men said nothing for a few minutes. The general stood erect. The inspector sat back with his eyes closed. Finally, Rostnikov sighed deeply and sat up.

"Let us play a military game," he said. "I'll propose a hypothetical situation, problem, and you provide a solution."

Krasnikov did not answer. Porfiry Petrovich shifted in his chair, looked at the general and went on.

"Military strategists like games, at least that's what Marshal Timeshenko said."

"I do not argue with Marshal Timeshenko," said Krasnikov.

"Suppose a military man fascinated by military strategy, feeling, perhaps, that his country is pursuing a foolish military course were banished for his ideas. Having nothing to do and being a man of letters, this military man spends some time writing his criticism of the military course of his former comrades and their nonmilitary superiors."

"For what purpose?" Krasnikov asked evenly.

"For what purpose does he write or for what purpose does he intend the results of his labor to be applied?"

"Both," said Krasnikov.

"Perhaps he writes because there is no one to listen except some reader of the future. Perhaps he dreams of return and wants his thoughts in clear form for publication. Perhaps he is bitter and wants to present his ideas to the world in the hope that by so doing he will force his country to revise its military strategy, force his country through the voices of its critics in other countries, because its strategy has been compromised, to develop a policy closer to his own. So many reasons."

"And the game?" Krasnikov said.

"Where would he keep his manuscript? How would he get it out of the country?"

"This sounds more like a policeman's game than a military strategist's," said Krasnikov. "Would you like some tea?"

"No tea. And yes, perhaps it is a policeman's game."

"Inspector, you have probably been up all night. You are worried about your wife. You have a killer to catch, a mystery to solve. Perhaps you would be better off dealing with those problems than with hypothetical ones."

Rostnikov smiled.

"You've been talking to one of the sailors," he said. "That is how you know about my wife."

"The people I find most compatible in this compound are those of the military even if they are not men of rank," said Krasnikov.

"What about our game?"

"I don't wish to play your game, Comrade Inspector."

"It is possible that Commissar Rutkin in the course of his investigation of the death of the Samsonov child found himself playing the game," said Rostnikov.

Krasnikov looked down at Rostnikov, tilted his head and laughed.

"You are amused," said Rostnikov with a sigh. "I'm pleased that I can bring a moment of mirth into the life of a resident of Tumsk."

"I don't believe Commissar Rutkin found himself playing such a game," Krasnikov said controlling his amusement.

Rostnikov rose, smiled at Krasnikov and said, "If such a manuscript existed by such a man, I would have no interest in it other than its connection to the death of the child, the murder of Commissar Rutkin, and the shooting of Sergei Mirasnikov."

"I did not kill the child or Rutkin. Nor did I shoot Mirasnikov. I am a soldier."

"I understand," Rostnikov said, stepping toward the still erect general, "that in Afghanistan, Soviet soldiers are being told to shoot children and old men."

"A policy and strategy destined for failure. Afghanistan is a disaster, should never have been entered into. The Soviet army should leave immediately before more of our reputation is eroded and more of our men are needlessly killed. It is not like the American's Viet Nam. For us it is worse, far worse."

"And this book, if it existed, might point out this folly?" Rostnikov said, now no more than three feet from the taller general.

There was something in the barrel-of-a-man's voice that made Krasnikov pause.

"It might. It would," he said.

Rostnikov nodded and started for the door.

"I have a son in the army, in Afghanistan," he said.

"I see," said Krasnikov behind him. "I would imagine that a police inspector might have enough blat to get his son out of that death trap."

"Some police inspectors are not looked upon with favor by the KGB," said Rostnikov. "Some police inspectors have made the mistake of playing games of strategy not unlike the one I proposed we play."

"And some police inspectors are clever enough to be maskirovannoye, masked, to play games to trap naïve lawbreakers," said Krasnikov.

"Keep writing, Comrade General," Rostnikov said, opening the door and stepping into the morning.

The yellow navy plow was screeching up the slope past the porch. Rostnikov stood waiting for it to pass. The driver, thickly bundled in fur, waved to Rostnikov who waved back.

"You are sure?" Dr. Olga Yegeneva asked, her eyes magnified by the round glasses.

The two women stood talking in the hall of a small private medical facility, really an old two-story house near the small botanic garden off of Mirak Prospekt. The office Olga Yegeneva shared with two other doctors was occupied and so they had moved into the hall where the doctor offered to sit with her patient on a wooden bench. Sarah Rostnikov had indicated that she would prefer to stand.

Sarah Rostnikov looked at the serious young woman in the white smock who stood before her and thought for an instant that it might be better to find an older doctor, a man. Then the instant passed and she saw the younger woman's confidence, steadiness and, equally important, her sincere concern for the patient before her.

"I've thought about it. Better to get it done quickly, have it over when he gets back," she said. "You've said every day of waiting is an added danger."

"Perhaps, but . . ." Dr. Yegeneva said.

"He'll forgive me," Sarah said.

"Your son. We could make some calls, perhaps get him back here on leave," the young doctor said, adjusting her glasses.

The young woman was quite pretty, her skin clear, her short hair a clean straw-yellow, her magnified eyes a glowing gray. Sarah imagined her son meeting the woman, sharing a joke near Sarah's hospital bed, getting together. Even though her cousin had recommended Dr. Yegeneva, Sarah knew the young woman was not Jewish. It was possible that if Josef took a non-Jewish wife he would cease to be identified as Jewish, that his children, Sarah and Porfiry Petrovich's grandchildren, would not be identified as Jewish. She thought this and felt guilty at the thought, guilty and angry and the anger showed.

"I'd rather my son know nothing of this till the operation is over," she said. "If everything is fine, he need not come. If everything is not fine, you can try to get him to Moscow as soon as you can. He will need his father. His father will need him."

Olga Yegeneva took both of her patient's hands.

"I'm very good," she said softly.

Sarah looked back into the gray eyes.

"I believe you are," she said. "Alex told me you are."

"I'll make the calls, set up the surgery for tomorrow morning," Olga Yegeneva said.

"My husband will arrange for the remainder of the costs when he gets back," she said. "We have saved a bit. We'll have a bit left after."

Olga Yegeneva nodded. She didn't like talking about money. She didn't like talking about very much but her work. She had heard, read of the money, prestige of surgeons in the West. She would have settled for the respect she felt her skills deserved. Getting through medical school had required all of the influence of her father, a department head at the University of Leningrad. Her father had even joined the Communist Party when she was but a little girl in anticipation of ensuring the education of his only child.

In medical school, Olga and the other women were treated with tolerance rather than acceptance. Olga's interest in surgery had been discouraged but her skill couldn't be denied. She pushed, insisted, studied, proved herself and passed all of her surgery examinations, examinations which, she understood, were much more rigorous in the West.

In spite of what she had heard of western physicians, Olga Yegeneva never thought of emigration or defection even had they been possible. Russia was her country. She had no desire to be anywhere else.

Even her initial assignment to a public ward dealing with daily complaints of workers at a radiator factory in Minsk had not initially discouraged her. It was the fact that she was given no surgery, no promotion, no change and no recognition of commendation that prompted her to consider a private career. The main problems with a private medical career were the costs, the pressure and suspicion of the medical committees, and the fact that she would have to deal with those who could afford her services. Olga hated dealing with money, hated bartering for the health of her patients.

According to Article 42 of the Soviet Constitution, which was quoted to her throughout her medical education and in every medical meeting she had attended, citizens of the USSR have the right to "free, qualified medical care provided by State health institutions." However, the quality of that care was in the hands of health care professionals, nurses, therapists, doctors, who were overworked, underpaid and often underqualified. Many of the professionals were outstanding, but many lived a life of professional lethargy.

"What shall I do?" Sarah Rostnikov said.

"Go home, pack lightly and wait for my call. I'll try to clear an operating room for tomorrow morning," the young woman said still holding Sarah's hands.

"Yes," Sarah said looking around at a woman in a wheelchair being pushed by a serious young man.

There was nothing more to say. The younger woman hugged Sarah Rostnikov, and looked into her eyes with a confidence Sarah was sure she did not completely feel.

When Porfiry Petrovich Rostnikov returned to the People's Hall of Justice and Solidarity, he found three people in the assembly room, Emil Karpo, Dimitri Galich and a man kneeling in front of an open brown sack made of animal skins. Karpo and Galich had removed their coats and hats and stood still heavily clad in sweaters. Rostnikov noticed a most uncharacteristic piece of jewelry, a beaded necklace of amber, around the neck of Emil Karpo. He had no time or opportunity to comment on it at the moment. Rostnikov's attention was drawn to the man on his knees, who looked up for only an instant when Rostnikov stepped in. The kneeling man still wore his fur parka and hood.

"This is Kurmu," Karpo announced to Rostnikov who opened his coat and plunged his hat into his pocket.

Galich said something guttural to the kneeling man who grunted but did not look up again.

"I told him you were a representative of the Soviet government with full powers," Galich said.

"He does not appear to have been impressed," said Rostnikov moving across the wooden floor toward the kneeling Evenk. "What is he doing?"

"He says he is preparing," Galich said. "He hasn't told me what he is preparing for."

"We'll try not to keep him from his task too long," said Rostnikov. "Emil, I think it would be best if we had no visitors for a while. That includes Dr. Samsonov and Comrade Sokolov."

"You will have no visitors," Karpo said. "Shall I wait outside?"

"No," said Rostnikov, yawning. "We will go into Mirasnikov's room. My questions are few and simple."

Karpo nodded. Galich walked to the Evenk still kneeling on the floor.

"Will you ask him to join us?" Rostnikov said and Galich spoke the language again.

Kurmu, apparently satisfied that he had what he needed, closed the sack, nodded and got to his feet. For the first time, he looked at Rostnikov and a smile passed between the two men. Rostnikov liked the man instantly.

Inside the nearby room, Liana Mirasnikov lay on a bed in the corner sleeping soundly. Sergei Mirasnikov lay, eyes closed, breathing heavily, his face drenched with perspiration.

Rostnikov watched Kurmu whose eyes fell on the dying old man. Before Rostnikov could ask his next question, Kurmu moved to Mirasnikov's bedside, sat cross-legged on the floor and opened his sack. He paused to loosen his parka and toss the cape back to reveal his peppery-white hair that hung straight and shining to his neck.

"You want me to ask him what he is doing?" Galich offered.

"No," said Rostnikov watching the old man reach into the sack and pull out a small wooden bowl, a gnarled root and a brownish thick block.

"The root is ginseng," Galich said. "The other piece is panti, raindeer horn."

Rostnikov watched with interest as the shaman pulled out a large knife with a white bone handle and began to shave pieces of ginseng and panti into the bowl.

"That's wild ginseng," Galich said. "During the Mongol occupation, a natural root like that would have been worth thousands of rubles. Even now that root looks like it would bring a good price in Manchuria."

The shaman was rocking back and forth slowly as he reached into the sack again and pulled out a smaller jar that looked as if it had once held jelly. He opened the jar, took out a pinch of yellow, flaky material and mixed it into the bowl. While he mixed, he said something.

"He wants water," Galich said. "Water from snow. I'll get it."

"How are you feeling?" Rostnikov asked as Galich moved toward the door.

Galich's eyes were heavy, tired and dark, and the man's white stubble of overnight beard reminded Rostnikov that the bulky former priest was not a young man, that he had been drunk when he went out into the Siberian winter, that he probably hadn't had much sleep in at least thirty hours.

"Fascinated," Galich said with a grin and he left the room.

The closing of the door woke Mirasnikov who looked up at the wooden ceiling, blinked, wiped his face with his already soaked blanket and looked toward the sound of something moving at his side. When he saw Kurmu, Sergei Mirasnikov tried to scream. It was only the ghost of a scream because he had no strength, but his mouth and face made clear his intent.

Kurmu paid no attention and continued rocking and mixing his brew. Rostnikov moved to the bed quickly and looked down at Mirasnikov.

"Be calm, Sergei," Rostnikov said. "The shaman is trying to help you."

"He means to kill me," Mirasnikov said. "He means to kill me for telling you that he sent the demon."

Then Mirasnikov said something which Rostnikov didn't understand and the old shaman answered with what sounded like a single abrupt word that brought a dry laugh of disbelief from Mirasnikov.

"I say he means to kill me," Mirasnikov said, getting up on his elbows. The sheet fell back showing the old man's thin, white bandaged chest.

Galich returned with a pot of snow which he brought to the shaman who accepted it with firm, brown hands. Mirasnikov lay back moaning and his wife paused in her snoring for a beat during which Rostnikov feared she would wake up.

"Can he talk while he does that?" Rostnikov asked.

Galich asked the shaman something and the old man nodded.

"Ask him if he saw Commissar Rutkin killed last week," Rostnikov said.

"Time doesn't mean anything to an Evenk," Galich said. "I can ask him if he saw someone killed in town but to an Evenk a week ago is like ten years ago. It is the past and the past merges. They think the past, present and future are the same."

"Ask him, please."

While the shaman mixed and then poured his concoction into a tea cup, he answered questions Rostnikov put to him through the former priest and discovered that the shaman had, indeed, seen the death of the man from the West, that he had been murdered, that the murder had been done by a man and not a demon.

"Ask him if he knows who the man is, could recognize the man," Rostnikov said.

The shaman was holding Mirasnikov's head up and urging him with grunts and words to finish the cool brew. Mirasnikov, eyes closed, was drinking and gurgling. He opened his eyes, saw Kurmu and closed them again. A thin line of the dark liquid trickled out of the corner of the old man's mouth but most of it got into him.

Galich spoke and Kurmu, concentrating on his task, getting the last of the cup's contents into the old man, said something quickly, and nodded at Galich.

"My God. He says the man who killed the other man is the one with the black bag, the white shaman," said Galich.

The shaman slowly let Mirasnikov's head back onto the thin, moist pillow. Then he stood, looked around the room, saw what he wanted and moved to a shelf against the wall where he pulled down a jar half full of dry beans. He emptied the beans into a bowl on a lower shelf and brought the jar back to the bed where he began to fill it with the remainder of the liquid he had mixed. While he poured, he spoke.

"He says the old woman should give him a full glass every water cycle which means, approximately, three times a day till it runs out."

"Tell him we will see that it is done," said Rostnikov.

The information was passed on and the shaman reached into his sack and pulled out a small, very old red leather bag. With his ginseng root in one hand and the sack in the other, he walked up to Rostnikov.

"What does he want?" Rostnikov asked looking into the shaman's unemotional face.

"I don't know," said Galich.

Kurmu held up the ginseng root and nodded at it. Rostnikov reached up to touch the root and found it warm, almost hot to the touch.

"Hot?" asked Galich. "Not surprising. Hot ginseng roots have been reported for hundreds of years. Some think it's some kind of natural radiation."

Kurmu spoke softly, directly to Rostnikov, holding out the small sack.

"I didn't hear him," said Galich.

Rostnikov took the small sack, which contained something light that shifted like sand or grain, and pointed at Mirasnikov. The shaman shook his head no and pointed west. West, Rostnikov thought, toward Moscow. Porfiry Petrovich placed the red sack in his pocket and nodded his thanks. Kurmu smiled and looked over at Galich.

"So, Inspector," Galich said with a massive yawn. "Your killer appears to be Dr. Samsonov, which should come as no great surprise. You've seen his temper. Rutkin must have come to a conclusion about his daughter's death that he found unacceptable. Who knows? Samsonov certainly was bitter at Rutkin, at the entire Soviet system. In that, as you know, I am not in great disagreement."

Kurmu turned, moved back to the bed and began packing.

"And my only witness is an Evenk shaman who speaks no English and doesn't believe in time. What does he think about space?"

Galich smiled and said something to the shaman who was bending over his sack, back turned when he answered.

"It and time are endless, he said," Galich translated. "And there is no point to thinking about it."

The Evenk finished his packing, threw the sack over his shoulder and turned to Rostnikov, pointing at the jar of dark liquid. Rostnikov nodded and Kurmu headed for the door.

"I hope you're not going to stop him from going," said Galich. "I certainly won't help you."

"I'm not going to stop him," said Rostnikov. "I'm going to have Emil Karpo arrest Dr. Samsonov. I'm going to tell Mirasnikov's wife to give him the brew in that jar, and I am going to get a few hours of sleep."

At the door, Kurmu said something and left without looking back.

"What did he say?" asked Rostnikov.

"He said that we should tell Mirasnikov when he awakens that there is no longer a need for demons, that there has been no need for demons since the whites came across the mountains and brought their own demons within their soul."

"Religious philosophy," said Rostnikov.

"Of the highest order," Galich agreed. "Of the very highest order."

When Porfiry Petrovich Rostnikov awakened from his few hours of sleep, he was very hungry. He had slept on top of his bedding in his clothes, taking off only his boots. And now he awoke ravenous. He massaged his left leg into feeling, considered taking one of the pills Samsonov had given him and made his way past Karpo and Sokolov's doors and down the stairs.

It was in the dining room, after he had gathered a bowl of cold soup and a half loaf of bread, that he found himself facing a quivering Sokolov who stood in his unbuttoned coat, his fingers clutching his hat. Sokolov's mustache was drooping slightly on the left side.

"Comrade Inspector," Sokolov said, his voice barely under control. "I have been informed that you have asked the commander of the weather station to allow no phone calls out of Tumsk."

"You understand correctly, Comrade," Rostnikov said putting his food on the table and sitting. "Join me."

"I'm not hungry," Sokolov said. "I am angry. You have arrested Samsonov, announced a public hearing this afternoon, informed me of nothing. Your actions are not those of an investigator but of a jailer."

"A situation not unheard of in Siberia," said Rostnikov dipping a torn piece of bread into the soup and taking a bite. The potato soup wasn't as good as Sarah's but it was better than just acceptable. The thought of Sarah brought him abruptly back to the small dining room in Siberia.

"You do not have the authority," Sokolov hissed. "I wish to call the Procurator General's Office in Moscow. I doubt that the government wishes to arrest Samsonov. I was under the impression that we were sent here to placate Samsonov, reassure him about his daughter's death before he left the country. You are threatening . . . threatening glasnost."

Rostnikov paused in his eating to look at Sokolov.

"Glasnost?"

"Better relations with the West," Sokolov said impatiently.

"A very good idea," Rostnikov agreed, putting the bread aside to get at the soup with the spoon he had brought from the kitchen.

"Then let Samsonov go," shouted Sokolov.

"Even if he killed Commissar Rutkin?" asked Rostnikov.

"You have no evidence that he committed the murder."

"A man named Kurmu is reported to have seen the murder and identified Samsonov as the killer," said Rostnikov.

"Kurmu. Kurmu. Galich says he's a native medicine man," Sokolov shouted, pounding on the table. The bowl in front of Rostnikov rattled and a bit of soup splattered onto the table.

"Comrade, I was under the impression that you were here to observe my investigative methods, not to ruin my humble meals. And I thought I was here to find the person responsible for the death of Commissar Rutkin."

"It is not that simple," Sokolov said, making a fist for another assault on the table.

His hand started down but was intercepted by Rostnikov's fingers which caught the fist as if it were a falling ball. Rostnikov had a spoon full of soup in his other hand. Not a drop spilled.

"No," said Rostnikov releasing Sokolov's fist. The investigator for the Deputy Procurator staggered back holding his aching fist.

"You attacked me," he shouted. "As God is my witness, you attacked me,"

"God is not considered a very reliable witness in a Soviet court, Comrade," said Rostnikov. "And I'm rather surprised that you, an officer of the court, would invoke the name of God. I might have to put that in my reports, though it is an invocation I encounter with surprising frequency."

With a combination of fear and face-saving front, Sokolov pulled himself together as he backed toward the door and muttered that things would be quite different when they returned to Moscow.

"Let us hope so, Comrade," Rostnikov said, finishing the last of his soup by scouring his bowl with the remainder of the loaf of bread. "I'll be over at the People's Hall for the hearing as soon as I get my boots on."

The killer paced back and forth across the room glancing from time to time at the window, trying to decide what to do. The hearing had been a disaster.

The People's Hall had been set up by Famfanoff complete with chairs and a table behind which Rostnikov could sit like a judge conducting the hearing. To the left of Rostnikov the man from the Procurator's Office, Sokolov, sat brooding throughout, his hands folded except when his left hand moved up to stroke his mustache. To the right of Rostnikov sat the ghost, the pale unblinking creature with the straight back who examined everyone, seemed to register everything. They looked like a comic version of the jury in the Pudovkin movie, Mother.

Famfanoff had served as warder of the court, hovering warningly over those who might shout, giving stern looks to those who coughed or whispered.

Samsonov had protested, shouted, screamed, claimed that he was being railroaded to cover his daughter's murder. He had shouted that the western press would be incensed, that glasnost would be dealt a serious blow.

Rostnikov had sat there without the slightest hint of emotion, his eyes focused far off, though they occasionally scanned the faces in the hall and fell frequently on that of the killer.

When Rostnikov repeated that the primary evidence against Samsonov was the testimony of an Evenk shaman, Samsonov had to be restrained by Famfanoff who, surprisingly, found enough strength within his abused body to control the furious doctor.

The entire hearing had lasted no more than an hour. There were no speeches and very little evidence.

The hearing had closed with Rostnikov's announcement that he was holding Samsonov for removal to Moscow for possible prosecution, that Famfanoff would keep the doctor under guard in a spare room volunteered by the commanding officer of the weather station. He further announced that no phone calls would be permitted for the next twenty-four hours.

The situation was a disaster. The killer's mission would be ruined if Samsonov were brought to Moscow, tried and convicted or even refused the right to leave the country. The ultimate irony of the situation was that the killer knew Samsonov to be completely innocent of the crime.

Something had to be done and very quickly.

TWELVE

BY THE END OF THE DAY PORFIRY PETROVICH ROSTNIKOV would hear two confessions, watch someone die, conspire against the government and nearly meet his death for the second time since his arrival in Tumsk. At the moment, however, he stood over the bed of Sergei Mirasnikov who drank the dark liquid Kurmu had left for him.

Liana Mirasnikov held the cup in her shaking hands and the old man, who was already looking much better, complained constantly that she was trying to drown him.

"How are you feeling, Sergei Mirasnikov?" Rostnikov asked.

"Hungry," gurgled the old man. "Hungry and stiff in the arms."

"Good signs," said Rostnikov.

"Good signs," repeated Mirasnikov sarcastically after another sip from the cup. "If I died you would feel guilty the rest of your life because I got shot instead of you. So you feel relieved because it looks like I might live. Am I right or am I right?"

"You are right," Rostnikov agreed.

That seemed to satisfy the old man who finished off the last of the drink and gave his wife an angry look as if the taste of the liquid were her doing. She shuffled away silently and Mirasnikov, who was no longer perspiring, looked up at the Inspector.

"I'm sick but I'm not deaf," the old man said. "I heard things that happened. I remember seeing Kurmu."

"He didn't command a demon to kill Commissar Rutkin," said Rostnikov.

"I know that," said Mirasnikov irritably, and then he called to his wife, "Food. I need food, old creature." And then to Rostnikov again. "And I know that Dr. Samsonov didn't kill him either. How do you like that?"

"I am aware of that too," said Rostnikov.

"You are . . . All right. All right. Lean over here and I'll tell you something you didn't know. I'll tell you who your killer of Commissars is," croaked Mirasnikov.

And so Inspector Rostnikov leaned forward, smelling the bitter warmth of the brew on Mirasnikov's breath, and listened to the old man's whispered information, information which did not surprise him in the least.

"So, what are you going to do?" Mirasnikov said when Rostnikov stood up. "Go. Go make your arrest. End this. Get out of my town. It may be a frozen hell here in the long winter and a bog of insects in the short summer, but no one tries to kill me when you are not around."

"We will be going soon," said Rostnikov. "Very soon."

The old woman came hurrying back with two plates of food, small pieces of meat cooked soft, potatoes, beans.

"Well," grumbled Mirasnikov. "You might as well eat something before you go. Sit down."

So Rostnikov sat and thought and ate. Immediately after the hearing, Ludmilla Samsonov, her eyes moist, holding back tears, had asked Rostnikov to please let her speak to him as soon as possible. Rostnikov had nodded his agreement uncomfortably knowing that the woman would probably plead for her husband.

The first confession of the day came when Rostnikov returned to his room an hour later after hearing Mirasnikov's accusation. Karpo was busily preparing reports in his room. Sokolov was off somewhere, probably, thought Rostnikov, trying to talk the naval officer into letting him use the phone.

Rostnikov wasn't surprised to find General Krasnikov standing at the window in full uniform, his coat neatly draped over his left arm.

"I've come to confess," the general said.

"Please take a seat, General," said Rostnikov who had left his coat, hat and boots inside the downstairs door. "I'll sit on the bed."

"I'd prefer to stand," Krasnikov said.

"So I have noticed," said Rostnikov sitting on the bed, feeling the twinge in his leg.

"I killed Commissar Rutkin," the general said.

"Yes."

"That is all. I killed him."

"Would you tell me why you killed him?" Rostnikov asked reaching for the pillow and hugging it to his chest.

"He was an insulting, meddling bureaucrat," said Krasnikov.

"If we were to murder all the insulting, meddling bureaucrats in the Soviet Union, we would have to issue new incentives for women to replenish the depleted population," Rostnikov said.

"I killed him. This is a confession and I demand that you release Samsonov immediately," the general insisted.

"Would you still confess if I said that we would confiscate all of your property immediately and search through Samsonov's possessions the moment you were arrested?" asked Rostnikov. "Would you like some tea? Everyone in Tumsk has been filling me with tea for two days. I'd like the opportunity to return the favor."

"No tea," said Krasnikov. "Arrest me. I demand, as a Soviet citizen, to be arrested for murder."

"You did not kill Commissar Rutkin," said Rostnikov, leaning over to scratch the bottoms of his feet through his thick wool socks. "I know who killed Rutkin."

Krasnikov paused, looked at the man on the bed scratching his feet and said, "I don't believe you."

Rostnikov shrugged.

"Nonetheless, I know, and the killer is not you."

He stopped scratching, started rubbing, and went on.

"I admire your patriotism and conviction, however, Comrade General. To be willing to spend one's life in prison or possibly to be executed for one's beliefs is indeed admirable. One might guess, and mind you I am not doing so, that somewhere among the belongings of Lev or Ludmilla Samsonov is a manuscript, and that a military man who wrote that manuscript would do a great deal to get that manuscript carried to the West among the belongings of a notable dissident whose belongings are not likely to be searched carefully by a government wishing to let him leave as a sign of conciliation with the West. Does that not make sense?"

"Perhaps," agreed Krasnikov.

"In what form would you guess this manuscript would appear? I know it does not exist but if it did?" Rostnikov asked leaning back against the wall.

Krasnikov looked out the window, bit his lower lip and paced the small room once, from the window to the wall and back to the window where he turned to Rostnikov who looked up at him attentively.

"You have a son in Afghanistan?"

"I have."

"And you agree that the military operation there is improper for political, economic and humanitarian reasons?"

"I do," said Rostnikov.

"I am concerned primarily with the military error," Krasnikov said, looking as if he were about to resume pacing. "If I were to try to have a manuscript-length work carried out of the country by a departing citizen, a citizen who might not want to carry such a document, I would go through the painstaking process of actually printing one copy of the manuscript in book form and have it covered, bound and titled, probably giving it a title which an airport inspector or even a KGB officer would be likely to ignore."

"Printing one copy of a book would be most difficult, require special printing equipment, binding equipment," said Rostnikov, his eyes never leaving his visitor.

"It would probably take a year to do using crude equipment," said Krasnikov.

"And the idea would be that instead of hiding the manuscript, one disguises it and puts it in plain sight," said Rostnikov. "Clever."

"A traditional military tactic," said Krasnikov. "But it does no good if the carrier does not cross the border."

"Perhaps a miracle will happen very soon," said Rostnikov. "Perhaps a new killer will be identified and Samsonov will be freed and urged to leave the country within the week as he was scheduled to do."

Krasnikov examined the bland, flat face of the policeman and smiled.

"Then we will have to hope for a miracle," he said.

"Do you still wish to be arrested for murder?" Rostnikov asked.

"There seems to be a slight hint of sun this morning," said Krasnikov. "Perhaps I won't confess today."

The general moved to the bed and held out his right hand. Rostnikov took it.

"Forgive me for not rising, Comrade."

"Forgive me for underestimating you," Krasnikov responded.

"Always a tactical error," said Rostnikov.

"Just as Tolstoy said in his Military Strategy Through History," said Krasnikov releasing the inspector's hand.

"A book I should read some day," said Rostnikov with a sigh.

"Let's hope you do," said the General moving to the door. "Good morning."

It was Rostnikov's belief that only one copy existed of Tolstoy's Military Strategy Through History and that copy had most definitely not been written by Tolstoy. The general left the room, closing the door gently behind him. Rostnikov listened to his booted feet move across the short hall and down the stairs. When the outside door closed, Rostnikov sensed rather than heard another movement in the house and then a light knock at the door.

"Come in, Emil," he called, and Karpo entered the room dressed in black trousers, shoes, and a turtleneck sweater, and carrying a thick sheaf of papers. Rostnikov looked up. "Emil, how is it that you never need a shave?"

"I shave frequently, Comrade Inspector," Karpo said.

"Good," sighed Rostnikov, putting his feet on the floor and reaching out to accept Karpo's report. "I feared that you had found a way to remove facial hair but once in your life so you would not have to spend time removing it, time you could be spending at work."

"I don't think such a procedure exists, Comrade," Karpo said seriously. "If it were not time-consuming and were reversible, it might well be a consideration. A very rough estimate would yield thousands, perhaps tens of thousands of man-hours saved in the ranks of the MVD alone."

"You are not joking, are you, Emil? You haven't finally made a joke?" Rostnikov said with a smile as he stood.

"Not at all," said Karpo, puzzled. "The seemingly absurd can turn out to be the eminently practical. Invention often requires the creativity of the absurd."

"Do you ever practice such creativity, Emil?" Rostnikov stretched and looked toward the window.

"Never, Comrade. I am not creative. I leave that to others, like you, who have a genetic or developed ability in that direction," said Karpo.

"Perhaps you do have a sense of humor, Emil. The problem is that you don't know it. I think it is time to go catch a killer. Shall we go over it again?"

"If you think it is necessary," Karpo said.

"No," said Rostnikov. "Let's go."

Three minutes later Porfiry Petrovich Rostnikov left the house on the square, looked over at the People's Hall of Justice and Solidarity, glanced at the statue of Ermak and started once again up the snowy slope following in the plowed furrow that was almost refilled with drifting snow. He trudged past the weather station and moved to the door of the house of Dimitri Galich.

"It will grow back quickly," Olga Yegeneva assured her patient.

Sarah Rostnikov looked up at the young surgeon and nodded to show that she understood but she found it difficult to answer, to speak, for fear of crying. Porfiry Petrovich had always admired her dark hair with reddish highlights, her naturally curling hair which had recently developed strands of gray.

"Most of it is still there and it can be brushed over," said Olga Yegeneva. "I told them to be most careful of that."

Sarah looked around the small room. The room was white, rather old-fashioned. There were two other beds in the room, one empty, the other containing a sleeping woman with white hair who snored very gently. The winter sun beamed through the window making it difficult for Sarah to accept that the moment was nearing.

"It shouldn't be sunny," she finally said with a sad smile.

"It should," said the doctor, her eyes widening behind her round glasses. "Are you ready?"

Sarah shrugged.

"Why not?"

Olga Yegeneva took her patient's right hand in both of hers and told her again what the procedure would be, that she would be given an injection which would make her drowsy, that she would be wheeled to the operating room where the anesthetic would be administered. She would fall asleep and wake up back in this room, very sleepy, very tired.

"I will wake up back in this room," Sarah repeated.

"You will."

The doctor released her patient's hand and made way for a man in white who stepped to the side of Sarah's bed with a hypodermic needle in his hand.

Sarah tried to remember the faces of her husband and son. It was suddenly very important to do so and she wanted to stop this man, call the doctor back, explain that she needed just a few minutes more, a few minutes to remember the faces. It was like catching one's breath. The doctor would understand. She would have to, but Sarah felt the sting of the needle. The panic left her and Sarah gave in, closed her eyes and smiled because the image of Porfiry Petrovich and Josef came to her clearly and both were smiling.

Galich, smiling, clad in overalls and a flannel shirt under a thick green pullover sweater and carrying a brush in his thick right hand, ushered Rostnikov into the house.

"You want to use the weights?" he asked, moving across the room to his worktable cluttered with bits of metal, cloth and glass.

The mesh armor had been joined by a thick rusted metal spear which Galich held up for Rostnikov to see.

"No weights today," said Rostnikov. "I have much to do."

"Found this spear only this morning," said Galich. "Piece of good luck. It's definitely Mongol and seems to have belonged to a tribal leader. See the markings? Right here?" He brushed at them gently and went on. "Heavy, iron, but remarkably balanced."

He hefted the weapon in his right hand, showing how well it was balanced.

"An interesting weapon," Rostnikov agreed. "But there are more ancient ones which are also interesting."

Rostnikov had moved to a chair near the window about fifteen feet from the table.

"Such as?" Galich asked, working at the spear which he returned gently to the table.

"Ice. A simple, frozen spear of ice," said Rostnikov. "Such as the one that killed Commissar Rutkin."

"True," agreed Galich. "A spear of ice would be unreliable. It might break. But as you said at the hearing, Samsonov must have been insane with hatred."

"You are most happy this morning," said Rostnikov. "May I ask why?"

"Why?" Galich repeated and reached up to brush back his wild white hair. "Perhaps the spear, perhaps something internal."

"Does it have something to do with Samsonov being held for murder, something to do with the fact that if he is convicted he will not leave the country?"

Galich stopped brushing, the dim gray light of the arctic circle outlining him from the window at his back.

"I don't understand," the former priest said, the joy leaving his voice.

"Samsonov did not kill Commissar Rutkin," said Rostnikov. "You killed Commissar Rutkin."

"I . . ." Galich said with a deep laugh, pointing to his chest. "What makes you think . . ."

"When Kurmu pointed at you at Mirasnikov's bedside, he identified you as the man he saw kill Commissar Rutkin. I'm afraid your translation was a bit inaccurate, but Mirasnikov was awake and understands the language."

"He is wrong," Galich said, his voice now calm and even. "Mirasnikov is a sick man, an old man. He did not hear correctly."

"I wasn't sure why you did it though I had some idea. It wasn't till I came through that door a few minutes ago and saw your happiness that I was sure," Rostnikov said.

"This is ridiculous," Galich said, his jaw going tight, his hands playing with the brush, putting the brush aside, playing with the spear.

"No, it is not ridiculous," said Rostnikov. "The life of the spirit, of the past you came to pursue, to end your life with, was pushed to the side for the life of the body you thought you had put to sleep. Am I right, Dimitri? I've looked at your file, your history. You lost your church. You didn't quit. You lost your church because you were accused of seduction of four of the women in your church."

"I assume you are not asking me but informing me," Galich said evenly.

"I'm discussing it with you. I'm trying to decide what to do about this situation," said Rostnikov.

"I did not try to shoot you, Porfiry Petrovich," Galich said solemnly.

"Moments after the shooting, I had Emil Karpo get up to the slope. The person who shot at me made a series of trails in the snow, footprints leading to this house, Samsonov's house and General Krasnikov's house."

"I did not shoot at you. I did not shoot Mirasnikov," Galich said.

"I believe you, Dimitri, but I am sure you know who did the shooting. And I am sure you will not tell me. Didn't the attempt to shoot me, didn't the shooting of the old man make you suspicious?"

Galich said nothing, simply played with the spear before him.

"You killed Rutkin," Rostnikov said.

"Your evidence is absurd," said Galich softly.

"We are not talking about evidence here," Rostnikov said sitting forward in the chair. "We are talking about what you and I know."

"Why did you arrest Samsonov? Why did you have that hearing?" Galich asked softly.

"To deceive a killer," said Rostnikov. "A killer, I think, who has a great interest in seeing to it that Samsonov be allowed to leave the country."

"I don't know what you're talking about. You just said I don't want Samsonov to leave," Galich shouted.

"You don't, but I wasn't talking about you. Now, let's talk about you. I understand a man can live in those forests indefinitely if he knows what he is doing. I believe you told me that."

"One cedar tree can provide enough for a man for a year," agreed Galich with a laugh. "I might be able to live in the taiga, but I'm too old and too civilized. Is that the option you give me, Rostnikov? I run and disappear and you announce that I'm the killer. The case is closed and everyone is happy. Everyone but me."

"It is a chance to live, Dimitri," Rostnikov said softly.

"I've just come back to life," Galich said. "I'm too old for any more changes, too old to live alone in the cold and darkness."

"Dimitri . . ." Rostnikov began, but before he could say more the Mongol spear was in Galich's right hand, had been hefted over his shoulder and was whistling across the room. Rostnikov rolled to his right breaking the arm of the chair. He didn't see the spear break through the back of the chair but he did hear it clatter to the floor and across the room.

Rostnikov tried to rise quickly, but his leg would not cooperate and he had to roll back toward the chair anticipating another attack by an ancient weapon.

"Dimitri Galich," he called. "Stop."

"I lied," shouted Galich, picking up a rusted knife with a curved blade. "I did try to shoot you. I did shoot Mirasnikov."

Rostnikov was on his knees now as the former priest came around the table knife in hand. Using the remaining good arm of the almost destroyed chair, Porfiry Petrovich managed to stand ready to meet the attack of the advancing man. Galich stepped into the light of the window and Rostnikov could see his red eyes filled with tears. He could also see the ancient flecks of rust on the blade of the knife. He wanted to say something to stop the man, but Rostnikov had seen that look in the eyes of the desperate before. Words would not stop him.

The bullet cracked through the window as Galich raised the knife to strike and Rostnikov prepared to counter the attack. The bullet hit Galich under the arm and spun him around. A rush of frigid air burst through the broken window sending papers on the worktable flying like thick snow. Beyond the window, Emil Karpo stood, arms straight, pistol aimed. Galich recovered a bit and turned for another lunge at Rostnikov. The second shot hit him in the chest and the third and final shot entered his eye at approximately the same angle Galich had stabbed Commissar Rutkin with an icicle.

As he fell the former priest let out a massive groan that sounded almost like relief. When he hit the floor, there was little doubt. Dimitri Galich was dead.

"Come around," Rostnikov called to Karpo who put his pistol away and made his way around the house as Rostnikov bent awkwardly over Dimitri Galich's body to confirm what he already knew. The wind through the broken window suddenly grew angry, tumbled a book to the floor and whistled shrilly into one of the ancient bottles on the table.

Karpo came through the door and moved to Rostnikov's side.

"Did you hear?" Rostnikov asked.

"A little," said Karpo.

"He confessed to the murder of Commissar Rutkin," said Rostnikov, pulling his coat around him as the house quickly grew cold. "The reasons he gave were muddled. He was a bit mad, I'm afraid. I imagine living in Tumsk for several years does not minimize that risk."

"Shall I tell Famfanoff to free Dr. Samsonov?" Karpo said.

"Not yet. I have something to do first. Attend to Dimitri Galich's body and then prepare your report."

"Yes, Inspector. Shall I inform Procurator Sokolov and arrange for air transport back to Moscow?"

"The sooner the better," said Rostnikov, finally looking away from the body. "You know, Emil, I liked the man."

"So I observed," said Karpo.

And with that Rostnikov headed for the door and a meeting he dreaded.

A slight snow was falling as he stepped out of Galich's house, the first since Rostnikov had come to Tumsk. He wondered if a plane could get through the snow, if there was a chance that he would be snowed in and unable to get back to Moscow, back to Sarah.

He stepped off the small porch and walked the thirty or so yards to the Samsonovs'. He didn't have to knock. Ludmilla Samsonov opened the door as he neared the house.

She was dressed in white, her dark hair tied back, tiny earrings of white stone dangling from her ears. He lips were pink and shiny and her eyes full of fear.

"I've been hoping you would come," she said fighting back a chill.

"Let's get inside," he said stepping in, close to her, smelling her, unsure of whether the smell was natural or perfume. She closed the door and smiled at him uncertainly.

"I have some coffee ready," she said nervously. "Would you like some?"

"No, thank you," Rostnikov said removing his hat and unbuttoning his coat.

"Please have a seat," she said pointing at the sofa. "Let me take your coat."

Rostnikov removed his coat, handed it to the woman who brushed his hand as she took it. He sat on the sofa and made room for her when she returned from placing his coat on a table near the window. She straightened her dress, revealing her slim legs, and looked into his face.

"I heard something," she said. "It sounded like shots."

"Yes," he said. "I heard it. I'll have Inspector Karpo investigate. You said at the hearing that you wished to speak to me?"

"Yes," she said leaning close, almost weeping. "My husband did not kill Commissar Rutkin. He didn't shoot Mirasnikov. He has been distraught by Karla's death. That is true. But he is a gentle man. You must be mistaken. I would do anything for him, anything."

"Anything?" Rostnikov asked.

"Yes," she said, holding back the tears.

"Even be very friendly to a rather homely old police inspector?"

"I believe in my husband's innocence," she said, her eyes pleading, her mouth quivering.

Her teeth, Rostnikov noted, were remarkably white and even. Rostnikov took her hand. She didn't resist.

"And how would I do this? How could I let him go after the hearing?"

"You could find new evidence, evidence that the murderer is the Evenk, the one Mirasnikov saw, the one you talked to," she said eagerly. "The Evenk accused Lev to protect himself. Someone, Dimitri Galich, could tell the Evenk, tell him to go away. I'll ask Galich right away."

She looked into his eyes, squeezed his hand.

"Dimitri Galich is dead," he said.

Ludmilla Samsonov withdrew her hands and shuddered.

"Dead?"

"Inspector Karpo had to shoot him no more than ten minutes ago," said Rostnikov. "He attempted to kill me after confessing that he killed Commissar Rutkin."

"That's . . . " she began. "Then my husband will be freed."

She breathed deeply and sat back. Rostnikov said nothing.

"I'm sorry," she went on. "I was so . . . My husband has been through so much."

"And it is very important that he be allowed to move to the West," said Rostnikov.

"It is what he wants, what he needs," she said. "He cannot contain, cannot control his beliefs. If he remains in the Soviet Union, he will get into more trouble. If he remains in Siberia unable to practice, to do his research, he will probably die."

"And that is important to you?" asked Rostnikov.

She nodded.

"Would you like to know why Dimitri Galich killed Commissar Rutkin?" Rostnikov asked.

"Yes," she said quietly.

"Dimitri Galich, before he died, said that he killed Commissar Rutkin because you asked him to," Rostnikov said.

"I . . . he said I . . . " she said, her eyes opening, her hand moving to her breast.

"Absurd on the surface," said Rostnikov, "but he claimed with the sincerity of a dying man that you and he were lovers and that you said Rutkin was going to reveal your affair as part of the hearing into the death of Karla Samsonov."

"That's ridiculous," she said clasping her hands together.

"I don't know," Rostnikov shrugged. "He swore and it sounded sincere to me and my assistant."

"Why would I have an affair with Dimitri Galich?" she cried. "He was old enough to be my father, maybe my grandfather."

"As am I," Rostnikov said, "and moments ago you appeared to be quite willing to be intimate with me to get me to free your husband. It is possible you knew about Galich's vulnerability, his background and weakness for women and you engaged him with the very thought of getting him to kill Commissar Rutkin. My experience seems to confirm Galich's dying claim."

"How would I know anything of Dimitri Galich's background, this weakness?" she said, standing and fishing into the pocket of her dress for a package of cigarettes. She pulled one out, put it to her lips and lit it, her eyes fixed on the placid face of the seated policeman.

"My guess," said Rostnikov, "is that you are a KGB agent, that you have spent some time in getting close to Samsonov, marrying him. My guess is that Samsonov is finding it relatively easy to leave the country not only as a gesture of glasnost, but because he will be in a position within the western scientific community to learn a great deal about people, developments which would be of great value to the KGB. My guess is that when Karla died, and according to the reports her death was quite natural, quite accidental, and Samsonov went wild in grief and anger, it threatened your plan. Rutkin was sent because he was incompetent. It was assumed he would be fed information, probably most of it true, to prove that Karla died by accident. With your help, it was hoped that Samsonov would believe it, would leave the country, would not go mad. You had invested too much in him to lose Samsonov. Am I close?"

"Go on," she said taking a deep lungful of smoke.

"Somehow Rutkin stumbled on information about you. Perhaps it wasn't much but it was enough to make it possible for your husband to become suspicious. And Commissar Rutkin was ambitious. Maybe you tried to persuade him to be quiet about what he knew. Maybe you even told him you were KGB. Maybe he didn't believe you."

"It was ridiculous," Ludmilla Samsonov said with a deep sigh, reaching over to put out her unfinished cigarette. "I told him to call Moscow. The phones were out. All that night. He didn't believe me. The fool didn't believe me and he was going to ruin everything. He confronted Galich, told him, told me that he would suggest at the hearing that we might have killed Karla. He came up with some nonsense about Karla having seen Galich and me together."

"And so," said Rostnikov still sitting. "You convinced Galich that he had to kill Rutkin and because he loved you he did it. He was quite happy this morning. He thought your husband was going to prison, that you wouldn't be leaving Tumsk. I'm sorry to say that you handled the situation rather badly. Your attempt to shoot me is a rather good example of what can only be described as incompetence."

"And what do you plan to do with this information?" she said.

Rostnikov pulled himself up from the sofa with a deep breath and looked at her. She was quite beautiful, even more beautiful now that the guise of vulnerability had been dropped.

"Nothing," said Rostnikov. "There is nothing I can do to you without destroying myself." He looked around the room. "I will announce that Galich was the murderer. I will order the release of your husband. And in a few days the two of you will leave the country with your belongings, your books, your memories."

"That is a wise decision, Comrade," she said, "and I will tell my superiors of your cooperation."

She held out her right hand but Rostnikov did not take it.

"I do not give my hand to murderers," said Rostnikov.

She dropped her hand to her side and shrugged.

"As long as you keep your word to them, Comrade," she said.

Rostnikov nodded, accepted his coat and hat and refused to let her help him put them on. He had learned patience. General Krasnikov's book would leave the country. He assumed the general had some contact in the West who could pick it up, probably get it published, maybe save some lives including Josef's.

As for Ludmilla Samsonov, Rostnikov was well aware of the need for such operations, the need for intelligence information. But he could not forgive her the seduction and death of Dimitri Galich. Perhaps some day a western embassy would receive a call or a note suggesting that Ludmilla Samsonov was not what she appeared to be. Perhaps and perhaps not.

Rostnikov moved quickly away from the house and down the slope. The snow had stopped. He was on his way home to Sarah.

THIRTEEN

Before he left Tumsk, Rostnikov ordered the release of Lev Samsonov with apologies and announced that for reasons unknown Dimitri Galich had murdered Commissar Rutkin and, when he was discovered, was killed trying to resist arrest.

Samsonov was presented with the information confirming his daughter's death by natural causes and his wife, in an emotional plea to her husband, helped to convince him that Rostnikov's report on Karla's death was accurate, that there was no conspiracy.

Procurator Sokolov brooded but could find no fault with Rostnikov's actions other than his lack of consideration for the representative of the Procurator General's Office.

Rostnikov said goodbye to the officer at the weather station and the Mirasnikov's. He promised Famfanoff that he would write the letter for him supporting his request for transfer.

The last resident of Tumsk Rostnikov saw before he left the town was General Krasnikov who was standing at his window when Rostnikov, Karpo and Sokolov came out of the house with their bags and headed for the waiting helicopter.

Krasnikov was holding a glass in his hand which he raised in a toast to the departing policeman. Rostnikov nodded almost imperceptibly in response.

Sokolov said nothing during the flight. When they arrived at Igarka and boarded the airplane to which they transferred, Rostnikov turned to Karpo seated at his side. Sokolov had chosen to sit five rows from them.

"You did well, Emil Karpo," he said.

"Thank you, Comrade Inspector." Rostnikov still had the feeling that Karpo had something to say or deal with, but he knew the man well enough to know that he could not ask again. So Porfiry Petrovich Rostnikov wrote his letter requesting Famfanoff's transfer and went to sleep.

When they arrived at the airport in Moscow, the temperature was a balmy 15 degrees above zero. Rostnikov didn't bother to put on his hat as they walked the hundred or so yards from the plane to the terminal. Sokolov left them without a word and Rostnikov hurried to a phone to call Sarah. There was no answer. It was almost five in the morning. He found the phone number of the woman doctor in his notebook and called it.

"Dr. Yegeneva?" he asked.

"Yes," she said sleepily. "Who . . . ?"

"Rostnikov. My wife?"

"She's at the clinic. I'm . . . We operated this morning. She insisted, wanted it over when you got back. She's fine, just fine. The tumor was benign though there were a few minor complications. She will be fine."

She gave him the address of the clinic and he hurried away from the phone.

"We should talk, Porfiry Petrovich," Karpo said. He had stood waiting a discreet dozen paces away.

"It will have to wait till tomorrow, Emil," he said. "Sarah had the operation this morning. I must go to the clinic."

"Is she . . . ?"

"She is doing well. I talked to the doctor. Go home. Get some sleep. Tomorrow we begin a new day. Tomorrow we talk."

Rostnikov resisted the urge to hug the brooding pale detective, to reassure him. It was not the thing to do with Emil Karpo.

Rostnikov hurried to the front of the airport, found a taxi, threw his suitcase on the back seat and got in. He gave the driver the destination and sat back feeling, even smelling the familiar presence of Moscow. He did not want to think.

The cab passed within two blocks of where Sasha Tkach, who had been up for two hours, sat hugging himself to keep warm in a ten-year-old Ahiguli while Zelach sat snoring next to him. They were waiting for a truck belonging to the son of one Viktor Ivanov, a truck they thought might be carrying the stolen goods stolen from the Volovkatin apartment.

While Rostnikov sat in the back of his cab, Emil Karpo placed a call from the airport to the KGB. He gave his name and rank to the man with the deep voice who answered and told the man that Major Zhenya should be informed that he was on his way. There was a one-minute pause at the KGB and the man came back on to tell Karpo that the major would be waiting for him when he arrived.

Thirty minutes later Emil Karpo, his small dark travel case in hand, once again accompanied by two burly men in dark suits, entered the office of Major Zhenya who sat with his hands folded on his desk like a disapproving school master about to discipline a troublesome student. No emotion showed on the major's face, but Karpo noted that a few strands of hair were out of place on the right side of the major's head, just above the ear.

"Your report," the major said.

"My written report will be in your hands in two hours," said Karpo. "If you like, I will write it here."

"Summarize," the major said. "I'm not concerned about the investigation itself. I've already been informed about that. The conclusion is satisfactory. I wish a listing of each error, indiscretion, delay in Inspector Rostnikov's investigation. We will be getting a similar report from Inspector Sokolov of the Procurator's Office."

"I will prepare the report on my observations of the investigation. I will also give you copies of my part of the investigation. I have that in my travel case. I will, however, inform Inspector Rostnikov, who is my immediate superior, that I have done so. This is in accordance with MVD and CID regulations."

"I am well aware of the regulations," Major Zhenya said. "In matters of national security, such regulations are superceded."

"National security?" asked Karpo. "I am unable to see how Inspector Rostnikov's conducting of this investigation deals with or compromises national security."

"It is not your place to understand," said Zhenya. "If you do not comply you will be obstructing an investigation dealing with national security, an investigation which involves much more that you do not see or understand."

"Then I will have to accept the consequences of my decision. It is also my responsibility to inform you that my report on Inspector Rostnikov will contain no citations of impropriety. His methods are not always within the borders of suggested investigatory procedure, but they are well within his rights of discretion and his results are undeniable."

Zhenya shook his head at the pale, unblinking man before him. He reached up to straighten the out-of-place hairs above his ear and reclasped his hands tightly. Karpo could see the major's knuckles go white with anger.

"Have you considered your future, Comrade?" Zhenya asked.

"I have no ambition, Comrade," said Karpo. "I wish only to do my work for the State. I do that work diligently and, I believe, efficiently according to regulations. To deprive the State of my training in retaliation for my unwillingness to perjure myself in a report would itself be disservice to the State. I am not, however, foolish enough to think that it is beyond your power to do so."

"Get out," Major Zhenya said evenly.

Karpo stood, said nothing more and left the room, closing the door gently behind him. One of the two men who stood outside the door of the major's office handed him his travel bag. Karpo noted that the zipper was almost fully closed, not one-half of an inch open as he had left it. They had been through his things, probably already copied his duplicate notes on the investigation of Commissar Rutkin. There was nothing in the notes to compromise Porfiry Petrovich Rostnikov.

When he reached the front of the building, Karpo checked his watch and found that it was slightly after five. It was also Wednesday. He had slept on the plane to Moscow and needed no further rest. He would work on several outstanding cases if there were no new assignments on his desk. And that evening he would be seeing Mathilde Verson. Emil Karpo came very close to smiling.

Porfiry Petrovich Rostnikov, meanwhile, had arrived at the clinic where a very thin woman in white, with a voice that reminded him of a teacher he had had as a child, met him as he came through the door. She had been called by Dr. Yegeneva and had been waiting for him.

The woman chattered away in a whisper and led him down a short corridor and pointed at a door on the left.

"First bed. Doctor said no more than half an hour." She went on smiling at him.

Rostnikov nodded, went through the door and put his case on the floor. The early morning sun was bursting brightly through the window on the three beds in the room. An older woman in the bed furthest to his right snored gently. In the center bed, a woman, possibly a child, lay curled up on her side, her dark hair covering her face. She breathed gently, asleep. In the third bed, the bed nearest him, lay his wife, her head covered by a turban of white bandages. Sarah lay on her back, eyes closed, hands at her sides.

Porfiry Petrovich moved to the side of the bed and reached down to hold Sarah's hand. It was cool. She stirred, her mouth moving, and her eyes fluttered open and found him. She smiled weakly and squeezed his hand and then closed her eyes.

Rostnikov touched the bridge of his nose, glanced at the other two sleeping women and reached into his pocket. He leaned over, kissed his wife gently on the forehead and under her pillow placed a very small, slightly odd smelling red sack of reindeer hide.

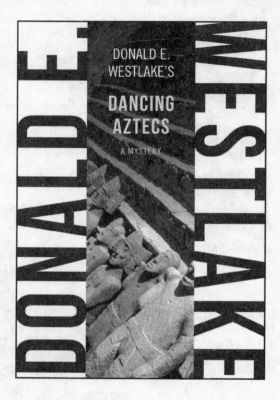

Washington on Foot

23 Walking Tours of Washington, D.C., Old Town Alexandria, Virginia,
and Historic Annapolis, Maryland

Second Edition

Edited by **Allan A. Hodges**, AICP, and **Carol A. Hodges**

For

National Capital Area Chapter,
American Planning Association

Smithsonian Institution Press
Washington, D.C. 1980

This book has been prepared under the editorial and design supervision of the following persons:

Allan A. Hodges, AICP, Editor
Carol A. Hodges, Author, "Restaurants and Carryouts"
Leo Schmittel, Production-Design Manager
Fred Greenberg, Graphics Designer

Library of Congress Cataloging in Publication Data
Main entry under title:

Washington on foot.

1. Washington, D.C.—Description—1951—Tours. 2. Old Town,
Alexandria, Va. 3. Alexandria, Va.—Description—Tours.
4. Annapolis—Description—Tours.
I. Hodges, Allan A. II. Hodges, Carol A.
III. American Planning Association.
National Capital Area Chapter.
F192.3.W335   1980   917.53′044   80-15844
ISBN O-87474-527-6

First edition: 1976; revised 1977;
Second edition: 1980; second printing, 1981; third printing, 1981

CONTENTS

---

  * Interesting
 * Recommended
*** Highly Recommended

18. Washington Cathedral***/Cleveland Park**

17. Woodley Park/National Zoo**

15. Kalorama***

19. Howard University*

20. Le Droit Park**

12. 16th Street, N.W./Meridian Hill***

13. Dupont Circle***

14. Shaw School Urban Renewal Area/Logan Circle**

16. Georgetown***

11. Midtown**

7. Foggy Bottom**

8. White House***

10. Downtown**

9. Federal Triangle**

3. The Mall-East***

4. The Mall-West***

5. Independence Ave.*/L'Enfant Plaza**

6. Southwest**

22. Old Town Alexandria, Virginia***

MAP OF TOUR AREAS

1. Capitol Hill***

2. Capitol Hill-East**

23. Historic Annapolis, Maryland***

21. Old Anacostia**

ABOUT WASHINGTON ON FOOT

Any city is best seen on foot. The unexpected shop window, a tile mosaic on a garden wall, a framed view of a church dome from a narrow street. These are the visual rewards for the pedestrian.

"Washington on Foot" will help you find these rewards in the nation's capital. Twenty-one informative walking tours will guide you through the preserved colonial and federal quarters, the booming commercial districts, the revitalized inner city neighborhoods, the new communities and employment areas created by urban renewal as well as to the familiar national memorials, public buildings and museums. Two more tours will escort you across the Potomac River to Alexandria, Virginia's restored Old Town and to the banks of the Chesapeake Bay to the historic capital city of Annapolis, Maryland.

"Washington on Foot" was first published in 1976 as a Bicentennial project by the National Capital Area Chapter of the American Institute of Planners (now called American Planning Association). The guide was specifically prepared for use by the 3000 urban and regional planners and planning officials who attended the National Planning Conference in Washington, D. C. in March 1976. Now it is in general use by thousands more visitors and residents interested in a close-up look at these three cities.

It was written by over two dozen volunteers who are urban planners, architectural historians and other professional city watchers. The tours have been updated and revised in each subsequent edition. City buffs interested in the city planning, historical and architectural features of Washington, Alexandria and Annapolis will find "Washington on Foot" an indispensible guide.

About the Editors

Allan A. Hodges, editor of "Washington on Foot", has practiced and taught professional city planning in Washington, D. C., Boston and Columbus, Ohio. He has written for professional journals, and was editor of "Practicing Planner" magazine published by the American Institute of Planners (AIP) and later by the American Planning Association (APA). In 1976-77 he was President of the National Capital Area Chapter of AIP. He is a member of the American Institute of Certified Planners and APA.

Carol A. Hodges wrote the restaurant descriptions included at the end of "Washington on Foot". She is a freelance writer and food consultant, has a master's degree in urban planning, and has studied cooking professionally in France and the U. S. Ms. Hodges also assisted in the editing and prepared many of the sketches in the guide book.

Leo Schmittel, Chief of the Graphics Branch, National
Capital Planning Commission, Washington, D. C., was the
Production-Design Editor of "Washington on Foot". He
has studied art at the D'Ambrosio Ecclesiastical Art Studio,
New York City, New York and the Corcoran Museum,
Washington, D. C.

Fred Greenberg, Graphic Designer for "Washington on
Foot", prepared all the freehand maps and most of the
sketches. He is Art Director of the American Institute
of Architects Research Corporation. Mr. Greenberg has
a degree in community planning and was an urban designer
with planning agencies in the Washington, D. C. area.
Presently, he is illustrating a book on Washington's architecture.

About the American Planning Association

The American Planning Association (APA) is a 1978
consolidation of two well established professional and
educational organizations; the American Institute of Planners (founded in 1917) and the American Society of
Planning Officials (founded in 1934). The purpose of
APA is to advance the art and science of planning for
the comprehensive development of communities, cities,
regions, states and the nation. Within APA is the autonomous organization of professional urban planners, the
American Institute of Certified Planners. APA's 20,000
members include professional urban and regional planners,
planning officials and citizens interested in planning. It
is headquartered in Washington, D. C. with a branch office
in Chicago, Illinois.

The National Capital Area Chapter of APA serves about
700 members in the District of Columbia as well as
Montgomery and Prince Georges Counties in Maryland.

For more information about the American Planning
Association please write APA, 1776 Massachusetts Avenue,
N.W., Washington, D. C. 20036 or call 202-872-0611.

Note

The opinions expressed by the authors of the guide are
their own. They provide the reader with a refreshing
subjective and objective look at Washington, D. C. through
the eyes of over two dozen professional observers. Their
observations add to the interest and value of the Guide.
However, their opinions should not necessarily be interpreted as official positions of the National Capital Area
Chapter, APA, or the Smithsonian Institution Press.

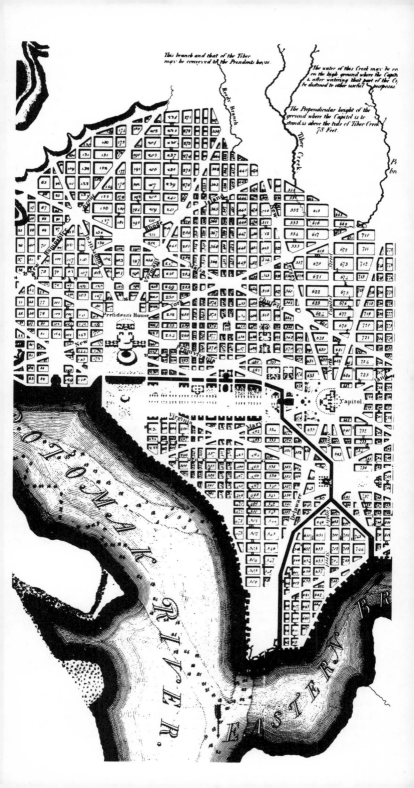

This branch and that of the Tiber
may be conveyed to the Presidents house.

The water of this Creek may be co
on the high ground where the Capit
& after watering that part of the C
be destined to other useful purposes

The Perpendicular height of the
ground where the Capitol is to
stand, is above the tide of Tiber Creek
78 Feet.

Presidents House

Capitol

POTOMAK RIVER

EASTERN BR

Washington, D.C.

Washington, D.C. is the largest city in the United States that has been virtually fully developed under the initial direction of an 18th century master plan. The plan for the new national capital of the United States was prepared in 1791 by Pierre Charles L'Enfant, a French engineer, at the request of George Washington* L'Enfant's plan called for the new city to be built along the banks of the Potomac River. The Plan primarily consisted of a physical framework for the majestic siting of the major government buildings and a pattern for the street system resembling Beaux Arts Paris. The boundaries of L'Enfant's capital city plan were the Potomac River to the west, the Anacostia River to the east and south, and a ridge rimming the city to the north. This central area, today, contains Washington's most historic places.

The original city of Washington, as envisioned by L'Enfant is now completely developed. Here one can appreciate the historic heart of the capital. Washington ranks as one of the most beautiful cities in the United States because of these early city planning efforts which resulted in broad avenues, great landscapes, beautiful national memorials and impressive public buildings. The observer can experience the basic structure of L'Enfant's city plan which is a grid pattern of streets threaded by diagonal avenues radiating from the White House and the U.S. Capitol Building. The intersections of the diagonal avenues with the grid system were reserved as circles and squares for public open space and have resulted in an abundance of beautiful and heavily used urban parks.

Areas located beyond the original historic limits developed in the late 19th and early 20th centuries. These neighborhoods include most of the District of Columbia that visitors usually never see. This area is home for most of the 700,000 residents of the city. A tour of these neighborhoods reveals humble early 20th century Victorian wood houses in old Anacostia sharply contrasting with the elegant Beaux Arts mansions of Kalorama. Historic Georgetown, which predates Washington by some 50 years, is located here. This other Washington includes the first

---

*Subsequent to the original city plan by L'Enfant, four significant plans have had major impact on the physical development of Washington, D.C. They were:

1. Downing's Plan for the Pleasure Gardens of the Smithsonian on the Mall (1851);

2. McMillan's Plan published as a reaffirmation that future development should proceed along the lines originally planned by L'Enfant (1902);

3. Comprehensive Plan published by the National Capital Park and Planning Commission (1950); and

4. Proposed Comprehensive Plan for the National Capital published by the National Capital Planning Commission (1967).

Since July, 1974, by Congressional Statute, comprehensive planning for the city of Washington became a joint responsibility between the Federal and District of Columbia governments. The National Capital Planning Commission, a Federal agency, is responsible for the Federal element of the plan. The Municipal Planning Office, under the Mayor of the District of Columbia, is responsible for the "District" or local elements of the plan.

Both agencies are charged with the responsibility by the District of Columbia Self Government and Governmental Reorganization Act of 1973 (Home Rule Act) to jointly publish a Comprehensive Plan which will reflect both Federal and District program and policy interests.

apartment districts of the city, such as Woodley Park, as
well as the long established single family residential neighborhoods, such as Le Droit Park. This other Washington
is, in fact, the real Washington to many of its residents.

Alexandria and Annapolis

*No visit to the Nation's Capital is complete without seeing the
nearby historic port cities of Old Town Alexandria, Virginia and
historic Annapolis, Maryland. Both of these colonial port cities,
along with Georgetown, are older than the District of Columbia.
Today, both cities are bustling with active commercial life while
retaining much of their 17th and 18th century residential
atmosphere.*

How to use the Guide

*Each of the 23 tours in "Washington on Foot" indicates
the name of the area and the major sights. The time to
walk the route (not including visits to museums and historic houses) and walking distance are listed to help you
plan your visit. Public transit information to the starting
point of each tour is provided by the Washington Metropolitan Area Transit Authority. Each tour includes a
map with the tour route and sights indicated by numbers.
The sketches highlight the tours' major sights. The stars
indicate a ranking for each tour and major sight, as
follows:*

*** Highly Recommended
 ** Recommended
  * Interesting

Selecting a Restaurant

*Some of the city's interesting restaurants and good carry-
outs are listed by tour area at the end of "Washington on
Foot". The list is provided as a service to visitors to aid
finding a place to eat while en-route. The suggestions
are those of the author. They should not be construed
to mean endorsement of those establishments by the
American Planning Association or the Smithsonian Institution.*

Taking the Right Bus

*The Washington Metropolitan Area Transit Authority Information
Service will provide you with information to take the right Metrobus to any destination. Call 637-2437.*

*When you board your bus, you will be expected to pay
the exact fare in tickets, tokens, or cash. Metrobus operators do not carry change, nor do they sell tickets or
tokens. Call 637-1328 to find out where you can purchase
commuter tickets or tokens. The basic fare within the
District of Columbia is 40 cents in non-rush hours, 50
cents in rush hours (defined as 6-9:30 AM and 3-6:30 PM
weekday non-holidays based on the time of boarding.)
The fare increases as you cross the various zones into the
suburbs.*

9

If you need to change from one bus to another in order to reach your destination, you will be given a transfer at no additional cost. You must ask your bus operator for it when you pay your fare. Your transfer permits you to change to three more buses, if necessary. Transfers are valid for two hours and they cannot be used for a return trip or stopover, but only for on-going connections.

Route numbers and letters accompanying each tour map in the guide refer to bus services available weekdays. These routes pass the beginning point of each tour or near it. Ask your bus operator if his or her route intersects with the above routes. Also, don't forget to ask for a transfer. Note, special rush hour and weekend routings are not listed.

Using the METRO Subway

Washington's subway system, called METRO, began operation in March 1976 and has revolutionized travel patterns in the city ever since. It is a pleasant and quick way to travel to and from the tour areas in the guide, particularly those in central Washington.

Three METRO rail lines serve the Washington area. The Red Line provides service between Silver Spring, Maryland, and Dupont Circle, N.W. The Blue Line links National Airport and the Stadium-Armory stations. The Orange Line's terminals are at Ballston in Arlington, Virginia, and New Carrollton, Maryland. The Orange and Blue Lines share tracks between Rosslyn and Stadium-Armory. (See Map of METRO Subway inside back cover). In early 1980, METRO service covered 34 miles of track; eventually it will reach 100 miles serving the far out suburbs. Please check maps in each METRO station and car for new extensions.

The three lines intersect at the Metro Center station in downtown Washington facilitating transfers between the Red Line (upper level) and the Blue and Orange Lines (lower level).

On each tour map in the guide, the name of each METRO station and the color of each line serving the beginning point of each walking tour is indicated. The "M" symbol on each tour map locates a station entrance.

METRO operates as follows:

Weekdays: 6:00 a.m. - 12:00 Midnight
Saturdays: 8:00 a.m. - 12:00 Midnight
Sundays: 10:00 a.m. - 6:00 p.m.

There is a two-tiered fare system on METRO based on time and distance travelled. As of March 1980, the fares during rush hours (6:00 - 9:30 a.m. and 3:00 - 6:30 p.m.

on weekday non-holidays) ranged between 45 cents to
$1.60. The fare during non-rush hours (all other times
on weekday non-holidays as well as Saturday, Sunday and
holidays) was a flat 50 cents between any two stations.
All METRO fares are paid using a farecard for sale in
machines in all stations; purchasable in any value between
25 cents and $20 and good until used. Exit gates auto-
matically deduct the fare and print the remaining value
on the fare card. Check the fare charts in each station
for the exact fare between stations you will use.

Transfers from METRO to bus with a discount up to
100% can be made only if the transfer ticket is acquired
from any other station than the one at which the
METRO-to-bus connection is to be made. Get your free
transfer ticket from the dispensing machine within the
paid area at the station where you enter the METRO
rail system. Remember that free transfers obtained aboard
a bus cannot be used on the METRO rail system.

Bon voyage!

On Not Getting Lost on Washington Streets

The four quadrants (N.W., S.W.,N.E.,S.E.,) must be explained.
The north/south axis through the Capitol, represented by South
and North Capitol Streets, divides the eastern and western sections
of the city. The east/west axis through the Capitol Building, represented by East Capitol Street and the center line of the Mall,
separates the northern and southern sections. All streets within
each of the four quadrants bears the quadrant designation and
the quadrant describes its direction on the compass from the
Capitol Building.

Street names are generally in alphabetical or numerical order.
State names are only used for the diagonal avenues. Measuring
from the center line of the Mall in either direction, north or south,
the parallel streets are designated by letters, (A, B, C, etc.). Two
syllable words follow the letters from A to about W (such as
Adams, Bryant, Channing, etc.). Three syllable words continue
the pattern from A to about W. (Albemarle, Brandywine,
Chesapeake, etc.). Beyond that point, along the longest north/south
line approximating 16th Street, N.W., the streets are named after
trees and flowers, also in alphabetical order (Aspen, Butternut,
Cedar, etc.). In a western and eastern direction from the line
representing North and South Capitol Streets, the streets are
numbered first, second, third, to somewhere in the fifties.

Address numbering is also orderly. Between First Street and Second
Street (on lettered and named streets) the house numbers are
between 100 and 199; between 40th Street and 41st Street the
house numbers are between 4000 and 4099. An easy rule in
locating an address on numbered streets is that 10 blocks from
A Street would be K Street; hence, 1000 15th Street would be
the intersection of K and 15th Street.

1 ***CAPITOL HILL (U. S. Capitol, Union Station-National Visitors Center, Library of Congress, Supreme Court, active residential restoration area)

By Clifford W. Moy

Mr. Moy is an environmental and energy planner, National Capital Planning Commission, Washington, D.C. He gratefully acknowledges the assistance of Mrs. Robert Kreinheder, Capitol Hill Restoration Society, Ms. Suzanne Ganschinietz, Ms. Charity Davidson and the staff of the Washington International Center.

DISTANCE: 2¾ Miles　　　*TIME: 1¼ Hours*

BUS: 16, 38, 40, 42, 80, 96, 98, D2, D4, D8, X2, X4, X6, & X8.

METRO: Union Station - Visitors Center (Red)

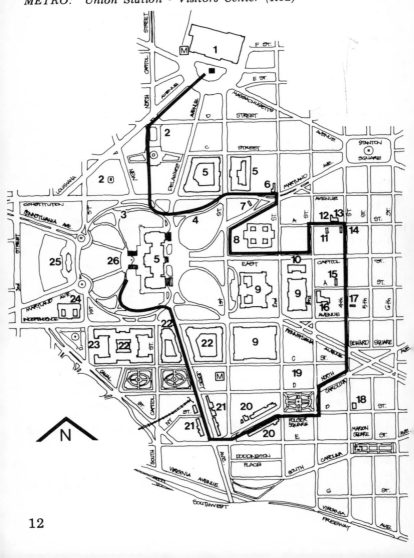

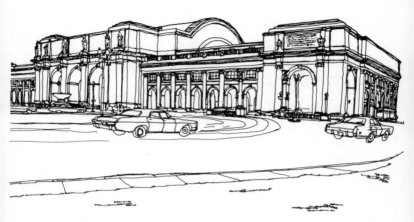

1. The tour begins at UNION STATION*** and the PLAZA***
Architect Daniel H. Burnham responded to one of the wishes of
the McMillan Commission to consolidate all the train stations
into one terminal by designing Union Station. Since 1908 it has
also served as a monumental gateway into Washington, D.C. To
further this end, the 40 million dollar NATIONAL VISITORS
CENTER* housed within the railroad terminal was dedicated
July 4, 1976. Preparation activities for the Bicentennial in conjunction with the National Park Service also included restoration
of the west wing, construction of a Metro subway station, a food
facility, book shop, tourist information booths and exhibits.
Also planned is the provision for a multitransportation facility to
include a four-level parking garage. Union Station Plaza received
a cosmetic touch. The re-design of the Plaza stresses "people-
orientation" (and hence, a rechannelization of the traffic) and
the placement of flag poles along the perimeter of the Plaza. An
impressive structure in the center of the Plaza is the COLUMBUS
MEMORIAL FOUNTAIN*, sculptured by Lorado Taft in 1912.

2. This Capitol Hill PARK** is one of the favorites of many
congressional aides, particularly the younger set, who brown-
bag their lunches. If you are here in the spring and summer
you can see why. The many red oak trees and a sparkling water
fountain are invitations one cannot refuse. To the west juts a
concrete MONOLITH HONORING SENATOR ROBERT A.
TAFT* of Ohio. Designed by Douglass W. Orr in 1959, this
memorial houses twenty-seven bells in its tower which chime
every quarter-hour.

3. The CAPITOL GROTTO** (1879) is one of the best features
of the Capitol grounds. Originally designed by landscape architect
Frederick Law Olmsted to tap fresh spring water, the Grotto now
provides municipal water.

4. Designed by Frederick Law Olmstead, landscape architect for the Capitol grounds, the TROLLEY WAITING STATION* (circa 1876) was served by horse-drawn trolley cars. The other waiting station is located on the southeast corner of the U. S. Capitol.

5. Asked by President George Washington to design a plan for the Federal city, Major Pierre Charles L'Enfant, French engineer and architect, elected to position the U. S. CAPITOL*** in one of two significant locations in the future city (the other for the President's House). Jenkins Hill, in Major L'Enfant's estimate, was like ". . . a pedestal waiting for a monument . . ." The cornerstone for the U. S. Capitol was laid in 1793 by President Washington. After being partly destroyed by the British troops in 1814, the U. S. Capitol was restored with the addition of a wooden dome. In 1857, two wings were added (the Senate and the House of Representatives) and an iron dome replaced the wooden one in 1865. Atop the dome stands the Statue of Freedom. According to Thomas Crawford, the sculptor, the statue represents "Armed Liberty"; her right hand grasping a sheathed sword while the other holds the wreath and shield. The CAPITOL GUIDED TOUR** is recommended. If possible, take the Capitol subway to either the Richard B. Russell Senate Office Building (Senate Caucus Room; scene of the famous Watergate hearings) or the Everett M. Dirksen Senate Office Building. (The subway schedule is generally 9:00 a.m. - 5:00 p.m. weekdays and 9:00 a.m. - 12:00 p.m. weekends; will stay open until 9:30 p.m. if Congress has a night session).

6. The SEWALL-BELMONT HOUSE*, 144 Constitution Avenue, survived demolition by a special Act of Congress and was subsequently entered into the National Register of Historic Places. Otherwise, the parcel would have given way to complete a Senate parking lot which now abuts the Sewall-Belmont House. Robert Sewall, from an illustrious Maryland family, in 1800 built this three-story townhouse which was characteristic of the federal period in style. His Capitol Hill home was leased to Albert Gallatin, Secretary of the Treasury (1801-1813). In 1929, the National Women's Party purchased the house from Senator Porter Dale. Reportedly, some of the unusual furnishings include desks once owned by Henry Clay and Susan B. Anthony. Visiting hours: 10:00 a.m. - 2:00 p.m. weekdays; 12:00 noon - 4:00 p.m. weekends and holidays.

7. The MOUNTJOY BAYLY HOUSE (known also as the Chaplain's Memorial Building) at 122 Maryland Avenue is also representative of the Federal period and listed in the National Register of Historic Places. Mountjoy Bayly was a former Sergeant-at-arms and doorkeeper of the Senate. Hiram Johnson, a progressive U. S. Senator from 1917 until his death in 1945 and vice presidential candidate to Theodore Roosevelt on the Bull Moose ticket, purchased the property in 1929 and resided there from 1930 to 1945. Since 1947, the House has been owned by the Headquarters for the General Commission on Chaplain and Armed Forces Personnel.

8. Built entirely of marble, the SUPREME COURT BUILDING*** was completed in 1935. A spacious 100-foot-wide oval plaza precedes the main steps of the building. On the east front of the building are a group of marble figures representing Confucius, Solon and Moses (sculpted by Herman A. MacNeil).

9. Created by an Act of Congress in 1800, the LIBRARY OF CONGRESS*** housed its materials in the Capitol for seventy-five years. In 1896, the Army Corps of Engineers constructed the main building. It serves not only the members of Congress, but also the government agencies and the general public. Outstanding collections of rare Chinese, Russian and Japanese books are among its many treasures. A visit to the main reading room is a must. Directly behind the main building is the Library Annex. The JAMES MADISON MEMORIAL LIBRARY, another annex on Pennsylvania Avenue between 1st and 2nd Streets, was opened in 1980.

10. The FOLGER SHAKESPEARE LIBRARY** (1932; Paul Cret, architect) on 201 East Capitol Street is certainly a must for Shakespeare followers; especially the reproduction of an ELIZABETHAN THEATER** which is in active use all year.

11. The use of the side entrance on 311 A Street, N. E. is quite refreshing.

12. FREDERICK DOUGLASS' FIRST WASHINGTON, D. C. RESIDENCE was at 316 A Street, N. E. According to a Capitol Hill Restoration Society plaque, Douglass was the "precursor to the Civil Rights Movement . . . (and) . . . resided in this building from 1871-1877."

13. Opening in a residential area in 1964, the MUSEUM OF AFRICAN ART* (318 A Street, N. E.) was the first museum to house and thereby promote African heritage. (Hours: weekdays, 11:00 a.m. - 5:00 p.m. and weekends and holidays 12:00 p.m. - 5:00 p.m.)

14. The townhouse on the corner of 4th and A Streets, N. E., a converted store built around 1869, is enhanced by the use of landscaping. Compare this with the same style, but unrestored, townhouse at 1100 Independence Avenue, S. E.

15. The BRUMIDI HOUSE, 326 A Street, S. E., was built circa 1850. It is purportedly the home of Constantino Brumidi an Italian artist, who at the age of 60, in 11 months painted the Apotheosis of Washington over 4,664 square feet of the Capitol dome. He is also responsible for the Rotunda frescoes and other Capitol decorations.

16. ST. MARKS EPISCOPAL CHURCH (1888) located on 3rd and A Streets, S. E., is listed in the National Register of Historic Places. A frequent visitor was the late President Lyndon B. Johnson.

17. The townhouse at 120 4th Street, S. E. (built circa 1876) is typical of the 1870's with flat facade, elaborate cornice and lintels.

18. The EBENEZER UNITED METHODIST CHURCH on 4th and D Street, S. E., originally known as the Little Ebenezer Church, was constructed in 1838 and rebuilt in 1897. From March 1864 to May 1865, the church served as the first schoolhouse for blacks in Washington, D. C. The church is also the oldest black church on Capitol Hill.

19. This vacant square is the site of the old Providence Hospital. It has been acquired by the Architect of the Capitol, George White, as one of the "Capitol Grounds." Should this be used for additional congressional office space? If so, how does one properly design it to harmonize with the residential area?

20. This stretch of NORTH CAROLINA AVENUE, S. E. ** is a fine example of the L'Enfant Plan for the Federal City: the superimposition of bold, diagonal avenues over a standard grid pattern. The side streets, particularly E Street, have been the scene of many touch football games.

21. This stretch of NEW JERSEY AVENUE, S. E. ** frames a magnificent sight. The transition between residential and federal buildings, along with the view of the Capitol dome, is a startling sensation. Sen. Metcalf (Mont.), Rep. Sikes (Fla.), and several Congressional staffers who reside in this area have taken extreme steps to restore their homes, as have other New Jersey

Avenue residents. Unfortunately, Congress is suffering from growth pangs and wishes to expand its office space into the residential area. According to the Congressional Quarterly, in the five year period ending in 1960, the House staff increased by 525 staffers, with additional increases of 1,524 between 1960 and 1965, 1,462 between 1965 and 1970, and a whopping 2,817 in the five years ending in April,1975. When will it level off?

22. The HOUSE OFFICE BUILDINGS along Independence Avenue are, from west to east, the Sam Rayburn Building, the Nicholas Longworth Building and the Joseph Cannon Building. You may want to stop by and visit your Congressmen.

23. The BARTHOLDI FOUNTAIN* (between Canal and 1st Streets on Independence Avenue, S.W.) was designed by Frederic Auguste Bartholdi in 1876.

24. The BOTANIC GARDENS (Independence Avenue, Maryland Avenue, and 1st Streets, S. W.) was constructed during 1931-1933 and is worth a visit. (For more details See Tour No. 3,The Mall-East).

25. The GRANT MEMORIAL* (1922) is the largest and most expensive statuary grouping in Washington, D. C. The CAPITOL REFLECTING POOL, directly over an interstate highway beneath the Mall, was designed by Skidmore, Owings, and Merrill and completed in 1970.

26. The tour ends at the steps of the west side of the U. S. Capitol. The VIEW*** across the Mall to the Washington Monument is stupendous. The site of the U. S. Capitol is truly like " . . . a pedestal" from which to view L'Enfant's capital city before you.

17

2 **CAPITOL HILL-EAST (active residential restoration area)

By Clifford W. Moy

DISTANCE: 2¾ Miles *TIME: 1¼ Hours*

BUS: 40, 96, 98 on East Capitol Street; 92 and 94 on 8th Street, S.E.

METRO: Eastern Market (Blue & Orange)

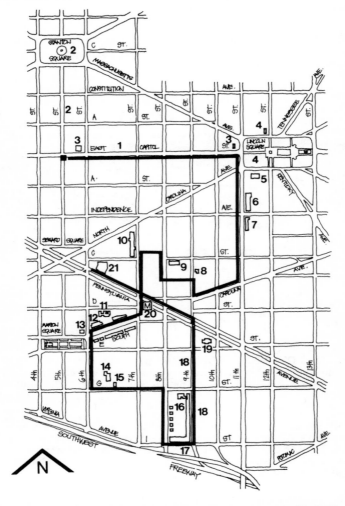

1. The tour begins at 5th and East Capitol Street. **EAST CAPITOL STREET****** is considered the "Grand Street" of the Capitol Hill Community. The smaller scale of development of adjacent streets north and south of East Capitol Street provides a sharp contrast. In 1974, Michael Franch prepared a report for

the Joint Committee on Landmarks for the National Capital in which he discovered that "the general area of elite residence (for the years 1888, 1889, 1909, and 1918) was a diamond-shaped district between the Capitol and Lincoln Park, Stanton Park and Seward Square." As was suspected, the heaviest concentration of elite residences was along East Capitol Street. The diversity of housing types and styles is tremendous, quite unlike the Georgetown Historic District. Everything from manor houses, Federal townhouses and brick rowhouses to the contemporary style of housing exists in the Capitol Hill Historic District. A Community group, the Capitol Hill Restoration Society, has done much to encourage and to maintain the "Capitol Hill" image.

2. The VIEW FROM EAST CAPITOL STREET looking north along 5th Street includes a statue of Major General Nathaniel Greene on horseback in Stanton Park. There are dashed green stripes which designate bike routes running the entire length of East Capitol Street. Under a proposed Bicycle Transportation Plan and Program for the District of Columbia (prepared by Barton-Aschman & Associates, March, 1975) bike routes are classified into three categories. In this instance, the 1.6 miles from the U. S. Capitol to RFK Stadium is categorized as a Class III bike route in which both the bicycles and the motor vehicles share the same street. In other words, the bicyclist is on his/her own.

3. The TOWNHOUSES AT 512 AND 514 EAST CAPITOL STREET* (1879) are representative of the 1870's with flat facades and elaborate cornices and lintels. Some of the town-houses, for instance 1014 EAST CAPITOL STREET* (1899), have balconies and/or roof decks on which to enjoy the hot summer evenings.

4. LINCOLN PARK* and the EMANCIPATION STATUE (completed and dedicated April, 1876; President Ulysses S. Grant and Frederick Douglass were present at the ceremony) were constructed in memory of Abraham Lincoln. The other statue (dedicated July, 1974) at the east end of the park is in honor of MARY McLEOD BETHUNE, black educator. The entire seven acre park was designed by Hilliard Robinson, landscape architect, in conjunction with the National Park Service. The homes surrounding Lincoln Park are predominately from the 1890-1895 period. Pay particular attention to the townhouse at 1126 EAST CAPITOL STREET* (1892) at the northwest corner of Lincoln Park.

5. The GRANITE ROWHOUSES with balconies (1111 to 1119 East Capitol Street) were built in 1892.

6. PHILADELPHIA ROW* (124 to 154 11th Street, S. E.) was built by James W. Gessford, circa 1866. He built 16 rowhouses in the style of Philadelphia to soothe his wife's homesickness for her native city.

7. This GROUP of 15 Rowhouses* (200 to 228 11th Street, S.E.) was built by Charles Gessford in 1891, some 25 years after Philadelphia Row had been built.

8. Constructed in 1967, the THOMAS SIMMONS HOUSE* (314 to 316 9th Street, S. E.) is a fine example of the contemporary homes which are in keeping with the physical scale of the Capitol Hill Historic District.

9. A set of CONTEMPORARY ROWHOUSES (801-819 C Street, S. E.) was constructed in the mid-1960's.

20

10.   A swing through an alley will lead directly to the EASTERN MARKET** on 7th and C Street, S. E. The open market activity will mesmerize even the most tough-skinned of individuals. Designed by Adolph Cluss and constructed in 1873, this market is the heart of the Capitol Hill community. Be sure to sample the spumoni at the bakery. More boutiques and shops line 7th Street into Pennsylvania Avenue, S. E.

11. The MAPLES HOUSE*, presently named the Friendship House Settlement, was built during the Federal period 1795-1796 by architect-builder William Lovering. Francis Scott Key was one of the many distinguished owners. The front entrance of the Maples House originally opened onto South Carolina Avenue but today it goes by the 619 D Street, S.E. address.

12.   This stretch of SOUTH CAROLINA AVENUE* provides a spacious yet charming residential atmosphere. The Capitol Hill community is a predominately stable, middle class group. This was the case even as far back as the 1880's and 1890's. Today, a large influx of professional people and those who work at the nearby Capitol provide an apparantly healthy white and black residential mix.

13.   The CARBERY HOUSE, 423 6th Street, S. E., was built circa 1813, and designated an historic site/structure by the Joint Committee on Landmarks. This stretch of 6th Street to G Streets, S. E. comprises some of the oldest houses on Capitol Hill, many built in 1840's-1850's.

14.   CHRIST CHURCH*, 620 G Street, S. E. (1806: Benjamin H. Latrobe, architect), was originally believed to be a Gothic Revival building. In the past, the Church had served many individuals from the Navy Yard and Marine Barracks and is believed to have been visited by Presidents James Madison, Thomas Jefferson, and James Monroe.

15.   The house at 636 G Street, S. E., the BIRTHPLACE OF JOHN PHILIP SOUSA, conductor, composer and bandmaster of the U. S. Marine Corps, was built in 1844.

16. The MARINE COMMANDANT'S HOUSE** and the MARINE BARRACKS** occupy the entire square. Constructed in 1801-1805 after George Hadfield's designs, the physical scale of the Commandant's house sets it apart from the nearby homes. The Marine Barracks surrounds an interior courtyard and parade ground which is extremely manicured in the traditional military style. The Marine Corps Band and the ceremonial units are housed at the Barracks. Along 8th Street, S. E., from Pennsylvania Avenue to the S. E. Freeway (also known as Barracks Row) signs of commercial rejuvenation have begun.

17. One of the textbook results of a major freeway splicing through a community is the creation of vacant lots. What should this space be used for?

18. Note the abrupt contrast of housing styles between the contemporary and the older housing in the 700 and 500 blocks of 9th Street, respectively.

19. Constructed in 1865-1866, the OLD NAVAL HOSPITAL (Temporary Home for Veterans of All Wars) on Pennsylvania Avenue, S. E., between 9th and 10th Streets, S. E., still retains what may be the original cast-iron fence.

20. The square at Pennsylvania Avenue, S.E., and 8th Street, S.E., is the site of the EASTERN MARKET METRO subway station. The design interface with the commercial strip along Pennsylvania Avenue could have been more interesting.

21. On the corner of Pennsylvania Avenue, S.E., and 6th Street, S.E., is the Eastern Liberty Federal Building (built entirely in conformance with existing zoning standards for Pennsylvania Avenue). Occupied in 1976, this building of 90,000 square feet of office space is heated by SOLAR PANELS.

23

3 ***THE MALL-EAST (Major axis of monumental core, Smithsonian museums, art galleries)

by Dr. Wilcomb Washburn and Kathryn Cousins, AICP

Dr. Washburn is Director of the Office of American Studies, Smithsonian Institution, Washington, D. C. Ms. Cousins is Regional Manager, North Atlantic States, Office of Coastal Zone Management, and a former member of the Board of Governors of the American Institute of Planners.

DISTANCE: 2 Miles   *TIME: 1 Hour*

BUS: On or near Independence Avenue; 16B, 16C, 52, V4, or V6.

METRO: Smithsonian (Blue & Orange)

1. The tour begins at the SMITHSONIAN BUILDING*** (James Renwick, 1855), Jefferson Drive between 9th and 11th Streets, S. W. The GREAT HALL*** contains an excellent exhibit on the history of the planning of Washington, D. C. It introduces planning concepts to laymen as well as orienting them to the city. Note particularly the innovative "perspective" models of the four major plans — L'Enfant (1791), Downing (1851), McMillan Commission (1902), and National Capital Planning Commission/Pennsylvania Avenue Development Corporation (1975). The original McMillan Commission Models are also on display.

24

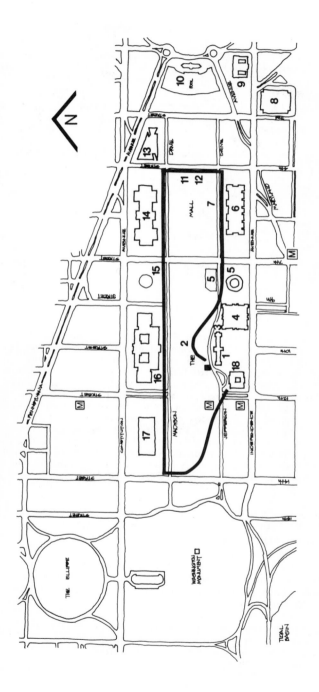

N

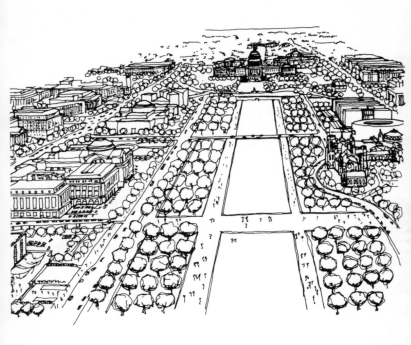

2. Walk outside to the center of the Mall***. You are midway on the major axis of the monumental core of this capital city as planned by Pierre Charles L'Enfant. (The Mall was extended beyond the Monument to the Lincoln Memorial in the twentieth century after the tidal flats and marshes west of the Monument were filled in.) The greensward was planned by L'Enfant as a broad avenue, 400 feet wide, lined with grand residences. The Mall now represents a sensitive compromise between the monumental plans of L'Enfant and the McMillan Commission (executed without the broad central avenue L'Enfant proposed) softened at the edges with humanistic touches suggestive of Downing (exemplified by the present-day ice rink, carousel, sports activities, Constitution Gardens and the Festival of American Folk Life).

3. Directly east of the Smithsonian Building is the URN COMMEMORATING ANDREW JACKSON DOWNING. His plan for the Mall created the first landscaped American public park. In the 1930's many of the mature trees planted in conformity with his plan were removed from the center of the Mall as it was "restored" to L'Enfant's more formal concept by the McMillan Commission. Behind the Smithsonian Building is a Victorian garden.

4. The ARTS AND INDUSTRIES BUILDING* (Cluss and Schulze after plans by Montgomery Meigs, 1881), Jefferson Drive and 9th Street, S.W. features exhibits from the 1876 Centennial Exhibition held in Philadelphia.

5.   Continue east along Jefferson Drive to 7th Street, S. W. to the JOSEPH H. HIRSHHORN MUSEUM AND SCULPTURE GARDEN** (Gordon Bunschaft: Skidmore, Owings and Merrill, 1974). Note the sunken outdoor sculpture garden north of Jefferson Drive as well as the controversial cylindrical building which contains paintings and sculptures from the late 1800's to the present.

6.   Continue on Jefferson Drive across 7th Street to the NATIONAL AIR AND SPACE MUSEUM***(Gyo Obata; Helmuth, Obata and Kassabaum, 1976). Since its official opening on July 4, 1976, it has become the most popular Smithsonian museum and the most heavily visited museum in the world.

7.   The elm trees on the north side of Jefferson Drive are part of a continuous band of trees on both sides of the Mall which serve to emphasize the east-west axis. Unfortunately, the barrenness of these deciduous trees in winter leaves the Mall dull and lifeless. Downing's argument that the Mall should be meaningful above all in the winter when Congress is in session has been lost to questionable arguments that evergreens are not tolerant of urban conditions, are messy or present security problems.

8.   At the corner of 4th and Jefferson Drive, S.W. one can view the HUBERT HUMPHREY FEDERAL OFFICE BUILDING* designed by Marcel Breuer who also designed the Housing and Urban Development Building (1968). The core of the building contains a 10-story exhaust shaft of the Interstate Highway 395 tunneled beneath the Mall.

9.   The BOTANIC GARDEN CONSERVATORY* to the north of the Health, Education and Welfare Building is better known in Washington for supplying an amazing number of free plants for congressional offices, than for some of its well-conceived attempts to experiment with innovative plantings around the Mall. Open to the public, the conservatory contains special exhibits, lush tropical plants, ferns, cacti and succulents.

10. Walk north on 4th Street. On your right is the GRANT MEMORIAL and REFLECTING POOL*, (See Tour 1, Capitol Hill) First Street between Maryland and Pennsylvania Avenues, N.W. The Reflecting Pool (Skidmore, Owings and Merrill, 1970) is directly over the Interstate Highway 395 that underlies the Mall.

11. Looking toward the Washington Monument, it is interesting to realize that this impressive open grassy version of L'Enfant's principal axial avenue was not completely implemented until 1975 when traffic and parking on the interior streets were replaced by the current pedestrian and bicycle paths. During the years between 1791 and 1972 the Mall has been the location of a cow pasture and slaughtering site, swamps, a civil war hospital, "murderers' row," a railroad station and numerous railroad tracks, a trash filled and stagnant canal and "temporary" government buildings that existed from World War I to 1972.

12. This is a good site to note how the position of the OLD SMITHSONIAN BUILDING offended the sense of order of the monumental minded park planners of the 1900's. The McMillan Plan assumed the building would be removed. But the "defects" of Renwick's Norman castle, as seen by the formal eye of 1900, have become assets in the eyes of those forced to live in marble halls. The warm rusty colors, which glow in the evening sun, serve as a standing rebuke to the colorless and lackluster whited sepulchres around it. Its irregular dimensions and projections — vertically and horizontally — give us welcome relief from the symmetrical boxes constantly spawning in the Federal City. Even its failure to stand back of the line prescribed by the turn-of-the-centruy planners warms our hidden rebelliousness.

13. This striking building is the widely acclaimed EAST BUILDING OF THE NATIONAL GALLERY OF ART** (I.M. Pei), which opened in 1978.

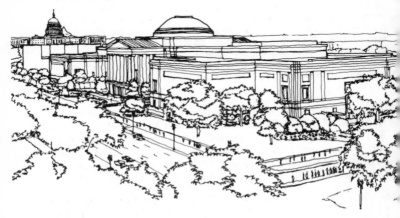

14. Turn west on Madison to the NATIONAL GALLERY OF ART, MAIN BUILDING** (John Russell Pope, 1941). It contains the richest COLLECTION OF FINE ARTS*** in the city.

15.   Continue west to the POOL AND ICE SKATING RINK*
(Skidmore, Owings and Merrill, 1974) between 7th and 9th
Streets. This joint project of the National Park Service and
National Gallery of Art has been extremely successful in hu-
manizing the edges of the Mall. An outdoor sculpture garden
is planned on the site which will balance the one at the
Hirshhorn across the Mall.

16.   In front of the NATIONAL MUSEUM OF NATURAL
HISTORY** (Hornblower and Marshall, 1911; Mills, Petticord
and Mills, 1965 wings), between 9th and 12th Streets, you will
see a few evergreens planted in conformity with the 1851 Mall
plan of Andrew Jackson Downing. The holly tree that you see
in the midst of the elms slightly to the southeast of the Natural
History building steps was scheduled for removal during the
leveling process. The tree was saved in the 1930's by Smithsonian Secretary Alexander Wetmore, an ornithologist, because it
was the nesting place of his pet mockingbird.

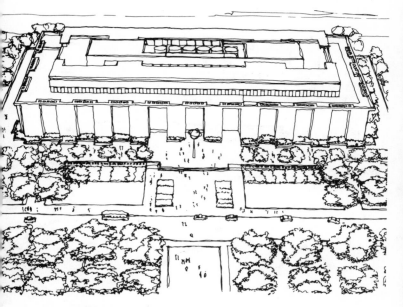

17. The NATIONAL MUSEUM OF HISTORY AND TECH-
NOLOGY*** (McKim, Mead and White, 1964), Madison Drive
between 12th and 14th Streets, is characteristic of the museums
of the 1960s. Note the contrast with the lighter, more "open"
Smithsonian museums of the 1970s. Popular exhibits include
the Star Spangled Banner, Benjamin Franklin's printing press,
and the First Ladies' gowns.

18.   Walk across the Mall to the FREER GALLERY OF ART**
(Charles A. Platt, 1923) at 12th and Jefferson Drive. Built around
a delightful interior court, the museum contains a small but choice
collection of oriental art, and the world's largest collection of
James Abbott McNeill Whistler's works (including the famous
Peacock Room).

4 ***THE MALL-WEST (National Memorials)

By Dr. Wilcomb Washburn and Kathryn Cousins, AICP

DISTANCE: 2¾ Miles   TIME: 2 Hours

BUS: On Constitution Avenue; 16A, 16D, and on 14th Street; 50, 52, 9, 11A, 11E and 11W.

METRO: Federal Triangle or Smithsonian (Blue & Orange)

This tour includes the Washington, Jefferson and Lincoln Memorials. Because of the tour length and inadequate parking, you may wish to buy a ticket for the Tourmobile which enables you to see each site at your own pace. You can get on and off the tourmobile at 11 sites along the Mall for the entire day of purchase. Adult tickets can be purchased at major tourist spots on the Mall, including the three memorials on this tour. Call 554-7950 for Tourmobile rates and information.

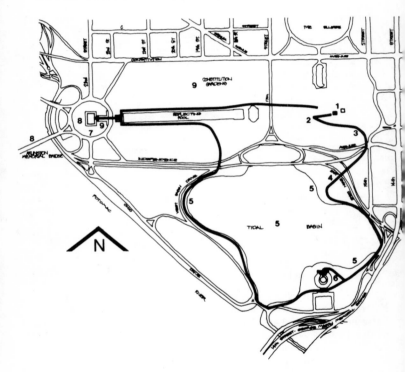

1.   The tour begins at the WASHINGTON MONUMENT*** (Robert Mills, 1884), 15th Street and Center of the Mall. Pierre L'Enfant chose this site to erect the equestrian statue proposed by Congress. George Washington approved the site. Because Congress failed to act decisively on the proposal, a group of private citizens organized in 1833 as the Washington National Monument Society offered a prize for the best design for a

monument. Robert Mills' design for a 600-foot obelisk rising from a colonnaded base won. The Society accepted the design minus its colonnaded base. Construction began in 1848. Funds for its erection ran out in 1854. Construction began again in 1876 after Congress authorized its completion at government expense. It was completed by the Army Corps of Engineers in 1884. If you look about one-fourth the way up you will see a distinct break in the color of the stone indicating the pause between construction phases.

L'Enfant's plan called for the monument to Washington to be located at the crossing of the north-south axis south from the White House at its crossing with the east-west axis due west from the Capitol. The ground at that point, however, was low and marshy and when the present monument was started early in the nineteenth century it was placed on more solid ground 360 feet east and 120 feet south of the planned position. Down the hill to the northwest you will see the "Jefferson Pier," a stone monument placed there in 1810 to mark the true intersection of L'Enfant's proposed north-south and east-west axes. It was later removed — but replaced in 1889. The Senate Park Commission planners sought to rectify the off-center Monument in its north-south axis by creating an elaborate sunken garden with a large circular pool west of the Monument. It was never built because engineers asserted that the Monument's stability would be threatened as a result. The Planners sought to rectify the off-center Monument in its east-west axis by slanting the Mall one degree south of its true east-west direction.

2. Walk to the west of the Monument and look west toward Lincoln Memorial. All of the land toward the Potomac was reclaimed from marsh and tidal land between the 1880's and the 1920's. Until then the Potomac occasionally flooded right to the south lawn of the White House. The McMillan Commission proposed extending the Mall from the Washington Monument to the proposed site for a Lincoln Memorial. The planners connected the two monuments with a reflecting pool and aligned the extension along the Park Commission's slanted new east-west axis.

3. Go south toward the Jefferson Memorial. The SYLVAN THEATER at 15th and Independence, southeast of the Washington Monument, is the site of open air summer musical, dramatic and dance productions. Shakespearean plays are favorites.

4. Continue south across Independence and walk west to East Basin Drive, near 17th Street to the TULIP LIBRARY *. This outdoor garden is planted with flowering annuals which are well identified. The tulips in the spring are spectacular.

5. The site of the TIDAL BASIN*** (designed by W. T. Twining, 1897), Independence and East Basin Drive, was originally part of the Potomac River. In 1882 the tidal basin was created as part of a plan to improve navigation on the Potomac and to reclaim some land for parks. The basin serves to flush clean the Washington channel, as gates between the basin and channel are opened at low tide to release the Potomac waters which have filled the basin in high tide. The CHERRY TREES*** surrounding the basin are

31

among 3,000 given by Japan in 1912. The Cherry Blossom Festival — held each year in early April — celebrates their enchanting but short blooming period.

6.   Continue along the Tidal Basin to the JEFFERSON MEMORIAL*** (John Russell Pope, Architect; Rudulph Evans, Sculptor, 1943). The McMillan Commission recommended a memorial center in this location but not specifically for Jefferson. There was considerable controversy on the design of the monument before approval. It was criticized as combining outmoded classic architectural styles, for being too similar to the Lincoln Memorial and for blocking the view of the Potomac from the White House. Defenders of the design said it was influenced by Jefferson's respect for classical styles which he introduced to this country and particularly by the Pantheon which much of his own architecture resembled. The grounds are landscaped after designs of Frederick Law Olmstead, Jr. The site forms the south end of the major cross axis of the Mall with the White House at the north. This axis is difficult to perceive on the ground because the Tidal Basin presents a barrier to direct access to the memorial from the north. It is readily apparent, however, on a map or from the air.

Take the tourmobile to the Lincoln Memorial or walk north-west across West Potomac Park to Independence Avenue.

7. The site of the LINCOLN MEMORIAL*** (Henry Bacon,
Architect; Daniel Chester French, Sculptor, 1922) had been de-
bated since 1867. Many early proposals stressed commemorating him as a war hero rather than as a humanitarian. Alternate
sites considered were a Lincoln Highway between Gettysburg
and Washington, D. C. and sites near Union Station and the
Capitol. In 1911, the decision was made to locate the memorial
here on the continuation of the axis of the Capitol and Washington Monument, as called for on the McMillan Plan, despite many
objections that the land was swampy and inaccessible. Designed
in a form derivative from a Greek temple, columns are tilted
slightly inward to avoid the optical illusion of a bulging top.
Many motifs representing Lincoln and America are incorporated
in the monument, including the 36 columns which symbolize
the 36 states of the Union while Lincoln was President. While
some people questioned the design of a Greek temple to commemorate someone who was born in a log cabin and who proudly acknowledged that heritage, Daniel French said, "The Greeks alone
were best able to express in their building . . . the highest attributes
and the greatest beauty known to man." The memorial pays hom-
age to "his simplicity, his grandeur and his power."

8. Walk around the Memorial to the rear or west side for the
VIEW*** across the Potomac. The ARLINGTON MEMORIAL
BRIDGE** (Architects: McKim, Mead and White; Sculptor: Leo
Freidlander, 1932) is considered to be one of the finest bridges in
the country. It was designed with the concept of symbolically
reuniting the North and South. It was recommended by the
McMillan Commission and built in the 1920's. The bridge con-
tains an operable (though rarely used) draw span cleverly con-
cealed in the center section. The bridge provides access to the
ARLINGTON NATIONAL CEMETERY*. About half way up
the hill straight ahead of the bridge is the GRAVE OF PRESI-
DENT JOHN KENNEDY* where the eternal flame can be seen
at night. Further up the hill is ARLINGTON HOUSE* (Custis-
Lee Mansion), home of Robert E. Lee. Looking back along the
Potomac the island to the right is a nature preserve and MEMO-
RIAL TO PRESIDENT THEODORE ROOSEVELT*.

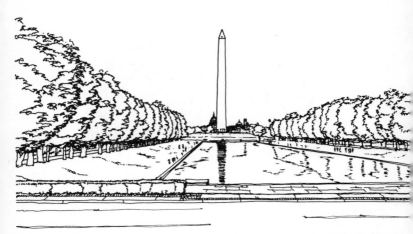

9. Walk around the Memorial to the entrance and look toward
the Capitol. The VIEW*** is one of the most photographed in
Washington because it is truly spectacular. It is here that the
current design policy maintaining a formal treatment of the
center of the Mall and a more people-oriented treatment at the
edges is most apparent. The REFLECTING POOL*** is designed
to mirror, and to link in a formal and inspiring setting, both monuments. When an artificial ice skating facility was proposed for the
pool in the 1960s, it was turned down by the National Park
Service as out of keeping with the dignity of the Mall. Such a
facility has more recently been installed in the area between the
National Gallery and the National Museum of Natural History
(see Tour 3, Mall-East). To the north (formerly the site of "Main
Navy"--temporary buildings from World War I which outlasted
World War II) is the site of CONSTITUTION GARDENS (Architects: Skidmore, Owings and Merrill). Originally planned as a
vibrant, day and night time attraction (modeled on the Tivoli
Gardens in Copenhagen) the proposed concessionary activities
were almost entirely eliminated to reduce initial costs. Since its
opening in 1976 the gardens have failed to attract the crowds
expected. An irregularly shaped lake forms the center of the
park. Note the total absence of evergreens, which makes the landscape barren in winter and monotonous in summer.

5 *INDEPENDENCE AVENUE, S.W./**L'ENFANT PLAZA (Federal office buildings, large commercial urban redevelopment project)

By Charity Vanderbilt Davidson

Ms. Davidson is the Urban Historian and Preservation Grants Manager with the Joint District of Columbia/National Capital Planning Commission Historic Preservation Office. She gratefully acknowledges the kind assistance of Mr. Donald E. Jackson of NCPC's Urban Design Office.

DISTANCE: ¾ Mile   TIME: 1½ Hours

BUS: 16B, 16C, 30, 32, 34, 36, 52, A2, A4, A6 and A8.

METRO: Federal Center, S.W. (Blue & Orange)

The Independence Avenue/L'Enfant Plaza area is the northern edge of Washington's southwest quadrant. During the first half of the 19th century, it was a desirable residential area with a smattering of commercial uses (including the most famous of the city's slave pens). After the Baltimore and Potomac Railroad laid tracks along Maryland and Virginia Avenues, S. W. in 1873, the western end of the area between B Street, S. W. (Independence Avenue) and the waterfront became a vast railroad yard, and its desirability as a residential section diminished.

Prior to 1900, the only government agencies with a strong interest in the area were the Department of Agriculture, with buildings along B Street, and the Bureau of Printing and Engraving. Federal interest in the northern fringes of the southwest increased during the first decades of the 20th century with the erection of more buildings for Agriculture and Printing and Engraving. The area retained much of its 19th century appearance because the departments rented space in existing structures rather than erecting new buildings.

During World War I, the federal bureaucracy mushroomed, and it became all too apparent that the departments could no longer "make do" with a multitude of offices scattered all over the city. This area was included in the kite-shaped monumental core proposed by the Senate Park Commission in 1902, but its use was undefined and little action was taken. By the 1920's, a new building program had become a necessity. Most of the attention was focused on the Federal Triangle between Pennsylvania Avenue, N. W. and the Mall. But by the 1930's, the newly created National Capital Park and Planning Commission (today the National Capital Planning Commission) was drawing up plans for similar developments in other parts of the city. One of the areas proposed was the Southwest Rectangle, bounded by B Street, S. W. (which was to be given the more pretentious name of Independence Avenue), 14th Street, the railroad tracks, and 2nd Street, S. W. Several large federal buildings (H.E.W., most of Agriculture, and Printing and Engraving) were erected before the outbreak of World War II. In addition, Independence Avenue (B Street) was widened to form a south parallel to Constitution Avenue on the other side of the Mall.

Nothing further was done until the 1950's, when plans for the redevelopment of the entire southwest were drawn up. Although an area roughly the same as the old Southwest Rectangle was set aside for development as government offices, no plan specified the location of any of the proposed buildings or their spatial relationship to one another. The awkward positioning of many of the offices in the redeveloped federal area is a result of this omission from the recent plans.

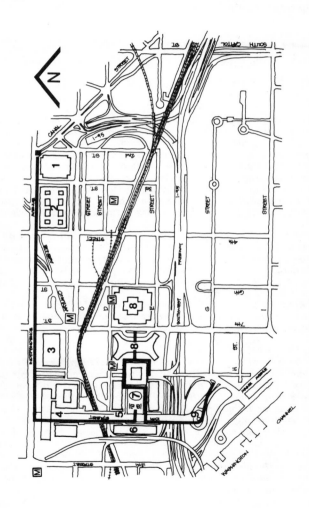

1. HUBERT HUMPHREY FEDERAL OFFICE BUILDING*
Independence Avenue between 2nd and 3rd Streets, S.W.
1976 - Marcel Breuer and Herbert Beckhard, architects
Nolen-Swinburne & Associates.

This 6-story rectangular building is the newest federal government
office building. It presented a particular challenge to the architect
because it spans part of the adjacent freeway and exhaust ducts
from the freeway tunnel and a large mechanical equipment shaft
had to be designed into the building. Interior offices are lighted
by two interior light wells (one of which can be entered from the
plaza). There are 3 levels of parking and mechanical equipment
spaces as well as the freeway under the plaza. The plaza itself,
like the HUD building, is notable for its crisp or hard urban finish
rather than the soft planting typical of Washington parks and
plazas.

2.   THE DEPARTMENT OF HEALTH, EDUCATION AND
WELFARE
Independence Avenue between 3rd and 4th Streets, S. W.
1939-41 Office of the Supervising Architect of the Treasury

Originally intended for the Social Security Administration, this
monolithic building was part of the Southwest Rectangle development. It is typical of federal architecture of the period, except
that its openings (for ventilation) are screened (Egyptian style)
for more overall massing (note later how this compares with the
rear of the south building at the Department of Agriculture).

3.   FEDERAL OFFICE BUILDING NO. 10
800 Independence Avenue, S. W.
1963 - Holabird & Root, architects
Burgee, Carroll, Grisdale and Van Allen

FOB No. 10 is probably the most conspicuous of the "universal
office buildings" constructed under the General Services Administration program of not assigning proposed buildings to any
specific government agency or department. Occupied by the
Department of Transportation, this building is an example of
the fallacy of the 1950's belief that two buildings were harmo-

nious if they had the same mass. It was hoped that the similarity in mass, height, and setback between FOB No. 10 and the the National Archives directly across the Mall, would emphasize the 8th Street axis as it crossed the Mall; unfortunately, there was no effort to relate such other features as fenestration, columns, portico, etc. The result was so visually unsatisfactory that few objected when the Hirshhorn Museum interrupted the vista between the two supposedly matching buildings. FOB No. 10's ground floor is raised, giving it the appearance of an arcade; the result in this building, with the loggia separated from the street by its landscaping, is markedly different from that achieved by the Forrestal Building, where it is part of the plaza.

4. THE JAMES FORRESTAL BUILDING (FOB NO. 5)**
Independence Avenue and 10th Street, S. W.
1970 - Curtis & Davis, architects
Fordyce and Hamby Associates
Frank Grad & Sons
Robert Zion and Harold Breen, landscape architects

The Forrestal Building, which is the only federal office building to have both a name and a number, is probably the most special of the "universal" buildings. It actually consists of three structures: the 660-foot long main building fronting on Independence Avenue, a taller office annex behind, and a separate cafeteria building. The large horizontal building originally was conceived as two of the General Services Administration's "universal office buildings," one on each side of 10th Street. The Department of Defense convinced Congress that the specialized nature of the Department's activities required that the majority of its facilities on this site be contained in a single structure. Congress then approved the concept of a single building spanning 10th Street, S. W. It finally was agreed that the first floor of the horizontal building would be lifted 30 feet above the street level in order to avoid blocking the 10th Street vista of the Smithsonian Castle tower. It was felt that the sense of space created by the horizontal opening between the plaza and the first floor more than compensated for the loss of the narrow view up 10th Street. The feeling of unity between the Forrestal Building and the developing 10th Street Mall/L'Enfant Plaza complex to the south was reinforced by the use of coordinated paving materials on all three projects. The presence of the surface railroad in Maryland Avenue required that the two building complexes be on different levels. A lower level passage serves as a circulation system for the three parts of the building and as a boarding area for commuter buses.

5. THE 10TH STREET MALL** AND L'ENFANT PLAZA**
1965 - 10th Street Mall; Wright & Gane, architects
1965 - 10th Street Overlook; Office of Dan Kiley, landscape architect
1965 - L'Enfant Plaza (North & South Buildings & Plaza); I. M. Pei and Partners, architects
1970-73 - L'Enfant Plaza Hotel; Vlastimil Koubek, architect

Original development plans for 10th Street, S. W. envisioned it as an esplanade lined with restricted commercial and residential uses. A slightly later plan proposed that 10th Street be widened

38

and serve as a thruway between downtown Washington and the
Southwest Expressway.

Early in 1954, Webb & Knapp, the New York developers, proposed a renewal plan for the entire southwest, including 10th
Street and L'Enfant Plaza. As originally worked out by William
Zeckendorf of Webb & Knapp and I. M. Pei, this proposal called
for widening 10th Street and developing it as a 1200-foot long
mall. This mall was to be flanked with public and semi-public
office buildings. L'Enfant Plaza, originally farther east of 10th
Street, was to be an enclosed square surrounded by private office buildings. It was also expected to develop as a cultural and
entertainment/convention center with a hotel, performance hall,
theater, and outdoor cafes. The mall itself was to terminate in
a semi-circular reflecting pool and waterfront park on the Washington Channel, balancing another large fountain treatment in the
Smithsonian yard.

By the time construction began, significant changes had been
made in the plan. In 1960, urban designer Willow von Molke
proposed the development of the 10th Street axis to a waterfront overlook. I. M. Pei & Associates drew up a master plan
for the mall and plaza which brought the plaza west to its
present location; after public hearings, this master plan was
incorporated into the official renewal plan approved by the
National Capital Planning Commission (NCPC). Webb &
Knapp had withdrawn and the project had been taken over
by the L'Enfant Plaza Corporation.

6. & 7.   Walk up the west side of THE 10TH STREET MALL
(6.) past the Postal Service building to the PLAZA**(7.). Note
that the mall bridges the railroad tracks which cut through the
site and that nothing has been done to develop the Maryland
Avenue vista toward the Capitol. The Pei proposal had included a major focal sculpture for the plaza, but this too has been
eliminated.

The paving for both the mall and L'Enfant Plaza is Hastings block inlaid with red granite. No effort has been made to visually differentiate between public and private property along the mall or in the plaza. The center strip down the mall was intended as a cascade of water flowing toward Independence Avenue, but leakage has forced its draining.

8. The buildings to the north and south of the plaza are office towers; and one to the east is the L'ENFANT PLAZA HOTEL, one of Washington's newest. There is parking for 1,300 cars under the plaza, with direct ramps on and off the nearby expressway.

Proceed across 10th Street and down the stairs on either side of the fountain. These lead to the 100,000 square foot underground shopping mall. As with the plaza above, this retail facility gets intensive use by workers from the surrounding buildings. Once the shopping mall has been explored, continue east along the main corridor of the shopping arcade to the exit to the curvilinear:

9. DEPARTMENT OF HOUSING & URBAN DEVELOPMENT**
451 7th Street, S. W.
1968 - Marcel Breuer and Herbert Beckhard, architects
Nolen-Swinburn & Associates
George Patton, landscape architect

Walk through the HUD building to the 7th Street, S. W. entrance and plaza. Commissioned in 1963, when HUD was still the Housing and Home Finance Agency, this was one of the first buildings constructed after President Kennedy issued his directive on "Guiding Principles for Federal Architecture." To raise the aesthetic standards of federal buildings, the General Services Administration provided that a percentage of the construction costs could be devoted to artistic embellishments (such as plazas and sculpture).

Breuer became involved with curvilinear buildings while designing a building for UNESCO and a research lab for IBM at LaGaude, France. The French favor such buildings because they permit a maximum amount of natural light in a maximum number of offices (thereby reducing the amount of electricity required) while keeping the distance between offices to a minimum. The architect selected a curvilinear shape for the HUD building partly because it would yield the best window-distance ratio in a large building on a restricted site, and partly because its lines would be sympathetic to the curves of the Southwest Freeway adjacent to it. The building is a double-Y, with each wing touching the property lines only at the corners. The building provides office space for over 6,000 employees and has 3 levels of parking under the plaza. The plaza itself is also an effort to relate the 7th Street connection to the Mall.

The rectangular white building (Edward Durell Stone, architect) directly across 7th Street was privately built but is occupied by the Department of Transportation. Return to the underground arcade and follow the overhead signs to the L'Enfant Plaza Hotel lobby. Exit from the lobby via the south doors in order to walk around the hotel's terrace. The section of terrace just south of the hotel is provided with umbrella-shaded tables, available to anyone wishing to use them; additional seating is provided elsewhere around the terrace.

Walk along the terrace in a counter-clockwise direction. Note the small, walled, grassy space which separates the hotel from the HUD building; small as it is, this open space also is used intensively. This juxtaposition of buildings results from the fact that there was never a single design plan for the section of the redevelopment area designated for office use; each building was developed without direct coordination with its neighbors.

Continuing along the terrace, the railroad track barrier is once again very evident. The north side of the terrace provides an excellent VIEW** of the Smithsonian's National Museum building and the downtown skyline beyond the Mall.

10.   Now walk back to the front of the hotel, across the plaza and back to the 10th Street Mall. Continue south along the mall to the BENJAMIN BANNEKER FOUNTAIN** where it terminates. This overlook provides a PANORAMIC VIEW** of the Washington Channel and the redeveloped southwest. Moving around the overlook in a counter-clockwise direction, one can see:

DEPARTMENT OF AGRICULTURE - South Building. This structure covers 3 city blocks. A portion was completed as part of the 1930's Southwest Rectangle project.

BUREAU OF PRINTING & ENGRAVING.

EAST POTOMAC PARK, created by the U. S. Army Corps of Engineers during dredging operations along the Potomac in the 1880's. The park includes facilities for active and passive recreation. Initial redevelopment plans for the waterfront area included provision for wharves and slips on the park side of the Channel; eventually it was decided to emphasize the sharp, park landscape instead.

CRYSTAL CITY, visible beyond East Potomac Park, is a privately developed complex of offices, apartments, and shops. Most of its tenants are government agencies.

The WATERFRONT. The major problem in the redevelopment of the waterfront was determining the intensity to which it should be rebuilt. At the time of renewal, most of the waterfront was taken up by commercial activities, dilapidated warehouses, the railroad yards, a hodgepodge of rotting piers. The Washington architectural firm of Satterlee and Smith prepared a tentative redevelopment plan, but it was rejected by the National Capital Planning Commission as too intense. NCPC then drew up a list of plan objectives for the waterfront. Some of these objectives have been realized — buildings in the commercial waterfront area have been kept low so that the interior buildings also have view of the Channel, streets ends kept open with parklets, and decking for underground parking and development was included as a public amenity. Unfortunately, most of the objectives have not yet been realized and the northern section of the waterfront leaves a great deal to be desired (see Tour 6 - Southwest).

The VISTA DOWN THE WASHINGTON CHANNEL to its juncture with the Potomac River.

FORT LESLIE J. McNAIR and the NATIONAL WAR COLLEGE (see Tour 6 - Southwest).

The SOUTHWEST EXPRESSWAY, which isolates the residential southwest from the rest of the city.

6 **SOUTHWEST (Waterfront urban renewal area)

By Charity Vanderbilt Davidson

DISTANCE: 2 Miles   *TIME: 1½ Hours*

BUS: To 7th & I (Eye) Streets, S.W.; 70, M8, V4, and V6.

METRO: L'Enfant Plaza (Blue & Orange) transfer to Bus 70 or V4

When the Federal City was laid out in 1791-1792, it was expected that the southwest would develop as a mixed residential/commercial center. During the last decade of the 18th century, a number of wealthy citizens built homes in the area and a real estate syndicate built several rows of substantial brick dwellings for speculative purposes. Unfortunately, the southwest's commercial dreams were never realized. It was hoped that the City Canal would enable the area to attract some of Georgetown's trade, but the mismanaged, decaying canal proved to be a barrier which isolated the southwest from the rest of the developing city, rather than a commercial link. During the 19th century, the central portion of the southwest became a working class residential area ringed by commercial uses such as the transporting and storing of goods and produce. The sections along B Street, S. W. (today Independence Avenue) continued to be occupied by more prominent citizens.

The area's isolation was reinforced and further emphasized in 1873 when the Baltimore and Potomac Railroad laid tracks along Maryland and Virginia Avenues, S. W. By the early 20th century, the type of services provided by the southwest's commercial waterfront had lost much of their importance, but the area where the Department of Agriculture is now located gained in importance when a railway depot was established nearby. However, the development of the depot led to the departure of the area's more wealthy residents. The area further declined and acquired a reputation for a high crime rate and innumerable inhabited alleys. The Army Corps of Engineers redeveloped part of the waterfront in the 1930's, but even this did not halt the downward spiral. Also during the 1930's, the federal government began to redevelop the northern fringes as the Southwest Rectangle, a complex of government buildings similar to the Federal Triangle development. The buildings for the Department of Health, Education and Welfare, the Department of Agriculture, and the complex of buildings for the Bureau of Printing and Engraving were the only ones completed before construction was halted. By the late 1940's, the southwest was considered a vast slum with three quarters of its buildings regarded as substandard.

Early in 1952, two plans were offered for the redevelopment of 427 acres in the southwest. The first plan, prepared by Elbert Peets for the National Capital Planning Commission (NCPC), called for the rehabilitation of many of the residential structures, but it was rejected as socially and financially impossible. The second plan, commissioned by the District of Columbia Redevelopment Land Agency (RLA, today part of the D. C. Department of Housing and Community Development) was prepared by the

43

St. Louis planning firm of Harland Bartholomew and Associates and by two Washington Architects, Louis Justement and Chloethiel Woodward Smith. The Smith-Justement Plan, as it is known, called for the demolition of nearly all existing structures and the erection of approximately 5,000 new dwelling units. NCPC then prepared a third plan, stressing redevelopment rather than rehabilitation. RLA began to accept bids for Area B, the section east of Canal Street and Delaware Avenue, S. W. reserved for public housing.

In 1953, President Eisenhower succeeded in persuading the New York development firm of Webb & Knapp to prepare a plan for 440 acres which had been set aside for private development. The plan developed by Webb & Knapp's architectural and planning staff, headed by I. M. Pei, and Chicago architect Harry Weese, was unveiled early in 1954. The area south of the freeway was to be residential, with highrise apartment towers interspersed among clusters of townhouses; this proposal for the mixing of building types was innovative since developers had previously segregated highrise and lowrise structures. The plans prepared by Peets and Smith-Justement called for the rebuilding of retail commercial streets. However, the new plan called for a Town Center, or shopping mall, designed to serve the entire southwest. The waterfront was to be completely redeveloped. In exchange for formulating the plan, Webb & Knapp were given their choice of areas to develop; they chose the area of the Town Center, what is today L'Enfant Plaza, and the residential section north of M Street. The basic concepts of the Webb & Knapp plan (sometimes also referred to as the Zeckendorf-Pei plan) were finally adopted by NCPC in 1956, but many of the details were altered. Webb & Knapp began work on their portion of the project, but were forced to withdraw later for financial reasons.

The Peets plan of 1951 had tried to work with the original street plan, but subsequent development plans called for substantial changes, such as the creation of "super blocks" by closing many of the streets. One of the recurring themes in the redevelopment area is the various ways in which different developers have used the old street spaces.

In an effort to insure variety in the redevelopment area, RLA divided the portions not already assigned to the government or to Webb & Knapp into development parcels, some of which were awarded on the basis of design/development competitions. One of the plan requirements was that there be no ground-floor residence in any of the highrise buildings; it is interesting to note the various efforts to utilize this under-building space; eg. from parking (Capitol Park, 17) to activity rooms and large lobbies (River Park, 9) or arcades (Town Center, 5).

1.   The SMALL URBAN PARK* between the Flagship and Hogate's restaurants was designed by Sasaki, Dawson and Demay. This section of the bulkhead along the water's edge is deserted even in nice weather. Both its landscaping and the amount of use it gets contrast markedly with the situation farther down the Channel.

44

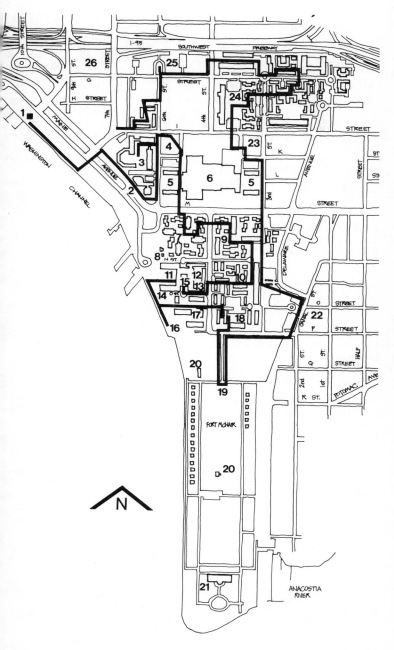

2. THE ARENA STAGE**
6th and M Streets, S. W.
1961 - Harry Weese & Associates, architects

THE KREEGER THEATER (Addition)
6th and M Streets, S. W.
1970 - Harry Weese & Associates

The Arena Stage's company was one of the pioneers of theater-in-the-round in America and is today one of the best resident theater companies in the country. The polygonal theater building, which seats 750, is separate from but connected to the elongated administration building which houses the supporting facilities.

The 3-story Kreeger Theater wraps around one corner of this administration wing. It seats 500 and allows the company to expand its program of experimental plays, children's theater, and teaching. Unlike the Arena Stage, which is truly theater-in-the-round, the Kreeger's stage is fan-shaped.

The exterior materials of both buildings are identical to make the two buildings "an aesthetic, functional whole," according to architect Weese.

3. WATERSIDE TOWERS*
905-947 6th Street, S. W.
1970 - Chloethiel Woodward Smith Associates, architects

This complex of townhouses and highrise apartments can be entered by walking down the driveway entrance. The townhouses serve as a wall around the large landscaped interior courtyard which covers the underground parking. The uninterrupted openness of this courtyard contrasts with the courtyard treatments in a number of other developments in the area.

4. The PARK** with the pond was designed by Ian McHarg, landscape architect

5. TOWN CENTER PLAZA* (apartments)
1100 block of 6th Street, S. W.
1961-1962 - I. M. Pei Associates, architects
Robert Zion and Harold Breen, landscape architects

Built in two phases, these apartments were part of the Webb & Knapp development. They were winners of an FHA Honor Award and are significant because they demonstrated that good residential architecture could be produced within the financial restraints set by developers and still meet the requirements for FHA Title I funds. They are the only apartments in the redevelopment area which do not have balconies and are not accompanied by townhouses. Their courtyards have been created from the old street space and trees of L Street, S. W.

6. WATERSIDE MALL
400 M Street, S. W.
1972 - Chloethiel Woodward Smith Associates, architects

The large office tower (housing the Environmental Protection Agency) is part of the office and retail development known as Waterside Mall. This still-to-be-completed commercial center expands the original Town Center Plaza development. Originally designed along the lines of a suburban shopping center, the mall was redesigned when it was determined that a more intensive facility was needed for the original shopping center. It appears that this extension was unwarranted by the Center's market area, for many of the original stores have closed and the developers are reluctant to complete the structure. The planned residential components of the Center have been changed to offices.

7. TIBER ISLAND**
Bounded by M, N & 4th Streets, S. W. and the waterfront
1965 - Keyes, Lethbridge and Condon, architects
Eric Paepcke, landscape architect

47

Tiber Island was the winner of the first RLA design competition and of a 1961 AIA Honor Award. It consists of four 8-story apartment towers (368 units) and 85 two/three-story townhouses. It is especially interesting because of the spatial relationship between its highrise and lowrise elements, and the way in which the District of Columbia zoning code was interpreted in order to permit the design's implementation.

The architects were particularly concerned with the organization and scale of the exterior spaces between and around the buildings. The principal exterior space, a large pedestrian court, is defined by the 4 apartment towers; the fringes of this space are subdivided into smaller courts surrounded by the townhouses. The central plaza and the courts are linked together by walkways, but variations in architectural detail and landscaping have given each court an individual character. The central pedestrian plaza covers a 280-car underground garage.

Local zoning regulations required that a rowhouse have its own lot, have off-street parking, front on a street, and have individual utilities. The D. C. Government was willing to view the Tiber Island townhouses as apartments. This meant that the 64 houses on the perimeter could be sold under condominium agreements and the 21 houses entirely within the complex could be rented.

8. The THOMAS LAW HOUSE* also known as the Honeymoon House, is located at 1252 6th Street, S. W., in the southeast corner of Tiber Island. Law was a major promoter of south Washington development. His Federal style house, built between 1794 and 1796, is among Washington's earliest extant structures and is listed on the National Register of Historic Places. It was rehabilitated in 1965 to serve as a community center for residents of Tiber Island and Carrollsburg Square.

9. CARROLLSBURG SQUARE*
Bounded by M, N and 4th Streets and Delaware Avenue, S. W.
1965 - Keyes, Lethbridge and Condon, architects
Eric Paepcke, landscape architect

Carrollsburg Square was the winner of the second RLA design competition. Like Tiber Island, it has a central pedestrian area over an underground garage, but here the plaza has been divided into a larger number of small residential courts. Here again, each court has been given its own character by means of variations in landscaping and architectural detail. Carrollsburg Square was intended as a transition between Tiber Island and the public housing immediately to the east.

10. RIVER PARK COOPERATIVE**
Bounded by 4th Street and Delaware Avenue, S. W.
1962 - Charles M. Goodman Associates, architects

River Park was the first owner-occupied development in the new southwest. It includes 134 townhouses and 384 adjacent apartments. The apartment slab was designed to serve as a barrier between the development's barrel-vaulted townhouses and the public housing across Delaware Avenue.

This wall-like quality can best be experienced by walking south between the apartment building and the townhouses. The former street spaces in the complex have been landscaped and terminate in cul-de-sacs.

11. HARBOUR SQUARE**

Bounded by 4th, N, and O Streets, S. W. and the waterfront
1966 - Chloethiel Woodward Smith Associates, architects
Office of Dan Kiley, landscape architect

The Harbour Square complex includes not only new highrise apartments and townhouses, but also has incorporated 3 of the late 18th/early 19th century structures which survived the extensive demolition carried out in the renewal area.

12. WHEAT ROW** at 1315-1321 4th Street is an important example of the conservative, vernacular domestic architecture constructed during the Federal Period. Built in 1794, it is believed to be the first speculative housing built in Washington City by the real estate syndicate of James Greenleaf (a former American consul in Amsterdam), Robert Morris (the Philadelphia financier) and John Nicholson (also of Philadelphia). It was rehabilitated in 1964-66 and included in Harbour Square as 4 townhouses.

13. The EDWARD SIMON LEWIS HOUSE* at 456 N Street was built circa 1817, and is typical of the early 19th century

brick houses in Washington. Originally built as a single family house, the structure was converted to apartments in the 1920's; during the 1930's, its tenants included journalists Lewis J. Heath and Ernie Pyle. After rehabilitation in 1964-66, the house was included in Harbour Square as a single family townhouse.

14. The DUNCANSON-CRANCH HOUSE*, 468-470 N Street, S.W., like Wheat Row, was built circa 1794 by the Greenleaf syndicate. It now serves as two townhouses in Harbour Square.

15. The WATER GARDEN** in the center of the complex is the dominant element in the development's pedestrian square. It includes sculptured forms, platforms, walks, and seating. Planting includes flowering water plants and willow trees. Hubert Humphrey moved to Harbour Square when he became Vice President.

16. WATERSIDE PARK**
1967-68 Sasaki, Dawson and Demay, designers

Walk around this park near a grove of willow trees and southwest along the seawall to the Titanic Memorial. This area is much more pleasant than the section of waterfront discussed earlier (1) and receives much more use (partly because people are drawn to the nearby tourist boats to Mt. Vernon and partly because of the nearby residential structures).

17. J. FINLEY HOUSE (Chalk House)
Bounded by 4th, O and P Streets and the waterfront
1966 - Morris Lapidus Associates, architects

This complex was the winner of the third RLA design competition. Walk along the O Street facade and between the buildings. The O Street side is cold, but the interior area has a parklike quality. Note the use of old street space for a greenway along O Street.

18. CHANNEL SQUARE
325 P Street, S. W.
1968 - Harry Weese & Associates

Channel Square, which consists of tan colored townhouses and an apartment tower, was designed as middle-income housing under Section 221 D3 of the Housing Act of 1949. This section of the Act subsidized the developer's interest rate, and in turn, rents have been kept well below existing market rates. The whole feeling of Channel Square is very different from that of other developments, especially Capitol Park.

19. FORT LESLIE J. McNAIR*
Estb. 1794 as the Washington Arsenal
1903 - McKim, Mead and White, master plan

Fort McNair, a feature of the L'Enfant Plan, has been known by a variety of names (Washington Arsenal, U. S. Arsenal at Greenleaf Point, the Washington Barracks). The first fortifications were erected in 1794 and the first arsenal buildings in 1803-04. It was

one of the earliest employers in Washington. All of the original buildings were destroyed by an explosion during the British occupation of Washington in August 1814. The arsenal buildings were rebuilt and served as a distribution center for arms.

20. The first U. S. PENITENTIARY, opened on the northern end of the arsenal grounds in 1826, is best known as the site of the trial and execution of 4 of the Lincoln conspirators and of the Commandant of the Confederate prison at Andersonville, Georgia. Most of the penitentiary buildings were razed in 1869, but a portion remains in the center of the greensward. The arsenal grounds were used for storage by the Quartermaster Corps after 1881. Between 1898 and 1909, the general hospital on the grounds was the site of many of Major Walter Reed's experiments on yellow fever and diphtheria.

21. In 1903, the New York architectural firm of McKim, Mead and White was retained to design a building for the new ARMY WAR COLLEGE and to develop a master plan for the entire installation. Most of the firm's plan, (which called for a long mall, flanked by white-columned officers' houses, with the War College at the end as the focal point) was implemented. An unconfirmed story relates that the designer was so angry when he learned that the War Department had refused to tear down the few remaining arsenal and penitentiary buildings in the middle of the proposed mall (thereby blocking the vista to the War College), he refused to set foot on the site again.

22. CANAL STREET, S. W. follows the route of the old James Creek Canal, part of the city canal system constructed during the first half of the 19th century to provide a protected all-water route for goods coming down the Chesapeake and Ohio Canal destined for the Navy Yard or the Anacostia River. The buildings on the east side of Canal Street are public housing erected during the early 1950's.

23. Note the PARK* by landscape designer Ian McHarg which occupies the northern half of the square along the north side of the Town Center. Walk west through the ELONGATED PARK* (also by McHarg) to the central plaza. These parks were intended

as low maintenance parks, but a great deal is still required. A variety of community facilities (library, churches, public transportation) are concentrated in this area. The large scale dislocation of people, caused by the renewal, raised particular problems for local churches. The National Council of Churches worked with the southwest's congregations in determining which would remain in the area, which would combine facilities if not congregations, and which would leave the area. Two of the congregations which remained flank the park.

24. CAPITOL PARK APARTMENTS & TOWNHOUSES**
Bounded by 4th Street, I Street, Delaware Avenue and the S. W. Expressway
1959 - Satterlee and Smith, architects
1963 - Smith and Associates, architects
Office of Dan Kiley, landscape architect

Built on the site of Dixon's Court, one of Washington's largest and most infamous inhabited alleys, Capitol Park was the first of the new projects erected in the southwest. It was awarded an AIA Merit Award in 1960. The apartment tower at 800 4th Street was the first building (402 units) of what was ultimately intended as 1600 units. Although it was built in stages, the complex was designed as a unified whole. The accompanying townhouses are FHA Honor Award winners. The development is best known for its parklike atmosphere. The use of glass and the feeling of openness which pervades Capitol Park contrasts sharply with the feeling of containment present in other, later southwest developments.

25. After exploring Capitol Park, cross 4th Street and walk west along G Street past the townhouses (1966-69 - Walter Peter, arch.) to the PARK at the end of 6th Street. Walk north across the park to the retaining wall on the far side of the parking lot. This offers one of the most spectacular VIEWS** of just how major a barrier the Southwest Freeway is and how it cuts off the residential part of the southwest from the office development areas. The townhouses are interesting since they are grouped around COMMON GREENS which are maintained and owned by the homeowners.

26. At the corner of G Street and 7th Street, S.W., there is a bus stop. Nearby, the tract (Parcel 76) now being used as a parking lot is the proposed site of a subsidized housing project - a selection the adjacent homeowners are successfully contesting in court. The proposed project will consist of 136 dwelling units within 36 row-house structures, most of which are to be 2-bedroom units. Louis Sauer is the architect and the Housing Development Cooperative is the developer.

7 **FOGGY BOTTOM (Watergate, Kennedy Center, George Washington University, State Department)

By Zachary Domike

Mr. Domike was a student of historic preservation at George Washington University when he wrote this tour for the original edition.

DISTANCE: 2¾ Miles　　　　　*TIME: 1¼ Hours*

BUS: 80, or H6 to 19th and G Streets, N.W. Or 30, 32, 34, 36 to Pennsylvania Avenue and 19th Street, N.W.

METRO: Farragut West (Blue & Orange)

In 1765 Jacob Funk, a German emigrant, purchased 130 acres of land which were within the limits of present-day Washington. Incorporated as Hamburg, but known as Funkstown, the citizens of Hamburg deeded all their lots to the "U. S. commissioners for the building of a Federal City" in 1793.

Laid out just west of the White House in an area which included unclaimed river marsh and was known, until draining, for its unhealthfulness, Hamburg became the site of a glass factory, brewery and gas works — all of which contributed to the unpleasant stench and smoke which befouled the air and led to the enduring nick name, Foggy Bottom.

In 1890 Franklin W. Smith proposed a plan for the District of Columbia's Centennial which would have established the area between F Street and Constitution Avenue, N. W. and extending west from the White House grounds to the Potomac River as the site for a gigantic National Gallery of History and Art. Here were to be displayed the great civilizations of the past, complete with an American Acropolis on the banks of the Potomac.

In 1901 the McMillan Commission Plan was submitted to the U. S. Senate. For a period of one hundred years Washington had developed more or less haphazardly with no single authority responsible for the planning and zoning of districts and control of building design or location. The McMillan Commission was appointed to report on existing conditions and presented a plan which was a unique statement in planning and one which had a significant impact upon the District's modern development. This report was prepared by Charles Moore and Frederick Law Olmstead, Jr. and was developed under the direction of Daniel Burnham, architect, Charles F. McKim, architect, and Augustus Saint-Gaudens, sculptor. The significance of this plan for Foggy Bottom was the reclamation of the Potomac Flats which increased the area into which Foggy Bottom could expand and improved the environment considerably.

1. Begin at 17th and G Streets, N.W. Heading west along G Street, one enters an area dominated by two major institutions: The WORLD BANK (International Bank for Reconstruction

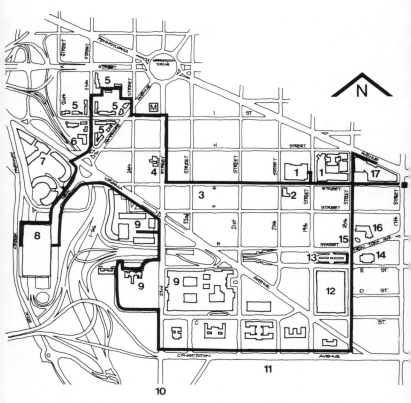

and Development) and the INTERNATIONAL MONETARY
FUND. The Bank complex was originally housed in a building
facing H Street; it has since expanded to occupy the entire block.
A recent addition (1974) is the Monetary Fund's building (NW
corner, 19th and G Streets) and its ENCLOSED INTERIOR
COURTYARD ** which is spectacular.

2. CONCORDIA LUTHERAN EVANGELICAL CHURCH (S.E.
corner, 20th and G), a surviving memento of the late 19th century
German ethnic community that occupied this area, still offers
German language services.

3. The GEORGE WASHINGTON UNIVERSITY, founded in
1821, occupied two sites before moving to 2023 G Street in
1912. Lacking funding for building, the University gradually
acquired the old homes of Foggy Bottom converting some for
classrooms and offices and replacing others with new academic
buildings. As the University grew it produced four distinctive
architectural styles: a red brick genteel building with Georgian
cupolas; barebones Depression-period white painted factory-
sash brick and concrete structures; limestone-faced buildings,
still much influenced by Depression architecture; and precast
concrete "element buildings" of the present day. The question of interest to planners is how to reconcile the University's
need for continued growth with the planning of the entire area.
Traffic and parking problems and the balance of old and new,

large and small, high and low buildings are significant for this area. The "campus" is surrounded by active commerical development to the east, an expanding medical district to the north, the federal establishment to the south, and office and apartment building pressures everywhere.

4.   23RD STREET, N. W., is a principal "edge" which divided the comfortable middle class neighborhood (now inhabited by the University, but previously tenented by civil servants and professionals) from the working class neighborhood which was supported by work in the brewery, lumber yard, gas works, coal depot and waterfront enterprises which used to exist in Foggy Bottom. At 730 23rd Street, ST. MARY'S CHURCH is the only church designed by architect James Renwick for blacks. Immediately west and south of St. Mary's stood one of the city's first public housing projects, demolished 5 years ago to make way for a University parking lot. Today this former working class neighborhood of slum housing has been transformed into expensively modernized row houses, a good example of which may be seen on New Hampshire Avenue north of G Street.

5.   Vestiges of an older style of living may be seen in the "alley dwellings" (now quite desirable and rehabilitated) of Snow's Court, which may be reached on 25th Street between I and K Streets, N. W.

6.   From the juncture of New Hampshire and Virginia Avenues one looks out upon "POTOMAC PLAZA." Once the site of the gas works and brewery, the area has been "reclaimed" by urban renewal initiated during the 1960's. Watergate and Columbia Plaza contain apartments, offices, a hotel, a shopping mall and a commercial strip — "packaged living" on the model of New York's UN Plaza or Los Angeles' Century City — and very much responsive to the nearby State Department and Kennedy Center for the Performing Arts. The design theme found here was much influenced by the expressways and approaches to the Roosevelt Memorial Bridge beyond.

7.   Cross the traffic circle into the shopping mall in the WATER-GATE** Complex; (Luigi Moretti, 1964-1972). The mall is a delightful respite amidst the overwhelming curves and jagged edges of the flamboyant architecture surrounding you. Return to New Hampshire Avenue. Continue south toward the Kennedy Center. Immediately on your right is a curved office building — a part of the Watergate complex. This building contains Les Champs, a swank interior shopping mall highlighted by haute couture boutiques, other small specialty shops, restaurant and bar. The office floors are occupied by several foreign chanceries and embassies.

56

8. Walk up the slight grade to the KENNEDY CENTER***
(Edward D. Stone, 1969) and enter the second door on your
right. This will take you into one of the three enormous lobbies. Half way down the hall proceed to the elevators on your
left. Go to the roof. Here you will find three restaurants, an
exhibit space and a huge terrace on all four sides of the building. The VIEWS*** of the monuments, Arlington, Georgetown
and the rest of Washington are memorable. Return to the first
level and turn left into the Grand Foyer — one of the largest
rooms in the world. At intermission as many as 6,000 persons
fill the foyer as they emerge from the acoustically perfect Concert Hall, Opera House and Eisenhower Theatre. Although the
Kennedy Center's bulk and location have been bitterly criticized
the center's excellent facilities have substantially enriched the
cultural life of Washington. The willow shaded terrace to the
west is beautiful and offers a fine view of the Potomac River.
More detailed information and tours of the Kennedy Center
are available at the information desk on the first level.

9. COLUMBIA PLAZA* and the STATE DEPARTMENT
occupy the ridge stretching along D Street from 23rd to 21st
Streets. An example of the architect's insensibility to topography is seen by standing at the 23rd Street entrance to the
State Department's auditorium and contemplating the blank
concrete retaining wall on the west side of the street. The

57

Naval Hospital grounds can be entered at D Street and it is
from here that one can admire the commanding and unusual
VIEW** of Georgetown and the Potomac Palisades.

10.   Continuing south down 23rd Street to Constitution Avenue
one enjoys an excellent view of the LINCOLN MEMORIAL***
It was this area which was developed following the plan of the
McMillan Commission, and its success gave rise to the national
"City Beautiful" movement. The plans of the Commission showed
the Lincoln Memorial and Arlington bridge substantially as they
were realized a quarter-century later (see Tour 4, The Mall-West).

11.   CONSTITUTION AVENUE, N. W. occupies the site of the
former Tiber Creek. Proceeding east one passes monuments to
the City Beautiful designed in classical and renaissance styles. The
south side of the Avenue was flanked until 1971 by the concrete
"Tempos" built during the first World War, and recently transformed into CONSTITUTION GARDENS, an innovative urban
park by the National Park Service and Skidmore, Owings and
Merrill architects and pressed to completion for the Bicentennial.
To the north stand the dignified and monumental buildings of (in
order of their appearance): the American Pharmaceutical Association, the National Academy of Sciences, the Federal Reserve
Board, the Bureau of Indian Affairs, the Interior Department, the
Pan American Union annex, and the Pan American Union.

12.   The large building on the west side of 18th Street, N. W. is
occupied by the DEPARTMENT OF THE INTERIOR. Across
the street is CONSTITUTION HALL, which used to be the capital's primary concert hall (see Tour 8, White House).

13.   Beautiful RAWLINS PARK** surrounded by 18th, 19th
and E Streets, N. W. is popular with government workers at
lunch time.

14.   The UNITED UNIONS BUILDING* facing Rawlins Park
from the east is a good example of how private initiative, by
providing a plaza and landscaping, can improve the environment
at the street level.

15.   OCTAGON HOUSE**
1741 New York Avenue
1800 - Dr. Thornton
Open to the public
Hours: 10 a.m. to 5 p.m. daily, except Monday

Originally the home of General John Tayloe, the Octagon House
was the temporary residence of President Madison when the
British burned the White House in 1814. The Treaty of Ghent
was signed here, ending the War of 1812.

16. HEADQUARTERS BUILDING, THE AMERICAN INSTITUTE OF ARCHITECTS*
1735 New York Avenue, N. W.
1973 - The Architects Collaborative

Wrapped around the Octagon House, the new A.I.A. building provides a strong architectural juxtaposition while enhancing the prominence to the corner. The color, texture and materials used provide a pleasant contrast to the Octagon House. Occasional art exhibits are located in the lobby.

17. This block of PENNSYLVANIA AVENUE, N. W. has been virtually redeveloped privately into office use during the past decade. The colorful shops and open plazas have generated lively street level activity.

8 ***WHITE HOUSE (Renwick Gallery, Lafayette Square, Treasury and Ellipse)

By Fred H. Greenberg

DISTANCE: 2 Miles   *TIME: 1½ Hours*

BUS: 30, 34, 36, 38, 42, 80, X2, X4, and X6.

METRO: Farragut West (Blue & Orange)

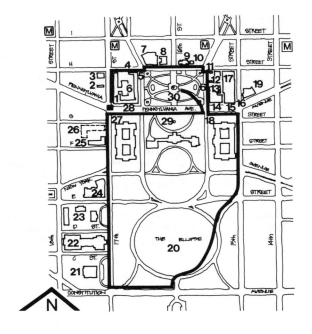

1. RENWICK GALLERY* (Old Corcoran Gallery and Court of Claims)
17th and Pennsylvania Avenue, N. W.
1859 - James Renwick
1972 - Restoration by John Carl Warnecke and Hugh Newell Jacobsen
Hours: 10:00 a.m. to 5:30 p.m. daily

Originally designed as an art gallery for W. W. Corcoran, the Renwick was used by the government during the Civil War. When he was able to occupy his own buildings, Corcoran found

that it was too small for his collection, and he built a larger gallery at 17th and New York Avenue. Later, the building was used as the Court of Claims. The meticulous exterior and interior restoration took several years, and the building was returned to its original function as an art gallery. The Renwick Gallery exhibits crafts, industrial design, architecture and city planning.

2. SANS SOUCI Restaurant
    726 17th Street, N.W.

Sans Souci was one of the "in" spots for big shot politicos during the Nixon years. Henry Kissinger and Art Buchwald, an unlikely pair, used to eat there.

3. METROPOLITAN CLUB
1700 H Street, N. W. (at 17th Street, N. W.)
1908 - Heins and Lafarge

This social club is the club for some of Washington's statesmen, politicians and most monied men.

4. TRUXTON-DECATUR NAVAL MUSEUM*
1610 H Street, N. W.
Hours: 10:30 a.m. to 4:00 p.m. daily
Free Admission

This small and interesting museum presents an unusual collection of historic sea going memorabilia.

5. DECATUR HOUSE**
Southwest corner of Jackson Place and H Street, N. W.
1818 - Benjamin Latrobe
Hours: 12:00 p.m. to 5:00 p.m. daily

The house of Commodore Stephen Decatur, the suppressor of the Barbery pirates, now serves as offices for the National Trust for Historic Preservation. (Be sure to visit the preservation book store next door.) Decatur House was the first private house to be built on Lafayette Square.

6. LAFAYETTE SQUARE RESTORATION**

With new plans to demolish the rowhouses along Lafayette Square already designed, President Kennedy engaged architect John Carl Warnecke to study the problem. The result was a splendid solution; the integration of taller elements with the restored and infill row houses. The "bookends" not only saved, but enhanced the scale, fabric and marvelous sense of space of Lafayette Square. The two office buildings referred to as "bookends" flank Lafayette Square on the west and east and contain lovely courtyards with fountains. They are:

West - NEW EXECUTIVE OFFICE BUILDING*
17th and H Streets, N.W.
Hours: 9:00 a.m. to 5:00 p.m. Monday through Friday

East - UNITED STATES COURT OF CLAIMS* (See No. 13, this tour)
1968 - John Carl Warnecke and Associates

For more on Lafayette Square see No. 30, this tour.

7. U. S. CHAMBER OF COMMERCE BUILDING
1615 H Street, N. W.
1925 Cass Gilbert

The Chamber of Commerce and Treasury Annex (see 14, this tour) buildings are the only completed portions of a plan to unify the architecture of Lafayette Square in the Neo-Classic style of the older Treasury Building.

8. HAY-ADAMS HOTEL*
Northwest corner of 16th and H Streets, N. W.

This elegant hotel was the site of H. H. Richardson's houses for Henry Adams and John Hay.

9. ST. JOHN'S CHURCH**
16th and H Streets, N. W.
1816 - Benjamin Latrobe
1883 - James Renwick

In the church, also known as "the Church of the Presidents," a pew has been set aside for the President and his family. The original architect, Benjamin Latrobe, was the first organist.

10. ST. JOHN'S PARISH BUILDING (Old British Embassy)
1525 H Street, N. W.
1822-1824 St. Clair Clarke

(See Restaurant Guide for description of French lunch here on Wednesdays)

11. BENJAMIN OGLE TAYLOE HOUSE
21 Madison Place, N. W.
1828

12. Cutts Madison House (DOLLY MADISON HOUSE)*
H Street and Madison Place, N. W.
1820

The Dolly Madison and the Tayloe House are mentioned more for their historic value than their architectural contributions.

13. The UNITED STATES COURT OF CLAIMS*
717 Madison Place, N. W.
Hours: 9:00 a.m. to 5:00 p.m. Monday through Friday

An arcaded passageway leads pedestrians from H Street through a pleasant courtyard to Madison Place, N.W. and Lafayette Square. The entrance to a "colonial style" cafeteria faces the courtyard.

14. TREASURY ANNEX
Pennsylvania Avenue and Madison Place, N. W.
1919 - Cass Gilbert

The unified facade treatment of these buildings (14-18) and
their massive columns give the old financial district a rather
stolid appearance.

15. RIGGS NATIONAL BANK
1503 Pennsylvania Avenue, N. W.
1898 - York and Sawyer

16. AMERICAN SECURITY AND TRUST COMPANY
Northwest corner of 15th Street and Pennsylvania Avenue, N. W.
1899 - York and Sawyer

17. UNION TRUST BUILDING
Southwest corner of 15th and H Streets, N. W.
1906 - Wood, Donnard and Deming

This classic bank building sets the tone for Washington's old
financial district along 15th Street.

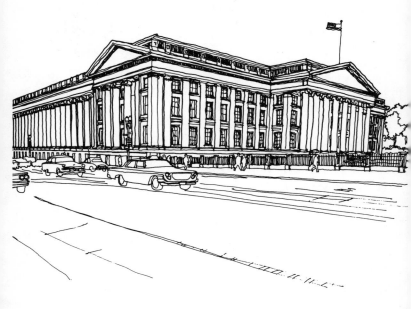

18. TREASURY BUILDING*
1500 Pennsylvania Avenue, N. W.
1836-1869 - Robert Mills, Thomas U. Walter

The site, selected by Andrew Jackson, destroyed L'Enfant's vista
between the Capitol and the White House. The Treasury is the
third oldest federal building in Washington.

19. NATIONAL SAVINGS AND TRUST COMPANY*
Northeast corner of 15th Street and Pennsylvania Avenue, N. W.
1880 - James Windrim

The red brick Victorian style structure occupies an important position in the financial district across from the Treasury Department. Its architectural style and color contrasts sharply with its rather stolid neighbors.

20. THE ELLIPSE

Like Lafayette Square, the Ellipse (between 15th, 17th and Constitution Avenue) was the southern portion of the presidential grounds included in the L'Enfant Plan. Note the visual relationship between the White House and the Jefferson Memorial; the strong axial relationship along 16th Street, through the White House to the Jefferson Memorial. L'Enfant intended the monument to George Washington to be located along this north-south axis, yet soil conditions prevented its construction there (see Tour 4, Mall-West).

21. PAN AMERICAN UNION* (Organization of American States)
17th and Constitution Avenue, N. W.
1910 - Albert Kelsey and Paul Cret
Hours: 8:30 a.m. to 4:30 p.m. Weekdays and Saturdays

The interior court filled with many tropical plants creates a lovely space.

65

22.   CONSTITUTION HALL (Daughters of the American Revolution Hall)
1778 D Street, N. W.
C. 1930 John Russell Pope
Revolutionary Period Museum with tour
9:00 a.m. to 4:00 p.m., Monday through Friday

Home of the National Symphony prior to the opening of the
Kennedy Center; the D.A.R. Hall's program now consists of
varied concerts.

23.   AMERICAN NATIONAL RED CROSS
17th, D and E Streets, N. W.
1929 - Livingston
Hours: 9:00 a.m. to 4:00 p.m., Monday through Friday

Note the imposing yet rather pleasingly harmonious variety of
styles of the buildings along 17th Street north of Constitution
to Pennsylvania Avenue.

24.   CORCORAN GALLERY OF ART**
17th and New York Avenue, N.W.
1897 - Ernest Flagg
Hours: 10:00 a.m. to 4:30 p.m. Tuesday through
Sunday
Closed Mondays, Christmas and New Years Day

2:00 p.m. to 5:00 p.m. Saturday and Sunday
Free admission on Tuesday and Wednesday

Clearly, this is one of Washington's finest art galleries. A fine example of Beaux-Art style, the Corcoran has a magnificant interior atrium gallery.

25. WINDER BUILDING
604 17th Street, N. W.
1847-1848

Although the building pioneered the use of central heating, steel beams and was a veritable high rise in its time, its significance is more historical than architectural. It was the first, among many more to come, of the inexpensive, speculative office buildings designed to be leased for use by the federal government — its use today.

26. Headquarters Building, FEDERAL HOME LOAN BANK BOARD
17th and G Streets, N.W.
1977 - Max Urbahn and Associates

A wonderfully innovative and attractive design, the Headquarters is well integrated with the GSA renovated Winder building, harmonizing new with old. The building features a lively urban park with an ice skating rink in the winter that converts into a fountain in the summer, an outdoor restaurant and retail uses at the street level. The project is significant in that it represents an effort by GSA to upgrade the quality of federal architecture, and to incorporate lively, nightime uses into the deserted downtown area.

27. EXECUTIVE OFFICE BUILDING** (Old State, War and Navy)
Pennsylvania Avenue and 17th Street, N.W.
1871-1888 - A. N. Mullett

Behind the 900 doric columns was the world's largest office building at the time it was built. The building, a veritable wealth of detail, is probably the most eloquent government building in Washington. In an effort to beautify the Nation's Capital, President Kennedy saved the Old Executive Building from demolition and initiated planning for the improvement of Pennsylvania Avenue in the 1960's.

28. BLAIR-LEE HOUSES*
1651 Pennsylvania Avenue, N. W.
1824
1931 - Restored, W. Faulkner

These fine houses are used by the government for entertaining distinguished visitors from foreign countries.

29. THE WHITE HOUSE***
1600 Pennsylvania Avenue, N. W.
Begun 1792 - James Hoban, Benjamin Latrobe and others
Hours: 10:00 a.m. to 12:00 p.m., except Sunday, Monday and holidays

The simple, yet dignified home of our President has over 132 rooms, including the 54 rooms and 16 baths in the living quarters. The Adams were the first to occupy the White House and soon after in 1814, it was burned by the British. It is speculated that the building was first painted white at this time to cover the charring from the fire.

30. LAFAYETTE SQUARE***

The park was included in the President's Park according to L'Enfants Plan in 1791. Jefferson authorized its separation into a park for public use. In 1824, the park was named in honor of Major General Marquis de Lafayette, a hero in the American Revolution.

The central statue of Andrew Jackson, cast from the cannons captured by Jackson during the War of 1812, was the first equestrian statue in Washington; second in the U. S. The four other statues are of American Revolutionary heroes. General Lafayette (southeast corner, 1890); Comte de Rochambeau, (southwest corner, 1902); General Thaddeus Kosiuszko (northeast corner, 1910); and Baron Van Steuben (northwest corner, 1910).

Lafayette Square, probably one of the loveliest urban spaces in any American city, is actively used most of the year, especially during the summer when many free lunch time concerts are sponsored by the National Park Service.

9 **FEDERAL TRIANGLE (government office buildings, Old Post Office)

By Sally Kress Tompkins

Ms. Tompkin's Masters Degree thesis dealt with the development of the Federal Triangle.

DISTANCE: 1¼ Miles   *TIME: ¾ Hour*

METRO: Federal Triangle (Blue & Orange)

BUS: On 14th Street: 50, 52, 9, 11A, 11E, 11W; on Pennsylvania Avenue: 30, 32, 34, 36, 38, and 54.

The Federal Triangle is formed by the intersection of Constitution Avenue, N. W. with the diagonal Pennsylvania Avenue, N. W. and is bounded on the west by 15th Street, N. W. and on the east by 6th Street, N. W. When Pierre L'Enfant imposed his grand design on the tobacco fields, farms and wilderness that were to become the capital, the Triangle was a swamp, subject to frequent flooding from the nearby Tiber Creek. Nevertheless, its exceptional location, south of Pennsylvania Avenue and north of the Mall between the White House and the Capital, made it of obvious importance. L'Enfant marked it as the future site of municipal buildings.

After the construction of the Tiber Canal in 1816 alleviated the flooding, the Triangle area developed rapidly but as a commercial rather than as a governmental center. The Center Market, between 7th and 9th Streets, N. W. and dating from 1801, was replaced in 1870 by a large modern brick market whose stalls spread out as far as 11th Street, N. W. Hotels, taverns, rooming houses, printing and newspaper offices filled the area.

After the Civil War the Triangle began to deteriorate. In 1899 the Old Post Office was erected at 12th Street and Pennsylvania Avenue, N. W., and it was hoped that this would be the beginning of a Renaissance for the area. The McMillan Commission plan of 1901 pictured the Triangle as a park dotted with various government buildings of a municipal nature; and, in 1908, the District Building was erected at 14th and E Streets, N. W. but no further action was taken. Conditions became increasingly scandalous: tatoo parlors, gas stations, cheap hotels, and chop suey signs were prevalent, and Ohio Avenue (eliminated by Triangle construction) was lined with brothels. At the same time the government's need for more office space was growing acute. The Public Buildings bill allocating 50 million dollars for buildings in the District was finally passed by Congress and signed by President Calvin Coolidge on May 5, 1926. Two years later, Congress appropriated the money to buy the entire Triangle.

Secretary of the Treasury, Andrew Mellon, was responsible for the construction and design of the buildings, and in 1927, he appointed a Board of Architectural Consultants to draw up a plan for the entire Triangle area. The original members were Edward H. Bennett, Chairman, Louis Ayres, Milton Medary, William Adams Delano, Arthur Brown, Jr. and Louis Simon. John Russell Pope was included later.

The architects and the members of the National Commission of Fine Arts who took an active role in formulating the plan, accepted the prevailing premise that the neoclassic style was the proper one for public buildings. They saw in the Triangle development a rare opportunity to plan a group of monumental buildings designed and related to constitute a single great composition. Public enthusiasm was high for the project, and the capital was caught up in a quest for grandeur. They looked forward to Washington becoming the "Paris of America" and talked of a capital, "worthy of a great nation."

In 1929, the model of the Triangle composition designed by the Board of Architectural Consultants went on display. The architects had given the Triangle a treatment somewhat similar to the Louvre, with buildings reflecting a high classical style. They had designed a series of courtyards of which a central circular court was pivotal. Vistas from this court extended into the other plazas, one of which, the Great Plaza, was to be as large as Lafayette Square. The main entrances were planned to open onto these courts so that a sense of quiet would pervade the scheme. The buildings had a uniform cornice line drawn from the Natural History Museum and followed the diagonal of Pennsylvania Avenue. Pylons at the entrances and specially designed sidewalks served to unify the composition.

Unfortunately the Triangle would never achieve the perfection for which its designers strove. The depression and the automobile would sadly alter the final composition. The Great Plaza became a parking lot. The sweeping drives turned into major traffic arteries, and the pylons that were to flank them were declared a traffic hazard and never constructed. The circular court was never completed because the Old Post Office, anathema to the Triangle's designers, was never demolished. Depression economies put the future of the final structure, the Federal Trade Commission building at the apex, in doubt. When it was finally constructed in 1937, it was a simplified version of the original design. By that time the neoclassic style was out of favor and there was little interest in the buildings or in completing the design. The Triangle's imperial facade was deemed inappropriate for a democratic country.

Today the Triangle presents a confused and ill-defined image. The finished facade along Constitution Avenue is somewhat forbidding, and the Pennsylvania Avenue side is a nightmare of cut up space and chaotic traffic patterns. Too much monumentality, robbed of its planned interludes of green, voids itself in a sea of limestone and columns. The individual Triangle buildings, with the exception of the Archives, lack architectural distinction; they draw their importance from their relationship to one another. It is the overall design of the Triangle that lays claim to those unique qualities which mark an important artistic contribution. Completion of that design would turn what is at present a liability to downtown Washington into one of the finest areas in the Capital. As the redevelopment of Pennsylvania Avenue gets underway, proposals have been made to restore the Great Plaza and put the automobile under ground. Hopefully this will mark the beginning of a movement to at last complete the Triangle's design.

Start your walking tour at the Oscar Straus Memorial Fountain across 14th Street from the Commerce Department building.

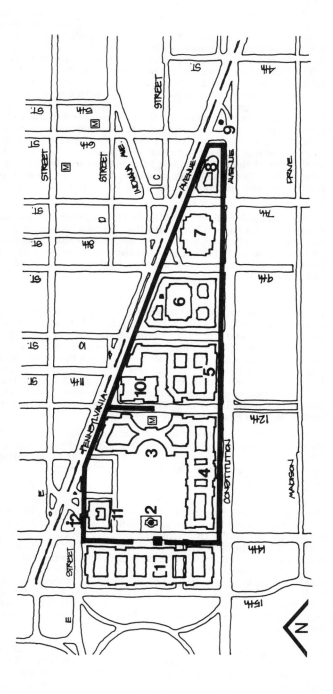

71

1. The COMMERCE DEPARTMENT BUILDING* was designed by Louis Ayres of the firm of York and Sawyer and was intended to house all the bureaus of the department under one roof, which it did, excepting the Bureau of Standards. At the time of its construction it was the largest government office building in the world, 1,050 feet in length, exceeding the Capitol by 300 feet. It has five miles of corridors and 5,000 windows. The building is essentially three complete rectangular buildings each with a large inner courtyard. Arched gateways two stories high give direct access through the building at what used to be C and D Streets, but above the gates the structural mass is unbroken. The central section of the 14th Street facade is patterned after the Perrault facade at the Louvre and has 22 doric columns with flanking pilasters — the other sides of the building have 16 columns each, bringing the total to 70. The relief panels represent the various agencies of the department and were designed by James Earle Fraser.

2. The OSCAR STRAUS MEMORIAL FOUNTAIN* was designed by John Russell Pope with the figures sculpted by Adolph A. Weinman. The large parking lot behind it is the Great Plaza. Picture the space as the designers envisaged it, landscaped as a formal garden with a sunken panel and balustrade, planted with oak trees.

3. At the eastern end of the parking lot is the hemicycle building, housing the POST OFFICE DEPARTMENT *. It was designed by the firm of Delano and Aldrich and meant to form a fitting terminus to the Great Plaza. The sculptured pediment is the work of Adolph A. Weinman. The bricks visible at the Pennsylvania Avenue side of the Post Office Department building mark the place where a final wing was to adjoin the building and enclose the Plaza. The opposite or eastern facade of the building forms half of the proposed circular court. The dark tower visible behind it is that of the Old Post Office.

Walk south on 14th Street and cross Constitution Avenue. The elaborate neoclassic facade of the Triangle buildings along Constitution Avenue is best viewed from a distance. It is particularly impressive at night when the facades are illuminated.

4. Arthur Brown, Jr. of San Francisco, designer of the City Hall and War Memorial Opera House in that city, was the architect of the complex made up of the U. S. CUSTOMS SERVICE (originally built for the Labor Department), the DEPARTMENTAL AUDITORIUM and the INTERSTATE COMMERCE COMMISSION BUILDING. Of particular interest is the second story relief panel of the Departmental Auditorium which diverges from the neoclassic allegorical sculpture typical of the buildings' exteriors. Designed by Edmond Romulus Amateis it depicts General George Washington with Major Generals Nathanael Green and John Sullivan. Green's face is that of architect Brown and Sullivan's is that of sculptor Edgar Walter.

5. Crossing 12th Street you are now looking across Constitution Avenue at the INTERNAL REVENUE SERVICE BUILDING and the comforting words of Oliver Wendell Holmes inscribed on it: "Taxes are what we pay for a civilized society." The building was designed by the Office of the Supervising Architect of the Treasury

Department under the direction of Louis Simon. It was completed in 1930, the first of the group to be finished. It is constructed of Indiana limestone and granite with columns of Tennessee marble. The building has four inner courtyards handsomely landscaped. The final wing, which was to form the eastern side of the circular court, was never completed.

6. When you have crossed 10th Street you are opposite the JUSTICE DEPARTMENT BUILDING. It was designed by the Philadelphia firm of Zantzinger, Borie and Medary, and completed in 1934. The metal doors are fine examples of the Art Deco style. A statue of Nathan Hale by Bela Lyon Pratt, stands in front of the building. The relief panel above the door depicting "law and order" was designed by Carl Paul Jennewein, who also sculpted the fine neoclassic figures of The Four Winds which decorate the largest of its four inner courtyards.

7. As you proceed across 9th Street there is a bench in the center of the block which offers a place to rest and admire John Russell Pope's ARCHIVES BUILDING*** and to understand why he was reduced to tears by the request of the Archivist of

73

the United States to reverse the building so that his office would have a view of the mall. The structure is purely classical with completely plain walls, except for windows to accommodate the offices on the Pennsylvania Avenue side. It is adorned by 72 Corinthian pillars, 52 feet high, grouped in colonnades about the building. The great pediment on the Constitution Avenue facade displays a figure representing the Recorder of the Archives and two eagles standing guard at the sides. The sculptor was James Earle Fraser who also designed the large seated figures which flank the monumental steps. The steps lead into a public hall which houses the DECLARATION OF INDEPENDENCE *** the CONSTITUTION*** and the BILL OF RIGHTS *** all on display along with a changing special exhibit. The Archives' less notable records are housed in a central steel shaft.

8. Crossing back to the other side of Constitution Avenue and proceeding to the last of the Triangle group, the FEDERAL TRADE COMMISSION* or Apex Building, be sure to notice the specially designed sidewalks which surround most of the Triangle. This building, designed by Bennett, Parsons and Frost, was considerably altered from the original model to be acceptable to a nation in the throes of a depression. It is still a very satisfying building, however, and its eastern end, a ROUNDED COLONNADE* of doric columns reminiscent of a blunted ship's bow, makes an excellent terminus to the Triangle composition. The Art Deco style becoming increasingly popular in the 1930's is much in evidence in the relief panels, the decorative medallions, the aluminum doors, and most dramatically in Michael Lantz's horses which flank the eastern colonnade.

9. The ANDREW MELLON MEMORIAL FOUNTAIN* across 6th Street from the Federal Trade building is an exclamation point to the Triangle. The fountain, completed in 1952, could not be in a more appropriate position, filling the last sliver of the great Triangle which Mellon's influence brought to fruition and situated directly across from the National Gallery of Art which he gave to the nation. The fountain was designed by Otto R. Eggers in bronze and granite; the signs of the zodiac, visible under the sheet of water formed by the overflow from the basins, are the work of Sidney Waugh. There are also benches to

rest on before beginning the walk back along Pennsylvania Avenue.

The Pennsylvannia Avenue side of the Triangle reveals all its weaknesses as well as its great potential. It is noticeable here that John Russell Pope did not follow the diagonal of the Avenue as did the other architects. The resulting triangular slice of land is a small park, a memorial to Franklin Delano Roosevelt, located there according to his wishes. The flanking statues at the Archives entrance are the work of Robert Aiken. The Justice Department building presents no surprises, neatly filling the entire block. The short, truncated facade of the IRS building testifies that the design here was never completed.

10. The OLD POST OFFICE** was designed by Willoughby Edbrooke in the Richardsonian Romanesque style popular at the time of its construction in 1899. It was considered an "object of permanent regret" by the neoclassicists, and the Triangle designers drew up a plan that demanded its demolition. Its bulk cuts across the space that would have been the pivotal circular court designed after the "gay fashion of Paris." It is worth walking down 12th Street to see the great eastern facade of the Post Office Department building that was to form half of that court. A small segment of the opposite side of the circular court is visible on the IRS building behind the old Post Office. A metro station is being constructed there at the present time, and the Old Post Office, saved from the bulldozer, will be remodeled for government offices and commercial activities — producing a multi-use character seldom offered in government buildings.

Continuing down Pennsylvania Avenue past the unfinished wing of the Post Office Department one has another view of the Great

75

Plaza — what the President's Temporary Commission on Pennsylvania Avenue called "potentially one of the finest urban land spaces in the country," now filled with cars.

11.   The DISTRICT BUILDING* was designed by Cope and Stewardson in 1908 in a style described as "Beaux Arts classicicism." The original 1929 model of the Triangle did not include it, but later plans did, using landscaping features to relate it to the Great Plaza.

12.   In front of the District building is a statue of Alexander Robey Shepherd, governor of the territory of Washington, D. C. from September, 1873 until June, 1874, and the city's most famous administrator (see Tour 23, Shepherd Park).   He brought about a remarkable program of public improvements.   The statue, by U. S. J. Dunbar, was erected in 1909.

Museums:

The AQUARIUM
Located in the basement of the Commerce Department Bldg.
Enter from the 14th Street side.
Hours: 9:00 a.m. to 5:00 p.m. daily

The NATIONAL ARCHIVES***
Enter from Constitution Avenue.
Hours: 9:00 a.m. to 6:00 p.m. Monday through Saturday
1:00 p.m. to 6:00 p.m. Sundays

10 **DOWNTOWN (central business district, pedestrian malls, National Portrait Gallery, Ford's Theatre, FBI Building)

By Robert N. Gray, AICP

Mr. Gray is Director of Operations and Manager of Business Development of The Greater Washington Board of Trade. Formerly Mr. Gray was planning director of Downtown Progress, an action group for the revitalization of downtown Washington.

DISTANCE: 4 Miles   TIME: 2 Hours

BUS: 42, 60, 62, 80, B6, D2, D4, D8, L2, L4, L8, M8, D2, S2, S4, X2, X4 and X6.

METRO: Metro Center (Red, Blue & Orange)

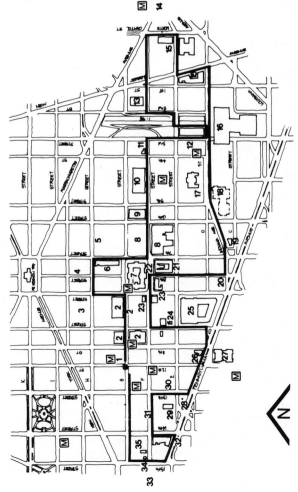

1. METRO CENTER** is the largest and expected to be the most heavily used of the 86 METRO stations in the 100-mile regional rapid rail transit system. Above the station, at 12th, 13th, and G Streets, N. W., are publicly-acquired urban renewal sites totalling 4.13 acres which have a reuse potential of more than 1.7 million gross square feet of floor area for mixed-use development. Subway service on a limited 4½ mile segment through downtown started March, 1976.

2. The 900 block of G Street, N.W., east of Woodward & Lothrop, one of Washington's major department stores, is part of the STREETS FOR PEOPLE* pedestrian improvements. The project includes special paving, lighting, signing, plantings, and fountains. Along this block are a number of significant institutions and facilities, including the MARTIN LUTHER KING MEMORIAL LIBRARY* at 9th and G Streets, N.W., the only work of architect Mies van der Rohe in Washington. It was completed in 1972 and is eight times larger than the old D.C. Central Library at Mt. Vernon Square which it replaced.

3. The area south of Mt. Vernon Square is the site for a major civic and convention center. The center will contain 300,000 square feet of multipurpose exhibit space and 30 meeting rooms.

4. In the L'Enfant Plan for the City of Washington, 8th Street, N. W., located midway between the White House and the Capitol, is a major axis. Its vista in this location is broken by two important buildings: the old D. C. Central Library to the north, dedicated by Teddy Roosevelt in 1901; and the National Portrait Gallery/National Collection of Fine Arts (Old Patent Office) to the south.

5. In 1970, Washington's CHINATOWN included approximately 500 dwelling units, 1,000 residents and 30 businesses. The Chinese Consolidated Benevolent Association and others have been working for the creation of a Chinese Cultural Center and housing for elderly within the area to help strengthen the existing base of Chinese activities. The Chinese New Year parade, complete with dragons and firecrackers, attracts 10,000 people to H Street each year.

6. The buildings along the west side of the 700 BLOCK OF 7TH STREET* between G and H Streets, N. W. were erected in the 1880's. These three and four-story Victorian brick commercial structures have remained substantially unchanged except for the street floor windows. This business frontage is a Category III landmark.

7. The NATIONAL PORTRAIT GALLERY/NATIONAL COLLECTION OF FINE ARTS*** building at F, G, 7th and 9th Streets, N. W. was formerly the U. S. Patent Office, a patent museum, then a repository for the Declaration of Independence, and a Civil War hospital before its renovation and reuse by the Smithsonian Institution in 1968 as a public art gallery. An excel-

lent example of Classical Revival architecture and a Category I landmark, the building now contains two excellent art collections plus a popular cafeteria with seating in its interior, landscaped courtyard where lunch is anything from a "sandwich" to a "Yogurt Sundae" (see Restaurants and Carryouts).

8. Publicly acquired for redevelpment is the entire block located between 6th, 7th, F and G Streets, N. W. across from the Hecht Company, another large department store. Provision for access into the site from the METRO mezzanine below grade enhances its development potential. Redevelopment of this 2.77 acre site is expected to include a mixture of commercial uses totalling potentially 1,208,380 gross square feet.

9. The Washington Metropolitan Transit Authority (WMATA) — builders of METRO and operators of Metrobus — moved into their new building in 1974. (Keyes, Lethbridge and Condon, a local firm, designed the building.) It accommodates METRO's 1,100-person headquarters staff and houses the fare collection and central computer facilities for the entire rapid rail transit system.

10. The OLD PENSION BUILDING** (1882), a Category I landmark in JUDICIARY SQUARE*, was designed by retired Col. Montgomery C. Meigs, engineer of the Capitol Dome and the Cabin John Bridge. Its huge central hall, an innovation for lighting and ventilation at the time, was used for presidential inaugural balls in the 1800's. The building has been proposed as a museum and center for the building arts including American architecture, landscape architecture, and construction.

11. The ADAS ISRAEL SYNAGOGUE*, dedicated in 1876, was the first building constructed as a synagogue in the District of Columbia. It was moved to its present site in 1969, and its restoration was completed in 1974. A small museum inside is open Sundays 10 to 4 and weekdays by appointment (789-0800).

12.   Designed by Victor Lundy, the new U. S. TAX COURT, east of 3rd Street between D and E Streets, N. W., utilizes innovative structural concepts of post-tensioning to support a cantilevered courtroom on six columns. A landscaped pedestrian plaza with a lily-pond will span the adjacent Center-Leg freeway.

13.   Designed by Edward Durrell Stone (architect also of the John F. Kennedy Center for the Performing Arts), the GEORGETOWN UNIVERSITY LAW CENTER* opened in 1969 with facilities for 1,700 students.

14.   The landmark UNION STATION*** has been converted to the National Visitors Center providing information, orientation, exhibits, and eating facilities. (see Tour 1, Capitol Hill).

15.   Several new commercial buildings have been constructed in the vicinity of North Capitol Street, New Jersey Avenue, E Street and F Street, N. W. in recent years. Capitol Mall North, an eight-story office building; 400 North Capitol Plaza, providing office space for 3,500 employees; and the 900 room Hyatt Regency Hotel illustrate the revitalization occurring downtown between the White House and the Capitol.

16.   The new DEPARTMENT OF LABOR BUILDING, located between 2nd and 3rd Streets south of D Street, N. W. accommodates approximately 4,000 employees. Below this large federal building is the eight-lane Center-Leg freeway which crosses the mall entirely in tunnel. The Department of Labor Building incorporates ventilation shafts for the freeway tunnel as does the new HEW building across the Mall.

17.   The OLD CITY HALL* (begun in 1820 and successively added to until completed in 1916), a Category I landmark in Judiciary Square, was the first public building constructed to house the District of Columbia Government. It has been put to various other uses, including a "jail lot" and a Civil War Hospital. The D. C. courts presently occupy the building.

18.   The new home for the DISTRICT OF COLUMBIA COURT OF APPEALS AND SUPERIOR COURT at Indiana Avenue, John Marshall Place, 6th and D Streets, N.W., opened in 1977. It has one appellate and 44 trial courtrooms plus ancillary space and totals 375,000 net square feet. Continuing a Washington architectural tradition, it has a large exterior courtyard with extensive plantings.

19.   The Richardsonian-style NATIONAL BANK OF WASHINGTON BUILDING* at 7th Street and Indiana Avenue, N. W. (1886), a Category III landmark, is proposed to be retained in the Pennsylvania Avenue Plan. Notice the TEMPERANCE MONUMENT* located in front of Apex Liquors, one of Washington's interesting juxtapositions.

20. L'Enfant designated the area between 7th and 9th Streets on Pennsylvania Avenue as an open space called Market Square. According to the Pennsylvania Avenue Plan, shops, offices and 750 residential units are to be built east of 7th Street, N.W.

21. The Greek Revival-style Tariff Commission Building (Robert Mills - 1839), a Category II landmark, was originally to be the District of Columbia's Post Office. It has provided space for a variety of government departments since then. The International Trade Commission currently occupies the building and a Post Office is located on its main floor.

22. Between 7th and 9th on F Street, N.W. — "GALLERY PLACE" — a portion of downtown Washington's STREETS FOR PEOPLE pedestrian system provides space for sitting, watching an occasional performance by street musicians or others, enjoying a casual lunch, and relaxing. Fountains and pools add excitement to the area. The Gallery Place METRO station underlies G Street—one block north.

23. At the corner of 9th and F Streets, N. W., are several noteworthy commercial and architectural landmarks: the Richardsonian-style RIGGS NATIONAL BANK* (1891), a Category II landmark; Lansburgh's Furniture Store (1870), a Category III landmark; and the buildings on the south side of the 800 BLOCK OF F STREET, N. W., including the LeDROIT BUILDING*, all Category II landmarks. These facades compliment that of the National Portrait Gallery. The Le Droit Building, an early nonelevated Victorian office building, now contains the studios of approximately 30 D. C. artists. Many of D. C.'s well-known artists have had studios in this building.

24.   FORD'S THEATER***, a Category I landmark, where President Lincoln was assassinated, was restored by the National Park Service and reopened as a museum and a live theater in 1965. Across 10th Street, N. W., the PETERSEN HOUSE* has also been restored to its appearance on April 14, 1865, when the dying President was carried there for treatment.

25.   The J. EDGAR HOOVER FBI BUILDING was completed in 1975 at a cost of $126 million. The building provides space for more than 8,000 employees, 850 parking spaces, and has an interior courtyard. The FBI TOUR* is a popular visitor attraction.

26.   The Pennsylvania Avenue Plan calls for a building setback of 50 feet along the north side of the avenue. This would result in a 76-foot wide sidewalk to be lined with three rows of trees. All new buildings are to conform to this setback. However, several significant existing structures which extend into this space may remain, including the OLD EVENING STAR BUILDING and the WASHINGTON and WILLARD HOTELS*.

27.   The OLD POST OFFICE BUILDING** (1899), a Romanesque Revival Building and a Category II landmark, contains a

handsome interior courtyard and a distinctive clock tower 315 feet high. The National Endowment for the Arts has proposed that the building become its headquarters. Public use areas would be provided in and around the interior courtyard on the lower floors (see Tour 9, Federal Triangle).

28. The Statue of Brigadier General Count Casimir Pulaski, a Revolutionary War patriot, stands in the park at 13th and E Streets, N. W.

29. The nearby NATIONAL THEATER** (Washington's oldest theater) opened in 1835 with the comedy, "Man of the World," and "Turnout," a musical farce. The National Theater is to be incorporated in the major redevelopment taking place on this block as part of the Pennsylvania Avenue Plan.

30. The WARNER THEATER at 13th and E Streets, N.W., has a long history as an entertainment center in downtown Washington. An ornate movie palace in earlier decades, the Warner is now a live stage for various theatrical and musical productions.

31. Dedicated in 1966, F STREET PLAZA* demonstrated that vehicles and pedestrians can co-exist more favorably. F Street Plaza has stimulated business activity and has become a downtown Washington landmark. Its success served as an impetus for Streets for People. Opposite the Plaza at 14th Street, N. W. is Garfinckel's, Washington's largest fashionable specialty store.

32. The WILLARD HOTEL*, at 14th Street and Pennsylvania Avenue, N.W., a Category III landmark, opened in 1901 and served as one of Washington's top visitor accommodations for many years. On the site of the Willard, Julia Ward Howe composed the "Battle Hymn of the Republic." The hotel is to be restored as part of the Pennsylvania Avenue redevelopment plan.

33. The TREASURY BUILDING** was designed between 1836 and 1839 by several period architects. It is an outstanding example of Greek Revival Architecture and has influenced civic building design throughout the United States (see Tour 8, White House).

34. Constructed in 1800, RHODES TAVERN* (only about one-third of the original structure remains) is the oldest commercial building in downtown Washington. A Category II landmark, it was used as a polling place in the first municipal election in 1802. British officers ate dinner in the tavern while the White House burned in 1814. The Rhodes Tavern building may be demolished in the course of the redevelopment of this block.

35. Adjacent to Rhodes Tavern is the OLD EBBITT GRILL*, the interior of which is a Category III landmark. The Old Ebbitt Grill was moved to this location from its original site where the National Press Building now stands. The reconstructed interior includes the original mahogany bar and much of the old grill work (see Restaurant Guide).

84

11 **MIDTOWN (office, hotel, high quality restaurant and retail area)

By Allan A. Hodges, AICP

DISTANCE: 2¾ Miles   *TIME: 1¼ Hours*

BUS: 38, 42, D2, D4, D8, H6, L2, L4, L8, M8, N2, and N4

METRO: Farragut North (Red)

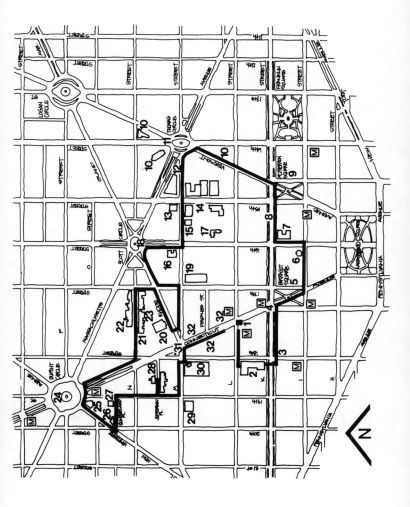

1. The increased accessibility that METRO has brought Washington has channelled new development near certain well located stations. At this key Midtown corner, a private developer has leased the air rights above the Farragut North METRO Station and has built an attractive red brick office-retail building. Because it has a direct underground connection to the station, no automobile parking spaces were required by the city, an innovative development incentive.

2. The huge block-long office building at 1801 K Street, N. W. contains an ATTRACTIVE TWO LEVEL RETAIL MALL which can be entered from L Street or K Street, N. W. Greek submarine sandwiches, salads with feta cheese and splits of wine are available at the Port of Piraeus on the K Street Level. Have an al fresco lunch at nearby Farragut Square.

3. The corner of K and 18th Streets, N.W., is a good position to view the visual effect of the 130 foot HEIGHT LIMIT* for buildings in the city. Restricted by the Height of Buildings Act of 1910, a congressional statute, Washington has developed a flat, low skyline unique for large U.S. cities. Some have complained that the height limit has restricted good architecture. But well designed buildings built here during the late 1970s and early 1980s have proven otherwise.

4. The corner of CONNECTICUT AND K STREETS, N. W.* is the center of Washington's booming private office district. This area, referred to by some as Midtown, accounts for nearly one third of the total employment in the central employment area of the city. In addition, Washington's major hotels, better restaurants, quality shops and much of its growing night life are located here. Midtown is also a good place to experience the main features of Pierre L'Enfant's plan for Washington: diagonal radial avenues super-imposed over a grid street system with circles and squares at their intersections.

5. "Damn the torpedoes! Full Speed Ahead!" said David G. Farragut during a Civil War battle in 1864 in Mobile Bay. A sta-

tue to the Admiral is the centerpiece to lovely Farragut Square, and a roosting place for scores of pigeons. With good reason. FARRAGUT SQUARE** is one of the most heavily used urban parks in Washington. At noon, the "lunch bunch" congregates to eat brown bag lunches and be entertained by events ranging from concerts by the National Symphony to Karate exhibitions. A metro tunnel underlies the park.

6. The striking hexagonal THIRD CHURCH OF THE CHRIST SCIENTIST* and the CHRISTIAN SCIENCE MONITOR BUILDING* (N. W. Corner of 16th and Eye Streets, N. W.) were designed by I. M. Pei and Partners in 1972. The Plaza between them is rarely used by pedestrians because it lacks benches to sit on and the exit is not clearly marked. However, the whole setting is visually satisfying.

7. The SHERATON CARLTON HOTEL* (Mihran Mesrobian — 1926) is as elegant on the main floor as is its facade. Have a look at the ceiling details in the lobby. Across the street is the busy Capital-Hilton Hotel which caters to the convention/business trade.

8. Busy K STREET, a heavily travelled bus route, is the major east-west axis of the Midtown business district. The street channels commuter traffic westward to Virginia and Maryland. Many airline offices and business services are located here.

9. McPHERSON SQUARE*, the eastern counterpart of Farragut Square, is one of the many public reservations provided in the L'Enfant plan. A statue to Brigadier General McPherson who commanded the Tennessee Army was erected in 1876. During the summer months, many local workers and tourists relax in the park while eating lunches and listening to free outdoor concerts.

10. VERMONT AVENUE, N. W., the diagonal twin to Connecticut Avenue, N. W., is not nearly as busy as the other since it

leads into a residential area, (see Tour 14, Shaw School Urban Renewal Area/Logan Circle) instead of a major commercial corridor. Vermont Avenue, however, provides a good VIEW* of the steeples of the colonial style National City Christian Church (John Russel Pope - 1930) and the neo gothic Luther Place Memorial Church (Judson York - 1870). Recently constructed motor-hotels have added new life to this northeast corner of Midtown.

11. THOMAS CIRCLE** is one of fifteen major circles in the original L'Enfant Plan. The circle was intended as a quiet park, but now forms the junction of four of the city's busiest arteries. To relieve congestion, an underpass was built in 1940. In the late 19th and early 20th centuries, two and three-story private dwellings surrounded the area. The low density residential area has been replaced by apartment, hotel and office complexes. An equestrian statue of Major General George H. Thomas, a Union hero of the Civil War, commands the circle.

12. The NATIONAL HOUSING CENTER* (Vincent Kling and Associates - 1975) serves as the spectacular headquarters of the National Association of Home Builders. The first floor features an imaginative exhibit of housing in the U.S.

13. The PUBLIC CITIZENS VISITORS CENTER, 1200 15th Street, N. W., offers free information about congressional sessions, city tours, D. C. City Council Affairs, transit, etc. Visitors are welcome.

14. 15th Street, N. W., between L and M Streets, N. W., has been redeveloped privately during the past decade. Dominated by new office buildings, not unlike 13 story "boxes," the street is made more interesting by the huge new WASHINGTON POST headquarters and the posh MADISON HOTEL.

15. The METROPOLITAN AFRICAN METHODIST EPISCOPAL CHURCH*, known as the National Cathedral of African Methodism by its followers, is a Victorian Gothic structure — a style popular in America in the 1880's. Completed in 1886, the structure is more known for its importance to Black Washington as an influential church still prospering in central Washington than its architectural style. The church is a Category II landmark listed in the National Register of Historic places.

16. The JEFFERSON HOTEL*, a small quiet European style hotel, offers visitors a pleasant contrast to the big convention hotels or chain motels. The lobby area is flanked by an interesting use of air shafts. A little known restaurant within is a favorite of workers in the area. Originally built as an apartment house, the Jefferson has been a hotel for more than 35 years. It has been popular with artists and entertainers. Over the years guests at the Jefferson have included Victor Borge, Carol Channing, Vivian Leigh and Van Cliburn.

88

17. The Russians have outgrown their EMBASSY* on 16th Street, N.W. and have built a huge complex on Wisconsin Avenue north of Georgetown. Through a joint agreement, the Americans were to build a new embassy complex in Moscow at the same time.

18. SCOTT CIRCLE** is a good vantage point to view the WHITE HOUSE*** (see Tour 8, White House) and the WASHINGTON MONUMENT*** (see Tour 4, The Mall-West). Together, the White House and the Washington Monument provide a terminal view to a great avenue — a typical feature of L'Enfant's city plan for Washington. North of Scott Circle, the street is lined with imposing churches, embassies and mansions. (See Tour 12, 16th Street/Meridian Hill).

19. The "new" National Geographic Society building was designed by Edward Durell Stone in 1964. The first floor "EXPLORER'S HALL"* museum is fascinating and worth a visit.

20. ST. MATTHEW'S CATHEDRAL** (1899) is somewhat hidden by the large office buildings surrounding it. But good views of its dome are available from Scott Circle, the courtyard of the Iron Gate Inn Restaurant off N Street, N.W. and Jefferson Place, N.W. East of the cathedral is what remains of a row of elegant 19th century townhouses which continued to 17th Street, N.W. Half of the block was demolished to make room for the new Metropolitan YMCA.

21. N STREET, N.W.**, between 17th and 18th Streets, represents an almost contiguous block of beautiful 19th century townhouses. The street retains its historic charm despite continual pressures for redevelopment to higher density

uses. This block is located in the Dupont Circle Historic District which has been designated a Category II landmark and is on the National Register of Historic Places. This, plus a 1979 D. C. preservation law requiring an official review of demolition permits in the historic district, provides a limited measure of protection of this unique streetscape in Midtown.

22. The street contains two small european style hotels. One of them, TABARD INN, consists of three private residences built in 1860 and converted to a hotel in the 1920's. Edward Everett Hale wrote "The Man Without a Country" on the top floor in the 1860's.

23. Across the street from the Tabard Inn, tucked away in a courtyard, is an old stable turned into a restaurant — The IRON GATE INN* (see Restaurant Guide). The stables were on the estate of General Nelson A. Miles.

24. DUPONT CIRCLE** is Washington's largest circle park and one of its livliest - at all hours of day and night. The circle is located at the center of a cosmopolitan neighborhood. The area surrounding it has been designated a historic district. The view from the Circle down busy Connecticut Avenue toward the White House is impressive (see Tour 13, Dupont Circle).

25. The EURAM BUILDING*, 21 Dupont Circle, was designed by a local firm, Hartman-Cox, and opened in 1970. This striking departure from the "Washington box" shows that imaginative design can be accomplished, even within a rigid zoning envelope. The inner courtyard is a pleasant surprise upon entering.

26. The Columbia Historical Society occupies the HEURICH
HOUSE* (1892-94), a splendid example of Victorian architecture for which Washington is a treasure house. Threatened by
demolition to make way for an office building, a development
rights transfer was negotiated. The unused air space within
the zoning envelope of the Heurich House site was sold to the
adjacent site, permitting greater floor space in the office
building. The proceeds of the sale are to be used to restore
and maintain the mansion as well as to support the scholarly
activities of the Society.

27. The SUNDERLAND BUILDING, by another local firm
(Keyes, Lethbridge and Condon - 1969), is an example of good
design possible within the confines of the city's height limit.

28. Quiet JEFFERSON PLACE, N. W.*, lined with 19th century townhouses occupied by small professional offices, frames
a magnificent view of the dome of St. Matthew's Cathedral.

29. An office building with a mirrored facade sports a mid-
1970s office building fad in D.C.

30. A walk along the southside of M Street, N. W. towards
Connecticut Avenue, N. W. leads you to the entrance courtyard of 1800 M Street — a huge new office building opened
in 1975. The ground level contains an interesting SHOPPING
ARCADE and landscaped open space which relieves the mo-
notony typical of most new office buildings in Washington.

31. Across the street, in a little triangular park, is a STATUE
OF HENRY WADSWORTH LONGFELLOW*. Since 1909 he
has gazed over his "neighborhood" which has completely
changed from townhouses to high rises.

32. A stroll down CONNECTICUT AVENUE*, will take you
past some of Midtown Washington's most fashionable specialty
shops and boutiques.

91

12 ***SIXTEENTH STREET, N. W./MERIDIAN HILL
(Elegant mansions, street of churches, active restoration area)

By Perry G. Fisher

Mr. Fisher is Executive Director — Librarian of the Columbia Historical Society — a scholarly organization devoted to the history of the District of Columbia.

DISTANCE: 1½ Miles   TIME: 2 Hours

BUS: S2 and S4

METRO: Farragut North (Red)

Sixteenth Street, N. W. is the most prominent of the numbered streets of Washington, D. C., and is laid out along the north-south center line of the White House, just slightly east of the central meridian of the District of Columbia. The impressive boulevard mounts a series of gentle terraces shaped in the glacial period. One of the highest terraces encircling the original City of Washington is that stretching across Meridian Hill and Mount Pleasant at an average elevation of about 200 feet; a terrace which Sixteenth Street bisects in its route from Lafayette Square to Silver Spring, Maryland.

The lower Sixteenth Street corridor and the Meridian Hill district occupy land that at the time of the establishment of Washington, D. C., was part of three large estates stemming from 17th century patents from Lord Baltimore. When Pierre Charles L'Enfant submitted his Plan for the City of Washington in July, 1791, development in this section of the Territory of Columbia was rather typical of the tidewater region of the time. Minor plantation houses occupied the higher elevations overlooking the Potomac River. There were some widely scattered clusters of frame, shack-like houses near the streambanks which developed with the active milling enterprises along the larger, swifter tributaries of the Potomac. Settlement was sparse despite a good deal of speculation and subdivision of land in expectation of a real estate boom to accompany the move of the Federal Government to Washington. However, most of Sixteenth Street above K Street remained vacant throughout the first three-quarters of the 19th century. Before the Civil War small cottages near M and Sixteenth Streets were built and occupied by semi-skilled craftsmen and laborers. Many of these workers were black and employed in the light industrial and commercial businesses that depended on the streams flowing through the area.

Under the territorial form of government imposed upon the District of Columbia in 1871 and the ambitious public works programs of Alexander Robey Shepherd, executive officer of the Board of Public Works, the fortunes of Sixteenth Street and Meridian Hill took a different direction. The foundations of the impressive later development which still sets the physical character of the street and district were laid. Shepherd, as a successful local builder and real estate speculator, had a decided interest in the improvements of the West End of Washington. He began a program in the mid 1800's of deliberate cultivation of that section of the city as the most important residential and diplomatic quarter of the booming post-Civil War capital.

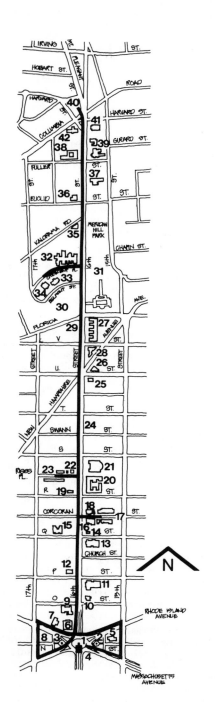

1.   SCOTT CIRCLE** (Massachusetts Avenue, Rhode Island Avenue and 16th Street, N. W.)

Scott Circle is one of the original federal reservations planned by L'Enfant, although Andrew Ellicott subsequently modified its configuration. It was not until the early 1870's that a park was laid out and an upper class residential neighborhood developed. The park area has been eroded continuously until today there is no meaningful public gathering space in Scott Circle. The present chaos is a perfect illustration of the problems of adapting Washington's many multiple-street intersections to the demands of automobile traffic. The diagonal avenues and Sixteenth Street are major commuting routes converging on this section of booming office construction. The automobile underpass along Sixteenth Street was completed in 1942.

Scott Circle takes its name from the statue of General Winfield Scott in the center of the space. The sculptor was Henry Kirk Brown and the figure was cast from a cannon captured in the Mexican War. The statue of Scott was first erected in 1874.

2.   In the small triangular park just to the east is the interesting MEMORIAL TO S. C. F. HAHNEMANN* (1775-1843), founder of the homeopathic school of medicine. The memorial was designed by Charles Henry Neihaus and erected in 1900 by the American Institute of Homeopathy.

3.   In the corresponding small triangular park just to the west of Sixteenth Street is Gaetano Trentanove's STATUE OF DANIEL WEBSTER* cast in bronze. The founder of the Washington Post, Stilson Hutchins, presented the statue to the city in 1900.

4.   1500 Massachusetts Avenue Apartment House; original SITE OF THE LOUISE HOME

The Louise Home stood until replaced by the present, bland apartment house in the early 1950's. The Louise Home was erected in 1871 through the generosity of William Wilson Corcoran, Washington banker, art patron, and philanthropist, as a refuge for "Protestant women of refinement and culture who have become reduced in circumstances in their old age."

5.   1500 Rhode Island Avenue, N. W. — NATIONAL PAINT AND COATINGS ASSOCIATION**

The present 1912 exterior of this building is John Russell Pope's classical entombment for most of architect John Fraser's 1879 house for John T. Brodhead, wealthy Marine Corps officer from Detroit. In 1882 Brodhead sold it to Gardiner Green Hubbard, founder of the National Geographic Society. Hubbard bought it for his daughter and son-in-law Alexander Graham Bell, who lived there until 1889.

For an example of architect Fraser's great domestic commissions in Washington, one may still view the James G. Blain mansion (1882) at 2000 Massachusetts Avenue, a building in all its essentials very much like the Brodhead-Bell mansion (see Tour 13, Dupont Circle). In 1889 Levi P. Morton, newly-elected vice president, purchased the Rhode Island Avenue house.

6.   1601 Massachusetts Avenue, N. W. — EMBASSY OF
AUSTRALIA CHANCERY*

Built in 1965, the Embassy of Australia Chancery firmly anchors
Embassy Row at Scott Circle, despite the continuing move of
embassies to the upper Northwest section of Washington. The
undistinguished building by Australian architect Bates Smart
McCutcheon is in no way an aesthetic contribution to an
important crossroads. The Australian government recently
doubled the size of the building to the rear, along Sixteenth
Street, after demolishing three fine rowhouses.

7.   1619 Massachusetts Avenue, N. W. — The FOREST INDUS-
TRIES BUILDING*

The Forest Industries Building is a much-praised work of the
local architectural firm of Keyes, Lethbridge, and Condon. The
order and polish, the dignified restraint in the use of materials,
and the proportioning of the main blocks and elements of the
facade have pleased both critics and laymen. A real understanding of the character of Washington and the design constraints it
imposes is evident here.

8.   West side of Scott Circle; cleared site

The vacant site on the west side of Scott Circle between Massachusetts and N Street, Seventeenth Street, and Bataan Place, N. W.,
awaits the construction of the new Embassy of the Philippines
Chancery. The distinctive turn-of-the-century rowhouses formerly on the site housed a long list of notable persons. But, Scott
Circle is an area that has been totally transformed in the years
since the Second World War. The district is now overwhelmingly
one of institutional and professional office uses.

A major factor in the changes that have taken place is the RE-
ZONING OF THE DISTRICT OF COLUMBIA*, which was prepared in 1954-1956 by Harold M. Lewis of New York City, and
which became effective May 12, 1958. Among the several zoning categories was the SPECIAL PURPOSE CATEGORY*; a
classification which has had particular importance for areas like
Scott and Dupont Circles, Sixteenth Street, and the major diagonal avenues. The intent of the Special Purpose zoning district
was to stabilize areas of special architectural, historical, or functional character adjacent to districts of high intensity commercial or Central Business District supporting uses. The conversion
of existing buildings to chancery, nonprofit organization, or
professional office use is a matter of right within an S-P zone,
and this provision has resulted in the conversion of many former residences to handsome adaptive uses. However, within an
S-P zone, a new hotel or apartment house of a height of ninety
feet is also a matter of right. Construction of new ninety-feet
high office buildings for chancery, nonprofit organization, or
professional use requires the approval of the Board of Zoning
Adjustment of the District of Columbia, and the Board has been
willing to grant such variances all too often. The result has been
a continual erosion of rowhouse districts in Washington. The
potential preservation benefits of Special Purpose zoning are
rarely realized.

9. Southwest Corner Sixteenth and O Streets, N. W. — FIRST
BAPTIST CHURCH*

This church building in a pseudo-Gothic style was designed in
1955 by Philadelphia architect Harold Waggoner. However, a
different style church once occupied the site. In 1890, architect W. Bruce Gray designed a red brick and sandstone church
which combined Romanesque and Italian Renaissance styles.
An impressive square campanile, flanking the main church on
the north, reached a height of 140 feet. A magnificent arched
recess sheltered the main entrance to the building.

The First Baptist Church building of 1890 marks the period
when many downtown congregations sought new sites in the
developing Sixteenth Street and Dupont Circle areas for their
church buildings, in an attempt to escape the increasing commercialism of the older parts of downtown. Washington.

10. 1401 Sixteenth Street, N. W. — Ingersoll and Bloch (former
GURLEY HOUSE*)

This is a fortunate case of adaptive use in a S-P zone. The house
was built in 1888 as a residence and was designed by one of the
builders, Samuel and Charles Edmonston. This firm was responsible for the construction of two Sixteenth Street houses designed
by H. H. Richardson. The Edmonstons borrowed heavily from
Richardson in their plans for the house, which has recently been
put to use as law offices and the office of syndicated columnist
Jack Anderson. Restoration costs proved cheaper than rental
rates in newer speculative office buildings nearby.

11. Southeast Corner Sixteenth and P Streets, N. W. — THE
CARNEGIE INSTITUTION*

The Carnegie Institution is an internationally respected philan-
thropy devoted to research in natural science. The home of the
institution is a rather uninspired Beaux-Arts design of the New
York architectural firm of Carrere and Hastings. It was built in
1908 of Indiana limestone and the portico, at least, deserves
some recognition for its impressive adaptation of the Ionic order and magnificent urns. It is an important structure since it
marks the spread of institutional uses to Sixteenth Street in the
early part of this century, and the growth of the scientific community in Washington.

12. Northwest Corner of Sixteenth and P Streets, N. W. —
FOUNDRY METHODIST EPISCOPAL CHURCH*

Foundry Methodist is from the period of Sixteenth Street development in which the boulevard began to be referred to as the
Street of Churches. Following the common pattern of wealthier
congregations of the era, Foundry Methodist — founded by
Georgetowner Henry Foxall who operated the Foxall-Columbia
Foundry on the Potomac — moved uptown from a downtown
location. The present Foundry Methodist Church was built in
1903-1904 on the plans of prolific and versatile Washington
architect Appleton P. Clark, who was the man largely responsible for an important revision of the D. C. Building Code at the
turn of the century.

Foundry Methodist has always been a socially-active congregation and developed a wide variety of programs to serve the so-called "free community" which grew up in this area in the 1960's. It has worked well with the black population that increased dramatically in the post-World War II years. The congregation remains one of Washington's largest, even though most members actually live in the suburbs.

13. Southeast Corner Sixteenth and Q Streets, N.W. UNIVERSITY OF THE DISTRICT OF COLUMBIA BRANCH; Former JEWISH COMMUNITY CENTER*

It was quite an achievement in 1910 for the Jewish community in Washington (then centered in the old Southwest section) to be able to build an imposing building on Sixteenth Street. The limestone structure - a work of B. Stanley Simmons - is in the classical manner, and perhaps its style and mass were inspired by the Carnegie Institution built two years earlier. The classical tradition was rarely employed in the design of the religious structures of Jewish people.

The Jewish community in Washington has continued to move north in the District of Columbia and into the suburbs.

The University of the District of Columbia, which now occupies the building for one of its many temporary branches, is to be consolidated into a new campus. The future of the building at Sixteenth and Q Streets is uncertain.

14. 1601 Sixteenth Street, N. W. — C. C. HUNTLEY HOUSE*

This bracketed, stuccoed house is notable as one of the earliest examples of brick rowhouses on Sixteenth Street and because its important stable building survives. The house was built in 1878 for C. C. Huntley, one of the principal owners of land along Sixteenth Street, and the estimated cost of construction was $9,000.

15. 1615 Q Street, N. W. — THE CAIRO HOTEL**

This building was designed and built in 1894 by Thomas Franklin Schneider, who eventually built more than 2,000 structures in

Washington, most in a very idiosyncratic interpretation of the Richardsonian Romanesque. Schneider here combines neo-Moorish and Art Nouveau elements in the facade of what is still the city's tallest non-monumental building. Note especially the wonderful carved elephants.

The Cairo Hotel's 165 feet so shocked turn-of-the-century, row-house Washington that Congress imposed severe height restrictions in 1910. The Cairo was opened as a first-class residential hotel, fell on hard times in the mid-20th century, and was restored as rental apartments in 1976. The sponsor of the restoration was the Georgetown Inland Corporation and the architect was Arthur Cotton Moore.

Although the partial 221(d) funding of the rehabilitation requires a percentage of low-moderate income apartments, only high-rent apartments were offered in the remodeled Cairo; a building located very close to the commercial core of Washington and in the center of an active restoration area. The structure was converted to condominiums in 1979.

16. Southeast Corner Sixteenth and Corcoran Streets, N. W. — CHURCH OF THE HOLY CITY**

Dedicated May 3, 1896. Built as the Church of the New Jerusalem, it is constructed of Bedford limestone, designed on the English perpendicular order, with a good deal of French Gothic influence. The gargoyles are worth a careful look. The tower is modeled after the tower over the main entrance to the Magdalen College in Oxford, England. The architect of this fine church was Prof. H. Langford Warren, head of the Department of Architecture at Harvard University, and Paul Pelz of Washington was construction overseer.

17. THE 1500 BLOCK OF CORCORAN STREET, N. W.**, immediately adjacent to the Church of the Holy City, is an interesting composite of late-19th century domestic architectural styles in Washington rowhouses. A speculatively-built "minor" street (originally an alley), Corcoran Street has been

virtually totally restored within the last decade by young white professionals, reflecting the recent trend of black displacement from the rowhouse blocks near Sixteenth Street.

18. 1623 Sixteenth Street, N. W. — DENMAN-HINCKLEY HOUSE*

This is one of Washington's finer Romanesque Revival houses and was built in 1886 for Judge H. P. Denman. The architects were Fuller and Wheeler of Albany, New York.

19. 1601 R Street, N. W. — The Foxtrappe, former MULLIGAN HOUSE*

The house was built in 1911 for Navy officer Richard T. Mulligan and designed by Jules Henri de Sibour, Washington's most gifted Beaux-Arts eclectic architect. The Mulligan house reflects the importance of the Georgian Revival in the large-scale domestic architecture of early-20th century Washington. The building recently was converted to a somewhat elite black professional club; an interesting use for one of the many mansions along Sixteenth Street looking for owners with ideas for adaptive uses.

20. 1701 Sixteenth Street, N. W. — THE CHASTLETON APARTMENTS

The Chastleton opened in 1919 as an apartment hotel. It was built by Harry Wardman, the Britisher who came to the U. S. almost penniless in the 1890's and eventually built a Washington real estate empire. Wardman specialized in lavish apartment houses and luxury hotels, noted for the quality of materials and workmanship. It was Wardman who did much to introduce Washingtonians to apartment house living. The Chastleton, however, with its somewhat silly Gothic elements, is hardly noteworthy architecture.

21. 1733 Sixteenth Street, N. W. — SCOTTISH RITE TEMPLE***

This is Headquarters of the Supreme Council of the Southern Jurisdiction of the Thirty-third Degree of the Ancient and Accepted Scottish Rite of Freemasonry. The Scottish Rite Temple is one of the most architecturally significant buildings on lower Sixteenth Street. John Russell Pope's design borrows from the famed Mausoleum of Halicarnassus. The cornerstone was laid in 1911 and the Temple was dedicated in 1915.

The main space is beneath the ziggurat surmounting the Greek-temple base. Two sphinxes by A. A. Weimann flank the main entrance to the building and represent Divine Wisdom and Power. The symbolism of the Masonic order is displayed in many facets of the design. For example, the Ionic columns of the colonnade are 33 feet high, representing the thirty-third degree of Masonry. Despite the relation of architectural elements to the symbolism and work of the order, it is interesting that the Temple is but a version of Pope's design for the Lincoln Memorial site.

The wealthy Masons recently have angered the local community by using their tax-exempt status to aid in the purchase and demolition of much-needed residential units to the rear of the Temple building. The District of Columbia Council has introduced a controversial bill which would remove the real property tax exemptions of organizations like the Masons, and thus, partially prevent such city-destructive abuse of privilege.

22.   1720 Sixteenth Street, N. W. — JUSTICE BROWN HOUSE, now TOUTORSKY ACADEMY OF MUSIC**

The 1880's German Renaissance-style mansion of Associate Justice of the Supreme Court, Henry B. Brown, is a rare design in Washington. The wings and carriage house along adjoining Riggs Place are superb.

23.   **RIGGS PLACE, N. W., is one of Washington's more charming side streets, and largely a product of the speculative building activities of the 1890's. The stained glass and copper work of these modest rowhouses are worth noting.

24.   Proceed north on Sixteenth Street through an area that is a mixture of late-19th century rowhouses and small early-20th century apartment buildings. There is considerable deterioration of some of the properties in this vicinity, but considerable restoration as well.

Blocks to the east of Sixteenth Street tend to house predominantly black populations, while those to the west tend to be whiter and somewhat more affluent.

The Sixteenth Street corridor in this area is zoned for medium to high density residential use (90 feet is the height limitation; 75% lot occupancy). Thus, from the realtor's standpoint, most of the existing structures are an underutilization of the land. At the present time there seems to be no intense developer interest in new high-rise residential construction along this stretch of Sixteenth Street. The fact that the as yet unrebuilt 14th Street riot corridor is but two blocks to the east may be a factor in the static development situation.

As Sixteenth Street crosses U Street, it enters the Meridian Hill district. The U Street intersection is poorly defined in terms of an architectural frame. Washington architect Chlothiel Woodard Smith has proposed raising the height limit at such key intersections to twenty-five stories in order to enhance the drama of entering the center of the city and to make a positive architectural statement more feasible where several very wide streets cross, as they do here.

25. & 26.   At this intersection are two organizations' headquarters which point out the complex nature of modern Washington society. On the southeast corner of Sixteenth and U Streets is the building of PRIDE, INC., a highly successful black, self-help enterprise. On the northeast corner of U Street and New Hampshire Avenue is the WOMEN'S CONGRESSIONAL CLUB*, erected in 1914 as a center for the social activities of the wives of Congressmen, Senators, Supreme Court Justices, and Cabinet officials.

27. & 28.   2001 SIXTEENTH STREET APARTMENT HOUSE and 2101 Sixteenth Street, N. W., the ROOSEVELT HOTEL FOR SENIOR CITIZENS*

Two of Harry Wardman's mammoth residential buildings of about 1916. The Roosevelt was originally an apartment hotel for the well-to-do, but since the early 1960's has served as a home for senior citizens.

29. FLORIDA AVENUE, N. W.*

Florida Avenue (the original city limit of Boundary Street) marks the location of the Fall Line, which divides the older and harder Piedmont Plateau from the softer deposits of the Coastal Plain.

Merchant and Mayor of Georgetown Robert Peter had assembled by 1760 a number of parts of a patent for land in this vicinity to form Mount Pleasant. His country farm house in the square bounded by 13th, 14th, W Streets, and Florida Avenue stood until the 1890's. Meridian Hill was originally referred to as Peter's Hill.

In 1821, Columbian College (which grew into the George Washington University) built its first building on Meridian Hill, where the institution remained until moving to the downtown financial district in the 1870's. Another educational institution on Meridian Hill was the Wayland Seminary for the training of Negro Baptist preachers, which was built in the northeast corner of the present Meridian Hill Park in 1873.

The Meridian Hill area remained a combination of woodlots, orchards, and fields until after the Civil War. In 1867, Isaac Messmore subdivided Meridian Hill into building lots selling at ten cents per square foot, but in those years there were few purchasers. Today land on Sixteenth Street and Meridian Hill sells for an average price of $5.00 per square foot. Real estate values in this section of Washington peaked (with relation to the rest of the city) in the mid-20th century. In 1925, for example, so prestigious had the area become that the large houses on Sixteenth Street itself sold for $250,000 and more. It was the extension of Sixteenth Street north of Columbia Road along the true north-south line and the bridging of Piney Branch Valley at the turn of the century which prompted intensive development.

30. Northwest corner of Sixteenth Street and Florida Avenue, N. W. — HENDERSON CASTLE TRACT**

It was Mrs. Mary Henderson, wife of John B. Henderson (the Senator from Missouri who authored the Emancipation amendment and cast the deciding vote that saved Johnson from conviction in his impeachment trial) who began and maintained the cultivation of Sixteenth Street as the premier residential and embassy boulevard of Washington from the late 1880's until her death in 1931.

In 1887 the Hendersons bought the tract for about $31,000. The purchase was the first in what would be the eventual assembly by Mrs. Henderson of a real estate holding of some 300 city lots in the Meridian Hill area. The wall is all that remains of the turreted, crenellated, red Seneca sandstone house built in 1888 and popularly known as Henderson Castle. J. E. Gardner was the architect of the pile and J. H. Lane the builder.

From her Meridian Hill tower Mary Henderson directed her architect, George Oakley Totten, in the upbuilding of Sixteenth Street;

fought busses on the Avenue of the Presidents (she succeeded in having the street's name changed for one year) and Harry Wardman's apartment houses which obstructed her view of the White House and degraded the capital city of villas; preached the evils of alcohol; and oversaw the planning and partial construction of the great Meridian Hill Park opposite her home.

After many other plans and false starts, including proposals for a colony of homes for the elderly, the Henderson Castle tract has been developed into "colonial-style" townhouses in the $150,000 price range. The townhouse project has attracted the growing market of returnees from the suburbs and young couples already living in the city.

31. MERIDIAN HILL PARK*** east side of Sixteenth Street between Florida Avenue and Euclid Street, N. W.

At the turn of the century, when the White House was in a bad state of repair, it was Meridian Hill that was seriously considered for a new Presidential Residence. Mrs. Henderson was one of the most vocal supporters of the movement.

When it became clear that the Presidential mansion would not be moved to Meridian Hill, Mrs. Henderson pressured Congress to buy the site for a public park. The purchase of the 12 acres that became Meridian Hill Park was authorized in 1910.

The park is one of the most important examples of formal garden design in the United States. Actual construction did not begin until 1917, and the lower part of the park was not opened until 1936. George Burnap was the original landscape architect and Horace W. Peaslee was responsible for the final plan and architectural design. The magnificent concrete work, in which aggregates were selected for varying sizes and colors, and the concrete washed with muriatic acid quickly after it began to set in order to expose the aggregates, was begun as an experiment at Meridian Hill Park.

The use of massive retaining walls heightens the drama of the natural topography. The upper two-thirds of the park is designed in the formal French manner with a large tapis vert bordered by promenades. The lower part of the park is inspired by the great Italian formal gardens of the 18th century. An artificial cascade of thirteen waterfalls of graduated size, representing the location of the park on the Fall Line, is the principal feature of this section.

The Meridian Hill Park is still administered by the National Park Service. Although not especially abused by local residents, upkeep in recent years has been minimal. The neglect of the park is a national tragedy.

The local black community refers to the park as Malcolm X Park. In warm weather it is the site of many musical entertainments and political rallies.

32. 2400 Sixteenth Street, N. W. — ENVOY TOWERS APARTMENTS*

The Envoy Towers opened in the early 20th century as Meridian Mansions, a very fashionable apartment hotel, and later acquired the name Hotel 2400. The enormous structure, some of the apartments of which have dining rooms that seat 24 people, changed hands a number of times in the early 1960's. After the 1968 riots, the District of Columbia leased much space in the building to house displaced vicitms of the 14th Street civil disturbances. The handsome structure's use as this kind of housing angered many of the nearby residents. The building has continued to deteriorate.

33.   CRESCENT PLACE — WHITE AND LAUGHLIN HOUSES**

On the high ridge between Belmont and Crescent Places, opposite Meridian Hill Park, stand two of John Russell Pope's loveliest'domestic commissions. Both represent departures from the usual ascetic classicism of Pope's work.

1624 CRESCENT PLACE, N.W., in something of a Georgian Revival mode, was built about 1912 for Henry White, Ambassador to France, and was long the residence of Eugene Meyer, publisher of the Washington Post. The building, which takes such command of a fine site, is now part of the Antioch School of Law's Washington facilities.

34.   1630 CRESCENT PLACE, N. W. is a richly decorated limestone house in the manner of an 18th century French pavilion. It was built for Irwin Laughlin, Ambassador to Spain, in 1915. The manicured garden with its beautiful canopy of pollarded trees is a rare example of landscaping art. The house is now the Washington International Center.

35.   2460 Sixteenth Street, N. W. — EMBASSY OF GHANA CHANCERY**

The Embassy of Ghana Chancery was built through the joint efforts of Mrs. Henderson and her architect, George Oakley Totten. It was the first of thirteen major mansions erected speculatively in order to attract embassies to Meridian Hill. Totten, adept Beaux-Arts architect though he was, never escapes the late Victorian exuberance, vitality, and curiosity that shaped his early career.

36.   2600 Sixteenth Street, N. W. — INTER-AMERICAN DEFENSE BOARD; THE PINK PALACE**

A fanciful Venetian palace on Sixteenth Street built by the Henderson-Totten team in 1906. The first occupant was Oscar Straus, Theodore Roosevelt's Secretary of Commerce and Labor. Mrs. Marshall Field was another prominent occupant, and for a long time the pink stuccoed house was the headquarters of the District of Columbia Order of the Eastern Star.

37.   2633 Sixteenth Street, N. W. — WARDER-TOTTEN HOUSE**

Originally constructed in the 1500-block of K Street, for a prominent Washington real estate developer, Benjamin Warder, the sandstone house is a product of H. H. Richardson's office. George Oakley Totten bought the shell of the house from the wrecker in 1902 and stored the parts of the building until he was able to reconstruct it as his own residence. The mansion makes a far better detached villa than part of a rowhouse block, which it originally was. The Warder-Totten House is now an element of Antioch College's Washington facilities.

38.   2700 Sixteenth Street, N. W. — EMBASSY OF ITALY**

Designed by the architects of Grand Central Station, Warren and Wetmore of New York City, 2700 Sixteenth Street is an especially fine adaptation of the Italian Renaissance palazzo. The interiors are rich in works of Medieval Italian art and the walled garden to the rear is an elegant, formal outdoor space that creates the illusion of being in Italy.

The Italian government is building a new Embassy-Chancery complex west of Rock Creek Park. A crime wave that peaked about 1970 frightened many of the diplomats who live and work on Sixteenth Street. Poland (whose Embassy is immediately south of the Italian Embassy) is also looking for new quarters.

39.   2801 Sixteenth Street and 2829 Sixteenth Street, N. W. — EMBASSY OF SPAIN and EMBASSY OF MEXICO***

The Spanish Embassy at 2801 Sixteenth Street was built by Mrs. Henderson and designed by George Oakley Totten in 1923. Mrs. Henderson built the mansion in the hope that the Federal Government would purchase it as the official residence of the Vice-President.

2829 Sixteenth Street, the Mexican Embassy, was built in 1911 for Franklin MacVeagh, Taft's Secretary of the Treasury, by his wife as a Christmas present. The architect was Washington designer Nathan Wyeth. The Italianate house is one of the most elaborate in Washington and has perhaps the largest private dining room in the city: it will seat 250. The music room has an exact copy of the pipe organ at Fountainbleau. Beginning in 1934, Roberto Cuerva del Rio began his great series of murals within for the new owners, the Mexican government.

Together, these two great houses and the chancery buildings to the rear facing 15th Street form one of Washington's largest diplomatic complexes.

40.   HARVARD SQUARE; the intersection of Sixteenth Street, Columbia Road, and Harvard Street, N. W.**

This intersection was originally planned as a circle in honor of Civil War hero, General George Meade. The pleasant landscaped area which actually developed just west of Sixteenth Street is known, to however few, as Harvard Square. It was landscaped about 1915.

Around the busy intersection are three important church buildings, erected during the years when the neighborhood was one of Washington's best residential neighborhoods. Columbia Road was here long before anything else manmade. It was an Indian route and later a post road to Georgetown from Baltimore.

41.   Southeast corner Sixteenth and Harvard Streets, N. W. — ALL SOULS' UNITARIAN CHURCH**
The architects of this skillful copy of James Gibbs' St. Martin's in the Fields, in London, were Coolidge and Shattuck of Boston. The church was constructed in 1924 at a cost of almost a million dollars.

Previous to the completion of the Sixteenth Street church, the congregation was located downtown at 14th and L Streets. Today the congregation is integrated and something of a status church among Washington blacks.

42.   Southwest corner Sixteenth Street and Columbia Road, N. W. — MORMON WASHINGTON CHAPEL**

A very interesting architectural period piece designed by Ramm Hanson and Don Carlos Young of Salt Lake City, and completed in 1933. Young was the grandson of Brigham Young.

Until September 1975, the Washington Mormons used the elegant Utah marble edifice for worship, but decided to sell. A gleaming, gold-leaf covered statue of the Angel Moroni which rested atop the lovely spire until the Mormons vacated the building was a landmark seen from all parts of Washington. The building is now a branch of the Unification Church.

13 ***DUPONT CIRCLE (cosmopolitan neighborhood, specialty shops, embassies, hotels, pubs, cafes)

By John Fondersmith, AICP

Mr. Fondersmith is with the District of Columbia's Department of Planning and Development and is a long time resident of the Dupont Circle area.

DISTANCE: 2¾ Miles   TIME: 3 Hours

BUS: 42, L4, and L8

METRO: Dupont Circle (Red)

Dupont Circle is a fascinating area offering a variety of points of interest to the urbanist. It was the prestige neighborhood in Washington at the turn of the century. The large mansions built by the newly wealthy from across the country were a reflection of Washington's increasing importance on the national and world scene at that time. The mansions reflect the Beaux Arts influence of the period and help give the neighborhood a special character. These are supplemented by smaller townhouses and row houses along many streets, providing a more intimate scale.

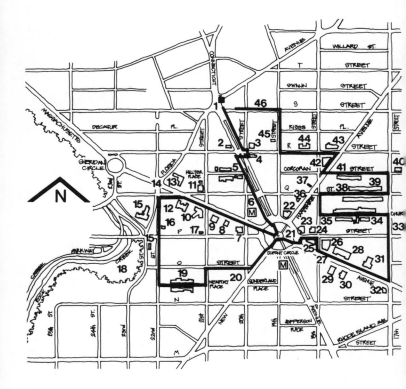

Today, Dupont Circle is again undergoing transition. The question is how to retain historic quality, scale, a mix of residents and commercial activities while accommodating some change. The D.C. Department of Planning and Development was recently preparing a plan for the area, in close consultation with citizens and businessmen.

The tour winds through the neighborhood, and at places connects with or approaches the routes of the adjacent tours: 15, Kalorama; 12, 16th Street/Meridian Hill; 11, Midtown. The visitor can therefore branch off to other tours or can take an abbreviated tour of Dupont Circle.

1.   The tour begins at Florida Avenue, N. W., the NORTHERN BOUNDARY OF THE ORIGINAL CITY OF WASHINGTON. The three blocks of Connecticut Avenue north of the circle (and the block to the south) comprise one of the most interesting areas in the city. Located here is one of the largest concentrations of restaurants in Washington and a variety of shops, two theaters, nightclubs, and several fine bookstores. Present zoning along this section of the Avenue allows construction of 90 foot high office buildings, such as the one at Connecticut Avenue and R Street, N. W. A major planning issue is how to retain the character and activities in the face of that allowable change.

2.   SCHWARTZ DRUGSTORE is a neighborhood institution, with an old fashioned ambience and piles of papers.

3.   The small open space at Connecticut and R Streets, N.W., has long been one of those special places in the city - the location for a FLOWER STAND and other vendors. Across 20th Street is the old Thorpe mansion, now converted to a restaurant.

4.   The Gargamelle Restaurant's SIDEWALK CAFE is a good place to pause and watch the world go by. A fast food restaurant was interested in the site, but neighborhood pressure kept it out and Gargamelle acquired the building.

5.   HILLYER PLACE*, N. W., is an attractive short street worth a detour.

6.   The north entrance of the DUPONT CIRCLE METRO STATION** has one of the most unusual designs of any in the system - a kind of funnel shape. The conflict between maintaining existing uses and scale, or allowing more intense development keyed to Metro, is an issue here as at other points in the city.

7.   The BLAINE MANSION*, 2000 Massachusetts Avenue, N. W., was one of the first large residences in this part of the city. It was built in 1881 for James G. Blaine, a three-time candidate for the presidency.

8.   The BEALE HOUSE, 2012 Massachusetts Avenue, N. W., was one of the plainer residences along Massachusetts Avenue. A similar house (Litchfield House) to the east was replaced several years ago by the new headquarters building of the American Home Economics Association. The AHEA Building was designed to relate well to the 19th century mansions on either side in materials and form.

9.   The INDONESIAN EMBASSY*, built in 1903 for Thomas Walsh, is reported to have been the most expensive mansion in the neighborhood.

10.   The quiet FAIRFAX HOTEL houses one of the city's most expensive restaurants - the Jockey Club.

11.   The PHILLIPS GALLERY** is housed in several residences and annex buildings. It is one of the nation's outstanding private art collections.

12.   The ANDERSON HOUSE**, 2118 Massachusetts Avenue, N. W., was constructed in 1900 and is now the headquarters of the Society of Cincinnati, an organization of descendants of the American officers of the Revolution. The walled entrance court of this large Beaux Arts mansion is unusual in Washington. A museum in the building is open to the public.

13.   The Cosmos Club**, 2121 Massachusetts Avenue, N. W., is one of the city's most prestigious private clubs. The original build-

ing was constructed for Mrs. Townsend in 1900, and has been remodeled and expanded.

14. Florida Avenue, again, is the original boundary of the city planned by L'Enfant. Massachusetts Avenue extends west to Sheridan Circle and beyond, bordered by large town houses and mansions now largely converted to embassy use. The Avenue is known as "EMBASSY ROW" (see Tour 15, Kalorama).

15. The CHURCH OF THE PILGRIMS* is a landmark on the west edge of the neighborhood. Note the gas station south of P Street, designed to be compatible with the church.

16. The BRICKSKELLER, a bar/restaurant, 1523 22nd Street, N. W., is a real find for beer lovers. It offers some 300 different beers from across the U. S. and around the world.

17. P STREET, N. W. is the site of several new apartment houses, with zoning allowing first floor commercial use. This area has developed as a center of private art galleries. Though several have been displaced, others have opened in the new apartment buildings, and several remain in older structures. The exhibitions at the Henri Gallery, 21st and P Streets, N. W., are often of special interest.

18. West of 23rd Street, N. W. is an open meadow known as the "P STREET BEACH," a favorite spot for concerts, sunbathing and frisbee games by neighborhood residents.

19. NEWPORT PLACE, N. W. is a block-long street of small row houses where rehabilitation is underway.

20. NEW HAMPSHIRE AVENUE, N. W. between Dupont and Washington Circles is lined with high-rise apartment buildings, primarily constructed in the 1960's (see Tour 11, Midtown for descriptions of the Heurich Mansion and the Euram Building).

21. Take time to walk around DUPONT CIRCLE** and reflect on the changing city. Originally called Pacific Circle, the name was changed to Dupont Circle in 1884 after Admiral Samuel F. Dupont. The present fountain, designed by Daniel Chester French, was placed here in 1921. The circle was once ringed with impressive mansions. Only three face the circle today. Others have been replaced with office buildings and a hotel. The tree shaded park with its chessboards is a popular gathering place; one of those "city rooms" that most area workers and residents pass through almost daily. It is often the starting point for demonstrations which then proceed to the White House or to a nearby embassy.

22. The HOTEL DUPONT PLAZA (1949) is typical of a type of design, especially for apartments, which was popular after World War II. The Hotel replaced the famous Leiter mansion.

23. The WASHINGTON CLUB* (Patterson House), 15 Dupont Circle, N. W., was designed by Stanford White in 1902. It is now somewhat overshadowed by the adjacent new dark brick office building.

109

24.   EMBASSY OF IRAQ* (Boardman House) at 1801 P Street, N. W., is considered one of the finest remaining Romanesque Revival houses in the city.

25.   SULGRAVE CLUB (Wadsworth House) was built circa 1900 and houses one of the city's prestigious private clubs.

26.   The McCORMICK APARTMENT BUILDING was constructed in 1917 to be the most exclusive apartment building in the city (five apartments, one per floor). Andrew Mellon lived here. It is now the headquarters for the National Trust for Historic Preservation.

27.   The 1700 BLOCK OF MASSACHUSETTS AVENUE, N. W., is a study in old, new and change. The Avenue is zoned Special Purpose — a classification that allows institutional buildings and apartments intended to serve as a buffer between the business district and the residential areas (see Tour 12, 16th Street/Meridian Hill for a more complete description of this SP zoning category).

28.   THE BROOKINGS INSTITUTION, 1775 Massachusetts Avenue, N. W., is an important national research center, but the building is architecturally dull. Neighborhood residents often cite the Brookings building as a symbol of the kind of development they oppose.

29.   The national headquarters of the AMERICAN PLANNING ASSOCIATION is located on the seventh floor of 1776 Massachusetts Avenue, N.W.

30.   The CANADIAN CHANCERY*, 1746 Massachusetts Avenue, N. W., occupies the Moore residence (1906), one of the great man-

sions of the area at the turn of the century. Next door to the east is the Johns Hopkins Center for International Studies.

31.   The buildings at 1755 and 1717 Massachusetts Avenue, N.W. house many RESEARCH ORGANIZATIONS of interest to planners. For example, Resources for the Future is located at 1775, and the Washington Center for Metropolitan Studies is located at 1717. The Georgetown University Research Center (1717) is an especially attractive contemporary building.

32.   The gap on the south side of block near 17th Street, N.W., is the scene of a recent preservation setback. Several old townhouses that helped form the streetscape were demolished in 1975 to provide space for a proposed new office building.

This section of Massachusetts Avenue has now been incorporated in an historic district. The building at the southwest corner of 17th and Massachusetts Avenue has recently been renovated to serve as the EMBASSY OF PERU.

33.   Seventeenth Street, N.W., in contrast to Connecticut Avenue, serves more of a neighborhood function, and is sometimes referred to as a "peoples street." As elsewhere, the issues deal with where new development should be encouraged and what should be retained. Notice the fine trees along this street.

34.   CHURCH STREET, N.W., is another attractive block-long street of small townhouses.

35.   ST. THOMAS' EPISCOPAL CHURCH, formerly the site of an impressive gothic church constructed by the elite of the turn of the century, was destroyed by arson in 1970. The congregation decided to stay and has carried on services in the renovated parish house "behind the ruins." The use of contemporary art in the present worship space is especially interesting.

Earlier this year the ruins received an architectural treatment to stabilize them. An earlier informal park in front of the ruins was replaced by a more permanent park, relfecting the congregation's commitment to be part of the neighborhood.

36. The Weeks House (1892), now the WOMAN'S NATIONAL DEMOCRATIC CLUB, is interesting. Notice the contemporary addition to the west. Next door is the New Left "think tank," the Center for Policy Studies.

37. The main offices of the NATIONAL PLANNING ASSOCI- ATION are located at 1606 New Hampshire Avenue, N. W.

38. The vacant lot on the north side of Q Street, N. W. is a site of a proposed high rise apartment building that has been resisted by neighborhood groups.

39. The STONE TOWNHOUSES* along the 1700 block of Q Street, N. W. are of special interest. They were the product of an early architect-developer, Thomas Franklin Schneider, in 1889. Schneider was also the designer-developer of the recently renovated CAIRO HOTEL** across 17th Street. (See Tour 12, 16th Street/ Meridian Hill.)

40. The interesting building at 17th and R Streets houses two fine restaurants - El Bodegon (Spanish) and La Fonda (Mexican). (See Restaurant List.)

41. The buildings on the south side of CORCORAN STREET, N. W., were among the first in the neighborhood to be rehabili- tated. Notice the mural on the wall mid-way down the south- side of the block.

42. The BELMONT HOUSE (1908) on this triangular site is another of the great houses of the area. It is now the headquarters of the Eastern Star.

43. The row of buildings on the north side of R STREET, N. W., between New Hampshire Avenue and 18th Street, are of interest. The major one — the THOMAS NELSON PAGE HOUSE by McKim, McKim, Mead and White (1897) — a Federal Revival Mansion — now serves as the French Military Mission.

44. The AMERICAN PSYCHIATRIC MUSEUM ASSOCIATION and the INTERNATIONAL STUDENT CENTER (north side of R Street between 18th and 19th Streets) are examples of old build- ings where recent additions have been designed to blend with the character and scale of the original buildings.

45. Turn north on 19th Street, N. W. This area was rezoned in 1974 to protect the scale of residential development. Notice the small wooden building at 1712 19th Street, N. W., which is reputed to be one of the few CIVIL WAR STRUCTURES remaining in the area.

46. Walk west on S Street, N. W., past buildings of somewhat different style, returning to Connecticut Avenue to the starting point of the tour.

14 *SHAW SCHOOL URBAN RENEWAL AREA/ **LOGAN CIRCLE (new moderate and low income housing, new school and library, historic circle)

By Dr. Audrey Parkinson

Dr. Parkinson, an Urban and Regional Planner, is an International Planning Consultant. Dr. Parkinson gratefully acknowledges the assistance of Mr. Robert Henderson, Area Director of the 14th Street Corridor, in providing topical information.

DISTANCE: 2 Miles   *TIME: 1½ Hours*

BUS: 70

METRO: Gallery Place (Red); transfer to bus 70 on 7th St. N.W.

It is suggested that persons taking this tour go as couples or small groups. For more on black Washington's heritage, you may wish to visit nearby LeDroit Park (Tour 20) and Howard University (Tour 19). A drive through all three areas is recommended.

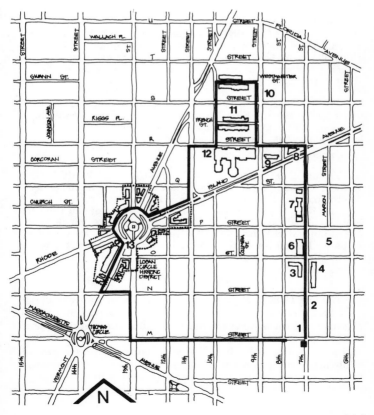

Shaw, located immediately north of Downtown, is a large part of the District's Model Cities Neighborhood. Largest of the urban renewal areas in the city with 675 acres of land, Shaw contains 33,000 residents.

The Shaw School Urban Renewal Area development has relied upon the involvement of black architects, attorneys and housing consultants as members of the development teams. The Small Business Guidance and Development Center at Howard University has provided training and assistance to small minority group contractors in order that they will have the opportunity to bid for rehabilitation work. In 1974, seventy-five percent of all contracting was with minority firms.

1. The tour begins at 7th Street, N. W. and M Street, N. W., scene of the 1968 civil disturbances along the 7th Street corridor. The Urban Renewal Plan for Shaw was adopted in 1969 to eliminate blight and renew and rehabilitate housing for low and moderate income families.

2. Initially planned as an interim park, the open space outlined by stump markers has returned to unused open space. Four such interim parks were initiated as an early action in the assistance program of 1969. CLIFFORD MEMORIAL PARK, a few blocks north, was developed with money left from President Nixon's Inaugural Fund.

3. The 10-story, 137 unit IMMACULATE CONCEPTION APARTMENT BUILDING, designed by Bryant & Bryant, was sponsored by the Immaculate Conception Community Partnership. This was the first limited dividend partnership to sponsor housing in Shaw. Twenty percent of the units are under the Rent Supplement Program.

4. GIBSON PLAZA, a 10-story, 217 unit building, was sponsored by the near-by First Rising Mount Zion Baptist Church. The open space with trees and benches adjacent to the building is used by residents.

5. The JOHN F. KENNEDY ADVENTURE PLAYGROUND was one of the first projects in the area. Children of the area use the park on Sundays when they climb and swing on the large replicas of a space ship and bus. The small size of the park and the black top surface of the playground leaves much to be desired in the creation of small adventurous places for children to play. The playground is run by the Recreation Department of the District of Columbia.

6. The O STREET MARKET*, built in 1886, has been designated a Category III landmark worthy of preservation. The O Street market is open for business, since completion of the restoration in early 1980. A visitor to the market will find delicacies, fruits, vegetables, fish and poultry displayed in stalls while lazy ceiling fans stir the rich aromas.

114

7. The SAMUEL KELSEY GARDEN APARTMENTS offer a more intimate scale to the housing built in the area. Sponsored by the Deliverance Church of God in Christ and financed under Section 236 of the Housing Act of 1968, this housing is for families with moderate incomes. The designer and builder are local firms.

8. Named for Watha T. Daniel, civic leader and first chairman of of the D. C. Model Cities Commission, this LIBRARY*, the first library in the Shaw area, was dedicated in September, 1975. The architectural design complements the triangular site and deserves a look inside.

9. FOSTER HOUSE APARTMENTS was financed under Section 236, which allows a non-profit corporation a 100% mortgage at low interest rates. The project was sponsored by the New Bethel Baptist Corporation.

10. This inner block park represents some of the difficulties encountered in urban renewal anywhere. Imaginative ideas meet headlong with the intricate procedures of implementation, unpredictable timing and economic changes. Housing rehabilitation along the sides of the alley has been started.

11. An increasing emphasis on home ownership for low and moderate income families is evident in Shaw. Neighborhood conservation and stabilization has been partially realized in the FRENCH-WESTMINISTER AREA*. Houses in this four block area have been rehabilitated and sold to individual owners as well as to the National Capital Housing Authority under the Section 235 program for moderate and low income families. The character of the area has been enhanced by new brick sidewalks, fencing and street paving.

12. The new SHAW JUNIOR HIGH SCHOOL** represents years of active citizen participation in the decision-making process. "Shameful Shaw," as the old school was known, was a central issue in the area much before the civil disturbances of 1968. The present site was selected after consideration of the number of households, buildings, non-resident establishments and owner-occupied houses required to be removed in clearing the site. Building the Shaw Junior High School was the uniting factor in the Shaw School Urban Renewal Area. This accomplishment represents a continued interest and involvement of many area residents.

13. The LOGAN CIRCLE HISTORIC DISTRICT** is a unique assemblage of 132 Victorian buildings. The importance of this district has been recognized by both federal and local governments. The Logan Circle Historic District is now listed on the Interior Department's National Register of Historic Places. The Circle, a basic part of the original L'Enfant geometry for the city, is a Category I landmark on the National Capital Committee on Landmarks list. The district itself is a Category II landmark and the STATUE OF GENERAL JOHN A. LOGAN* is a Category III landmark.

By the late 1880's most of the houses now standing in the Logan Circle area had been built. The neighborhood had become a racially mixed group of professionals and middle class businessmen. A third of the buildings in the Logan Circle Historic District have been designated for rehabilitation. These private restoration efforts are expected to bring medium and high income residents into the district. The building at 1318 Vermont Avenue, N. W., has recently been purchased by the National Council of Negro Women, Inc. to serve as headquarters and is undergoing rehabilitation.

15 ***KALORAMA (Embassies, Beaux-Arts Mansions)

By Perry G. Fisher

DISTANCE: 2 Miles   *TIME: 2 Hours*

BUS: N2, N4, or D2, D4, D8 on Q Street

METRO: Dupont Circle (Red); transfer to above bus routes.

Kalorama is the center of the foreign diplomatic community and contains one of the finest collections of Beaux-Arts-inspired mansions in the United States. Handsomely developed, richly treed and topographically varied, Kalorama is a pleasant island of quiet urbanity near central Washington.

For almost a century after the founding of Washington, D. C., much of the elegant district was part of a large estate of great natural beauty. Superbly-sited, the estate looked out over the Potomac, northern Virginia and the infant capital city. The estate bore the same name as the modern neighborhood, and was noted for its fine manor house, which stood until 1888. Kalorama was carved out of the widow's mite, a colonial patent of approximately 660 acres granted in 1664 to John Langworth by Lord Baltimore.

Kalorama, well-known for the concentration of embassies and chanceries in its large mansions, is a phenomenon of the early 20th century expansion of Washington, D. C. Its evolution into a beautiful and sophisticated neighborhood is closely related to several important developments: the termination in 1890 of the distinction between the City of Washington and the County of Washington (i. e., the area of the District of Columbia outside Florida Avenue); the extension of Massachusetts Avenue beyond Florida Avenue in the same period; the new bridges across Rock Creek; the commitment made in 1890 to preserve the Rock Creek Valley as a scenic and recreational resource; the proximity of Kalorama to established wealthy neighborhoods like Dupont Circle; and the filling up of older portions of the city in the dynamic post-Civil War years. From the outset, it was intended that Kalorama become a prime residential area. Intelligent and aggressive real estate promotion, very attractive building sites, and the astounding growth of the colony of wealthy people in Washington who wanted the most fashionable town residences, made Kalorama. These developments provided an opportunity for architects working in the Beaux-Arts-influenced styles of the general classical revival period following the Chicago World's Columbian Exposition of 1893.

1. SHERIDAN CIRCLE*** (Massachusetts Avenue at 23rd Street, N. W.)

In November, 1886 the Commissioners of the District of Columbia held public hearings to discuss plans for a Circle in honor of Stephen Decatur and the extension of Massachusetts Avenue. The widow of George Lovett, last private owner of the Kalorama estate, protested the proposed improvements affecting her property. However, a

New York real estate firm paid the Lovett heirs $354,000 for the remaining 60 acres of the estate. At $5,900 an acre (in 1887!), subsequent development by owners of the planned Kalorama Heights subdivision had to be either for a very wealthy population or for a very high density population. Standing in Sheridan Circle today it is clear that the former type of development turned out to be the actual case.

Decatur Circle became Sheridan Circle in 1890, when the Officers of the Army of the Cumberland received authorization to commission a statue of General Philip H. Sheridan, Civil War hero who died in 1888. Gutzon Borglum (sculptor of Mt. Rushmore) was commissioned and the model of his equestrian statue of Sheridan was accepted in January 1908. The statue was erected the following year. The statue in the past has been compared to a traffic cop stuck in mud, but the harshness of critical opinion of the work has lessened since. Mrs. Sheridan, of course, loved it instantly, and in fact had built 2211 Massachusetts Avenue in 1905 in order to be close.

Sheridan Circle is perhaps the only one of Washington's circles that has maintained its grand residential character. It was the earliest part of the Kalorama neighborhood to develop and the circle was a natural focus for neighborhood growth. Sheridan Circle is enclosed by a group of marvelous early 20th-century mansions whose mass, detailing, and styles are appropriate to the wide baroque boulevards of L'Enfant's original plan for the capital city.

2. 2306 Massachusetts Avenue, N. W. — ALICE PIKE BARNEY
STUDIO HOUSE**, now SMITHSONIAN INSTITUTION OFFICE
OF TRAVELING EXHIBITIONS SERVICE

Alice Pike Barney was a wealthy playwright and painter who built
this house in 1903 for her many artistic pursuits and informal entertainments. The wonderful house, influenced by the Mission
style of architecture, was designed by Waddy Butler Wood of Washington, and built for $18,000. It includes studio and stage facilities
and an interesting collection of 17th-century Spanish furniture.

The Barrymores, Caruso, and James Whistler were among those
Alice Barney entertained here.

3. 1606 23rd Street, N. W. (S.W. corner of 23rd Street and
Sheridan Circle) — EDWARD H. EVERETT HOUSE, now
EMBASSY OF THE REPUBLIC OF TURKEY**

Edward H. Everett was a multi-millionaire capitalist-industrialist.
Much of his fortune was the result of his patenting of the modern
fluted bottlecap.

The architect of the Everett mansion was George Oakley Totten,
Jr. The house was begun in 1910 but not completed until 1915.
As in so many of Totten's buildings, classical details are combined
in a totally personal and idiosyncratic manner. Totten was too
aware of architectural developments in America to remain unin-
fluenced by the pioneering work of Midwestern and California
architects that was contemporary with the full-blown Beaux-Arts.
This native influence shows in features like the trellised roof garden on the Q-Street side of the house. Similarly, the impact of
Totten's time in Turkey shows in such features as the elaborate
interior carving. It is hardly surprising that the Turkish Government admired this house and has occupied it since late 1932.

4. 2301 Massachusetts Avenue, N. W. — LIEUTENANT JOSEPH
BEALE HOUSE**, now U. A. R. INTERESTS SECTION OF THE
INDIAN EMBASSY.

The gently curved facade of this magnificent 18th century Italy-
inspired palazzo contributes a beautiful transition from R Street
to Massachusetts Avenue. The architect of the detached house
was Glenn Brown, who from 1899 to 1913 was Secretary of the

120

American Institute of Architects. The austerity of the exterior of the limestone and stucco mansion is not matched within. Instead, the interiors display some of the most remarkable and elaborate plaster work of any Washington building still standing.

In 1928, Egypt acquired the Beale house for its ambassadorial residence. The house now serves as the home of the Ambassador of the United Arab Republic.

5. 2253 R Street, N. W. — GEN. CHARLES FITZHUGH RESIDENCE, now the EMBASSY OF THE PHILIPPINES

The scale of the building is somewhat smaller than most of the houses around Sheridan Circle, but the Fitzhugh residence holds its important position by clarity of form, plain surfaces, clearly articulated openings and basic horizontality. The house was constructed in 1904 and the estimated cost was $38,000. Waddy Butler Wood, architect of the residence, used strong Mediterranean and even Wrightian influences. The unusual use of segmentally-arched windows under the eaves is a typical Wood curiosity.

6. 2225, 2223, and 2221 R STREET, N. W.**

Of this row of three houses, the central building was the first constructed. It was built in 1904 for Alice Pike Barney, who just a year earlier had opened her studio house on Sheridan Circle. In 1931, Chief Justice of the Supreme Court Charles Evans Hughes purchased the house and lived there until his death in 1948. The Government of Burma has been the owner since.

George Oakley Totten, Jr., was the architect of all three dwellings in the group. The smaller houses flanking the Barney residence were constructed in 1909. The houses are stuccoed, and in general treatment harmonize well with the Fitzhugh residence just down the street. The repeating porte-cocheres add great charm to the street.

7. 2201 R Street, N. W. — GARDNER FREDERICK WILLIAMS HOUSE**, now EMBASSY OF PAKISTAN ARMY, NAVY AND AIR ATTACHES OFFICE

This imposing, straightforward, clean-lined house was built in 1906-07 for Gardner Frederick Williams, a mining engineer who had been associated with Cecil Rhodes in Africa.

George Oakley Totten was the architect. It was once known for its lovely garden along R Street, but today, the entire garden and virtually all of the surrounding property is given over to diplomatic parking. The site is an eyesore. In recent years, the citizens of Kalorama have consistently fought the continuing spread of Embassy office uses to Kalorama, because the problems of traffic and parking in the area's narrow streets are insurmountable.

8. 2132 R Street, N. W. — the PALMER HOUSE

This handsome Georgian rowhouse was the home of A. Mitchell Palmer while serving as Wilson's Attorney General. Palmer was one of the chief figures in the "Red Scare" paranoia that swept the country after World War I. He saw Communists everywhere. On June 2, 1919 an unidentified terrorist tossed a bomb into the Palmer home and in the process destroyed himself. Palmer was in the house at the time, but uninjured. Police presence in quiet Kalorama has been notable ever since.

9. 2131 R Street, N. W. — FRANKLIN D. ROOSEVELT RESIDENCE, now EMBASSY OF MALI

Franklin Roosevelt lived from 1917 to 1920, while serving as Assistant Secretary of the Navy. The house has 17 rooms and 6½ baths, and was well-suited to the needs of the growing Roosevelt family. Now painted an inappropriate mustard color, the house serves as the residence of the Ambassador of Mali.

10. 2145 Decatur Place, N.W. - MARTHA CODMAN RESIDENCE**

In 1906, wealthy Boston spinster Martha Codman built her magnificent Washington home. The designer was New York society architect Ogden Codman, a relative of hers. The mansion is especially attractive because of its cherry-red brick and beautifully dressed stone. Although 18th-century England is the architectural inspiration, the approach to the house reminds one of a Parisian hotel. The superb garden terraces and the block of the house itself act as massive retaining walls for the Decatur Terrace slopes. The Codman House became the Louise Home in about 1950, when the original Louise Home for poor, but genteel Southern Protestant ladies was demolished to make way for the apartment house at 1500 Massachusetts Avenue, N. W.

11. DECATUR TERRACE STEPS AND FOUNTAIN** (22nd Street between Decatur Place and S Street, N. W.)

Designed and constructed by the Office of Public Buildings and Grounds in 1911-12, the delightful staircase and lions-head fountain solved the problem of linking Decatur Place with much higher S Street, and did so in favor of the pedestrian. It is a rare occurrence in an American city when a street becomes a staircase, and Washington's example is unknown to many residents.

12. 1743 22nd Street, N. W. — CHARLES D. WALCOTT HOUSE, now GEORGE WILMOT RENCHARD RESIDENCE

This home was built in 1904-5 for Charles D. Walcott, Secretary of the Smithsonian Institution and active real estate promoter in northern Washington, D. C. The architect was George Oakley Totten, in partnership with Laussat Rogers. The house has been modified and altered, but was originally a beautiful Italianate-Mission style home that took command of its fine site.

13. 2300 S Street, N. W. — GALES-HOOVER HOUSE**, now the EMBASSY OF BURMA

One of the earliest houses built on the Kalorama Heights, this house was originally the home of Major Thomas M. Gales, who was connected with the realty firm that developed the Kalorama section. The Gales house was built in 1901-02 and the architect was Washingtonian Appleton P. Clark. It is unmistakably a late 19th-century house trying desparately to become Georgian. It is far more famous as the Washington home of Herbert Hoover, who moved here in 1921, when he was appointed Secretary of Commerce by Harding, and he returned here after serving as President. Precisely in front of the Hoover House, in the middle of S Street, was the Kalorama mansion which stood until 1888 when it was demolished to accommodate the building of S and 23rd Streets.

14. 2301 S Street, N. W. — WILLIAM A. MEARNS RESIDENCE*, now part of the EMBASSY OF THE PEOPLE'S REPUBLIC OF CHINA

This house was built in 1906 for William A. Mearns, banker and President of the Washington Stock Exchange. The architects were Frost and Granger of Chicago. The house seems too informal for the location.

15. 2244 S Street, N. W. — FREDERICK A. DELANO HOUSE*, now EMBASSY OF IRELAND

GeorgianRevival architecture dominates the upper portions of Kalorama. It was the leading style of domestic design in early 20th-century Washington. Waddy Wood designed this house for Frederick A. Delano, an uncle of Franklin D. Roosevelt and President of the Wabash and several other Midwestern railroads.

16. MITCHELL PLAYGROUND** and the site of KALORAMA SQUARE development (North side of S Street between 23rd and 22nd Streets, N. W.)

The land for Mitchell Playground was donated to the city by Mrs. E. N. Mitchell in 1918. She and her husband had planned a large residence there, but his death terminated the project. The only proviso of Mrs. Mitchell's generous bequest was that the city care for the grave of her pet poodle, Bosque, perpetually. The dog's grave still remains, surrounded by a white chain fence, in the middle of the play area.

The fortress-like Kalorama Square townhouse project represents the most recent chapter in the long story of Kalorama. The pseudo-Georgian dwellings are the enterprise of Kalorama resident, architect Walter Marlow. Prices for the houses are in the $300,000 - 450,000 price range. A landscaped central mall covers the parking area between the rows of houses.

17. 1801-1809 PHELPS PLACE, N. W.*

Closer to Connecticut Avenue, the character of Kalorama changes. As early as 1873 streetcars ran along Connecticut Avenue from 17th Street to Florida Avenue. In the blocks of Kalorama adjacent to this major diagonal avenue of L'Enfant's plan, one notices speculative rowhouse development typical of a streetcar suburb. 1801-1809 Phelps Place is a good example of the pattern. The row was built for $55,000 in 1896 by William Alexander Kimmel, an active speculator and building contractor responsible for 17 Washington churches in addition to countless houses.

Most of the Phelps Place buildings now serve foundation or educational purposes. The rowhouses of the nearby blocks of S Street near Connecticut Avenue, Bancroft and Leroy Places have long been popular with government officials. There was an especially heavy concentration of prominent New Deal personalities in this section of Kalorama. Most of the pleasant rowhouses in this favored district were built between 1900 and 1915.

18.   1825 Phelps Place, N. W. — CONRAD MILLER RESIDENCE*, now OFFICE OF THE USSR AGRICULTURAL COUNSELLOR

Prolific Washington architect Thomas Franklin Schneider designed this 3-story, yellow-brick house for Conrad Miller, celebrated lecturer and publisher, and his wife Anna Jenness Miller, authoress and lecturer. It was constructed in 1896-7 for $35,000 and displays all of Schneider's full-blown mannerisms.

19.   SW corner of Phelps Place and California Street, N. W. — ST. ROSE'S INDUSTRIAL SCHOOL, now MACKIN CATHOLIC HIGH SCHOOL FOR BOYS*

Organized originally in a downtown location in 1872, St. Rose's Industrial School (for the training of orphan girls in home economics and 'feminine' manual arts) was built in about 1904 in what was then open country. Later the building became the St. Ann's Infant Asylum. In the 1960's it was the Cathedral Latin School, and today is the Mackin Catholic High School, whose enrollment is mostly black and non-resident in this section of Washington. The impressive Roman brick and brownstone structure is one of the few buildings in Kalorama not intended as a residence. A structure of this size would not be permitted in the area if built today.

20.   THE 2100 AND 2200 BLOCKS OF CALIFORNIA STREET, N. W.**

California Street, Connecticut Avenue, and Columbia Road are the only concentration of large apartment houses in the Kalorama district. At the turn of the century the heights above Florida Avenue attracted massive apartment house development which aroused the ire of many residents who felt that such structures were alien to the character of the city.

In the 1960's these enormous buildings — some of which had been neglected and overcrowded during the war years — received the overflow of the nearby Spanish-speaking immigrant population. Some of the structures continued to deteriorate, but in recent years condominium conversion and the attraction of the large, well-built apartments for a young professional population able to pay higher rents has resulted in the removal of a good portion of the Latino population.

21.   2205 California Street, N. W. — CALIFORNIA HOUSE APARTMENTS

Typical of the grander apartment houses of about 1905, California House has very large, handsomely-appointed apartments. Justice Louis Brandeis resided here for many years.

22.   2122 California Street, N. W. — THE WESTMORELAND APARTMENTS

Built in 1905, the Westmoreland is a fine example of Washington "apartment-house baroque" architecture.

23.   Connecticut Avenue and Columbia Road, N. W. — EQUESTRIAN STATUE OF MAJOR GENERAL GEORGE B. McCLELLAN

The completely personality-less bronze statue of the Commander of the Army of the Potomac was designed by Frederick MacMonnies in 1907 and rests on a base designed by James Crocroft. MacMonnies had attracted worldwide attention and praise with his sculpture for the World's Columbia Exposition in 1893, but so had some atrocious architecture at the same fair.

24.   NE Corner of Connecticut Avenue and California Street, N. W. — ALVIN MASON LOTHROP HOUSE**; now part of the U. S. S. R. EMBASSY COMPLEX

This 40-room, Italianate, limestone mansion was built in 1901 for Alvin Mason Lothrop, partner in the dry goods firm of Woodward and Lothrop (now Washington's largest department store). The architects were Joseph Hornblower and James Rush Marshall.

125

From the vantage point of the Lothrop house site, one can imagine what a wonderful view the early houses on Kalorama Heights must have had. The commanding view from Kalorama was possible until the development of the Washington Hilton Hotel site across Columbia Road from the Lothrop mansion.

25. Columbia Road and T Street, N. W. — THE WASHINGTON HILTON HOTEL-UNIVERSAL OFFICE BUILDING site

The large tract of land occupied by the Washington Hilton Hotel and large office buildings directly south was long called Oak Lawn, after the huge and ancient oak tree which stood there.

In the 1920's the site was proposed to accommodate a National Masonic Memorial which resulted in the submission of an interesting scheme by Frank Lloyd Wright. If constructed, this would have been a far better work of architecture and site design than the hideous, gleaming Washington Hilton Hotel. The erection of the hotel in the early 1960s totally upset the fabric of this neighborhood.

26. KALORAMA TRIANGLE and ADAMS MORGAN AREA**

Columbia Road (one of the oldest routes of land travel in the Washington area) runs through the heart of what is distinctly an early 20th-century community developed for the upper-middle and upper classes. The growth of the district was directly tied to the extension in 1896 of excellent streetcar service. This area was called Washington Heights. It is a neighborhood of well constructed rowhouses and apartment buildings. It is also one of the most racially, ethnically, and economically diverse parts of the capital.

Columbia Road itself is the eastern boundary of a largely-restored neighborhood known as the KALORAMA TRIANGLE (whose other two sides are Connecticut Avenue and Calvert Street). Kalorama Triangle is the western portion of a larger district known as ADAMS-MORGAN. The Adams-Morgan community takes its name from the two public elementary schools in the vicinity. In the late 1950's an experiment in community control of these schools led to an extremely controversial proposal for the large-scale renewal of this entire section. The plan was bitterly argued for several years, finally dying in the mid-1960's. Kalorama Triangle citizens, as residents of a sub-neighborhood being restored privately, objected to the inclusion of their area in the clearance and redevelopment schemes of the overall plan. Businessmen around the commerical hub of 18th Street and Columbia Road protested the displacement of small businesses and light industry required by the renewal project. In frustration, many businesses (including some of the long-established "carriage-trade" services) moved out of the area despite the lack of enactment of the Adams-Morgan plan.

In the process of debate about the future of the community and in the tumultuous years since the death of the official plan, several things have happened in Adams-Morgan:

— There has been a return of the young white population to the neighborhood in general;
— Kalorama Triangle has remained almost entirely white and prices for homes and apartments there have increased many

times since the onset of restoration. Restored rowhouses sell for an average price of $80,000.

— There has been an intensification of the political divisions within the community and a concomitant flood of emotional political rhetoric.

— There has been an intensification of the problems of the poor and Spanish-speaking people in Adams-Morgan, particularly in housing.

— There has been a revival of commerical life along Columbia Road and 18th Street; particularly there has been a growth in restaurants.

27. KALORAMA PARK** — Columbia Road and Kalorama Road, N. W.

One of the lovliest features of the Kalorama-Adams Morgan area is this small park with towering oak trees. The land was almost subdivided for housing development in the 1940's, but was saved by citizen pressure for public parkland. The site is well-used by the community and each summer is the scene of the annual Washington area Latino festival.

This brief circuit through the Kalorama Triangle to Connecticut Avenue gives the tour-goer a sampling of the variety and charm of housing in this section of Washington. Ashmead Place is the old route of Connecticut Avenue. The present alignment of Connecticut Avenue across Rock Creek Park dates from the construction of the great Taft Bridge, from 1897 to 1907.

28. 2101 CONNECTICUT AVENUE APARTMENTS**

Of all the mammoth luxury apartment buildings erected on this stretch of Connecticut Avenue in the early 20th century, 2101 is perhaps the most impressive. Built in 1928 by the same firm that built the Shoreham Hotel, it has only 66 apartments. All are at least 7 rooms with 3 baths and 3 exposures. Of special interest are the sculptured parrot gargoyles and lion's-head medallions above the entrance portals. On the roof are 8 atlantes.

2101 Connecticut Avenue has long housed some of Washington's most prominent people. In its art deco decorative flair and in its excess of elegant spaciousness, the building might be considered the last gasp of the truly lavish and significant phase in grand apartment house construction in Washington. Just compare it to Watergate for example — a recently-constructed "luxury" apartment building (see Tour 7 - Foggy Bottom).

29. 2131 Wyoming Avenue, N. W. — MORTIMER J. LAWRENCE HOUSE, now Brewster Residence**

Mortimer J. Lawrence was the publisher of The Ohio Farmer, The Michigan Farmer, and The Pennsylvania Farmer. He was a Cleveland bank president as well. The house was Lawrence's wedding gift to his bride, Carrie Snyder. Both were infatuated with Italy and had their architect, Waddy Wood, model the house after a Tuscan villa. It was constructed in 1907. Throughout there is fine marble and mosaic work; barely a surface, interior or exterior, is wood. Note the beautiful copper soffiting, which is seriously decayed. Overall, the condition of the building is quite poor, but the present owner hopes to restore the house.

30.   2215 Wyoming Avenue, N. W. — WILLIAM HOWARD
TAFT HOUSE**, now part of the U. A. R. Embassy complex

This house was the home of ex-President Taft from the time he
returned to Washington as Chief Justice of the Supreme Court,
in 1921, until his death in 1930. Mrs. Taft lived on in the house
until her death in 1944.

Taft purchased the large, Georgian Revival-style house from Massachusetts Congressman Alvin Fuller. The building was constructed about 1904.

31.   2300 Wyoming Avenue, N. W. — ANTHONY FRANCIS
LUCAS RESIDENCE**, now Embassy of Zambia

The cost of this delightfully-pretentious house at the time of its
construction in 1913 was an incredible $20,000. The architect
was Clark Waggaman, a local resident, who during his short career specialized in large suburban homes for the wealthy.

Undoubtedly, this house is one of the most unusual in the city.
So closely is it tied to the products of Italian Mannerism, particularly the work of an architect like Giulio Romano. The most
important space in the building is the two-story room behind the
loggia on 23rd Street. It is roofed with groin vaults and splendid-
ly articulated. The dining room is noteworthy for its richly carved
oak paneling.

32.   2314 Wyoming Avenue, N. W. — WARREN G. HARDING
RESIDENCE*

Warren G. Harding lived here as Senator from Ohio from 1917
until   becoming President in 1921. The house is more important for its historical than for its architectural values. However,
the use of a side entry is unusual in Washington, and the interesting use of classical elements and overall sculptural quality
make the building more intriguing than a first glance might
acknowledge.

33. 2300 Kalorama Road, N. W. — ROYAL THAI LEGATION*

One of the few Kalorama buildings built for a foreign mission,
the Royal Thai Legation dates from about 1915. Note the Eastern symbolism incorporated in the concrete work: for example,
the garudas (mythological bird that was the vehicle of Vishnu)
atop the pilasters of the Kalorama Road facade.

34. 2221 Kalorama Road, N. W. — W. W. LAWRENCE HOUSE***,
now the Embassy of France

Occupying a dramatic and beautiful site high above Rock Creek, the
residence of the French Ambassador is the largest house in Kalorama.
It was built in 1911 and was originally the mansion of W. W. Lawrence
whose fortune was in mining.

The Government of France purchased the house in January 1936
for about $400,000, including furnishings and household equip-
ment. The Kalorama Road mansion has served as the residence
of the French Ambassador ever since.

The architect of the splendid Tudor house was Jules Henri de Sibour, who was born in France in 1872. Although raised in the United States, de Sibour studied architecture at the Ecole des Beaux Arts. His Washington career was extemely successful. De Sibour worked most often in eclectic borrowings from French classicism, and thus, the house for W. W. Lawrence marks an unusual venture into the Tudor country manor house heritage. The mansion is actually perfectly symmetrical, but creates the impression of a rambling asymmetry, because it is impossible to approach head-on from any of the surrounding streets.

35. 2401 Kalorama Road, N. W. — THE LINDENS*** (Mrs. George Maurice Morris Residence)

The section of Kalorama west of the French Embassy dates entirely from the period since 1925. Kalorama Circle is unusual among the circles of Washington in that it was planned for development, rather than as a public park. None of the houses on the Circle is especially good architecture, but the overall quality of development, the superb VIEWS ACROSS ROCK CREEK PARK, and the cut-off, quiet character of the neighborhood keep this one of the city's most expensive and prestigious sections. Prices in excess of $100,000 for Kalorama homes are standard today. By way of comparison over time, the two charming Tudor, or Norman, stone houses at 33 and 29 Kalorama Circle were designed by Horace Peaslee and built in 1926 for Leslie F. R. Prince for a combined price of $45,000. And the decade of the 1920's was a period of extreme inflation.

In this neighborhood of recreated historical styles, the Lindens is an example of the real thing; or almost. The Georgian house was actually built in 1754 in Danvers, Massachusetts for Marblehead merchant Robert Hooper. The Lindens served as the summer home of Thomas Gage, the last Royal Governor of Massachusetts, and for this reason is sometimes known as the Gage House.

The Robert Hooper mansion was moved to Washington, D. C., by Mr. and Mrs. George Maurice Morris in 1936. At the time they were searching for a suitable home for their antiques, and by acquiring the Lindens, the Morris' spared the house from planned destruction. Walter Macomber, resident architect of Williamsburg, directed the disassembly of the building, which was carried out by Williamsburg workmen.

36. & 37.   2030 and 2000 24th Street, N. W. — DEVORE AND STEWART RESIDENCES**, respectively

These fine houses were built for two sisters whose father, Canadian-born Wisconsin lumber magnate Alexander Stewart, had in 1909 built the family's first Washington home at 2200 Massachusetts Avenue, on the site of the Kalorama estate cemetery. 2000 24th Street was built in 1931. The architect was New Yorker William L. Bottomley, who has been described as the "master of the old new house," and the Devore residence justifies his reputation. It is a limestone demi-palace in the style of a French hotel of the Louis XV period.

In 1961 G. Howland Chase offered 2000 24th Street to the U. S. Government as a permanent home for the Chief Justice of the Supreme Court, and an endowment to maintain it. The Government refused the gift offer. A minor scandal erupted two years ago when the public learned that the Roman Catholic Diocese of Washington planned to buy the home for its bishop. The building was recently purchased as a conference-reception center for a "Christian businessmen's" organization.

In 1938-39 the other sister, built 2030 24th Street, next door. The cost of the house was $100,000 and the architect was Philadelphian Paul Cret. Again France is the source of the design, although in the Stewart house there is a sort of Norman country house inspiration. The stonework and detailing are exquisite throughout. This building is probably the last great home of Kalorama.

38.   Proceed south on 24th Street to S Street. Terminate the Tour by visiting the WOODROW WILSON HOUSE** (2340 S Street, N. W.) and the TEXTILE MUSEUM* (2310-30 S Street, N. W.). Both are open to the public and are well worth seeing.

As one moves south toward Massachusetts Avenue, through this western part of Kalorama, the houses become quite a bit more modest. Until the mid-1920's most of this area was woodlands. Frances Hodgson Burnett, author of Little Lord Fauntleroy, was a major property owner. The land was rather rugged and not as attractive as property west of Rock Creek that was more accessible from Massachusetts Avenue and thus, developed somewhat earlier. Much of Kalorama is a far younger community than many people think, and it is a community of greater diversity than is commonly assumed.

130

French Embassy

16 ***GEORGETOWN (Historical residential district, specialty boutiques and restaurants, C&O Canal, Georgetown University)

By Robert H. Cousins

Mr. Cousins, who holds a planning degree from Yale, works for the National Capital Planning Commission, Washington, D. C. and is a longtime resident of Georgetown. He is a former officer of the National Capital Area Chapter, AIP

DISTANCE: 3½ Miles   *TIME: 2¼ Hours*

BUS: 62 to 27th and P Streets or D2, D4, D8 to 27th and Q Streets, N.W.

METRO: Dupont Circle (Red) then transfer to 62 on P Street, N.W. West of 20th Street, N.W.

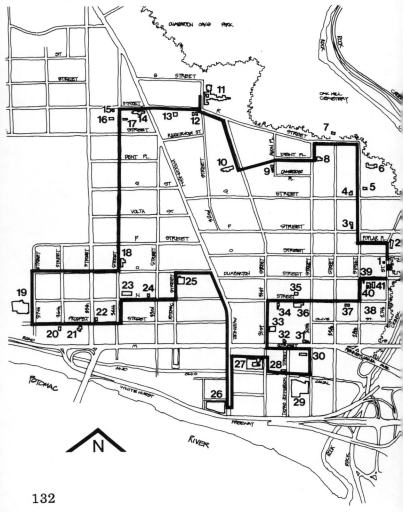

In 1751, the Maryland Assembly founded what they called Georgetown and drew up a plat for the land south of the present-day N-Street to the river. However, there is evidence that a grant of land, comprising what is now known as Georgetown, was awarded much earlier to Ninian Beall in 1703. In the 1740's, tobacco from nearby Maryland growers was being inspected, crated and shipped from warehouses along the Potomac River at Georgetown. Then in 1791, Georgetown was included in the area selected by President Washington to be the seat of government. By this time, work had started on the Chesapeake & Ohio Canal (1785) much further west, even though this important artery was not completed through Georgetown itself until the 1830's.

By the beginning of the 19th century, the men who were making money in commerce and government were building their fine residences in the area from N Street north (Dumbarton Oaks and Evermay were both built in 1801, and more modest, but handsome Federal houses still standing in the 3300 block, the 3100 block and the 2800 block of N Street were built in the period between 1813 and 1820). Despite a long and gradual decline toward the end of the 19th century and into the first quarter of the 20th century, Georgetown has been almost completely restored and today is at the top of the list of desirable places in Washington in which to live today. The mixture of almost blatant commercialism and fine old homes is no more of a contradiction than the mixture of formal Federal mansions cheek-by-jowl with 12-foot wide Victorian workers' homes. In fact, it is the variety and wide range of contrasts that make Georgetown so attractive.

Nevertheless, the battle of preservation and/or compatibility is a neverending process. The process is aided by the 'Old Georgetown Act' passed by Congress in 1950. The act calls for a very crucial review by the Commission of Fine Arts on all new development and all exterior modifications of existing development. Fortunately, the review has controlled exterior appearances (there are no neon signs, for instance, allowed in Georgetown) without having any negative effect on the area's liveliness and economic attractiveness.

Start your tour on 27th Street, N. W., between Dumbarton and O Streets, N. W.

1.   1350 27th Street, N. W. — The STEPHEN TRENTMAN HOUSE* was built in 1968 and designed by Hugh Jacobsen, a prominent Washington architect. This house represents an excellent alternative to the "Fake-Federal" style found elsewhere throughout Georgetown as new fill-in houses were added in the 1950's and 1960's.

2.   1411-1419 27th Street, N.W.   These townhouses were built in 1954 after a revision to the Zoning Regulations required off-street parking at the rate of one parking space for each dwelling unit.   Although parking is required to be provided, it is not required to be used (note the subsequent conversion of the garages to other uses).

3.   2805 P Street, N. W.   This is the home of MRS. DEAN ACHESON.   She and her late husband were among the vanguard

of the Georgetown restoration movement in the 1930's. The restoration of Georgetown was popular with the New Dealers of the Roosevelt administration, many of whom, like Harry Hopkins, lived here.

4. 2813 Q Street, N. W. This house, doubled in size and redone by Hugh Jacobsen in 1959, is one of the first attempts by this architect to renovate in a manner which combines contemporary ideas and materials with more traditional themes.

5. 1607 28th Street, N. W. This house was occupied by SENA-TOR EDWARD KENNEDY in the middle 1960's.

6. 1623 28th Street, N. W. EVERMAY is one of the showplaces of Georgetown and is the scene each year of a tea at the end of the Georgetown Garden Tour. It was built in 1801, was greatly modified over the years, and finally carefully restored to its original Georgian splendor.

7. R Street at 29th Street, N. W. THE RENWICK CHAPEL* of Oak Hill Cemetery was built in 1850 and is one of only four structures designed by James Renwick still standing in the District. Its simplicity is in strong contrast to other Renwick buildings, such as the original Smithsonian Museum on the Mall (see Tour 3, Mall East) or the Renwick Gallery next to Blair House (see Tour 8, White House) on Pennsylvania Avenue.

8. 2920 R Street, N. W. This is the home of KATHARINE MEYER GRAHAM, publisher of the Washington Post.

9. 1600 Avon Place, N. W. is the residence of ARTHUR COTTON MOORE, architect of the Canal Square project (see No. 27 this tour)

and the remodeled Cairo Hotel. The house was built in the late 1960's on a difficult sloped site and is notable for its arrangement on the site to insure family privacy.

10. 1644 31st Street, N. W. This great house, TUDOR PLACE, was built in 1815. The architect was William Thornton, the winner of the original competition for the design of the U. S. Capitol Building.

11. R Street at 31st Street, N. W. DUMBARTON OAKS*** is worth an afternoon visit. This magnificent 16 acre estate is now owned by Harvard University, but reflects the generosity and interests of its benefactors, the late Robert and Mildred Bliss. Mrs. Bliss was a very accomplished horticulturist and landscape architect. Note the extensive gardens ranging from a formal pebble mosaic pool to a romantic rustic pool shaded by lindens. Mr. Bliss was a former Foreign Service Officer and Ambassador to Argentina. He collected Pre-Columbian works of art which are now housed in a new handsome MUSEUM** designed by Philip Johnson. It is open to the public during designated hours and is reached from the 32nd Street side of the property. Not to be overlooked is the great Georgian mansion which was the original house at The Oaks and was built in 1801.

12. 3210 R Street, N. W. This is the home of ABE FORTAS, former Associate Justice of the Supreme Court and nominee for Chief Justice during the Johnson years.

13. 3238 R Street, N.W. The SCOTT-GRANT HOUSE* was built in 1858 and was once occupied by President Ulysses S. Grant as a "Summer White House." The property, which is quite large for Georgetown, has unfortunately been subdivided recently.

14. 3304 - 3310 R Street, N. W. This row of houses was a single house called "Friendship" and was occupied by the late EVALYN WALSH McLEAN, socialite and one-time owner of the Hope Diamond.

15. 3402 R Street, N. W. This was the home of H. R. HALDEMAN, close aide to former President Nixon. He was living here during the Watergate revelations. There were reports that a neighbor directly across the street hung a huge "Impeach Nixon" banner just opposite his front door.

16. 1686 34th Street, N. W. This large house, which until recently occupied an entire city block, was built in 1820 and is now the home of ROGER L. STEVENS, Chairman of the Board of Trustees of the Kennedy Center for the Performing Arts.

17. 1691 34th Street, N. W. This is the home of SENATOR CHARLES PERCY.

18. 1405 34th Street, N. W. DAVID K. E. BRUCE, the first Chief of the U. S. Liaison Office in Peking, China lives here.

19. 37th and N Streets, N. W. The relatively new LAUINGER MEMORIAL LIBRARY, GEORGETOWN UNIVERSITY** was the subject of prolonged and impassioned debate among the Fine Arts Commission, the Citizens Association of Georgetown, the National Capital Planning Commission, the University and others. The result, completed in 1970 and designed by John Carl Warnecke & Associates, now seems worth all the effort. Its fanciful profile and sympathetic color, texture and massing combine to make this addition a welcome one.

20. 3600 Prospect Street, N. W. This house, although of recent vintage and not the typical Georgetown house was, because of its unique location near a long flight of steep steps, chosen for the filming of THE EXORCIST. For the movie, however, it was necessary to have the house abut the steps and a temporary wing (making the house L-shaped) was added between the existing house and the flight of stairs.

21. 3508 Prospect Street, N. W. PROSPECT HOUSE* was erected in 1788. In the late 1940's it was the home of the late James E. Forrestal, the first Secretary of Defense.

22. 3425 Prospect Street, N. W. This handsome house, known as QUALITY HILL* and built in 1798, is the current home of Senator Claiborne Pell.

23. 3327 - 3339 N Street, N. W. This group of five houses, known as COX'S ROW* named after the owner-builder, was built in 1817. Their handsome doorways, dormers and facade decorations are characteristic of the Federal period.

24. 3307 N Street, N. W. The then Senator JOHN F. KENNEDY and his wife lived in this house at the time he was elected President. Mute testimony to the prominence of this house in the days just

136

before the Inauguration is evidenced by a plaque on the house across the street (the side wall of 3302) expressing appreciation from grateful members of the Press for comforts received there.

25.   Potomac and O Streets, N. W. — ST. JOHN'S EPISCOPAL CHURCH* (1809). This lovely old church is also attributed to William Thornton, the architect whose design for the Capitol Building was the foundation for many subsequent modifications. Like the Captiol, this church has seen many modifications; evidence of the last, the Victorian, is seen along Potomac Street.

26.   At the corner of Wisconsin Avenue & K Street, N. W. is DODGE CENTER*, a new 90-foot high office/retail building designed by Hartman-Cox. The rebuilding of the waterfront area has been the subject of bitter debate for more than a decade. The disagreement has been over height, density and even use. The permit for this structure was obtained before recently-adopted new zoning (the result of years of study) took effect and reflects what the old industrial zoning would allow. Despite the building's imaginative design, it is still the subject of some controversy. Integral in its design is the preservation of the OLD BRICK WAREHOUSES* at the corner of Wisconsin and K Street.

27.   CANAL SQUARE**, 1054 31st Street, N. W., is a lively and innovative office and specialty-shop complex which successfully incorporates some old warehouses along the C&O Canal into the project and is built around an inner court. It was designed by Arthur Cotton Moore and was completed in 1971.

28.   1058 THOMAS JEFFERSON STREET, N.W. The current office use is representative of one of the best aspects of Georgetown; the continuing use of old structures over a period of time even though the use may be different now. This little structure was built originally for use as a Masonic Hall in about 1810.

29. 1055 Thomas Jefferson Street, N.W. Like Canal Square this new building, called THE FOUNDRY*, uses red brick, combines its new construction with the preservation and adaptation of a landmark structure (an old foundry) and is oriented to the canal. Even further, Arthur Cotton Moore served as the principal architect. (See historic plaque in the canal side park for information about the C&O CANAL***.)

30. 3000 M Street, N.W. A gas station with its tree plantings, paving and low walls, was given much national publicity when it was built here during the 1960s. The colonial motif was probably a little overdone in gas station design, but with the additional features, the result was quite successful in fitting into the neighborhood scene. However, the gas station was demolished in 1979 to make way for a new hotel.

31. 3001 - 3009 M Street, N. W. This ROW OF FOUR HOUSES* (now retail uses on the ground floor) show the common 3-bay facade typical of the Federal period. The two houses on the right are dated about 1790; the two on the left a little later. The group was carefully restored in 1955.

32. 3051 M Street, N. W. The OLD STONE HOUSE** is believed to date back to about 1766. Regardless, it is generally accepted as the oldest building in the District of Columbia today and is now the property of the National Park Service, which maintains it as a public museum.

33. 1221 31st Street, N. W. Now the Georgetown Branch of the U. S. Postal Service, this Renaissance Revival building designed in the manner of an Italian palace was originally a CUSTOM HOUSE* for the bustling port of Georgetown. It was designed by Ammi B. Young and was constructed in 1857-8.

34. 3038 N Street, N. W. This fine old Federal house was built in 1816 and is presently the home of W. AVERELL HARRIMAN.

138

35.   3017 N Street, N. W. This is the house which JACKIE KENNEDY bought and occupied for a short time after becoming a widow. She complained of hordes of sight-seers which came by and invaded her privacy and subsequently moved to a more anonymous high-rise apartment building in New York City.

36.   3014 N Street, N. W. This large house was built in 1799, but with obvious later additions. It is notable for its nicely detailed round-top windows on the first floor. Supposedly President Lincoln's son lived here for a time.

37.   2806, 2808 & 2812 N Street, N. W. These three houses make one of the most outstanding groups of fine FEDERAL ARCHITECTURE* in the Georgetown area. They were all built between about 1813 and 1817. 2806 and 2808 are almost identical except that they are opposite-handed. 2812 is a larger house and has symmetry. It is referred to as the Decatur House because it is said that the Commodore's widow lived here after his death. All of these houses have been highly desirable as in-town residences and have, over the years, served as such for John Walker, former Director of the National Gallery of Art, Chester Bowles and others.

38.   2726 N Street, N. W. In the rear yard of this house, there is a brick wall up against the neighboring house on 28th Street that contains a large colored MOSAIC* designed by Marc Chagall. The artist is reportedly a friend of the residents of the house and, on a recent visit there, recommended that that spot was perfect for some alfresco art. The best place to see the mural is from the SW corner of the street intersection and it is best seen in the winter.

39.   2728 Dumbarton Avenue, N.W. This is the home of former SENATOR CLIFFORD CASE.

40.   2720 Dumbarton Avenue, N. W. This was the home, until recently, of JOSEPH ALSOP, the syndicated columnist and confidant of former Presidents.

41.   2716 Dumbarton Avenue, N. W. The ROMAN CATHOLIC CHURCH OF THE EPIPHANY has Masses in French and is very popular with the Embassy crowd. The little church was once highly favored by Jackie Kennedy.

17 **WOODLEY PARK/**NATIONAL ZOO (Early 20th Century apartments, Zoo, prestige residential area, Rock Creek bridges)

By Ms. Floy Brown

Ms. Brown is with Technical Preservation Services, Heritage Conservation and Recreation Service, Department of Interior. She gratefully acknowledges the assistance of Charles Szoradi, architect-planner, and Lindsley Williams, President of the Cleveland Park Association in designing this tour.

DISTANCE: 1¾ Miles   *TIME: ¾ Hour*

METRO: Farragut North (Red) and transfer to L2, L4, or L8 on K Street, N.W.; get off at Connecticut Avenue and Calvert Streets.
BUS: 92, 94, 96, 98, L2, L4, L8

Woodley Park was originally part of a 1000 acre tract of hilly, wooded land purchased by General Uriah Forrest shortly after the American Revolution. Around 1800 the General transferred 250 acres to a wealthy Georgetown lawyer named Philip Barton Key, uncle of Frances Scott Key. The house that Key built was

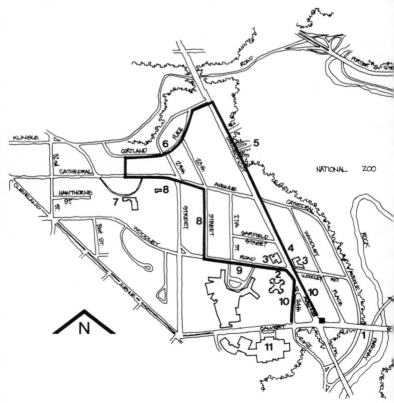

known as Woodley House, named after the old bachelor hall in Mrs. Elizabeth Gaskell's novel, Cranford.

Natural topographical borders locate Woodley Park on the peak of land which rises from the valley of Rock Creek, extends northward for a mile, and then slopes downward to a spring branch of the creek. The altitude and cooler summer temperatures made the area a desirable summer retreat from the city during the nineteenth century.

In the 1890's Woodley Park was purchased by Senator Francis G. Newlands of Nevada, owner of the Chevy Chase Land Company. Newlands was also principal owner in the newly chartered Rock Creek Railway of the District of Columbia, a line which would connect Chevy Chase with downtown Washington. Put into operation in 1892, the street-car route opened the area to suburban development.

1.   The original steel deck truss bridge crossing Rock Creek Valley at Calvert Street has long since been replaced by the existing concrete structure, now known as the DUKE ELLINGTON MEMORIAL BRIDGE*. The "million dollar" CONNECTICUT AVENUE BRIDGE* opened in 1907. At that time it was the largest concrete bridge in the world, and its name and presence highlighted the appeal of Woodley Park.

2.   At the corner of Connecticut Avenue and Woodley Road stands the WARDMAN TOWER* now part of the Sheraton Washington Hotel. Harry Wardman, the master builder of Woodley Park, constructed the luxury hotel in 1913. Washingtonians called it "Wardman's Folly," little realizing that a hotel in the suburbs would prove to be so popular. Formerly a residential wing of the larger complex, the Tower served as home to many of the nation's vice presidents and other VIP's.

3.   The APARTMENT BUILDINGS at 2700 and 2701 Connecticut Avenue and the extensive Cathedral Mansions at 3000 Connecticut Avenue are also Wardman's work. By constructing reasonably-priced houses and apartments along the street-car line, Wardman converted rural property into comfortable town living.

4.   Retracing the street-car route up Connecticut Avenue, one encounters its contemporary equivalent in rapid transit, Metrorail. The Woodley Park-Zoo Metro station, was scheduled to open in late 1981.

5.   At the crest of the hill is the entrance to the NATIONAL ZOOLOGICAL PARK**. Designed by the famous landscape architect, Frederick Law Olmsted, the world-renowned 175-

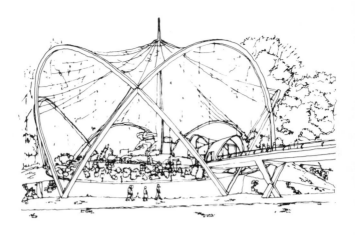

acre Zoo recently celebrated its 83rd birthday. It exhibits
nearly 3,000 animals of more than 800 species and sub-species,
many rare and not exhibited elsewhere in the country. The
Zoo's most famous residents, Hsing-Hsing and Ling-Ling, giant
pandas, were a gift to the American people from the People's
Republic of China following former President Nixon's visit
there in February, 1972.

6. Turn left to Devonshire Place and left again to Cortland
Place. Many of the homes in this mixed residential neighborhood were part of the exclusive Wardman subdivision north of
Cathedral Avenue known as ENGLISH VILLAGE. The cres-
cent-shaped streets give a picturesque effect.

7. Continue on Cortland Place past the playground which
adjoins Klingle Creek Valley. Turn left at the alley and cut
through to Cathedral Avenue, High on a hill behind a row of
stately oaks stands elegant WOODLEY MANSION*. The

white stucco Georgian house served as the summer home of four 19th century presidents, including presidents Van Buren, Tyler, Buchanan, and Cleveland. Henry L. Stimson lived there while serving as secretary of state for President Hoover and secretary of war for President Franklin D. Roosevelt. The building is now owned and operated by the private Maret School.

8. Proceeding down Cathedral Avenue towards Connecticut Avenue, one passes SINGLE OAK*, now the home of the Swiss ambassador, which was built by Sen. Newlands as a residence for a married daughter. Turn right onto 28th Street, The neo-Georgian brick townhouses, many of which have been modernized to contemporary standards, are characteristic of the Wardman subdivision south of Cathedral Avenue, known as Woodley Park. No longer a suburb, the area is desirable now to old and young alike, offering a variety of lifestyles.

9. The new SHERATON WASHINGTON HOTEL (1980) replaced the sprawling main building of the Sheraton Park Hotel (1931). Adjoining the original Wardman Tower at the corner of Connecticut Avenue, the complex now includes 16 acres of landscaped grounds, and large convention facilities.

10. Turn right at Connecticut Avenue. Reflective of the heterogeneous residential character of Woodley Park, the shops and restaurants along Connecticut Avenue include everything from the neighborhood drugstore to international haute cuisine. Numerous SIDEWALK CAFES* provide a congenial resting place.

11. Turn right to 24th Street and walk down to Calvert Street. The SHOREHAM HOTEL*, constructed in 1930 by Harry Bralove, proved a worthy rival to the Wardman Park. It has been said that the Shoreham attracted so many prominent Washingtonians that one could ring a bell there anytime and summon a quorum of senators.

143

18 ***WASHINGTON CATHEDRAL/**CLEVELAND PARK (Turn of the century residences, huge gothic cathedral)

By Charity Vanderbilt Davidson

DISTANCE: 2 Miles   TIME: 2 Hours

BUS: 30, 32, 34, 36, 96, 98, N2 and N4.

METRO: Dupont Circle (Red); transfer to N2 or N4 on Massachusetts Avenue, N.W. west of 20th Street, N.W.

Cleveland Park is significant as a neighborhood with a strong sense of community and a unique architectural quality. With its tree-lined streets, brick sidewalks, and large frame houses, it has successfully retained much of its late 19th/early 20th century atmosphere. Many of the architectural styles which gained popularity in the late nineteenth century are represented in Cleveland Park's houses. (Note: Most of the houses are not discussed individually, but some of those of particular interest are indicated on the tour-map.)

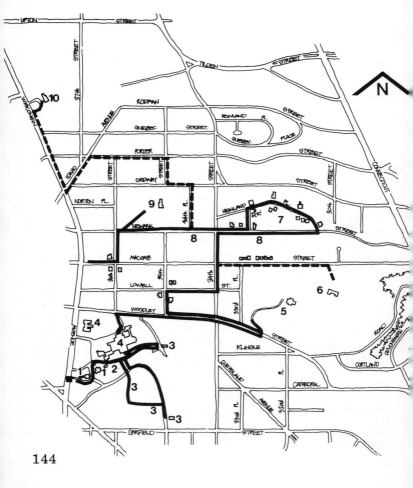

Cleveland Park and the Close of the Washington Cathedral (officially known as the Cathedral Church of St. Peter and St. Paul) were originally part of the almost 1,000 acres purchased in 1790 by two Georgetown merchants, Benjamin Stoddert (who was also the first Secretary of the Navy) and Uriah Forrest. Forrest bought Stoddert's share in the property, which he called Rosedale, in 1794 and moved his family to the house he built (see No. 9). The area remained rural until the late 1880's and early 1890's, when it became a fashionable retreat from Washington's hot, humid summers. Wealthy Washingtonians, including President Grover Cleveland (from whom the area derived its name after he established his summer White House at "Red Top" — since demolished — in 1886), built large, rambling "cottages," a few of which are extant. By 1900, with the extension of trolly lines up Connecticut and Wisconsin Avenues, N. W. and the completion of the Connecticut Avenue bridge across Rock Creek, Cleveland Park became a desirable area for year-round residence. Housing starts in what is today Cleveland Park (but then consisted of three subdivisions — Oak View, Cleveland Heights and Cleveland Park) mushroomed in the years between 1900 and 1914. It has remained a popular residential area ever since. Its residents consistently have been professionals, high level government officials, academicians, and journalists.

The 57-acre Close is a portion of the land Joseph Nourse is believed to have purchased from Philip Barton Key in 1804; Nourse called his holding Mt. Alban, after St. Alban's in Herefordshire. The Close was first opened to the public in 1901. Enter the Close from Wisconsin Avenue, N. W., near Massachusetts Avenue, N. W. It is recommended that visitors walk around the Close before entering the Cathedral proper. Walk through the wooden archway between St. Alban's Church and Satterlee Hall.

1. ST. ALBAN'S EPISCOPAL CHURCH
Consecrated 1855

After Joseph Nourse's death in 1841, this portion of his estate was sold to an Episcopal clergyman, who established a school on the property. Services at the school chapel were opened to the public after 1847; they were so well attended that St. Alban's parish was established and a small frame church erected with a bequest from one of Nourse's daughters. This original church was enlarged and encased in stone in 1926. St. Alban's and its buildings are not part of the Cathedral Foundation property, but the two jurisdictions work together closely.

The buildings off to the right, behind Satterlee Hall and the rectory, are St. Alban's School for Boys (founded 1903), one of the five Cathedral Schools on the Close.

Walk along the roadway past the Peace Cross (dedicated 1898). Turn left and then right and continue past the Episcopal Church House (1913-Henry Vaughn, arch.) and the Herb Cottage (one of the earliest buildings on the Close; originally built to house the Cathedral's baptistery, it now serves as a gift shop). The stone wall on the right encloses:

2. THE BISHOP'S GARDEN**
1928-1932 — Landscape design by Mrs. G. C. F. Bratenahl

Turn right through the Norman arch. The Garden actually consists of several gardens, including a rose garden and a medieval herb garden, connected by boxwood-lined, stone paved walkways. With its pools and ivy-covered gazebo, it is among the city's most pleasant and peaceful places.

Return to the main roadway and continue east to the Pilgrim Steps and the equestrian statue of George Washington (Herbert Haseltine, sculptor). Those wishing to, should descend the 40-foot wide steps, cross Pilgrim Road, and follow the:

3. WOODLAND PATH*

This curvilinear walk, which is maintained by local garden clubs leads either to St. Alban's School or to a lower section of Pilgrim Road. The branch to Pilgrim Road includes a large wooden foot bridge (1961 - Walter Dodd Ramberg, arch.); the bridge is particularly noteworthy for its composition, the size of its members, and its overall character. Cross the foot bridge to Pilgrim Road and then walk south on Pilgrim Road to Garfield Street, N. W. to the St. Albans Tennis Club (1970 - Hartman and Cox, arch.); this small, well-ordered building is notable for its varied, but dignified, facade.

Return to the main road. Beyond the Pilgrim Steps and the deanery (1953 - Walter G. Peter, arch.) is the Greenhouse, which offers a great variety of herb plants for sale (catalogues are available on request).

The low, modern building (1964-Falkner, Kingsbury & Stenhouse, arch.) to the right of the greenhouse is Beauvoir, the Cathedral elementary school (founded 1933). Other structures on the western end of the Close include buildings for administration, the College of Preachers, the Cathedral Library, and canons' housing (all 1924-1929 - Frohman, Robb & Little, arch.).

4. THE CATHEDRAL CHURCH OF ST. PETER AND ST. PAUL***
(Also known as the National Cathedral and the Washington Cathedral)

1906-1917 - George F. Bodley, architect
Henry Vaughn, supervising architect

1922-1971 - Philip H. Frohman, supervising architect
1971- Goodwin & Beckett, supervising architect

Late in 1891, a group of Washingtonians "interested in planning a cathedral" in the city met at the home of Charles Carroll Glover, a prominent local banker and the prime mover in the effort to establish Rock Creek Park. Two years later, in 1893, Congress chartered the Protestant Episcopal Cathedral Foundation to oversee the construction and operation of such a cathedral and to carry out an educational program. Mt. Alban, rising above the flat lands of the city, was selected as the site, and in 1906, Bishop Henry Yates Satterlee selected the Gothic design submitted by George Frederick Bodley, then England's leading Anglican church architect. Henry Vaughn, a prominent American proponent of the Neo-Gothic style was selected as the supervising architect. More than 20,000 people attended the laying of the foundation stone in 1907. The Bethleham Chapel and the sanctuary, opened in 1912, were the first sections completed. Construction was halted during World War I, but was resumed in 1922, under the supervision of Philip Hubert Frohman of Frohman, Robb & Little. Frohman, who continued as the supervising architect until 1971, modified the original design of the nave and the central

146

tower. The choir, apse and north transept were opened in 1932, the south transept in 1962, and the Gloria in Excelsis tower (which rises 301 feet above grade) in 1964.

There is a museum of czarist art treasures, "considered by experts to be one of the finest of its kind outside of Russia" in the crypt (basement) level of the Cathedral. This collection of icons, eucharistic vestments, chalices, and jeweled Easter eggs was brought to the United States by Ambassador Joseph E. Davies during the late 1930's.

The funerals of such famous Americans as Woodrow Wilson (who is also buried there), Dwight D. Eisenhower and Gen. Douglas MacArthur were held at the Cathedral. Dr. Martin Luther King's last sermon before going to Memphis in April 1968, was preached at the Cathedral.

The Cathedral itself can be entered from the north or south transepts or from the west end. The Cathedral Foundation conducts 30-45 minute guided tours of the interior, Monday thru Saturday, 10:00 a.m. to 3:15 p.m.

Leave the Cathedral by the north transept. Hearst Hall, the Renaissance Revival building visible at the northwest corner of the Close (corner of Wisconsin Avenue and Woodley Road, N. W.), was the first building erected on the Close (1900-1901 - Robert W. Gibson, arch.). Until recently, it served as a dormitory/classroom for the National Cathedral School for Girls (founded 1900). The two large brick buildings across Woodley Road, N. W. (Founder's Hall and Proctor Hall) are also part of NCS.

147

5. TWIN OAKS*
3225 Woodley Road, N. W.
1888 - Allen Kenway

Until recently the residence of the ambassador of the Republic of China, Twin Oaks is typical of the private estates and
summer "cottages" for which Cleveland Park was noted late in
the nineteenth century. The estate is part of the 250 acres
which Philip Barton Key (Francis Scott Key's uncle) purchased
from Uriah Forrest ca. 1800. Late in the 1880's, the property
was acquired by Gardiner Green Hubbard, a founder and the
first president of the National Geographic Society. Hubbard
improved the property by building the large frame house and
outbuildings (1890 - James G. Hill, architect). When Hubbard
died in 1897, the property was divided between his two daughters
(one of whom had married Alexander Graham Bell); one of the
daughters lived on this portion of the estate for a number of
years before it was sold to the Chinese government in 1947. It is
private property and therefore not open to the public, but the
house, its wooded site, and rolling lawns are visible from the lower
end of the driveway.

6. TREGARON
(Washington International School)
3100 Macomb Street, N. W./3029 Klingle Road, N. W.
1912 - Charles Adams Platt

This 20-acre portion of Gardiner Green Hubbard's estate was sold
in 1911 to James Parmelee, an Ohio industrialist. Parmelee built
the large Neo-Georgian residence (which is virtually unaltered) and
called his estate the "Causeway." The property was acquired by
Joseph E. Davies (U. S. Ambassador to the Soviet Union, 1934-1938)
in 1940, and renamed "Tregaron." Davies, who occupied the house
until his death in 1953, added the Russian dacha (cottage). At one
time, the house was proposed as a residence for the Vice President.
The property is currently being leased by the Washington International School, which hopes to purchase the property eventually.
Because of its size the Tregaron tract is of vital importance to the
future of Cleveland Park's neighborhood quality. An unsuccessful
attempt was made several years ago to acquire the property and
develop it as an apartment complex, and Cleveland Park residents
are greatly concerned by the possibility of the property being subdivided and developed. As in the case of Twin Oaks, Tregaron is
private property to which public access is limited. However, a
walk part of the way up the curvilinear drive does offer a view of
the house. It also is an excellent vantage point for observing the
tremendous differences in the topography of Cleveland Park.

7. HIGHLAND PLACE, N. W.**

This curvilinear, tree-lined street was one of the first built up when
Cleveland Park began to develop at the turn of the century. It is a
showcase of typical late-nineteenth century architectural styles.

8. NEWARK STREET, N. W.**

A large number of the houses along Newark Street were built between 1900 and 1912 and offer a cross section of the architectural
styles of the era.

9. ROSEDALE**
3501 Newark Street, N. W.
1794 - Uriah Forrest, owner-builder

This 8-acre tract is all that remains of the 990 acres Uriah Forrest
originally owned. It can be entered from the drive near the corner
of Newark and 36th Streets. A stone building on the property
(referred to as the "old kitchen") is believed to have been built in
1740, while the weatherboard farmhouse, typical of the 18th Century, was built by Forrest in 1794. Originally intended as a summer retreat, Rosedale quickly became the Forrests' permanent
home. George Washington is believed to have been a guest at
Rosedale while the new capital was being built, and L'Enfant,
also a personal friend, is rumored to have helped design the original gardens.

Forrest lost most of his money when the Greenleaf real estate
syndicate collapsed in 1797, and sold all but 130 acres of the
Rosedale holding before his death in 1805. His descendents
sold other sections of the property over the years, but the
house remained in the Forrest family until 1917, when it was
rented to Avery Coonley, a Chicago philanthropist, and his
wife; the Coonleys purchased the remaining 11 acres of Rosedale in 1920. Finally, in 1959, the Coonleys' daughter and
her husband, architect Waldron Faulkner, sold the house and
8 acres to the National Cathedral School for Girls. In 1978,
the house was purchased by an international student exchange
program, Youth for Understanding, which intends to use it as
a museum.

The brick buildings which now surround the farmhouse (1968 - W.
Faulkner, arch.), were intended as dormitories and faculty housing
for NCS. Although Rosedale's interior has been altered greatly, its
exterior has retained its integrity.

Those who wish to can walk south along 36th Street, N. W. and
then west along Macomb Street to Wisconsin Avenue, N. W., where
public transportation is available, (The corner of 36th and Macomb
has a number of interesting houses and offers an unineterupted view

149

of the Cathedral.) Those wishing to get still more of the flavor of Cleveland Park should retrace their steps east along Newark Street to 34th Place, walk north one block on 34th Place to Ordway Street, N. W., and then west on Ordway or Porter Street, N. W. (one block north) to Wisconsin Avenue and the bus. Two short blocks north of Ordway on Wisconsin Avenue, N. W. is:

10. THE HIGHLANDS*
(Zartman House, Sidwell Friends School)
3825 Wisconsin Avenue, N. W.
1817-1827 - Joseph Nourse, owner-builder
1926 - Peabody, Wilson & Brown

This is one of Washington's few extant late Georgian country houses. Built by Joseph Nourse, a Treasury Department official, the house remained in the Nourse family for nearly a century. Residents during the 20th century included such nationally prominent men as Adm. Cary T. Grayson, John Hay Whitney, and Allen Dulles. It is currently owned by the Sidwell Friends School and used as an administratio building.

19 *HOWARD UNIVERSITY (Major Black University)

By Deborah A. White

Deborah White, an urban planning graduate of Howard University, is with the National League of Cities, Washington, D.C.

DISTANCE: 2 Miles　　　　　　　*TIME: 1 Hour*

METRO: Gallery Place (Red); transfer to 70 on 7th Street, N.W.

BUS: 70

For more on black Washington's heritage, you may wish to visit nearby LeDroit Park (Tour 20) and Shaw School Urban Renewal Area/Logan Circle (Tour 14). A drive through all three areas is recommended.

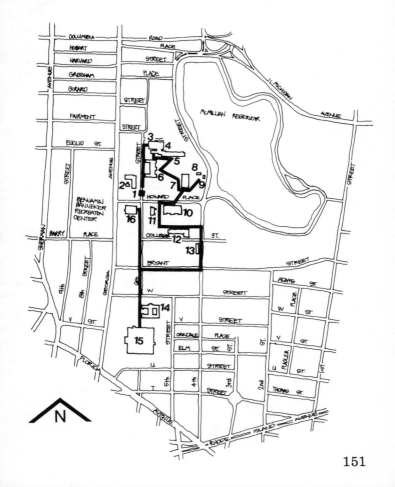

1. The ADMINISTRATION BUILDING includes the Office of the President and Vice-Presidents. Howard has been described as America's most cosmopolitan and integrated educational community. Among the more than 10,000 students and 4,600 faculty and staff members are individuals from all 50 states and more than 90 foreign countries. Their varied customs, cultures, ideas, and interests contribute to the University's international character and vitality.

2. HOWARD HALL* is considered an historical landmark on campus. It was the original building where classes were first held in 1867.

3. CRAMTON AUDITORIUM, with a seating capacity of 1,500, is the scene of concerts, plays, dance workshops, lectures, and other university-wide programs throughout the year.

4. IRA ALDRIDGE THEATER, as a part of the Fine Arts School, offers dramatic productions by the Howard Players and other groups.

5. The first floor of the Fine Arts School includes ART GALLERIES which present individual and group shows. Most notable is the James V. Herring Gallery which features African sculpture bequeathed to the University by Dr. Alain Locke. Works by students in the art department, exhibitions from the University's permanent collection, and work by outside artists are also featured. To the left of the Fine Arts Building is the future site of the new University Center which will feature many modern facilities for the enjoyment of the entire University community.

6. FREDERICK DOUGLASS MEMORIAL HALL is a liberal arts classroom building. The University is made up of 17 colleges and schools. Some trace their history to the University's founding and others have opened within the past year. There are 57 undergraduate majors and 33 advanced degree programs. Classroom visitation during tours is prohibited.

7.   LOCKE HALL, another liberal arts building, houses the University Computer Center. The main campus occupies seventy-five acres with buildings representing a variety of architectural styles from Georgian to contemporary.

8. & 9.   SCHOOL OF EDUCATION and the CENTER FOR ACADEMIC REINFORCEMENT. The latter program was begun this past September, 1975 with emphasis on supplementing the education of the student with english and mathematics deficiencies.

10.   The University Libraries System encompasses FOUNDERS LIBRARY* and 11 branch libraries in the colleges and schools. Founders, the main library, has more than 360,000 volumes, and the combined holdings of the University libraries exceed 750,000 volumes. Founders Library houses two collections of particular interest. The Channing Pollock Theater Collection spans the development of theaters around the world and is acquiring additional materials related to the black contribution to the dramatic arts. The Bernard B. Fall Collection is one of the finest collections of materials on Southeast Asia, particularly North and South Vietnam. It includes books, microfilms, periodicals, and writings accumulated by the late Dr. Fall, a professor of government at Howard and a recognized author and expert on Southeast Asia. The world's most comprehensive collection of materials on Africa and persons of African descent is found in the Moorland-Spingarn Research Center. The center's collections focus on black life, literature, and history, and include works by black authors from the 16th century to the present.

11.   RANKIN CHAPEL holds interdenominational services every Sunday, often featuring guest speakers from around the country.

12.   The BIOLOGY GREENHOUSE along with the College of Pharmacy, Chemistry and Physics Buildings are located in "The Valley" or "Death Valley." Across Fourth Street from the "Valley" are women's dormitories.

13.   The COLLEGE OF ALLIED HEALTH SCIENCES is at the corner of College Street, N. W., and Fourth Street, N. W. Part of Freedmen's Hospital, which is no longer in operation having been replaced by the new Howard University Hospital, is also on this street. The buildings of the old hospital will be utilized as office space for the University and as training laboratories for medical students.

14.   At Sixth and W Streets, N. W., are the COLLEGES OF DENTISTRY AND MEDICINE. The latter is connected by a glass enclosed corridor to the Howard University Hospital.

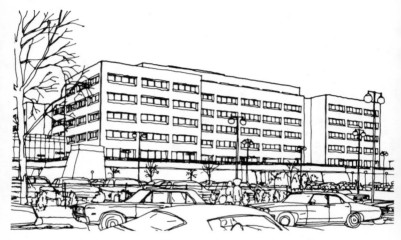

15.   The new 500-bed HOWARD UNIVERSITY HOSPITAL, facing Georgia Avenue, was erected on the site of the old Griffith Stadium. This modern facility, with its four-fold emphasis on teaching, research, education, and patient care, replaces Freedmen's Hospital. The new hospital is a major component of the University's Center for Health Sciences including the Colleges of Medicine, Dentistry, Pharmacy and Pharmacal Sciences, Allied Health Sciences, and Nursing. The Cancer Research Center is also planned for construction on the hospital grounds.

16.   The SCHOOL OF ARCHITECTURE AND PLANNING, on Sixth Street, N. W., prepares its students to become active in the search for solutions to the major problems facing urban communities in this country and throughout the world. The SCHOOL OF SOCIAL WORK is across from this building.

In addition to the main campus, other points of interest not included in the tour, are the 19-acre Dunbarton Campus near Rock Creek Park acquired by the University in 1974. This campus houses the School of Law, Howard University Press, several of the institutes, and the administrative offices. The beautifully landscaped grounds provide a setting of unusual serenity in the midst of the bustling city. This campus can be reached by a shuttle bus leaving from Founders Library every hour on the half hour.

The University also owns a 108-acre site at Beltsville in Prince George County, Maryland. Plans call for its development as a campus for research in the life sciences and training in veterinary medicine.

154

20 **LE DROIT PARK (Historic Black Residential area, Howard Theatre)

By Suzanne Ganschinietz

Ms. Ganschinietz is with the District of Columbia Historic Preservation Office. She gratefully acknowledges the assistance of W. Ray Luce, Kate Cole, Ward Jandl and Jan Thorman, all on the staff of the National Register of Historic Places, National Park Service, in designing this tour.

DISTANCE: 1½ Miles　　　　*Time: ¾ Hour*

BUS: 92, 94, 96, 98, 62, 64 and 66

METRO: No convenient station open.

For more on black Washington's heritage, you may wish to visit nearby Howard University (Tour 19) and Shaw School Urban Renewal Area/Logan Circle (Tour 14). A drive through all three areas is recommended.

Le Droit Park is a category II landmark of the National Capital and is listed in the National Register of Historic Places. It is a small unified subdivision built during the 1870's in Washington, D. C. Over sixty detached and semi-detached houses in the district were designed by James H. McGill, a well-known local architect, in the Calvert Vaux cottage tradition. The area, which was adjacent to the boundaries of Washington when built, was advertised as offering the advantages of city living with the open space of the country. No fences were erected between the homes although the entire area was enclosed by a fence. The character of the area changed in the 1880's and 1890's as the developers sold the remaining land within the district for the erection of row houses. An additional change occurred near the turn of the century as the area became a predominantly Black community.

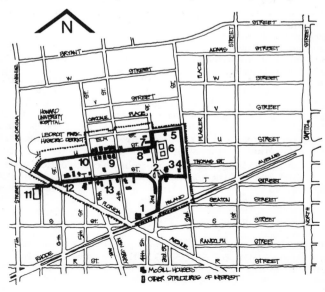

155

For many years the area has been the home of a number of prominent Black citizens. Located between Howard University and Howard Theater, two nationally significant Black educational and cultural centers, the neighborhood has served as an important cultural and political center for the entire city of Washington.

Today Le Droit Park retains much of the same scale and character and most of the architecture that it had at the turn of the century. Many of the original detached houses scattered among the slightly later brick and frame rowhouses are still standing. The rowhouses, constructed in the late 1880's and 1890's, are primarily low rise brick structures with fine terra-cotta and decorative brickwork. They have rooflines which are frequently accented with turrettes, towers, pedimented gables and iron cresting and combine to provide a varied and rhythmic pattern to the streets. Many of the houses and rowhouses retain decorative iron work fences and balustrades. One feature unique in Washington is the twisted porch columns found in the rowhouses on Third Street near the circle.

1. 301 Florida Avenue, N. W. (Safeway Store)

This site was the residence of David McClelland, one of the original owners and developers of Le Droit Park. The site, now used by an Elk Lodge and Safeway store, marked one of the major entrances to Le Droit Park.

2. Third Street, N. W., VISTA

The developers of Le Droit Park were responsible not only for the architecture and the landscaping of the subdivision but also for the design of the streets and sidewalks (which remained in private hands until 1901). The CIRCLE ON THIRD AVENUE* was part of the original street pattern, although the rationale for it is not entirely clear. One of the early advertisements for the Park referred to Harewood Avenue (3rd Street) as a projected main thoroughfare for trolleys from the city out to the Soldier's Home further north. Early maps, however, show that this throughway did not develop and that 3rd Street terminated just above Elm Street. It may be that the designers wished to imitate the L'Enfant plan with its monumental circles. Indeed, we know that the houses envisioned for Harewood Avenue were to be the most lavish and the most expensive in the Park. The original vista of Third Street was quite different from the present day view as most of the McGill houses have disappeared. Despite this change the circle remains a strong identification and orientation point for Le Droit Park. Although the street has retained its relatively low scale, the openness and sense of "refined elegance" envisioned by the developers is gone, replaced by the long mass of modern brick construction on the east, rowhouses on the west, and the new elementary school at the end.

3. 1901-1903 Third Street, N. W.*

The large white and gray house on the northwest corner of the circle was a McGILL DESIGNED HOUSE and belonged to General William Birney and Mr. Arthur Birney. It is virtually unchanged from its original state.

4. 201 T Street, N. W.**

This was the HOME OF DR. ANNA J. COOPER, who graduated
from Oberlin College in 1884 and came to Washington to teach
high school. She later received an honorary master's degree from
Oberlin and a doctorate from the Sorbonne in Paris. She became
associated with Frelinghuisen University, founded by Dr. Jesse
Lawson in 1906, to provide evening education classes for employed
blacks. When the University needed a permanent home, Dr. Cooper
donated her house which remained the location of the school until
it closed in the early 1960's.

5. Vista at Elm and 2nd Street, N. W.

At the northern end of Le Droit Avenue, nonconforming buildings
such as the elementary school and the Howard University dormi-
tory facility are examples of recent intrusions which have changed
the original residential character of Le Droit Park.

6. 1915 Third Street, N. W.

At the present site of the Howard University dorms was the house
of James H. McGill, the architect for many of the Le Droit Park
houses.

James H. McGill enjoyed a brief but prolific architectural career.
At 19 he joined the office of Henry R. Searle, a Washington architect, and during the next six years he climbed from draftsman to
architect. He opened his own office in 1872 and was soon associated with A. L. Barber in the development of Le Droit Park. In
addition to designing the homes in the Park, he designed sixty
homes, five churches, two markets, a roller skating rink, and
four major office buildings, including the Le Droit Building still
a downtown Washington landmark. He moved out of the Le Droit

Building in 1881, advertising both as an architect and a building supply salesman. He left architecture altogether the next year, and for the next twenty-five years ran a prosperous building supply business.

1900 block of Third Street, N. W.

Also on Third Street was the house (now demolished) of Mr. A. L. Barber, the builder of most of the McGill designed houses in Le Droit Park.

Amzi L. Barber, like his father, was trained for the ministry at Oberlin College. He came to Washington in 1868 to head the normal department at Howard University. He was later elected to a professorship of natural history and, at age 29, was appointed acting President of Howard. He left Howard to spend full time developing Le Droit. His business interests included the building and management of the Le Droit Building and other real estate interests. During the 1880's he developed Columbia Heights, north and west of Le Droit Park, constructing "Belmont" which he rented to Chief Justice Fuller of the United States Supreme Court. Barber's major interest changed in the mid-1880's to the Barber Asphalt Paving Company, which made him a very wealthy man.

7. 1938 Third Street, N. W.

This house was the BOYHOOD HOME OF MASSACHUSETTS SENATOR EDWARD W. BROOKE.

8. 1910 Third Street, N. W.*

This house is the former residence of Mr. J. J. Albright, and a McGill designed building. Mr. Albright also owned the St. Cloud Building (now demolished) which was designed by McGill. Mr. Albright was a prominent Washington businessman and was a dealer in coal. The STABLE which is also intact is the focus of a restoration project by the Le Droit Park Preservation Society.

9. 400 Block of U Street, N. W., VISTA

This is the ONLY REMAINING BLOCK IN LE DROIT PARK WHICH IS ORIGINAL TO THE 1870's development and which contains no intrusions. All the houses in this block were designed by architect McGill.

406 U STREET, N. W.

This is the home of Dr. Garnet C. Wilkinson, educator and Assistant Superintendent of Colored Schools until 1954, then Assistant Superintendent of the integrated system. Dr. Wilkinson was a graduate of Oberlin College.

414 U STREET, N. W.

Clara Taliaferro, a pharmacist and daughter of John H. Smyth (appointed minister to Liberia in 1890 and a lawyer and educator) lived in this double house.

158

419 U STREET, N. W.

Oscar DePriest, a black Congressman, lived here while in Congress.
When elected in 1928, DePriest was the first black Congressman
since 1901.

10.   500 Block of U Street, N. W., VISTA

HOWARD UNIVERSITY (see Tour 19 Howard University) and
Le Droit Park have traditionally had a close relationship. Howard
University was founded in 1867 by General Oliver O. Howard, head
of the Freedman's Bureau to provide an institution which would
welcome all students, including freedmen. A. L. Barber, developer
of Le Droit Park came to Washington to head the Normal Department at the school and later served as acting President of the University. Faculty members, administrators, and students have always
lived and worked in the district. The growth of the school, however,
now represents one of the major threats to the Park. This threat is
dramatically visible in the new medical building which looms over
the district north of U Street.

11.   HOWARD THEATRE, 620 T Street**

Le Droit Park housed many of the entertainers who performed
at Howard Theatre, which is located just across Florida Avenue
from the neighborhood. The Howard Theatre, along with the
Apollo in New York City, the Pearl in Philadelphia, and the Uptown in Baltimore, provided the stage on which many of the most
prominent entertainers in the past half-century made their debuts.
Segregation created barriers which made it difficult for black artists to develop and receive recognition, and the Howard thus played
a very important role in the development and promotion of black
talent. The theatre not only played host to the big names and big
bands but introduced new talent by its amateur night contests.
Winners of these contests include Ella Fitzgerald, Billy Eckstein,
and Bill "Ink Spots" Kenny. The theatre not only played host to
stars like Pearl Bailey, Sarah Vaughn, Lena Horne, Sammy Davis,
Jr., Billie Holliday, and Dick Gregory, but moved in the 1950's
and 1960's into rock and roll and the Motown sound. The Platters,
Gladys Knight and the Pips, Smokey Robinson and the Miracles,
James Brown, the Temptations, and the Supremes (who made their
first stage appearance at the Howard) all appeared at the Theatre.
The Theatre is quiet now, but money is being raised to reopen the
building as a viable Washington cultural institution.

12.   T Street, N. W., VISTA

525 T STREET, N. W.*

This house, complete with stable, is one of the FINEST REMAIN-
ING HOUSES in the historic district which was designed by James
McGill. Now vacant and deteriorated, the restoration of this house
would greatly benefit the district.

517 T STREET, N. W.*

This finely detailed and WELL-PRESERVED HOUSE is another
good example of McGill's work.

13.   400 Block of T Street, N. W. VISTA

420 T STREET, N. W.

Professor Nelson Weatherless, an early advocate of equal rights,

160

teacher and activist lived here. His daughter still resides in the house.

418 T STREET, N. W.

This was the home of Dr. Hattie Riggs, a black woman from Calais, Maine who taught at the M Street High School. Although she earned a medical degree she never practiced medicine.

408 T STREET, N. W. (Maple Avenue)**

This is the HOME OF WASHINGTON'S FIRST ELECTED MAYOR, WALTER WASHINGTON. It is the family home of his wife, Bennetta Bullock Washington, a descendant of Reverend Bullock a prominent minister and social worker.

14. 4th Street, N. W., VISTA

4th Street, formerly Linden Street, the only north-south thoroughfare in Le Droit Park which was aligned with the street pattern to the north, was the first area to be subdivided. The northwest corner of Florida Avenue and 4th Street is shown on an 1887 map as having been divided into twelve small lots. The large red-painted brick building on this corner is one of the oldest post-McGill buildings in Le Droit Park. Today much of 4th Street has been filled in with rowhouse development.

15. 300 Block of T Street, N. W.

330 T STREET, N. W.

Fountain Peyton, one of the first ten black lawyers in Washington, resided here. His daughter, Esther Peyton, still lives here.

326 T STREET, N. W.**

This was the HOME OF MARY CHURCH TERRELL, a woman of great importance to the black community, who was active in the women's suffrage movement, and who was the first black woman appointed to the D. C. Board of Education. This house has been designated a National Historic Landmark.

21 **OLD ANACOSTIA (Black Residential area, late 19th century buildings, Anacostia Neighborhood Museum)

By Sam Parker

Mr. Parker gratefully acknowledges the assistance of Ms. Cam Stiver, Anacostia Community Development Consortium and Mr. Peter Fuchs, Savings Associations Financing Enterprises, Inc. in designing this tour.

DISTANCE: 1½ Miles   TIME: ¾ Hour

BUS: 92 (best), 94, A2, A4, A6, A8, B2 and B4.

METRO: Eastern Market (Blue & Orange), transfer to 92 Garfield bus on 8th Street, S.E.

Incorporated in 1854 as one of Washington's earliest residential subdivisions, Old Anacostia retains considerable historical, architectural, and environmental appeal. The area had evolved from an ancient settlement of the Nacotchtanke (Anacostine) Indians to rich farmland. By the latter half of the century, a subdivision called Uniontown developed into a working class neighborhood and encompassed other minor subdivisions. Though the composition of its residents has changed over the years, many of its social and physical resources endure and continue to influence the community. Old Anacostia derives it distinctive sense of place from its rolling area, views to downtown Washington, the charm and human scale of its buildings and an appealing neighborhood environment.

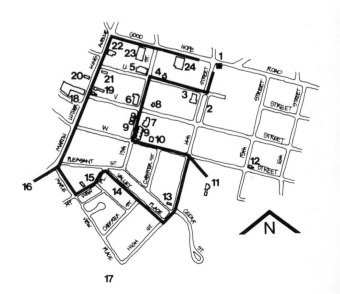

1. The Tour begins at 14th and Good Hope Road, S. E.

Old Anacostia first began to develop as a residential community after 1854, when John W. VanHook and two other men purchased 240 acres of farmland from the Chichester Tract for development into a residential subdivision. The original grid of streets laid out by the Union Land Association has survived to the present day and is framed by Good Hope Road to the north, 15th Street to the east, W Street to the south, and Martin Luther King, Jr. Avenue to the west. Known initially as Uniontown, the development was aimed at the middle class employees of the nearby Washington Navy Yard across the Anacostia River.

2. At 14th Street between U and V Streets, S. E., is the striking OLD MARKET SQUARE*, a block long and 40 feet wide. It was part of the original layout for Uniontown and was the prime focal point of the community.

3. The belfry of the ANACOSTIA METHODIST CHURCH provides an interesting visual reference along the square.

4. The house at 1312 U Street, S. E., represents one of the EARLY DWELLINGS still remaining. Featuring an elaborate bracket cornice, window pediments, and a handsome cubical cupola, this striking residence stands in pronounced contrast to the later houses around it.

5. The houses at 1230-1250 U Street, S. E., though dilapidated, are potentially handsome. Called "ROSE'S ROW", their form and detail are remarkably well integrated.

The architectural character of Old Anacostia is, in many ways, unique when compared to other communities in the Washington area. Nowhere else does there exist such a homogenous collection of late nineteenth century small-scale frame and brick buildings. The pleasant environment of Old Anacostia is less the product of outstanding architecture than the result of average buildings working together with remarkable success to create a cohesive and expressive whole.

6. The victorian gothic is represented by two churches each on a diagonally opposite corner of V and 13th Streets, S. E. ST. TERESA'S CATHOLIC CHURCH* was designed by E. Francis Baldwin, partner in the Baltimore firm of Baldwin and Pennington, and was built by Isaac Beers in 1879. A stucco building of simple form, the Church is embellished by a large rose window on the front facade decorated with a simple circular tracery.

7.   EMMANUEL EPISCOPAL CHURCH*, in contrast, is more irregular in form. Erected in 1891, the building employs rustic stonework with varied earthen brown tones. Its highly picturesque massing adds considerably to the building. The massive corner belfry, with its tall spire and spreading eaves makes Emmanuel Church one of the most prominent visual landmarks in Old Anacostia today.

8.   At 1308 V Street, S. E., is NEIGHBORHOOD HOUSING SER-VICES, a private nonprofit organization made up of area residents, representatives of financial institutions, businesses and the District of Columbia Government working together for neighborhood improvement. NHS provides long term, low interest loans to property owners to repair code violations. Visitors are welcome at the NHS office.

9.   A walk along 13th between V and W Streets, S. E., shows an ATTRACTIVE STREETSCAPE with its canopy of trees, row of brick duplexes set off by white frame porches and iron fences, and picturesque churches and church yards.

The exterior of the frame houses in Old Anacostia were embellished, often interchangeably, with varying degrees of Cottage Style, Italianate, or Mansard details of the period. The decoration of these buildings was simplified from that of the more elaborate brick townhouses built elsewhere in Washington at this time. Yet these small houses, with their repetitive rhythm of regularly spaced porches, windows, and doors succeeded in achieving great expressiveness and neighborhood homogeneity. These buildings provided the setting for lively and interesting streetscapes and a community environment of great pride and appeal.

10.   The duplex at 1310 - 1312 W Street, S. E., is an example of the prevalent WORKER'S COTTAGE built after the turn of the century. Notice the rooflines which reinforce a strong geometrical appearance.

164

11.   CEDAR HILL**, 14th and W Streets, S.E., built around 1855, was the home of Frederick Douglass, a noted Black Anti-Slavery editor and leader of the abolitionist movement. The handsome brick house, with its commanding VIEW OF WASHINGTON**, is listed in the National Register of Historic Places. It is open to the public from 9:00 a.m. to 4:00 p.m.

12.   From the front of the Douglass home notice the Queen Anne house at 15th and W Streets, S. E., built between 1887 and 1894.

13.   The house at 2248 14th Street, S. E., was recently remodeled with the assistance of NHS.

14./15./16.   An interesting walk down VALLEY PLACE and MT. VIEW PLACE will take you to the ANACOSTIA NEIGH-BORHOOD MUSEUM**, 2405 Martin Luther King, Jr., Avenue, S.E. It is a successful experiment in community involvement in the growth and development of a museum. The museum includes an educational department which serves schools, churches and hospitals. The museum has a series of continuing changing exhibits. Call 381-5656 for information about current exhibits. The Museum is open weekdays 10:00 a.m. to 6:00 p.m.; Satur-days and Sundays 1:00 p.m. to 6:00 p.m.

17.   If a car is available stop at Our Lady of Perpetual Help School, 1602 Morris Road, S. E. It offers one of the most beautiful VIEWS OF WASHINGTON**.

From 1854, what is now called Martin Luther King, Jr. Avenue and Good Hope Road were earmarked for commercial development. The first establishments, which included the legendary Duvall's Tavern and

George Pyle's Grocery, tended to concentrate at the intersection of these two streets.

18./19. Two later additions include an interesting ART DECO BUILDING at 2122 King Avenue, S. E., and the COLOSSAL CHAIR of the old Curtis Brothers Furniture Store. Although an architectural eyesore the chair has become a neighborhood landmark.

20. The first home of the Anacostia Bank, 2021 King Avenue, S. E., was built between 1903 and 1913 and is a marvelous expression of the GEORGIAN REVIVAL mode.

21. The monumental building at King Avenue and U Street, S. E., is an example of NEOCLASSICAL REVIVAL built between 1913 and 1927 as the second home of the Anacostia Bank.

22. Three storefronts at 1918 - 1922 King Avenue, S. E., highlight a new treatment of commercial buildings that appeared between 1936 and 1943. Notice the pediments over each store. The unit at 1922 retains the original window sash panels, revealing the richness of the initial composition.

Notoriety was brought to Good Hope Road, in 1865, as it provided JOHN WILKES BOOTH an escape route after he assassinated President Lincoln.

23. Several of the two-story commercial buildings, such as 1227 Good Hope Road, S. E., may be converted residences. Though heavily modified on the first floor, the upper portion of the building remains substantially intact, revealing handsomely proportioned brick detailing in the corners and arches crowning the windows.

A number of structures have been built in Old Anacostia over the past twenty-five years. In that time, the commercial area has undergone changes of varying scope; sometimes as minor as an addition of updated and often tasteless signs, at other times as major as the replacement of existing building with new ones. Many of the new buildings, unfortunately, are unarticulated structures that add nothing positive either to the streetscape or to the community as a whole. Some of them at least make an effort to maintain the scale and setback of the surrounding buildings.

24. Perhaps one of the most offensive of the new buildings is the C&P Telephone building which displays an alarming mediocrity of design and disregard for its surroundings. Notice the parking lot that cuts a hole, in the residential block on U Street.

Old Anacostia, as you have seen, has a positive and readily identifiable character. This cohesive quality is apparent in the physical evidence of a pleasant and remarkably intact low density late nineteenth-century neighborhood.

22 *** OLD TOWN ALEXANDRIA, VIRGINIA (18th Century Port City, Specialty Shops and Restaurants, Torpedo Factory Art Center)

By James L. Wilson and Andrea Lubershane

Mr. Wilson is a planner with the city of Alexandria and is on the Board of Directors of the Virginia chapter of the American Planning Association. Mrs. Lubershane is a planning consultant and author.

DISTANCE: 1-1/3 Miles 　　　　*TIME: 1¼ Hours*

BUS: 6B, 9, 10, 11, 12, 14, 15, 25A, 29K, and 29N.

METRO: National Airport (Blue), transfer to outbound 11 bus.

AUTO: Immediately after crossing the 14th Street bridge, follow signs to Mt. Vernon or Alexandria southbound via the George Washington Memorial Parkway alongside the Potomac River. The Parkway becomes Washington Street in Old Town Alexandria. Market Square is two blocks east of Washington Street and faces King Street.

Founded by John Alexander, a Scottish merchant, Alexandria was established in 1749, by an act of the Virginia General Assembly. It became a flourishing seaport and trading center, surpassing the port of New York and rivalling Boston in shipping activity. Rich merchants and shipowners built fine homes on the bluff overlooking the Potomac River. Until 1846, Alexandria was part of the District of Columbia. During the Civil War, Union soldiers occupied this Confederate City, but fortunately, little damage was done.

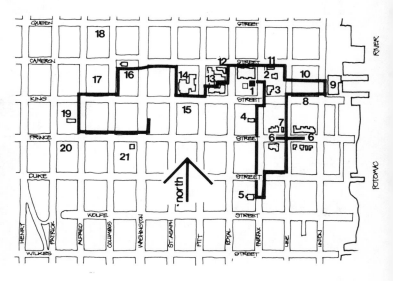

With the advent of railroads, the economy of Alexandria declined as the port of Baltimore garnered the lion's share of foreign trade and shipping activity. Warehouses and wharves along the Potomac deteriorated through disuse and lack of repair. Although a shipyard and torpedo plant were built during World War I, these activities ceased at the end of the war. Early housing also became dilapidated.

During the early 1960s, a City Council-appointed Citizen's Advisory Committee surveyed city housing needs and conditions of blight. They recommended a pilot urban renewal project in the downtown business district - the site of many historic buildings and early businesses. In 1962, City Council approved the six block Gadsby Urban Renewal Project. The Holiday Inn in the 400 block of King Street opened in 1975, completing the fifth block of the Gadsby Urban Renewal Project. A new City Courthouse in the 500 block of King Street completed the Gadsby project in 1980.

1. The tour begins at the MARKET SQUARE FOUNTAIN**. Established in 1749 by the founding fathers, City Hall and the market place occupy an historic block, where, among other things, British troops paraded during the French-Indian War. Annual reactments of this event are held in front of Gadsby's Tavern.

The urban renewal plan for this square contained numerous controls on the redeveloper, including provisions for open space, architectural style, underground parking, streetscape, height limitations, efficient traffic circluation, offstreet service and loading, and landscaping. The plantings are arranged to provide a blooming cycle from early spring to late fall. The square often hosts concerts, exhibits, and a Saturday morning farmer's market.

Construction of Market Square was completed in June 1967, at a cost of $1,600,000. Market Square was financed by a Federal capital grant of about 2/3 of the cost, with City financing for the other 1/3. Due to increased tax revenues, this was repaid in about 7 years. The City received from the U. S. Department of Housing and Urban Development a Merit Award for Excellence of Design for Market Square.

2. CARLYLE HOUSE**: Built in 1752 by John Carlyle, this restored historic house served as the meeting place of General Braddock and five British governors when they proposed the Stamp Act of 1755 — taxation without representation — the spark that ignited the American Revolution. Restoration of the Carlyle House was completed by the Northern Virginia Regional Park Authority in January, 1976. The house is the centerpiece of a unique urban park.

3. RAMSAY HOUSE*: "Alexandria's Oldest House" was built in 1724 as home to the City's first Lord Mayor, William Ramsay, a Scottish merchant and City founder. The house is restored and now occupied by the Visitors' Center of the Alexandria Tourist Council. For further information on the City and for a historic film, step inside the Ramsay House.

4. STABLER-LEADBEATER APOTHECARY SHOP*: Founded in 1792 and closed as an apothecary in 1933 after 150 years of continuous operation, this building now serves as a museum and antique shop. The old shop contains a remarkable collection of early medical ware and handblown glass. All furnishings are authentic.

5. OLD PRESBYTERIAN MEETING HOUSE*: Built in 1774 by Scottish founders of the City, this meeting house was the site of memorial services for George Washington, when impassable roads made the journey to Christ Church impossible. The interior is well-preserved. In the cemetery stands the tomb of the unknown soldier of the American Revolution.

As you walk in this area, you can sense the general character and atmosphere of colonial times. Look down Duke Street to the Potomac, which affords an interesting and attractive view.

169

6. GENTRY ROW AND CAPTAIN'S ROW*: Brick paved Gentry Row is lined by homes of early merchants and many important Alexandria patriots of the American Revolution. Cobblestoned Captain's Row contains 18th and 19th century homes of colonial sea captains. It is said that Hessian prisoners of war laid the cobblestones here. Layers of asphalt cover cobblestone streets in other parts of the City.

7. ATHENEUM*: The Atheneum is one of Alexandria's two surviving significant examples of Greek Revival architecture. It was built as a banking house in 1850, subsequently became a place of worship, and currently serves as the Gallery of the Northern Virginia Fine Arts Association. The original pumpkin color was restored in 1974.

8. LOWER KING STREET presents a variety of shops, sights, and sounds. It is a highly successful commercial area, using traditional style shopfronts in renovated Alexandria warehouses.

9. The torpedo plant, built during World War I and vacated subsequently thereafter, became host to art galleries, studios and classes in 1974. The TORPEDO FACTORY ART CENTER** continues to grow in popularity. The entire Torpedo plant building, which houses the Torpedo Factory Art Center, is currently an active planning issue as it is located on a choice piece of waterfront property. The Alexandria Waterfront Restoration Group was selected in 1979 to make significant future physical changes to the torpedo plant.

10. Walk up cobblestoned RAMSAY ALLEY, once trodden by George Washington. It was named after William Ramsay, Alexandria's first Mayor.

11. Next to the Carlyle House is the Bank of Alexandria, constructed in 1807. It is the second oldest bank building in the U.S. Restoration of the property by the Northern Virginia Regional Park Authority was completed in 1980.

12. GADSBY'S TAVERN**: Originally a small coffee house built in 1752, because it was so popular, a second smaller building known as the City Hotel was added in 1792. A jewel of Georgian architecture, Gadsby's Tavern was the site of the preparation of the Fairfax Resolves of George Mason, predecessor document of the Bill of Rights. The tavern was popular with George Washington throughout his life. It also was important to the entertainment world of colonial America as travelling troups of players came frequently and presented their plays in the tavern. Gadsby's Tavern was restored for use as a working tavern. Opening date was appropriately George Washington's Birthday in the Bicentennial year (see Restaurants and Carryouts).

13. TAVERN SQUARE*: This project takes its name from historic Gadsby's Tavern. Have a seat on one of the benches, rest a moment and enjoy the sights and sounds. Part of Phase I of the urban renewal project was subject to the same stringent planning controls as Market Square. The cost was $5,100,000 for this retail-office complex of 150 firms. The City purchased

the properties in the block, razed all structures except Gadsby's Tavern, relocated the former tenants and resold the cleared land to a private developer who arranged private financing. With the same architect and developer as Market Square, Tavern Square received an architectural award from the Washington Metropolitan Board of Trade in December 1967.

14. BANKER'S SQUARE*: Phase II of the Gadsby project included four more blocks along King Street, adjoining Phase I. In the 500 block of King Street, the First and Citizens National Bank completed in 1967 a new central downtown bank as a private renewal undertaking - one that conformed to the City's renewal plan for the area. For the remainder of the block, the designated redeveloper, Banker's Square Associates, developed a project which houses retail businesses and offices.

15. COURTHOUSE SQUARE: A new courthouse was completed here in 1980, marking the end of the Gadsby Urban Renewal Project.

16. CHRIST CHURCH**: Completed by John Carlyle in 1773, this church served as a place of worship for Washington and Lee. It is an English country style church, with panels inscribed by James Wren with the Lord's Prayer and the Ten Commandments. In the old churchyard are many graves of confederate soldiers who died in City hospitals.

17. This is a transitional area: to the east, the mostly renovated and historic town center; to the west and north west, mostly unrestored homes in a state of disrepair; and to the south, a typical urban shopping area. The contrast between Christ Church and the block directly behind it is striking.

18. National Endowment for the Arts Project: Small parks, trees, streetlighting and some brickwork were added to the POTOMAC EAST NEIGHBORHOOD IMPROVEMENT PROJECT. This area has since received funds for the conservation of housing. The object is to provide low interest home loans for low and middle income people to repair and renovate their homes. In this manner, they can continue to live there if they wished, rather than to sell and move out.

19. FRIENDSHIP ENGINE HOUSE* and Firehouse Square: The Friendship Fire Company, a volunteer corps of citizens organized in 1774, included George Washington as an early member. Together with the City, developers have placed utility lines underground and have installed brick sidewalks and attractive street lamps, beautifying and upgrading upper King Street as Banker's, Tavern, Courthouse, and Market Squares have done for lower King Street.

20. THE DIP: So-called because of its topographic situation, this 13-block area bounded by Duke, Washington, Henry, and Franklin Streets was originally brought to public attention by the local neighborhood and by the Alfred Street Baptist Church. It was characterized by its dilapidated houses, incompatible land uses and undeveloped land. In 1970, the City Council approved an Urban Renewal Project for this area. Ground breaking occured in September 1975. Because it was basically a low-income area, the intention was to build new housing that the current residents could afford. The project is expected to double the amount of housing available in the Dip area, to more than 400 housing units, providing additional opportunities for people now living in other low income areas. Unfortunately, inflated building costs have driven prices up, drastically changing the nature of the Dip project from that of homeowner to renter occupied. This project was completed in 1980.

21. THE VIRGINIA BICENTENNIAL CENTER***: Also called the Lyceum (circa 1842), offers information and films about Virginia. For several years the Lyceum remained a boarded-up dilapidated eyesore. It was restored in 1973. A visit here can be an interesting and worthwhile experience.

To return to Washington, D. C., take any bus in front of Hahn's Shoe Store on Washington Street. While waiting for the bus, you can observe the heart of downtown Alexandria, King and Washington Street.

23 ***HISTORIC ANNAPOLIS, MARYLAND (17th-18th Century Port-Capital City, U.S. Naval Academy)

By Carol D. and Gary L. Barrett

Ms. Barrett is a Project Director with the National Association of Counties. Mr. Barrett is a Program Manager with Public Technology, Inc. Both are members of APA and are residents of Annapolis.

DISTANCE: 1½ Miles   TIME: 2½ Hours

BUS: To Greyhound Bus Terminal, 12th and New York Ave., N.W.; 60, 62, 80, B6, D2, D4, D8, K4, L2, L4, L8, P2, S2, X3, X4 and X6.

Call Greyhound Bus Terminal (289-5100) for schedules. Trip takes one hour one way.

METRO: To Greyhound Bus Terminal; Metro Center (Red, Blue and Orange)

AUTO: Take New York Avenue, N.W., in Washington to Route 50 and get off at Rosco Rowe Blvd. Annapolis is about 30 miles or a one hour drive.

Only the historic district of Annapolis is included here because the Naval Academy offers free walking tour brochures available at the visitors center. Visitors who wish to see the noon formation of midshipmen at the Naval Academy should plan to take the walking tour of the Academy no later than 11:30 a.m.. Formation is at 12:05 p.m. on weekdays and 12:30 p.m. on Sundays, if the temperature is above 55° and it is not raining. As an alternate to your own walking tour, Historic Annapolis offers 90 minute tours from 10:00 a.m. to 3:30 p.m. everyday

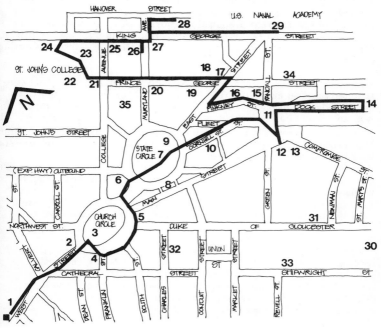

at a cost of $3.00 for adults and 50¢ for children. Tours start from the Treasury building on the State House grounds. You might also consider the purchase of "Colonial Annapolis" which contains a number of full color photographs and interesting anecdotes ($3.95 at Historic Annapolis). Wear comfortable walking shoes for navigating sidewalks. Please remember that, unlike most colonial cities, Annapolis is a living city and most of the homes are still in use; respect for the owners privacy will be appreciated.

Annapolis' colonial heritage and 16 miles of waterfront make it a unique American city. The town is justifiably proud of its numerous 18th century colonial homes, considered to be among the finest architectural elements of our history, nestled among a tangle of quaint narrow streets. In 1965, the National Park Service designated the down town area a National Historic District.

First settled in 1649 and known as Providence and then Anne Arundel Town, the city took on its final name of Annapolis in honor of Princess Anne, later Queen of England, and became the provincial capital of Maryland.

Annapolis prospered in the 18th century maintaining a flourishing trade with Europe and the West Indies and exporting tobacco. During the second half of the century, the city was the commercial, political, and social center of Maryland. Many of the great homes built during that era still stand. Among the fine homes were those of the four Maryland signers of the Declaration of Independence; William Paca, Charles Carroll, Samuel Chase, and Thomas Stone. As you walk through the town, note the markers placed on buildings of State and National importance by Historic Annapolis.

1. GREYHOUND STATION — Turn left on West Street and walk toward Church Circle. This area is currently undergoing renovation by the Annapolis Urban Renewal Authority. A number of decaying structures have been renovated or revitalized. The building at 26 West Street is where Thomas Jefferson and James Monroe had rooms during the Continental Congress of 1783.

2./3. CHURCH CIRCLE** — ST. ANNES CHURCH** was first constructed in 1700 and supported by an annual tax of 40 pounds of tobacco levied on every taxpayer. The first church fell into disrepair and was torn down before the Revolution. The second church burned. The present building was built in 1859. The last Colonial Governor of Maryland is buried in the church yard. A silver Communion Service presented by King William III is still used.

4. REYNOLD'S TAVERN* was built about 1747 and operated by William Reynolds as a tavern and hat-making business. The header pattern of burned blue bricks is characteristic of 18th century Annapolis homes. It was used as the Annapolis library for many years.

5. The MARYLAND INN** is located on the former site of the Drummer's lot, where the Town Crier, in earlier times, called the populace together with a roll of drums to hear official proclamations. The Inn was built during Revolutionary times and the King of France tavern was presumably named in honor of France's support during the War (see Restaurant Guide).

Chase-Lloyd House

6. Continue around the circle to GOVERNMENT HOUSE* home of Maryland's governors since 1869. It was built in a Victorian design in 1860 and was remodeled in 1935 to match the Georgian structures surrounding it.

7. Continue down School Street and walk into the STATE HOUSE*** started in 1669. It burned in 1709 and was replaced with a similar structure which was used until 1722 when the present building replaced it. Since 1775, only one session of the Maryland Legislature has been held elsewhere. (The 1861 session was held at Frederick, Md. because of the strong Confederate sentiment of people in Southern Maryland.) It is the oldest capitol in the Nation still in continuous legislative use. It has the largest wooden dome in the United States and was built entirely without nails. The old Senate Chamber served as the Capitol of the U. S. from November 1783 to June 1784. George Washington resigned his commission as Commander-in-Chief in 1783 and in 1784 the Treaty of Paris, officially ending the American Revolution, was ratified here. Later, Thomas Jefferson was appointed Minister to European Courts. Other interesting artifacts include historic oil paintings by Charles Wilson Peale, one of the foremost artists of his time, portraits of the four Marylanders who signed the Declaration of Independence, a painting of the "Burning of the Peggy Stewart" (described later), and a flag carried by Maryland troops during the Revolution. On the grounds is a cannon from the ships which brought Maryland's first settlers to these shores.

8. From the grounds can be seen the SHAW HOUSE with its captains walk along the roof. Shaw was an expert furniture maker and built the chairs and desks in the old Senate Chamber. (His desks sell for $10,000 - $15,000 today!)

9. On the Capitol grounds is the OLD TREASURY BUILDING* (beginning of the Historic Annapolis tours). Constructed in 1737, this is the oldest public building still standing in Maryland. Inside is displayed an iron money chest which once held the Treasury's money during the colonial times.

10. Walk down CORNHILL STREET* which shows excellent examples of private restoration of old homes. Note the iron insignias of fire companies hanging on the fronts of many of the homes. If a fire started, the company would extinguish the flames only if the home had their logo on it. At the apex of Fleet and Cornhill Streets is an old barber shop. It is said that George Washington was barbered and shaved here before his appearance at the State House in 1783.

11. The CUSTOM HOUSE** building is the third market at this location. The first was built in 1788, the second in 1856. The present structure was completed in 1972. Inside, there are a variety of stalls featuring different edibles (see Restaurants and Carryouts).

12. To the right can be seen a tall brick building (now called the Sign o' the Whale) thought to be the Shaw Blacksmith Shop built in 1728.

13. Further down is a colonial tobacco warehouse, and the MARKET HOUSE, now the home of the Summer Garden Theater.

14. The CITY DOCK*** area is a pleasant place to rest and watch the working oyster and clam boats. The blue Maryland Lady, which is the yacht belonging to the Governor of Maryland, is berthed to the left.

15. Also in the Market Space is the MIDDLETON TAVERN which is actually two colonial structures beneath the brick exterior. The original Middleton Tavern was built as a seafarers inn in 1750 and was the point of departure for ferry trips to the Eastern Shore.

16. Proceed up Pinkney Street past another tobacco warehouse to the SPICER SHIPLAP HOUSE built about 1723 as an ordinary for sailors. This building was the Harp and Crown Tavern during the Revolution and later, in the 19th century, home of Frank Mayer, painter of the "Burning of the Peggy Stewart." The name Shiplap is taken from the wooden siding on the facade. The front yard is planted as a kitchen and medicinal herb garden of the 18th century.

17. The BRICE HOUSE*, built in 1776, is one of the largest Georgian homes in America. The home was partly designed by William Buckland who came to this country as an indentured servant and later designed many of the best homes in Annapolis. The home once had gardens which stretched to the water and George Washington and Marquis de Lafayette were frequently entertained here. The house has a number of legends attached to it and residents claim to have seen ghosts and heard knockings in the library where the son of the builder was killed. Removal of a brick wall during the installation of electricity in part of the house exposed a secret stairway going from the library to an upstairs roof. Revealed with the stairwell removal was a woman's skeleton. Legend has it that an insane female relative was hidden away in the house, and when she died, was bricked in the secret stairwell. Note the tombstone used as a step just inside the gate on the Prince George Street side. (House is closed to visitors.)

18. The PACA HOUSE* was built in 1763 for William Paca, one of the signers of the Declaration of Independence and Governor of Maryland. This is one of the plainest homes designed by Buckland and is being completely restored. The gardens in the rear were covered by asphalt and buildings but have since been restored to their original condition.

19. The LITTLE BRICE HOUSE, 195 Prince George Street, was purchased from Amos Garrett who was the first mayor of Annapolis in 1708. This house is only part of the original structure — the wings were torn down a number of years ago.

20. THE DORSEY HOUSE, 211 Prince George Street, was the site of meetings of the Maryland Provincial Government before the State House was erected. The house was later used as a residence for Maryland's Governors.

21. Walk up Prince George Street to ST. JOHN'S COLLEGE**, begun as King Williams' School in 1696 and one of the first public schools in America.

22. The building in the center of the campus called McDOWELL HALL was originally known to townspeople as Bladen's Folley. Bladen, who was provincial Governor, was intent on building a Governors palace more magnificent than the one at Williamsburg. In 1746, four years after it was begun, the lower house of the general assembly was so aghast at the bill that they unanimously voted to stop all building funds. It was completed fifty years later in 1789.

23. To the right is the famous LIBERTY TREE*, a large 600 year old tulip poplar. It is said that under this tree the treaty of peace with the Susquehannock Indians was signed in 1652. Later colonists gathered under the tree to protest British taxation and were known as 'Sons of Liberty.' General Lafayette and George Washington were honored at picnics beneath this tree.

24. Walk down to the CARROLL-BARRISTER HOUSE built on Main Street in 1722. Carroll was the author of the Maryland Declaration of Rights in 1776.

25. Proceed down King George Street to the OGLE HOUSE built in 1739 for Governor Samuel Ogle who was known for his love of horse racing. George Washington often visited here when he attended the races.

26. Walk down the brick sidewalk to 235 King George Street, thought to have been the summer kitchen of the CHASE-LLOYD HOUSE. Walk around the corner to the front of the home which was begun in 1769 by Samuel Chase, one of the signers of the Declaration of Independence. Chase was originally one of the Sons of Liberty, then a speculator in available flour during the War, and finally a Justice of the U. S. Supreme Court who narrowly avoided impeachment. Chase ran out of money in 1771 and sold the unfinished structure to Edward Lloyd. Lloyd, who later became Governor of Maryland, wanted the grandest house in Annapolis. He immediately hired William Buckland to complete the house. The grounds contained extensive stables of race horses, coachhouses, and servants quarters. Francis Scott Key was married in this house in 1802.

27.   Across the street is the HAMMOND-HARWOOD HOUSE**, built during 1769-1774, and was the last home designed by Buckland. The first owner was Matthias Hammond, one of the Sons of Liberty. Legend notes that he built the house for his fiancee, but she grew impatient with his long involvement with the construction and eloped with another man. The home, which is open to the public, contains a large number of the original pieces of furniture.

28.   The PEGGY STEWART HOUSE, 207 Hanover Street, was built about 1740. Anthony Stewart, the owner, was a gentleman of Tory sympathies. In October 1774, Mr. Stewart received a shipment of tea aboard his brig, the Peggy Stewart, named after his daughter.

Annapolitans were so enraged about Stewart's tea and his payment of the tax, that they threatened to tar, feather and hang him from his doorway unless he burned both the brig and its cargo of tea. At first Stewart was defiant but later agreed to do as the crowd demanded.

He arranged to have the cargo (except the tea) removed under strict supervision and then he sailed the ship out (to an area now covered by the Academy playing field) and set fire to the ship while his wife and daughter watched from the house. (This Annapolis Tea Party took place long before the occurance in Boston.) This scene is portrayed in the painting in the Capitol painted by Frank Mayer who lived in the Shiplap House. The home was later sold to Thomas Stone, a signer of the Declaration of Independence.

29.   You may now enter the Naval Academy here or walk down King George Street to the main Academy gate. In either case, ask the Guard to direct you to the visitor's center where you may pick up a free copy of the walking tour of the Naval Academy. For those who have additional time, a number of other important homes have been added to the map (30-35) which you may wish to see.

30.   CHARLES CARROLL HOUSE

31.   RIDOUT HOUSE

32.   JONAS GREEN HOUSE

33.   UPTON SCOTT HOUSE

34.   SANDS HOUSE

35.   BORDLAY-RANDALL HOUSE

Restaurants
and
Carryouts

RESTAURANTS AND CARRYOUTS BY TOUR AREA

By Carol A. Hodges

Here is a list of restaurants in the tour areas provided as a service to hungry walkers. Check addresses to determine location on the tour maps. Menu descriptions and cost references are general, but will give you an idea of what to expect. The cost of dining in any restaurant can vary considerably, depending on how you order and what you consider to be expensive. Many restaurants are open on Sunday and some feature brunch; but call to be sure. In Washington, it is always best to call ahead for a table. I have included establishments in the list which would serve everybody's needs; whether for a special night out, a particular ethnic food, an inexpensive meal, or a snack to eat in a park.

RESTAURANTS

TOUR 1   CAPITOL HILL

Jenkins Hill
233 Pennsylvania Avenue, SE   544-6600

A bar-restaurant serving light meals and sandwiches. Popular with the "Hill" crowd every day and with Redskins fans on game weekends.

Toscanini
313 Pennsylvania Avenue, SE   544-2338

This moderately priced, lively establishment makes good things happen with pasta and veal. It's usually crowded into the late hours.

209 ½
209 ½ Pennsylvania Avenue, SE   544-6352

Small and expensive. The kitchen prepares some very imaginative food using the freshest ingredients. At dinner, there is a fixed-price menu with a few choices. Attentive service in intimate, beautiful surroundings.

American Cafe
227 Massachusetts Avenue, NE   547-8500

The large sandwiches, freshly-prepared soups and interesting salads are all inexpensive and very good. Desserts are fun and delicious. There is a small deli area where produce, pastries, and other foods from the menu can be purchased to take out.

La Brasserie
239 Massachusetts Avenue, NE   546-9154

A moderately priced French cafe which does exceptionally good things--especially with main course pastry dishes. Daily specials, beautiful salads, varied sandwiches and desserts all add up to good cafe fare.

TOUR 2   CAPITOL HILL - EAST

The Broker
713 8th Street, SE   546-8300

Lots of brick, skylights and an understated decor set the tone for this moderately expensive restaurant. The menu is interesting with several Swiss specialties such as fondue and emincee of veal with rosti potatoes, that are prepared exceptionally well. Save room for dessert.

TOUR 3   THE MALL - EAST

National Gallery of Art Cafe
Constitution Avenue at 6th Street, NW
737-4215

Located in the underground passage leading to the East Wing, the small cafe is set near a backdrop of skylights and a water cascade. The short menu of quiche, salads, crepes, sandwiches and pastry is a shade expensive for a museum. However, there is always the steam table fare at the adjacent cafeteria.

East Wing Cafe
East Wing - National Gallery

With a similar menu, this cafe has a more private setting than the one in the main building. Off the beaten path, sometimes you can be seated more quickly here, and it's not as noisy.

TOURS 4, 5   NONE LISTED

TOUR 6   SOUTHWEST

Pier 7
Maine Avenue and 7th Streets, SW   554-2500

View the Chesapeake Light Ship across the Washington
Channel while enjoying moderately priced, well-prepared
fresh seafood. Rather than emphasizing the fried seafood
platters so predominant elsewhere along the Maine Avenue
waterfront, fresh fish at Pier 7 may be skewered, served
Florentine-style, or broiled. Sauces are well executed.

TOUR 7   FOGGY BOTTOM

Coleman's
832 20th Street, NW   331-9430

Like an Irish pub in atmosphere, this popular retreat
features a wine bar and many imported beers and ales.
Food offerings include puffy fish and chips and corned
beef and cabbage, plus varied beef and seafood dinners.

Le Gaulois
2133 Pennsylvania Avenue, NW   466-3232

This jam-packed, bustling small French restaurant serves
exceedingly good food at moderate prices. Its popularity is evident when you try to get in; you must
reserve ahead, and you'll be glad you did.

Dominique's
1900 Pennsylvania Avenue, NW   452-1126

Design ingenuity has turned a subterranean well into an
attractive restaurant. The food is good; there is a general feeling of conviviality; and with the likes of roasted
hippopotamus, rattlesnake and other diverse offerings,
there is something for everyone. On the expensive side,
there is a pre-theater dinner which is a good value if you
dine early.

Foggy Bottom Cafe
924 25th Street, NW   338-8707

A pleasant place to stop en route to or from the
Kennedy Center. Open for breakfast as well as lunch
and dinner, it is relatively inexpensive for sandwiches,
croissants and coffee, or a light meal.

TOUR 8   WHITE HOUSE

Corcoran Cafe
Corcoran Gallery of Art
17th and New York Avenue, NW   638-3211

This tiny eatery is located in a delightful room in the midst of the Gallery. Quiche, soups, salads and pastry are among the light offerings. Service is painfully slow, and it is not inexpensive.

St. John's Church - Le Dejuner Francais
16th and H Streets, NW, at Lafayette Square
(H Street Entrance)

If you happen to be in this area at noon on Wednesday and you speak some French, this is a unique experience. Francophiles line up for a light French lunch including a glass of wine and animated conversation, then listen to a short talk and perhaps view slides on a topic presented by a volunteer. Ends promptly at 1:00.

TOUR 9   NONE LISTED

TOUR 10   DOWNTOWN

English Pub - Woodward & Lothrop
11th and F Streets, NW   347-5300

Tucked away in a corner next to Woodie's main tearoom is a small antique-filled pub. Sandwiches and quiche, salad bar included. Drinks, beer and wine available.

Patent Pending
National Collection of Fine Arts
Portrait Gallery
8th and G Streets, NW   628-4422

Sandwiches, cold plates, soups, pastry, wine and beer are served in this tiny cafeteria-cafe. In warm weather, tables are placed in the adjacent courtyard; a delightful place for breakfast, lunch or snack.

Kowloon Restaurant
1105 H Street, NW   628-4243

Ask for the regular menu rather than the lunch menu, and also for the Dim Sum list. Then you may choose from an array of extremely interesting Cantonese dishes. If you're on a budget, one dish, supplemented by soup or appetizers, or two Dim Sum choices, is adequate for children or moderate appetites.

Golden Palace
726 7th Street, NW   783-1225

Located in Chinatown and very popular. The menu offers
specialties, such as crabmeat with spring onions and ginger,
not found on many Cantonese menus. Choose carefully;
as staff are sometimes too busy to be helpful.

Szechuan Restaurant
615 I Street, NW   393-0130

Menu selections such as huge Dim Sum, steamed pastries filled
with meat, unusual cauliflower and asparagus specialties, and
other fiery, colorful dishes from China's western provinces
make this one of Washington's top oriental restaurants.

Greenbriar Room
Garfinckel's
14th and F Streets, NW   628-7730

This is several steps above the average department store
tearoom. In addition to very good salads and a few OK
sandwiches, several special entrees and several standard
dishes, such as well-prepared liver and bacon, round out
the menu. The food, mostly with a French emphasis,
is quite appealing and moderately priced.

Old Ebbitt Grill
1427 F Street, NW   347-5560

A cozy, crowded pub which excels in hamburgers, thick
sandwiches, and chili - or omelettes cooked to order in
the upstairs omelette room. History of the Grill, a
former boarding house, dates to 1856. It was once home
to President William McKinley and journalist Ben Perley
Poore. Be sure to stop; if only to have a beer, see the
mahogany bar, the Ebbitt Bear imported by Alexander
Hamilton, or the stein collection. Detailed brochures
inside. (Note: proposals call for demolishing the building
and relocating the Grill in a new complex. Be sure to
call first.)

TOUR 11   MIDTOWN

Harvey's
1001 18th Street, NW   833-1858

In 1858, it was T. M. Harvey's Ladies and Gentlemen's
Oyster Saloon; later the Restaurant of the Presidents.
Now in an attractive subterranean location, Harvey's still

serves fresh seafood and strong drinks. Warming chowders and soups are accompanied by goblets of beaten biscuits; however, it is expensive. The bar is a favorite with the after work crowd enjoying the large and also expensive drinks and free hors d'oeuvres.

Le Pavillon
1850 K Street, NW   833-3846

Nouvelle cuisine at extremely high prices. The gifted young French chef creates light, elegant, but not necessarily less rich, dishes. The menu is built around the freshest market produce and features beautifully composed and unique selections. There are fixed price menus, and an individually planned "tasting menu" can be arranged at your request.

Tiberio
1915 K Street, NW   452-1915

Northern Italian cuisine served in a pleasantly understated room enhanced with flowers and contemporary art. You won't go wrong with freshly made pasta--perhaps the fragile agnolotti in cream sauce. Main courses are expensive and well prepared. End with a dessert from the beautiful display. Dress well. Your expense account will be handy here.

Le Bagatelle
2000 K Street, NW   872-8677

Named after a popular restaurant in the Bois de Boulogne in Paris, this is as expensive--exchange rates not withstanding. Seafood entrees are particularly enticing and salads are beautifully composed. Service can vary from excellent to perfunctory. The dining areas are airy and cheerful.

Sholl's Cafeteria
1900 K Street, NW   296-3065

This is an old Washington institution in a new setting--the Esplanade Mall. The clientelle ranges from octogenarians to families with kids, to office workers to "street people." Anyone who appreciates freshly prepared, home-style food at very reasonable prices will see why the lines form early. Food is cooked and replenished continuously. Choose your fresh vegetables and home baked goodies fast as they hustle you along.

Iron Gate Inn
1734 N Street, NW   737-1371

Ask for a table downstairs, and if it's cool, by the fireplace in the cozy carriage house dining room. Booths on
one side were once horse stalls. Placemats tell the history.
In warm weather, enjoy the lovely courtyard with a view
of the dome of St. Matthew's Cathedral. Moderately
priced middle eastern food featuring tasty lamb and eggplant dishes. The desserts are excellent. Try the pudding
or the bird's nest pastry with thick black coffee.

Cafe Sorbet
1810 K Street, NW   293-3000

Very popular with the office crowd during the week,
Sorbet's seating arrangement packs you in. It is noisy,
bustling and hardly relaxing; but if you're in the mood
for a fast lunch, it's also fun. French servers, French
photos, French on Muzak. Authentic cafe fare is offered
such as quiche, salade Nicoise, and daily specials including
Cassoulet and sauteed scallops. Inexpensive.

Cafe Vie De France
1990 K Street, NW   659-0055

Another very popular French cafe, with long lines at
lunch. The ambiance is relaxing and the food quality is
quite good for the price. Fresh breads and croissants are
baked continuously in large ovens adjacent to the dining
area, and may be purchased to take home. At dinner
the menu features both light cafe fare and complete
fixed price dinners.

The Prime Rib
2020 K Street, NW   466-8811

If you want good beef and don't mind paying for it, this
is the place. Stick to the special for which it is named,
and enjoy the piano music. The decor is a bit dark and
heavy, matching the food and prices.

The Bread Oven
1220 19th Street, NW   466-4264

Another French cafe-bakery that is extremely popular.
The bright, cheerful room is comfortably appointed.
Daily menu items are rotated and offer two entree
choices and a cold plate. Prices are in the $5 range at
lunch; dinner is a better value. Service sometimes falters.
Breads and pastries may be purchased to take out. On
weekends, the price goes up at dinner when the chef has
free reign to prepare special dishes.

Kramer Books and Afterwords
1912 I Street, NW   466-3111

Sandwiches, salads and light entrees are served at small
tables amidst a bustling, well-stocked bookstore. Books
may be better buys than the food, but it's a good idea
for a snack. Sidewalk cafe in good weather.

La Marais
1919 I Street, NW   659-4447

Intimate, elegant, and a favorite with World Bank clientelle
at both lunch and dinner. The French food is well prepared and professionally served. Expensive.

Luigi's
1132 19th Street, NW   331-7574

Small, crowded and poorly ventilated, Luigi's is popular
for somewhat heavy pizza with a puffy crust and as
much cheese as you can handle. Other dishes are featured, but stick with pizza. Red-checked tablecloths and
candles in wine bottles provide the rustic charm of the
main floor dining room and outdoor cafe.

Astor
1813 M Street, NW   331-7994

This townhouse consists of a myriad of rather well-worn
rooms. However, the Greek food is inexpensive, if
rather carelessly prepared. Servings are large, the spana-
kopeta, chick pea salad and daily specials being the best.

Le Lion D'Or
1150 Connecticut Avenue, NW   296-7972

Very expensive, but absolutely the finest of classical
French cuisine. The menu ranges from exquisite **truite**
souffle au champagne to robust wild boar. A handsome
and sophisticated restaurant reflecting the owner-chef's
uncompromising standards.

Cantina D'Italia
1214-A 18th Street, NW   659-1830

The consistently high quality food served in this subterranean Washington favorite has withstood competition
from neighborhood newcomers. Decor is not inspiring,

but sophisticated pasta dishes and well-executed seafood and veal dishes are. Excellent wine collection, and very expensive. Not open on weekends.

Bacchus
1827 Thomas Jefferson Place, NW   785-0734

A moderately priced meal of interesting Lebanese dishes may be enjoyed in two very attractive small dining rooms. Lamb and chicken are skewered or molded with wonderfully perfumed, spiced rice. Hummus, Kibbeh and other appetizers comprise a tasty beginning or light meal. Try a cool orange-water flavored pudding for a light dessert.

TOUR 12   16th STREET

Blue Nile
1701 16th Street, NW   232-8400

One of an increasing number of African restaurants in Washington. This features authentic peppery Ethiopian stews served by waitresses in long robes. Eaten by scooping portions in thin pancakes, the often fiery stews are the only menu items, and are accompanied by vegetables and hot pepper paste. The variety is sometimes lost in the spiciness, but they are great fun to sample.

TOUR 13   DUPONT CIRCLE

Paru's
2010 S Street, NW   483-5133

This small vegetarian restaurant features wonderful Indian food in a small serve yourself hole in the wall off the beaten track. The curries, filled pancakes and pilafs are worth the detour from Connecticut Avenue. Very inexpensive.

Nora's
2132 Florida Avenue, NW   462-5143

Charming and cheerful, with a serious kitchen. Ingredients are fresh, vegetables remain firm, fish and meats are imaginatively prepared. The menu changes daily and also features large salad, pasta and vegetable main courses. The desserts are wonderful. An instantly likeable restaurant with a helpful staff and very reasonable prices. The wine list includes several very moderately priced selections. A charming garden cafe for warm weather is located in a rear courtyard.

Kramer Books and Afterwords
1517 Connecticut Avenue, NW   387-1400

This bookstore-cafe will satisfy both intellectual and gusta-
tory cravings at all hours. Try a tomato and ricotta salad
with anchovies, olive oil and oregano and a croissant or
pastry. Out back is a popular warm weather cafe.

Golden Temple
1521 Connecticut Avenue, NW   234-6134

Small and bright with a pleasant young staff, this vegetarian restaurant serves imaginative salads and sandwiches,
freshly-made soups and hearty main dishes. Whole grain
breads and desserts are especially good. Service can be
slow.

Timberlakes
1726 Connecticut Avenue, NW   483-2266

A popular, informal neighborhood pub specializing in huge
hamburgers, sandwiches, nice whole meal salads and several
dinner entrees. Good hearty food at very modest prices
served in attractive surroundings.

Le Manouche
1724 Connecticut Avenue, NW   462-8771

French and a few other ethnic dishes are served with an
imaginative flair in a simple, but pleasant room. It is
moderately expensive, but a welcome addition to the
upper Dupont Circle area.

El Bodegon
1637 R Street, NW   667-1710

Beam and stucco decor, friendly and informal with a
wide ranging menu of robust Spanish food. The colorful
dishes include a well-endowed paella, and chicken, veal
and beef dishes. You will be entertained by a flamenco
dancer and guitarist; and also the owner, who makes the
rounds with a spouted flask, pouring wine into the mouths
of those who trust his aim. Spanish cheesecake, pudding
and flan round out a modestly priced meal.

La Fonda
1639 R Street, NW   232-6965

Best for an inexpensive lunch, if you order a light meal
of perhaps tostados and a glass of wine. A Mexican cafe
with white stucco walls and attractive tile floor.

TOUR 14   NONE LISTED

TOUR 15   KALORAMA / ADAMS-MORGAN

Omega
1856 Columbia Road, NW   460-1730

This scruffy-looking place has been serving good Cuban
food for a long time. Asopaos, popular meat-rice dishes,
pork dishes and stuffed or fried squid are good choices.
Of course, those delicious black beans accompany it all.

El Caribe
1828 Columbia Road, NW   338-3121

Tiny and dark, this spirited restaurant offers an extensive
menu of Latin American specialties. All of the dishes,
mostly served in casserole, are robustly interesting. Appetizers and soups should not be overlooked--especially a
soup with yucca root, which appears again in a wonderful
pork dish. Black beans and rice, of course, accompany
your meal. There is a guitarist in the evening. Fun and
very modestly priced.

La Fourchette
2429 18th Street, NW   332-3077

This small, informal French restaurant offers exceptionally
well-prepared dishes from a menu of light entrees and
more robust daily specials. Try a vegetable tart or a fish
dish and a dessert. The tab will be modest.

TOUR 16   GEORGETOWN

Old Europe
2434 Wisconsin Avenue, NW   333-7600

German food is hearty and generally well-prepared here.
It is a lively place with a good selection of beers and a
variety of excellent seasonal offerings if you happen to
hit an asparagus festival, game festival, etc., etc. Dumplings, kraut, red cabbage and potato salad all round out
the menu. The extensive list of German wines and beers
is moderately priced as are the entrees with the exception
of several pedestrian schnitzels.

Au Pied Du Cochon
1335 Wisconsin Avenue, NW   333-5440

A most authentic French brasserie with food to match.
Its namesake dish, pig's foot, is not often found on menus
and is quite good cold with sauce ravigote. Other relatively
inexpensive dishes are crepes, coq au vin, fresh fish, salads
and egg dishes. Order simple foods, for sauces leave a lot
to be desired. This is a fun, crowded eating and drinking
spot.

Aux Fruits De Mer
1329 Wisconsin Avenue, NW   965-2377

Under the same management as Au Pied Du Cochon, this
small, equally crowded eatery features seafood. The lob-
ster is a bargain, and the daily specials are usually fresh
and good. Accompaniments are run-of-the-mill coleslaw
and oversalted French fries, so forget them and start with
the crusty onion soup. Inexpensive to moderate.

Bamiyan Afghan
3320 M Street, NW   338-1896

A former chef at the Embassy of Afghanistan is cooking
at Bamiyan. Two cozy candlelit dining rooms upstairs are
strikingly enhanced by persian rugs, wall tapestries and
plants. Deliciously light and intriguingly flavorful, the cuisine relies strongly on fresh vegetables, lamb and yogurt.
Since prices are low, order an appetizer and vegetable side
dish in addition to entrees. Sauteed pumpkin with yoghurt
meat sauce is delightful as are small leek filled dumplings
with the same sauce plus mint. Try stuffed turnovers and
a lamb palow or kebob.

Chez Maria
3338 M Street, NW   337-4283

Vietnamese and French dishes highlight the menu in this
modestly priced restaurant-wine bar. Spring rolls are crisp
and well stuffed. An unusual cold noodle dish is particularly interesting. Charcoaled meats are delicious. Wines
are very moderately priced and a variety may be ordered
by the glass.

Clyde's
3236 M Street, NW   333-9180

A jam-packed bar, pub, airy atrium room and omelette
room share this "in" establishment. Huge hamburgers and
sandwiches, dinners and egg dishes are all good. It is
always crowded and is great for brunch or late supper.

Nathan's
3150 M Street, NW   338-2000

Beyond the bar there is an intimate room with linen and
fresh flowers. Freshly made pasta dishes and well-executed
veal dishes are usually excellent. On the expensive side if
you order several courses.

The Big Cheese
3139 M Street, NW   338-3314

Huge fig trees, tiled tables, unusual artifacts and fabrics
personalize the decor. The menu, which changes bi-monthly,
is one of the most imaginative in town, featuring international cheese specialties. Absolutely fresh ingredients
are used and each dish is a strikingly handsome presentation.
Generally moderately priced with a few more expensive
choices.

American Cafe
1211 Wisconsin Avenue, NW   337-3600

The original that spawned the newer branch on Capitol
Hill serves the same menu. Delightful fresh salads, soups,
sandwiches and desserts at moderate prices are the main-
stay of this crowded cafe.

Apana
3066 M Street, NW   965-3040

Intriguingly spiced, visually exciting Indian food is served
in an intimate, well appointed dining room. Knowledge-
able waiters will help you with choices from the comprehensive menu. Do not omit excellent appetizers and
beautiful breads. Side dishes are interesting accents to the
varied main courses; some are abbreviated forms of the
vegetarian entrees. Moderately expensive.

Le Steak
3060 M Street, NW   965-1627

A good place when you don't feel like making decisions.
One entree-a boneless steak cooked precisely to order with
a nice mustard-tarragon sauce- is accompanied by an excellent house salad, crisp extra-thin French fries, cheese or a
sweet dessert and coffee. Small and crowded with lively
Parisian ambiance. Moderately expensive, depending on
drinks and wine.

192

Chez Odette
3063 M Street, NW   333-9490

A longtime Georgetown fixture, this inexpensive restaurant serves simple French food in two very attractive rooms. A good value.

Charing Cross
3027 M Street, NW   338-2141

Inexpensive, robust Italian food. There are a variety of interestingly sauced pastas and daily specialties. Entrees are accompanied by a salad. Very informal.

La Chaumiere
2813 M Street, NW   338-1784

The fireplace, country inn ambiance and the unpretentious French food add up to a very popular restaurant. The moderately priced menu features bourgeois dishes that are quite rewarding. There are also daily specials, such as North African Couscous.

La Ruche
1039 31 Street, NW   965-2684

Its name means the beehive, and it certainly does buzz with activity. You can relax, however, over quiche, saucisse en brioche, fresh artichokes, special entrees and a freshly baked, jumbo strawberry tart. Desserts are of exceptionally high quality, as is most of the food here. Prices are low, portions large.

Foundry
1050 30th Street, NW   337-1500

A circa 1856 foundry building adjacent to the C&O Canal has been virtually turned on its foundation and completely renovated into a restaurant. Fascinating interior spaces are enhanced with lots of glass, natural wood siding and much greenery. Choose a table overlooking the activity on the canal or an enclosed private banquette. Moderately priced entrees vary in quality. There is a drinking bar and a raw bar on the first floor where you can sink into overstuffed sofas or sit at tables and have a light snack.

Geppetto
2917 M Street, NW   333-2602

Named for Pinocchio's master, this crowded Italian cafe
mingles marionettes with plants. The inexpensive menu
offers daily Italian specialties and sandwiches such as fried
eggplant. The deep dish Sicilian pizza is delicious. A
rich chocolate-chip ricotta pie is heresy after such hearty
food, but worth every bite.

El Tio Pepe
2809 M Street, NW   337-0730

This popular Spanish restaurant highlights paella and seafood. Linens, beam and stucco decor, and sophisticated
service. Try concitas--a hot mixture of crab, olives and
other savories in clam shells for an appetizer, and finish
with a cool flan. The flamenco dancer and guitarist are
superb. Moderate to expensive, depending on the number
of courses ordered.

Viet Nam Georgetown
2934 M Street, NW   337-4536

Very interesting and attractively presented food bordering
on the inexpensive. Try crab and asparagus soup or citron
marinated skewered meats. Pungent fish sauce, shredded
cabbage and rice are accompaniments.

Enriqueta's
2811 M Street, NW   338-7772

Not a Tex-Mex establishment, but a serious cocina mexi-
cana producing a full range of delicious colorful dishes:
fresh fish in coriander sauce, chiles stuffed with pork and
fruits--as well as the more familiar enchiladas, tamales
and tostadas. The menu changes daily, offering a moderately priced selection of the regional dishes of Mexico.
The small dining room is cheerful, as are the helpful
waiters.

TOUR 17   WOODLEY PARK / NATIONAL ZOO

Arabian Nights
2915 Connecticut Avenue, NW   232-6684

A family run, small and plainly appointed restaurant.
There is nothing plain about the moderately priced food--
fragrant shish kebob, kifta and spicy stuffed eggplant.
Try the combination plate--it is nicely presented and offers
an array of appealing food. Desserts are freshly baked
and should not be missed.

194

Calvert Cafe
1967 Calvert Street, NW   232-5431

Ignore the exterior appearance (the inside is not much better) and enjoy shish kebob, couscous, and other interesting lamb and eggplant dishes. Call ahead and talk to Mama Ayesha to inquire about specialties such as Mensaf. Good desserts, very thick coffee, inexpensive.

Khyber Pass
2309 Calvert Street, NW   234-4632

A branch of Bamiyan Afghan in Georgetown; the menu is the same. The excellent lamb and intriguing vegetable-yogurt dishes are modestly priced. Be sure to order the unusual appetizers and desserts, too.

L'Escargot
3309 Connecticut Avenue, NW   966-7510

Same ownership as Chaumiere in Georgetown and the same good value; country French food at moderate prices.

Yenching Palace
3524 Connecticut Avenue, NW   362-8200

Moderately priced, but more expensive than the downtown Chinatown restaurants, the Yenching offers Szechuan, Peking and Cantonese dishes. The dated decor includes blue mirrors and curved booths. House specialties should be ordered here instead of standard dishes.

Csiko's
3601 Connecticut Avenue, NW   362-5624

Moderately priced Hungarian cooking in this family establishment located in the Broadmoor Apartments. Appetizers include a piquant cucumber dish. Try rabbit, chicken paprikash with spaetzle, or goulash. Hot strudle is baked throughout the evening. Extensive list of Hungarian wines. Recorded zither music, faded carpet and starched linens create an old world atmosphere.

Cafe Italiano
3516 Connecticut Avenue, NW   966-2172

A small, cozy restaurant serving wonderful, freshly made pasta and veal dishes. Moderately priced. Be sure to explore the Italian deli nearby.

TOUR 18   WASHINGTON CATHEDRAL / CLEVELAND PARK

Serbian Crown
4529 Wisconsin Avenue, NW   966-6787
(About 1-¾ miles north of tour area)

In this Serbian-Croatian restaurant, start with a special
vodka drink or one of the 18 straight vodkas available,
in ice-jacketed bottles, by glass or 4-ounce carafe. Zakus-
kas, or appetizers, are excellent as are the impressive
Coulibiac of Salmon, Chicken Kiev and Pate de Sole
Vladimir. The dense Russian custard cake with fruits is
unusual and delicious, as is the vodka-laced Coupe General Dourakine with chestnuts. A romantic restaurant;
there are candles, linen napery, a highly professional
staff and a violinist some evenings. Expensive.

TOURS 19-21   NONE LISTED

TOUR 22   OLD TOWN ALEXANDRIA

Taverna Cretekou
818 King Street   548-8688

A delightful taverna where moderately priced Greek food
goes a step beyond familiar standards with Iyam Byaldi,
a cold eggplant appetizer; and Exohikon, lamb and vegetables in spicy phyllo crust. Lamb dishes are all excellent as is the fried or baked squid. Whitewashed walls
and bright wall hangings are a part of the tasteful renovation of the old building. There is a very interesting
brunch menu and a special celebration at Easter.

Geranio
724 King Street   548-0088

The name in Italian means geraniums, which grow in the
window of this small restaurant. Veal and chicken entrees
are particularly good. Desserts include lovely, but very
non-Italian fruit tarts. Moderately expensive.

The Wharf
119 King Street   836-2834

An interesting renovation of a 100 year old warehouse,
the Wharf openly retains original structural elements of
the building in a nautical decor. Moderately priced fin
and shellfish are well prepared and served with run-of-the-
mill cole slaw and French fries.

King's Landing
121 S. Union Street   836-7010

The warm ambiance of this restored old building makes up for the sometimes disappointing entrees. Dinner is expensive; however, the lunch menu is reasonably priced.

Chadwick's
203 S. Strand   836-4442

A lively California-style waterfront pub with well-prepared burgers, salads and American fare dinners. A good drinking spot.

Wayfarers
110 S. Pitt Street   836-2749

A wonderful little English pub. Eat in the pub room or the more formal candle-lit colonial dining room. Lunch with an imported draft beer is a good buy. Dinners are moderately priced, featuring many veal dishes. Some of the English pies and turnovers are more successful than others.

219 King Street   549-1141

Another impressive adaptation of an old building, especially the exterior. Inside, every inch has been decorated-- OK if you like velour and glitter. The expensive appointments are reflected in the prices, too, but there's a tiny pub downstairs which serves an abbreviated version of the upstairs menu for much less. The food is Creole and some dishes are excellent, others aren't. The server will steer you in the right direction--usually a seafood dish. Try brunch on the patio if the weather is warm.

Gadsby's Tavern
138 N. Royal   548-1288

This 18th century hostelry named for John Gadsby, an Englishman, is noted for its exquisite Georgian architecture and hanging musician's gallery. George Washington wined and dined often in the tavern, and his favorite meal was canvasback duck, hominy and madeira. This completely restored tavern is a must to see. Meals are served in several rooms authentically decorated to recreate an atmosphere of early America. Have lunch here because the food is average and dinner prices are high. Try peanut soup, salads, broiled fish, or the sandwiches. Sally Lunn bread and the rich desserts are good.

La Bergerie
220 N. Lee Street   683-1007

A moderately expensive French menu is accented with robust Basque specialties. The food is well executed and attractively presented, with some excellent seafood dishes. The decor, while quietly elegant in its own way, doesn't befit the restoration of this former warehouse. Downstairs, there is a crowded cafe serving quiche, crepes, pastries and specials from a chalkboard--all very reasonably priced.

TOUR 23   HISTORIC ANNAPOLIS, MARYLAND

La Crepe Normande
195 Main Street   263-3382

A small popular creperie also offering quiche, salads, sandwiches and one or two light entrees. The well filled entree and lovely dessert crepes are inexpensive.

Treaty of Paris - Maryland Inn
Church Circle at Main Street   263-2641

Although the food has its ups and downs, this nevertheless is a very charming place. Candles, fireplaces, and historic artifacts add to its warmth and coziness. The adjacent King of France Tavern, a popular night spot and home of jazz guitarist Charlie Byrd, reveals the 12-inch thick original walls and barrel-vaulted ceilings of this old room. Entrees in the dining room are expensive. The fresh broiled sea catch of the day is probably best. Hot freshly-baked corn sticks are great as is the crab soup. The Inn has very nicely appointed rooms in period style at reasonable rates. Now a historic landmark, the building is immune from detracting alterations.

Harry Brown's
66 State Circle   263-4332

An elegantly appointed 1920's decor with representative background music. Emphasis is on fresh seafood at moderately high prices. A few non-seafood items are less. Forget the overpriced desserts and start with a chowder or soup.

Riordan's Saloon
26 Market Space   263-5449

A favorite with natives and Midshipmen. This bustling bar-restaurant serves excellent large hamburgers, good seafood and several tempura dishes. Upstairs is more formal and prices go up considerably. Again, fresh seafood is the thing.

Mum's
136 Dock Street   263-3353

Another popular bar with less noisy dining in an upstairs loft. Prices are the same, wherever. Burgers, chili and seafoods are moderately priced, with seafood, of course, at the top of the range.

Custom House Market
City Dock

This is a fun place in which to browse at will, sampling fresh crabcakes, cheeses, pastries, or other goodies. Fresh seafood, produce, and cheeses are sold in separate areas. If it's warm, take food and picnic along the dock, or up by the Capitol--or munch as you browse. A great way to have fresh native crab and a light lunch. Remember that it is closed on Tuesdays.

Harbor House
City Dock   268-0771

There is a bar downstairs serving snacks. Upstairs, the dining room offers a view of the harbor. Seafood is what to order; try crab Norfolk-style. Moderately priced.

Chart House
Second Street at Spa Creek   268-7166

Go here for a drink by the fireplace and gaze across the water to old Annapolis. Then drive back over the bridge to eat dinner unless you want overpriced beef and Alaskan crab. The building is quite dramatic. Great marine shops nearby invite you to browse.

CARRY OUTS

TOURS 1 and 2

American Cafe
227 Mass. Ave.,   NE

Capitol Hill Wine and Cheese
611 Pennsylvania Ave., SE

TOUR 3

Hirshhorn Museum Outdoor Cafe
Box Lunches - Warm Weather Only

TOUR 4   NONE LISTED

TOUR 5

L'Enfant Gourmet
470 L'Enfant Plaza, SW

Gourmet Too
609 L'Enfant Plaza, SW

TOUR 6   NONE LISTED

TOUR 7

Lunch Box
1721 G Street, NW

Kay's
1733 G Street, NW

Outdoor Cafe in
Liberty Square
Federal Home Loan
Bank Board Headquarters
17th and G Streets, NW

TOUR 8

Lunch Box
1622 Eye Street, NW

TOUR 9   NONE LISTED

TOUR 10

Kay's
1410 New York Avenue, NW

Dutch Boy Deli
639 Indiana Avenue, NW

German Deli
814 11th Street, NW

TOUR 11

Port of Piraeus
1801 K Street, NW
K Street Level in Mall

Lunch Box
20th and H Streets, NW

Cafe Sorbet
1810 K Street, NW

Vie De France
1990 K Street, NW
2nd Level in Esplanade Mall

Dimitri's
1823 M Street, NW

Le Souperb
1221 Connecticut Avenue, NW

Bread Oven (Bakery)
1220 19th Street, NW

Connecticut Connection
Farragut N. Metro Station
Metro Level - bakery and several
fast food places
Connecticut and L Streets, NW

Dutch Treat
1710 L Street, NW
1901 L Street, NW

TOUR 12   NONE LISTED

TOUR 13

Golden Temple
1521 Connecticut Avenue, NW

Tastebuds
1605 Connecticut Avenue, NW

Paru's
2010 S Street, NW

TOUR 14

O Street Market
O & 7th Streets, NW

TOUR 15   NONE LISTED

TOUR 16

Booeymonger
Corner, Prospect and Potomac
  Streets, NW

Gourmetisserie
1624 Wisconsin Avenue, NW

American Cafe
1211 Wisconsin Avenue, NW

La Ruche
1039 31st Street, NW

TOUR 17

National Zoo
Varied, good quality food concessions

TOURS 18-23   NONE LISTED